Kingdom Gone

Frank Lean is the pen name of Frank Leneghan, who was born in 1942 and educated at Thornleigh College, Bolton and Keele University where he read history and politics. He has worked in education in Manchester and now lives in Manchester.

Also by Frank Lean

Red for Rachel
Nine Lives
The Reluctant Investigator

Frank Lean

Kingdom Gone

ARROW

Published in the United Kingdom in 2000 by
Arrow Books

1 3 5 7 9 10 8 6 4 2

Copyright © Frank Lean 1999

The right of Frank Lean to be identified as the author
of this work has been asserted by him in accordance
with the Copyright, Designs and Patents Act, 1988

This book is sold subject to the condition that it shall not, by
way of trade or otherwise, be lent, resold, hired out, or otherwise circulated without the publisher's prior consent in any
form of binding or cover other than that in which it is published
and without a similar condition including this condition being
imposed on the subsequent purchaser

First published in the United Kingdom in 1999 by William Heinemann

Arrow Books Limited
The Random House Group Limited
20 Vauxhall Bridge Road, London SW1V 2SA

Random House Australia (Pty) Limited
20 Alfred Street, Milsons Point, Sydney,
New South Wales 2061, Australia

Random House New Zealand Limited
18 Poland Road, Glenfield,
Auckland 10, New Zealand

Random House (Pty) Limited
Endulini, 5a Jubilee Road, Parktown 2193, South Africa

The Random House Group Limited Reg. No. 954009

www.randomhouse.co.uk

A CIP catalogue record for this book
is available from the British Library

ISBN 978-0-09-959487-7

To Cara Elizabeth Feely

All newspaper reports included in this book are purely fictional and never actually appeared in the newspapers named.

> Here lay Duncan
> His silver skin lac'd with his golden blood;
> And his gash'd stabs looked like a breach in nature ...
>
> *Macbeth*, Act II, scene iii

1

Saturday, 17 October

Fred Travis woke early. A squint at the Rolex watch on his reproduction Louis XIV bedside table confirmed that it was just after six. He stretched in the bed for a moment, thinking of what lay before him. It wasn't going to be easy but he'd fix any bastards who thought they could use him and his good name. 'By God, I'll fix them and fix them good,' he vowed.

He swung his legs out of bed and caught a glimpse of his hairy torso in the mirror that extended across one wall of his bedroom. 'Not bad for a man my age,' he thought. 'No bloody beer gut at least.'

Solid as a granite statue, Fred padded across the thick carpet towards his en-suite bathroom. Sternly rejecting any self-indulgent hovering, he stepped straight into the marble-lined shower bay and turned on the taps. He allowed himself a single yelp as chilling water drenched him before the automatic temperature control kicked in. With the blood flowing freely in his sixty-year-old veins, he stepped out of the shower bay. At the sink he applied shaving foam to his face with a lavish hand and wiped condensation from the mirror. His determined mood turned to sudden terror as he detected a blur of motion in the steamy air behind him. Disregarding the foam, his killer jerked Fred's chin down and neatly cut Fred's throat from ear to ear. Gurgling his last breath, the dying man dropped to the tiled floor and thrashed about for a moment or two in a widening pool of his own blood. A last thought reached his fading brain ... If only he'd acted earlier ...

Contented with his handiwork, the killer, who was a professional, sprinkled a variety of clues about the crime scene. He carefully left footprints from size-eleven trainers in the rapidly congealing pool. Hairs, with follicles attached, were removed from a plastic container and placed on the edge of the wash-basin. A Swiss Army knife – not the one he'd used for the job, but smeared with blood – was dropped between the dead man's feet. Before leaving, the killer took a card from his wallet and placed it in his victim's nerveless fingers. He then allowed himself a little smile of satisfaction at a job well done.

Neither the national media nor the Greater Manchester Police were prepared to treat the savage killing of such a controversial figure as Fred Travis lightly. By nine that morning, just an hour after his housekeeper had alerted them, both groups had their premier-league teams on the job. Cars, vans and TV trucks jostled in the leafy Didsbury lane which hid the entrance to Fred's mansion.

'You could describe it as a palace all right,' Detective Sergeant Peterson said to his superior. Both men were pacing up and down in the extensive wooded grounds outside the house while scientific investigation of the scene went on.

'Yeah, trust Fred Travis to do the opposite to everyone else,' DI Cullen agreed. 'Most of the people who owned these Victorian dumps sold them to be hotels or offices, but what does our Fred do? He buys a nursing home and reconverts the pile to an individual residence.'

'Are you saying he was a crank?'

'No, you're allowed to be a bit opinionated when you've made as much money as he did, but he was all of a piece was our Fred. He believed the best was in the past. Haven't you heard him spouting this repeal crap of his?'

'Not everyone thinks it's crap sir,' Peterson protested.

'What, wanting the Queen to repeal all laws passed since 1953 and hand over government to a panel of businessmen? Are you crazy?'

'Some people don't think that would be so bad,' Peterson persisted.

Cullen looked speculatively at his companion. Squirrels were leaping about in the pine trees behind them. He was spared the necessity of completing the sergeant's education by the breathless arrival of a white-overalled figure.

'It's all right for you to go in now, sir. Everything's preserved and recorded.'

'About time,' Peterson grumbled. His eyes narrowed as the forensic officer passed a small plastic wallet to Cullen.

'There was this, sir. We thought you'd like to see it right away. Mr Travis had it in his fingers but it was definitely placed there after death.'

As Cullen read the words written on the small business card an expression of shock and disbelief passed across his face.

'What, sir?' Peterson asked. Cullen passed him the card.

Dave Cunane
Detection and Protection Services
Personal Attention Guaranteed
Pimpernel Investigations
Manchester
0161 880 9191

'Case solved?' Peterson asked eagerly.

'If only,' Cullen sighed. 'Do you know many murderers who sign their work?'

'But this Cunane must know something.'

'If only it was that easy. If Cunane's involved, this job will be as simple as a ten-thousand-piece jigsaw. Still, I'd better notify the old man.'

'Who?'

'Assistant Chief Constable Sinclair, he's sure to want to know all about it if his old friend's son's involved.'

'Look Cunane, you must know something,' the frustrated detective said for the twentieth time.

I shook my head wearily. My inquisitor, Detective Sergeant Alan Peterson, was clearly a man destined for higher things. Calm and level-headed Alan, he looked the sort who'd mastered all facets of modern coppering . . . profiling . . . use of computers . . . working as a team . . . psychological torture. Maybe that was why my stubborn refusal to admit any degree of culpability for Fred Travis's death was making him behave like an absolute sod. Or maybe it was because I was who I was, dressed as I was. My father, ex-Detective Chief Superintendent Paddy Cunane, veteran of over two hundred murder investigations, had been chief of CID in this very building – Bootle Street, once the headquarters of the old pre-amalgamation City of Manchester Police. It upset some coppers that I'd not only evaded my inheritance to the extent of not becoming one of the guardians of the law myself but had set up in opposition as it were, with my own private detective agency, Pimpernel Investigations.

Certainly there was something about me that Peterson didn't find to his liking. He seemed to have caught his fingers, if not more intimate parts, in the wringer. Almost the first thing he'd asked me was where I had got my suit. The garment in question was an unremarkable and well-worn Hugo Boss business suit but the way he'd gone on . . . 'How can you afford to dress like this, Cunane? Do you know that a high-class gents' outfitters in Chorlton was ram-raided last month?' I'd had to show him the wear at cuffs and elbows, the dry cleaner's tickets still stapled into the labels before he relented. I guessed that he got his suits from Marks & Spencer's or C&A. Not that there was anything wrong with that. The guy was perfectly presentable, neat even . . . but there was nevertheless a ragged air about him. It was his face, worn looking with sunken cheeks and curly dark-brown hair receding at the forehead, that told you there was a very big insect somewhere in the Peterson ointment.

'He had your card in his hand. You must have an explanation for it.'

'How many times do I have to tell you that I've never met Fred Travis or hardly even heard of him. I tell you, I'm out of the private eye game now,' I croaked. 'That card was more of a joke than anything.'

'Not to Fred Travis it wasn't. He had it in his hand when he died,' my interrogator said.

'I know nothing about that.'

'What about this organization, "Repeal 98"? You must have been aware of that.'

'Their activities are a complete mystery to me.'

'Oh come on! Don't you read the papers?'

'I only read the sports pages.'

'OK, smart arse, that's enough. You have half an hour to write down names of people you gave your card to.'

'What if I can't remember?'

'Then you'll find yourself under arrest on suspicion,' he said, pushing a pen and pad across the desk at me.

'Oh,' I commented weakly.

'All of them, mind you. If I find you've left some out, I'm going to have you as an accessory.'

He then departed and left me staring at the familiar white-tiled walls of the interview room. Familiarity didn't mean comfort. Everything was screwed to the floor in case clients became 'emotional'. I knew how they felt, but getting up and walking out wasn't an option.

I sat in that oppressive little room for ten minutes. I wasn't moving but my mind was racing. It's funny how fear can stimulate the memory. Then I began writing feverishly. Names of solicitor's clerks, detective agencies, company executives and hotel security men jumped off the point of my pen. I'd circulated the card to a whole gallery when I was still hoping to stay in the detection business.

Finally and after much hesitation I added one last name to the list . . . Clint Lane, the handicapped brother of a friend of mine. Still, no one could seriously suspect him.

Exactly on the half hour, Peterson bounced back in, snatched up the list and went out. I remained in the hot seat with a dull ache spreading up my spine.

A few minutes later he returned.

'OK, Cunane, ta-ta for now.'

'Does that mean I can go?'

He gave me a cheeky grin which I took to mean yes.

With that I was allowed to leave the city-centre police station.

Outside, in Albert Square, it was a brilliant October day with the sun shining brightly and a few small clouds scudding along. A fresh westerly breeze had blown the stench of hydrocarbons and fast food out of the city streets and the citizens were moving about their business in a lively and buoyant way without their usual closed-up, miserable expressions. Skateboarders were jerking and jinking about in one corner of the square. I liked this end of town. The Town Hall, with its rhythmical profusion of arches and Disneyesque pinnacles high in the air, provided a pleasing contrast with the solid drum of the Central Library, squashed under its dome.

Yet I knew that five minutes' walk away from this architectural grandeur I could find pubs where crack, smack or coke was openly sold across tables on which dealers laid their six-shooters, Wild West style. You could arrange for a shipment of drugs, or for someone to have bones broken or worse, with almost childish ease; and now it seemed as if someone had done just that for one of the more prominent local luminaries.

The hostile chat with Alan Peterson had left me feeling as if I'd been sand-papered all over. I needed to draw a line under the experience. There was a pavement café across the way from the Town Hall. I gratefully settled into a chair and ordered a coffee and Danish pastry.

Despite what I'd told Peterson, I knew as much about Fred Travis as anyone else who watched local TV or picked up a paper – which is to say, quite a lot. Like the chairs in Bootle Street, Travis had been a pain in the backside for years. Poor old Travis, he was one of those sad figures who claim to hate publicity but who can't live for long without seeing their name in print . . . a fame junky.

Well, he'd certainly got his name in the papers now. A glance at the slogan on the street corner news-stand confirmed that: *'Mystery Killing of Tycoon'*. I was chilled by the thought that it wouldn't be a mystery for long. My name must be on the list of suspects. I felt wildly angry at myself and at Travis. How dare he die with my card in his hand?

I must have looked fierce because a meek little council-tax collector on the next table folded up his newspaper, put it down and hastily left. I reached over and picked it up. It was an early edition of the evening paper.

I scanned the headlines. Travis was everywhere.

'*Travis the Tractor* . . .' Yes, Fred had started his fortune by selling reconditioned tractors in Africa. That was enterprising if you like. Certainly it was more than I'd ever done, hawking a two-and-a-half-inch piece of cardboard round Manchester.

'*Much Married* . . .' Well, you could say that. From all accounts he'd had enough wives in his time to fill a People Carrier.

'*Local Benefactor* . . .' True enough, if you called it charity when the right hand knew only too well what the left had was doing. Fred had always made sure that none of his giving was overlooked by the recording angels of the press.

'*Strong Views* . . .' Strong, certainly; there aren't many multimillionaires prepared to finance their own national political movement. Both Fred and his followers knew what they were opposed to. It made a long list. You name it, they were agin it.

'*Political Ambitions* . . .' Possibly not. His programme wasn't very realistic: 'Back to 1953 now!' How many were going to vote for that?'

'*Provocative Attacks on Political Correctness* . . .' That wasn't an exaggeration. Someone had done for him, but who?

'*Anti-permissive Slogans* . . .' The Repeal Movement and the Repealers weren't much more than a very rich man's whim. Their demos outside clubs and pubs were treated as a joke by most of the hard-faced individuals who made money out of the Manchester scene.

As I left the café and walked slowly through the Square towards King Street I was in an angry turmoil. I studied the snowflake patterns left by gum-chewers on the smooth stone pavement. There was no clue there. Why should anyone want to link me to such a crime? I rolled up the paper and threw it into a litter bin.

My mobile phone chirruped. 'Cunane?' a plummy voice I didn't know enquired. I grunted affirmatively. 'My name's Aldous Arkwright. I'm a friend of . . . or I should say I *was* a friend of poor Fred's.' Coming as it did on top of my own confused thoughts about Fred, the coincidence made me shiver. There was something about the voice too. What was special about those elongated vowel sounds? Wilfred Hyde White on speed?

'I want to consult you about Fred's death.'

'Say that again, please.'

'Fred . . . I want to know what the police have been saying to you.'

'Fred Travis?'

'Of course.'

'If this is some trick that Sergeant Peterson's put you up to, you can forget it.'

'No trick.'

'Well, how do you know . . . ?'

'Don't worry about *how* I know, Mr Cunane. The fact that I *do know* should be sufficient to impress you.'

'It does, believe me,' I said before switching off the call. Whoever was playing games wasn't going to get some phoney admission out of me so easily.

The phone rang again almost instantly.

'You do ply for hire as a private detective, don't you?'

'I suppose so,' I admitted grudgingly. Actually my main source of income over the last year has come from lecturing part-time in the management department of UNWIST, the University of the North West Institute of Science and Technology, one of the many higher educational establishments which dot central Manchester like cherries in a cake or dog turds round a lamp-post, depending on your point of view. I incline to the former at the moment, but sometimes I have my doubts. I'm only just coming up to thirty-eight but I can remember when students were a rare breed. You spotted them coming a long way off in their brightly coloured scarves. Now a mass movement of population deposits tens of thousands of them in Manchester every September just when the starlings are ready to leave. It's getting hard to spot the local fauna.

'Well, do you or don't you?' Arkwright demanded.

'Yes, yes, I do,' I said irritably. It was a sore point.

'I can't talk over the phone. Can you come up and see me right away? 79 Meldrum Terrace, Blackley. In case you don't know, I'm the spiritual director of a movement known as the Children of Light which is linked to the Repeal Campaign.'

'Spiritual director,' I repeated stupidly. If he'd said he was a starship captain the words couldn't have had a greater impact.

'Yes, I lead a group of seekers after truth,' he said testily.

'I don't have much to do with organized religion.'

'We're not organized in the way you mean. Come to see me and I'll pay you well. I'm reliably informed that there's nothing illegal in you telling an interested third party what you know about the police investigation. I can promise you that they won't learn about anything you say from us, if that's what's worrying you. I'm told you've had a rather up and down relationship with the constabulary.'

So, somehow the word had already gone out. I've often suspected that there are more grasses inside the police force than there are outside it. That would explain some of the crime figures.

A cruise out to Blackley on a Saturday afternoon was the last thing I wanted. United were at home to Chelsea. They were having an early kick-off and the traffic at this time, one thirty, would be fierce, and anyway a visit to the crumbling terraced streets of Blackley is hardly an attractive proposition at the best of times.

'I don't know if you're aware of what you're asking,' I said brusquely. 'My call-out fee on a weekend is £200 and if I come up to Blackley I shall expect to be paid, no matter how long our chat is.' I find that a demand for cash usually puts off casual queries.

'Fine, that's what we expected. When shall I see you?'

God! This guy didn't intend to be put off.

'How did you get this number?' I demanded. I was more angry with myself than him. My job at UNWIST had been the chance to escape from the clammy grip of the world of private detection. Opportunities to investigate crime in the retail trade had dried up recently as more and more businesses went in-house for their security service. That and CCTV had effectively shut down opportunities for a one-man business like mine. Business cards such as the one that the unfortunate Travis had been clutching had been my last stab at making a go of detection.

'I got your number off a card. I phoned and was referred to this number.'

I groaned. That damned card again! And why hadn't I cancelled the answering service?

'Yes, but why me?'

'It has to be you. I'm reliably informed that my late colleague Fred was on the point of consulting you when he died.'

'What?' I gasped. Did he know about the business card in Travis's hand? This mysterious director seemed to have more information than the police. It crossed my mind to walk back to see Peterson but that would only get me in deeper.

I felt sick. It was only pride that had made me keep on the answering service. For months there'd not been a single commission and now this. It served me right. I should have been decisive and made a clean break with the past. My dear father, Paddy, is absolutely right . . . I am a fool to myself.

I had to find out what else this 'spiritual director' knew about me, but for the moment, whatever he knew, he wasn't answering my question.

'Are you there?' I asked and was rewarded with a grunt.

'How do you know Travis wanted to get in touch with me?'

Arkwright went into the heavy-breathing routine again. For answers I'd have to see him.

I looked at my watch and then back across the square at the town hall clock. They both agreed. It was still half one. A jaunt up to Meldrum Terrace and back might take a couple of hours, but what else had I got to do with my time? My lectures were all prepared. The groceries were all bought. My flat had been cleaned until the carpets were in danger of disappearing entirely into the rotating maw of my ultra-powerful Dyson carpet cleaner. No man or woman, no chick nor child, was waiting with bated breath for my arrival. Failure's like that, I told myself.

'OK,' I said to Aldous Arkwright, 'you're on.'

Possibly the peevishness in my tone was evident because he said, 'Look, Mr Cunane. We'll pay you more than two hundred. Money's not a problem. I realize that a drive up to Blackley isn't to everyone's taste. How about a wager? If you get here before two fifteen, I'll pay you three hundred for ten minutes of your time.'

'Charming,' I muttered as I broke the connection, but I knew I was hooked. That old devil that killed the cat had its claws in me again. I sprinted down King Street to the car park behind Kendal's where I'd left my battered three-year-old Ford Mondeo. What sort of name was Aldous Arkwright? What was he? Aldous sounded far too exotic for a plain Arkwright, and he was pretty free with his money too. There couldn't be many people in Blackley boasting that money wasn't a problem . . . the odd club-owner or publican perhaps.

Charismatic leadership is marked not so much by the success of the leader in achieving goals as by his success in persuading his followers to surrender all personal initiative to his superior wisdom and judgement. Thus Adolf Hitler remained a successful charismatic leader until his country lay in ruins around his feet. His followers believed in him to the last.

Rick Guthrie, *Seven Charismatic Leaders*, p 276

2

Saturday, 17 October

Thirty minutes later I was cruising up Rochdale Road almost blinded by the brilliant autumn sunshine. Meldrum Terrace was in the oldest part of Blackley, down by the smoke-blackened Anglican parish church, according to the street atlas I kept squinting at. This area lay in the valley of the aptly named River Irk. The trouble was, I couldn't find the small terraced street. Streets were aligned at odd angles on factories that had vanished along with the textile industry.

After much ducking and weaving I finally reached Meldrum Terrace with minutes to spare. At first glance, it was a well-maintained terrace of quite large, working-class houses. Number 79 was the end house.

Next to the door, a brass plaque gleamed in the afternoon sun.

> *Residence of the Children of Light*
> *Peace   Harmony . . . Reconciliation*
> *A. Arkwright*
> *Director*
> *The Children of Light are incorporated as a*
> *limited company*
> *and are registered with the Charity Commissioners*
> *Number 347632*

. . . it proclaimed in elaborately scrolled letters.

I rapped the brass knocker on the highly polished front door.

The door swung open before the last stroke of the knocker hit the striker. A charming blonde young woman whose neat cashmere sweater and black dress couldn't disguise a very interesting figure was standing in the doorway.

'Mr Cunane?' she asked in a voice like gently pealing wind-chimes.

I managed to nod my head. If this was a typical Child of Light I was definitely interested in what the group had to offer.

'Come in,' she said. I couldn't place her accent but it wasn't Manchester. The room I entered was as surprising as my hostess. It was much bigger than it ought to have been. For a second I shook my head in bewilderment before I realized that the interiors of several, if not all, of the cottages in Meldrum Terrace had been knocked into one big building.

'You'd like to sit here and change your shoes?'

She removed the shoes from my feet.

'That's all right,' I said in embarrassment as I tried to remember if I'd put on clean socks that morning. I had of course.

She laughed. Again I was reminded of wind-chimes tinkling in a gentle summer zephyr, or distant church bells on a frosty morning. 'It's my job,' she whispered in a confidential tone. 'I'm the porter for today.' She matched a pair of slippers with my shoe size, unwrapped them and put them on my feet.

'Are those comfortable?' she asked.

I nodded.

'And now this,' she murmured and opened the door of a cupboard to reveal several long garments that looked like green silk night-shirts. 'We all wear them in the presence of the Master. It cuts down the chance of contamination.'

'No way are you getting me into that,' I said, heading to the exit.

Instantly a microphone crackled, 'Mr Cunane may be excused the robe, Sister Melanie. Just show him into my room.'

Melanie looked stricken. Big Brother had been listening, if

not actually watching. She darted towards the interior door and signalled me to follow. Obediently I trailed after her. She led me through offices in which green-robed figures were bent over word processors and duplicators. No one looked up at us, all were industriously involved in their tasks.

Finally we passed through an assembly area and reached a closed door. Melanie timidly tapped on the door. We entered.

A large man was seated in the corner on a sofa. He was wearing what looked like a long white Russian peasant shirt tied with a red sash over bell-bottomed blue cords. His attention was not on us but on the screen of a Gameboy which he was playing. A window was open, revealing an exquisite but tiny walled garden.

'Mr Arkwright, I presume,' I said cheekily, hoping to break the weird aura of unreality that enveloped the place like incense at a hippie wedding.

He reluctantly put the Gameboy to one side. 'I find these things absolutely addictive. Don't you?' His plump face wrinkled into a kindly smile. To my prejudiced eyes, this didn't improve things.

'Can't say I've ever tried,' I replied honestly.

'Oh you should. It develops concentration and hand-eye co-ordination.'

'Really?' I muttered.

'Sit,' he said.

I looked round the room. Although it was thickly carpeted, Arkwright appeared to be occupying the only seat.

'Sit here,' he commanded, patting the sofa next to himself. 'You're not shy, are you?'

'Well actually,' I started awkwardly, but Melanie tugged my sleeve before I completed the sentence. Her expression was nervous. I felt that I had to do as I was bid.

'Well, what do you make of us then?' he asked mischievously.

'To be honest I'm pinching myself to make sure that I'm not dreaming,' I said.

'Then we're doing something right, aren't we, Sister Melanie?'

She reacted with a little tinkle of forced laughter, and a

wonderfully pleased expression.

'You must forgive us, Mr Cunane. Visitors from the world always find us strange.'

Arkwright smiled at me warmly. So warmly in fact that if smiles had been money I could have walked out of that room a rich man. I instinctively distrusted him. He had brilliant blue eyes and a carefully cultivated 'piercing look' somewhat in the manner of the late Adolf Hitler. Rich russet brown hair tumbled over his smooth forehead. His nose and ears were both prominent and his complexion was ruddy and tanned like that of a man who spent most of his time outdoors. I could have sworn that he was wearing make-up. If so, it would account for the unnatural smoothness of his face. He continued to radiate charm and pat the seat beside him.

'Melanie, have you forgotten something?' he said in a rich fruity voice.

Melanie jumped like a timid woodland creature. She felt her side and, raising the encircling robe, she drew out a brown envelope which she passed to me. I opened it. It was full of five-pound notes, at least three hundred pounds. I sat down heavily next to Arkwright.

'What have you got all these people dressed in big girl's blouses for?' I asked, looking at Sister Melanie who was retreating backwards towards the door like the slave of some oriental potentate.

'Oh come, call me Aldous, please,' Arkwright begged. He moved closer to me, closer than I was comfortable with. I shuffled awkwardly away, at the same time putting the cash into my inside jacket pocket. Arkwright was wearing some strongly spiced after-shave or perfume. It was quite distinctive and somehow seemed to set off gong-like reverberations in the back of my head. I struggled to remember what the recollection it set off was . . . then it came to me. It was that instant before consciousness fades when under an anaesthetic. I checked my watch. Ten minutes was all he was going to get for his three hundred and he'd already had two minutes' worth.

'I expect you're wondering why I asked you here,' Arkwright said in a more businesslike tone.

'That's putting it mildly. There's absolutely nothing I can do for you.'

'Fred Travis was a highly valued member of this society,' he said gravely, fixing me with his penetrating gaze.

'News to me.'

'I need to know why he was in touch with you. Was there something that had alarmed him?'

'I'm sorry, Mr Arkwright, I've never met the man or spoken to him on the phone. I've absolutely no idea why he had my card. The only reason I came here is to find out how you come to know that he had it. You'd better have your money back,' I said, placing the envelope on the sofa next to him. 'I don't want to take it under false pretences.'

Arkwright stroked his chin with the fingers of his right hand as if drawing an invisible beard to a point. No doubt he thought it gave him an appearance of sagacity.

'It's as I thought, Mr Cunane. Your openness confirms my impression that you're a man I can trust. Someone is out to destroy us. I need your help.'

'I'm sorry, chief, you've lost me.'

'You may know that we're associated with the Repeal 98 campaign for a return to civility, manners and good governance.'

I looked at him intently. By listening to what this fruit-cake had to say, I might learn something that would come in handy in keeping Sergeant Peterson off my back.

'Mr Cunane, the police may seek to give you an impression that they're solving the case, but I can assure you that there are powerful forces at play here. Sometimes things go beyond the powers of a local force.'

I nodded as if accepting this.

'Either Brother Fred got hold of my card from a third party – and I can tell you I haven't given out many lately – or his killer left it for a reason,' I offered.

'Yes, that seems reasonable, but why leave your name? Why you, Mr Cunane?'

'I could make any number of guesses, but I don't care to,' I said abruptly. 'Despite what I told you on the phone, I've given up being a private detective and I don't see why I should get involved because some loony chooses to stick my card in a dead man's hand.'

Arkwright waved his hand languidly as if whisking away a noxious insect.

'The only reason I can think of is that the killer wished to deter others from associating with you. Why he should do that, I can't imagine. Are you dangerous to know, Mr Cunane?'

'If I am, it doesn't seem to have upset you.'

'No, that's true. I'm consulting you now. Someone as experienced as you must have light to throw on the death of Fred Travis. I understand that your father was one of the most accomplished murder investigators in the North of England.'

I was about to tell him to mind his own business when a small bird flew in through the open window. It flew round the room several times and then battered itself against the glass. When it fell to the window-ledge I could see that it was a robin. Arkwright, whose eyebrows were converging on the top of his head in surprise, picked up the bird and gently deposited it outside.

'My goodness, I hope that isn't an omen,' he muttered. 'I don't think it's dead, but you can see why I need to consult an expert in these matters.'

I didn't know what he was talking about. Omens aren't my scene.

'You look pale, Mr Cunane. I can see the little bird's upset you. I must offer you some refreshment.' He picked up a little bell and rang it. Melanie appeared at the door in an instant.

'A glass of the special cordial for our guest and myself,' he ordered.

She must have had the cordial ready because she returned to the room immediately with two tiny glasses on a silver tray. I looked at the drink curiously. It was obviously alcoholic but it didn't appear to have made its mind up what colour it was. There were orange and purple hues and a greenish tinge when I held it up to the light.

'Merely a restorative compounded entirely of natural ingredients, Mr Cunane. I assure you it's completely safe.'

Mindful of what happened to Alice when she quaffed a

potion in Wonderland, I waited until Arkwright had downed his own glass before taking a cautious sip from mine. It was delicious, with a smooth taste of unidentifiable fruits. Once again Melanie departed, not forgetting to curtsy to her leader. I didn't find that spectacle entirely pleasing. Just who did Aldous Arkwright think he was . . . the Dalai Lama?

'We make it ourselves. It contains a tincture of digitalis to relax and soothe the heart muscle. I find it relieves stress but of course it can only be drunk in the most limited quantities.'

'You mean it's poisonous?' I asked incredulously.

'Only in large doses, but then so is alcohol itself,' he said casually. 'Can you throw any light on this murder? I'd feel happier knowing that we had our own expert following up on the police investigation.'

'You don't know what you're asking.'

'We'd support you with a lawyer.'

'No thanks,' I said quietly.

'Surely I can persuade you? My organization believes strongly in inheritance of certain skills . . . Your father was a remarkable investigator, a legend . . .'

'Leave him out of it,' I growled.

'Some of my followers found the body. We were intending to holding a joint Repeal 98/Children strategy meeting at 7 a.m. When Mr Travis didn't arrive, I sent my people to find him. It may be that their discovery of the crime came earlier than the killer had anticipated. He may have been intending to return and leave further clues pointing in your direction.'

At last I was hearing something the police didn't know. According to them, the corpse was found by Travis's housekeeper. I didn't rise to Arkwright's carefully strewn bait. Travis's death had nothing to do with me and that was that. It seemed that Arkwright, like DS Peterson, cherished the illusion that he only needed to push the right buttons and I'd go rushing round trying to find out just who had cut Travis's throat.

Throughout this prolonged interview Arkwright had been gazing at me the whole time as if expecting writing to appear on my forehead. I was getting a crick in my neck trying to look at him. He had the advantage of being perched in the corner.

This man didn't need any help from me. He was as cute as a bag full of snakes.

Suddenly I'd had enough. Looking at the self-styled 'spiritual director' curled up on his sofa with that smug, knowing look on his mush irritated me intensely. 'Whoever left that business card with Travis and for whatever reason, the killing had nothing to do with me. I don't want your money. I don't want to feel under any obligation to you.'

Taking money from Arkwright now seemed like a very bad idea. I picked up the envelope from where it lay beside him and dropped it on his knee so he'd get the message.

My gesture produced an enigmatic smile from the spiritual leader.

I got up quickly, fighting back the impulse to smack him in the face. As it happened, that was a wise move because the door opened and two men, also clad in the ridiculous green robes, walked into the room and took up positions on either side of me without saying a word.

'What's this? The heavy squad?' I asked.

'These are my colleagues, Rufus and John.'

'Is there any trouble, sir?' Rufus, the taller and heavier of the two asked in an American accent. I'm no expert but I'd say it was a Southern drawl. A real charmer. He looked as if he spent hours every day practising his scowl. His greying hair was shaved almost down to the scalp. It wasn't right to say he looked at me. He clenched his face in my direction as if it was a fist.

I smiled right back at him.

Arkwright gave a little flick of the hand to signify that my presence wasn't disturbing him.

The pair then folded their arms and looked at me impassively. They were not quite Tweedledum and Tweedledee; John was as broad across the shoulders as Rufus was long. His face was more chiselled than his companion's, the features more defined, as if there was some native American blood in his ancestry. Whatever their looks, it was clear that Rufus and John were in the intimidation business. It didn't take a genius to guess that they were good at it . . . pros, in fact. They had that air of loving familiarity with violence that no amount of steroid-enhanced muscle-building can provide.

'Don't go without your money,' Arkwright pleaded. 'It's a tenet of our movement that everyone should get his due. I'll feel very bad if you leave without yours.'

He passed the envelope to John, who walked over to me. He waved the cash in my face. I shook my head, but when I turned to leave my path was blocked by Rufus. Santa's Grotto was getting distinctly crowded.

'I'm sure we'll be in touch with you again, Mr Cunane,' Arkwright warbled in his velvety tones. Rufus took the money from John and tried to stuff the wad of notes into the top pocket of my jacket.

Unfortunately any peaceful intentions I might have had disappeared when the big American, not content with stuffing the money into my pocket, flicked his finger at the end of my nose. 'Don't annoy the master, little fella,' he drawled.

I raked my heel down the inside of his leg. I was only wearing the regulation slippers provided by Melanie and not hobnailed boots so the effect wasn't drastic but he snarled and jumped back. I followed through and was about to land a neat body punch when my arms were gripped from behind by John. I heaved but it was like being towed by the QE2. The man was a gorilla. I couldn't make him budge. So I pulled forward and then jumped back, hoping to catch him off guard. Some chance of that! John did stagger a bit, but recovered without releasing me. Meanwhile Rufus got me in a head lock. I struggled but he had me by the neck, bent double, while John forced my arms up my back.

'How does this grab you, little fella?' Rufus enquired pleasantly while he rotated my neck. I strained every muscle but I felt like a child in his hands. Another fraction of an inch and he would snap my neck.

'Let him go,' Arkwright commanded in a relaxed voice. 'Rufus, you made a mistake. Mr Cunane's a guest here, you shouldn't have provoked him by flicking his nose.'

What happened next was the most surprising thing of all. Rufus and John released me without hesitation. It was like a circus act, with me as the bundle being passed between the high-wire men. No sooner had Arkwright spoken than I was in a heap on the carpet, struggling to get my breath. Years of being mauled by a wide variety of thugs had conditioned me to expect a parting kick or nasty blow on release. A lot of those guys are like dinosaurs. It takes a long time for a message to pass from their brains to their limbs. Not so with Rufus and John. The master spoke – I was free, with no argument.

Rufus turned and begged Aldous Arkwright's pardon. He wasn't exactly like a grovelling little dog but the sincere regrets offered had an unusual, old-fashioned ring. I started breathing again. Rufus continued to apologize. 'I'm sorry sir, I misread the situation. Will you please correct me?' he asked. I gawked in astonishment.

The display of power didn't displease Arkwright. 'Correction's certainly in order,' he said, 'for myself as well as for you, Rufus I should have made the situation clear. Mr Cunane, will you please take the money as a token of apology, if nothing else. I insist.' The grin had disappeared from his tanned face. Something more inscrutable replaced it.

In the circumstances it seemed counterproductive to refuse his offer a second time. I bent and picked the packet of cash from where it had fallen.

'That's better, Mr Cunane,' he said. 'I feel that we're just at the start of a fruitful relationship. I do so want to get off on the right foot.' I looked at him and shrugged. Closely shepherded by the green-clad minions, I made my way out through the suite of offices. I worked out that a long annexe had been run along the rear of the old terrace. Pigeon lofts, privies and backyards had made way for high tech. It must have cost hundreds of thousands.

Pretty Melanie was no longer at her post. She'd deposited my Timberlands right by the door. I didn't care to lengthen my stay by taking the time to put them on, so I grabbed them and left, still wearing the slippers.

As I got into the Mondeo Rufus posed in the doorway, giving me the old hard eye. I smiled genially at him, wondering to myself what mysterious current had cast such a rare specimen up on this remote shore. This was Blackley, Manchester, not some tragedy-soaked piece of deep-fried southern turf haunted by the ghosts of slavery and a lost war.

*

Getting back to my flat in Thornleigh Court, Chorlton was not easy. Streams of cars were heading away from Old Trafford and with the curious selfishness which comes over football supporters when their team has won they weren't letting cross traffic through. I cursed Aldous Arkwright once again but eventually managed to force my way against the flow and nip into the car park outside my flat. What joy! A group of chanting red-shirted youths were directing jets of steaming yellow urine against the back wall. I knew better than to comment.

I kicked my front door shut with a slam. It took me twenty minutes of quiet work in my kitchen before my pulse rate returned to normal. I scrubbed out several pans and polished the top of the cooker until it gleamed before making myself a risotto. As usual I cooked too much. I'd not adjusted well to bachelor existence since the enforced departure of my former girlfriend to a psychiatric hospital. There was some kind of psychological mechanism at work . . . it made me cook twice as much food as I needed in case some beautiful lovelorn female should turn up needing succour and a portion of whatever I was cooking.

No such luck.

I chewed my way stolidly through the risotto. It wasn't quite cooked enough and my jaws began to ache from the effort of clearing my plate. I gave it up as a bad job, threw the remaining food into the waste bin and poured myself a tall malt whisky. It's at times like this that alcohol comes into its own.

I savoured the flavour, rolling the whisky round my mouth as I pondered the events of the day and tried to shake off my gathering sense of uselessness. How did Travis come to be clutching my business card? It didn't make any sense at all. As I kicked that question around in the empty space that passed for my brain, I was aware of underlying feelings of guilt. I should never have put Clint's name down on that list for Peterson.

I lay on the sofa and studied the ceiling. No great thoughts occurred. Eventually I must have dropped into a light doze because I woke with a start when the phone rang.

At first I thought it was a little girl, the voice was so squeaky and thin. But after a moment I realized it was Melanie, the woodland sprite I'd met that afternoon.

'What is it now?' I snapped. 'Has the grand panjandrum decided to summon me again?'

'No, no, it's nothing like that. I'm the one who wants to see you. There's something I need to discuss.'

'Look sweetie, if you need a male shoulder to cry on I should imagine you've plenty to choose from at Meldrum Terrace but there's no way I'm going up there again.'

'I need help. I want to get away from here and I thought you had a kind face.'

I gave a hollow laugh at this but I felt as if someone had just switched on a powerful light in the back of my head. I was fully awake. What kind of trick was Arkwright trying to pull now? Would I turn up on the doorstep of Blackley only to find the lads playing pass the parcel with a fresh corpse?

'Just walk down to the corner of the street and get on a bus. It's that easy,' I told her.

'It's not! They'll find me.' She sounded hysterical.

'Then phone the police if you feel you're in danger.' This time I spoke more slowly. Melanie really did sound at the end of her tether, definitely no wind-chimes.

'You don't understand,' she pleaded. 'If I go to the police they'll send their solicitors round and I'll be back in Meldrum Terrace in no time. You're my last hope.'

There was a long pause after this. My glass still had whisky in it and I swilled it down. What was she to me? I didn't know her. Then, as the spirit burned the back of my throat, thousands of years of primate evolution made my mind up for me. I seemed to be standing outside myself listening as I spoke.

'Right, it's eight o'clock now. At precisely nine thirty I'll drive down your street and slow down outside number 79. If you're on the doorstep I'll give you a lift but there's no way I'm going in there.'

This produced a sharp intake of breath from my caller.

'Yes, I'll be there,' she said with a helpless little gasp and then broke the connection.

'What the hell!' I threw my glass against the wall. Against my better judgement, I'd got myself involved. How many times had I told myself when lying flat on my back in hospital that I'd never get myself involved in anything again?

Concern growing over mind-bending cult

Numerous complaints of families divided, husbands turning their backs on wives, and vice versa; of children refusing to make contact with parents and of parents breaking away from their children have been raised at a conference of Catholic bishops in Birmingham. The Assistant Secretary of the Catholic Bishops' Conference, Arnold Greengage, stated that the clergy are facing an increased pastoral work-load because of family breakdown caused by individuals being brain-washed by proselytising cults. Mr Greengage slated the activities of the Children of Light as a particular cause of concern. A spokesperson for the cult, Mr R.J. Polk, dismissed the bishops' concerns as 'naïve'. He said, 'Those guys need to learn to stand up to honest competition and open their tiny closed minds.'

Report in the *Guardian*

3

Saturday, 17 October – Sunday, 18 October

It took me ten minutes to sweep the broken glass up and then I had to wipe the wall to try to minimize the stain. When I raked the broken glass into the kitchen waste bin my hand was trembling.

'Get a grip, Cunane,' I told myself. I was aware that I was breaking every rule in the old private detective's handbook . . . no commission, no fee. I was annoyed with myself, but then if you can't follow a whim you might as well be dead.

I went into the bedroom and had a look through my wardrobe. They may call it power dressing but choosing the right clothes is better for me than a visit to a psychiatrist or a prescription of Prozac. Leather jacket and chinos did the trick. I examined myself in the mirror.

'You're looking good, baby,' I said, anxiously checking my temples for signs of grey. There were none. My dark curly locks were as lustrous as ever. Time's only victories over the handsome Cunane features were the crow's feet under my bonny blue eyes. The slight twist in my nose produced by some long-forgotten blow gave my face a certain lived-in look that didn't detract from the image.

I let myself out of the flat and went down the stairs feeling slightly more pleased with myself than I had a few minutes previously. The Mondeo was where I'd left it; the football 'fans' hadn't done any damage apart from raising the ammonia levels in the flower beds. Whistling 'You'll never get to Heaven in an old Ford car', I slipped behind the wheel and began backing out of my parking space.

Suddenly there was a loud rapping on my off-side window. Startled, I swivelled to see a chunky-looking woman in her mid to late twenties flashing a press card at me. I stopped and wound the window down. Her mousy brown hair was cropped in a roughly cut fringe. Her regular features were on the fleshy side and there was an incipient double chin but what gripped my attention was the expression of fierce determination. It was a face that should have adorned some old-time battleship's figurehead. I felt a shiver of apprehension. They say troubles come in threes. Peterson... Arkwright... was this my third nut of the day? At least she wasn't wearing a green smock. What appeared to be an ample anatomy was swathed in a loose gabardine coat.

'Mr Cunane?'

I grunted affirmatively.

'My name's Janine White, I'm with the *Guardian*. I wonder if I can ask you a few questions.'

As my memories of the *Guardian* include being battered over the head with rolled-up copies wielded by a former girlfriend's mother, this statement did not produce quite the response that Janine White may have expected. I glanced at my watch. It was twenty to nine. My attempts to achieve mental harmony through sartorial elegance had taken longer than I'd expected. I'd have my work cut out to reach Higher Blackley in time.

'Sorry love, I haven't the time,' I rasped, in a passable

imitation of a dyed-in-the-wool inner-city Manchester accent. Genuine Mancunians have always resented the *Guardian's* defection to London.

'I need to talk to you about the Travis case,' she said portentously. 'You must know something. I saw you being frog-marched into the police station by that Sergeant Peterson.'

I shrugged my shoulders. This could get to be seriously annoying. 'I know nothing about the Travis case . . . the police have spoken to me and they let me go.' I started reversing again.

'You know something,' White insisted. She shoved her head and shoulders through the open window. I couldn't move without inflicting injury on her, not that that prospect would have deterred me. I'm never at my smoothest with the press. 'You were up at Blackley with the Children of Light this afternoon.'

'How do you know that?' I asked angrily.

'You're involved with Repeal 98, aren't you?'

'What?'

'Have you got any statement on the killing of Fred Travis?'

'I don't know what you're talking about.'

'Oh come on, Mr Cunane, you spent the afternoon conferring with Aldous Arkwright.'

'Talk about getting hold of the wrong end of the stick,' I said wearily. 'I can't imagine why my movements should be of any interest to you.'

'But you've admitted that the police have questioned you and then you went straight off to report to Aldous Arkwright, so you must be working for Repeal and the Children of Light.'

'No comment,' I mumbled.

'Right,' she replied. 'So let me get this straight. David Cunane, private detective now lecturing on management at UNWIST, did not deny that he had been questioned by police concerning the Travis case and when asked if he was working for the self-styled moral-majority reformer Aldous Arkwright replied "No comment".'

I groaned.

'You're twisting what I said.'

'But that's what's going in Monday's paper.'

'You're not being fair,' I bleated. 'Look, I've got a very urgent appointment now. If your story is only for Monday's paper, can't you see me tomorrow? I'll be in all day.'

'But not where I can find you, eh? Sorry, I've got to file my copy tonight.'

'Well, tell your editor to be careful about the libel laws, because I'll sue . . .'

'When pressed for a statement Mr Cunane threatened to sue,' she said with an air of satisfaction.

'Damn you to hell,' I shouted, thoroughly rattled, 'I was never at Arkwright's.'

'Yes, you were. A very reliable source from Cultwatch saw you.'

I felt as if someone had dropped a large stone through the bottom of my stomach. A temporary lecturer who was associated with a controversial political group would be as popular with the Management Sciences department as a Hitler Youth choir at a bar mitzvah.

'We're running a feature on Cultwatch,' White continued. 'An informant from Cultwatch informed me that you were identified leaving Meldrum Terrace and when I looked you up in the files at the *Manchester Evening News* I realized that I'd also seen you with Peterson this morning. The public's entitled to know what's going on.'

'Are they?' I asked, unconvinced.

'Yes,' she said fiercely.

'What's Cultwatch when it's at home?'

'Don't you read the papers?'

I revved the engine slightly.

'Look, don't go. You're the first lead I've had. I know all about your reputation.'

'What reputation?' I muttered. 'I'm late for an appointment.' At that moment our conversation was interrupted by someone hooting behind me. Another resident wanted to get out of the car park and I was blocking the exit. I put the car into gear. Janine White was having none of this. She swiftly opened the door and slipped in beside me.

'Bloody cheek!' I growled.

'Oh, don't be like that, Mr Cunane. From what I've heard you aren't exactly backward about getting yourself into places where you aren't wanted yourself.'

I looked at her. She gave me a slightly crooked grin and then laughed.

'Shyness gets you nowhere in my job,' she explained.

'And just suppose I'm a serial rapist or something. Where would it get you then?'

'You're quite a pussy cat, Dave Cunane. There's a thick file on you at the *Evening News* offices. From what I hear about you, rape is about the last thing you'd need to try.'

'Can I drop you off in town?' I asked my uninvited passenger.

'You haven't answered my questions yet, and in case you're interested Cultwatch is a voluntary organization that keeps an eye on these mind-bending cults of which the Children of Light are one of the most dangerous.'

'I thought they were political,' I said innocently.

'You're talking about Repeal 98. That's just a front. They've even been proscribed by the Tories, or hadn't you heard?'

'Who cares? . . . I've nothing to tell you.' I turned into Seymour Grove, heading towards Deansgate.

'There must be some reason why you were at the Children of Light headquarters.'

'Can I speak off the record?' I asked after a long drawn-out sigh.

'Yes,' she said excitedly.

'I know you won't believe me but I have nothing whatever to do with Repeal 98. I've never met, spoken to, or heard much about Fred Travis. It's just that . . . well, there was something to do with . . . Oh, I can't tell you. The police haven't released the news yet and it could be prejudicial to a trial.'

'I promise absolute confidentiality,' she said earnestly.

I took my eyes off the road for a moment and looked at her sceptically.

'Travis was found clutching one of my business cards in his hand.'

'Ah,' Janine White purred in satisfaction, revealing rather large teeth as she turned and smiled at me. 'Presumably the police were satisfied by your explanation or you wouldn't be free, but that still doesn't explain why you went to see Arkwright as soon as you left them.'

'He phoned and offered me money to tell him what was going on. I'd nothing better to do.' It sounded lame even as I said it.

'Pretty mercenary character, aren't you?' she commented.

'I suppose you work for nothing?' I asked peevishly. 'Arkwright wanted harmless information. I'd already wasted the morning thanks to the Travis killing. I didn't see any harm at the time, so I went. When I got there I found I didn't like his set up. I tried to refuse his money but he has some pretty forceful followers.'

'Hmm,' she murmured, taking what I'd said with a handful of sodium chloride. 'You haven't explained how Arkwright knew that you were involved.'

'No, I haven't. Arkwright claims that his followers found the body. They must have seen my card.'

I drove in silence as I negotiated the narrow section of Deansgate outside Kendal's. Saturday-night crowds were making their way to the clubs and pubs. A well-known footballer was ramming his Jeep Grand Cherokee through the traffic, his much-televised features clearly visible through the darkened glass of his windscreen.

'Isn't that . . . what's his name?'

'Yes, it is,' I said miserably.

'Lighten up, Mr Cunane,' the journalist said. 'It's not you we're after. What you've said confirms that there's some kind of internal power struggle going on between the Children and the Repealers. This killing could be just the lever I need to force open this whole can of worms.'

'You can't force open a can of worms,' I pointed out. 'Not that I've ever heard of anyone putting worms in cans.'

'Well, whatever,' she said. 'This whole thing should be out in the open. These Repealers want to take women back into the Dark Ages.'

'Listen,' I replied cautiously, trying to keep a note of

pleading out of my voice. 'The police thought there was some link between the unfortunate Travis and me. They were just clearing that up. I no longer work as a private detective.' That was putting things a little strongly, I thought, but what right had White to know anything about my affairs? Why is it that in this country private eyes are the butt of all kinds of jokes? I've heard them all.

'What a shame!' she commented. 'I heard that you were a very colourful character.'

'I'm sorry but I've no intention of talking to you so that you can spice up some sneering background piece with references to a down-at-heel gumshoe. I know what your game is . . . find some dreary little provincial that your Hampstead readers can feel superior to.'

'Ouch! Touchy, aren't you? Dreary little provincial you may be, but you've carefully avoided telling me the real reason why you needed to visit dear Mr Aldous Arkwright this afternoon and why his heavies had to escort you to his door. My informant saw it all.'

'You can get out at the next traffic lights,' I told her.

By this time I'd escaped from the gridlock along Deansgate and was in the centre of town near the Nynex Arena. I slowed and headed for the kerb. There was a police car parked on the forecourt of the former Exchange station.

'I shall say you've assaulted me if you put me out here. You're heading up to Meldrum Terrace again, aren't you?'

'It's none of your business and you're holding me up,' I said angrily. It was ten past nine. I stopped the car, got out and opened her door. She made no effort to move. I could sense the policemen's eyes boring into my back.

'Come on, this is crazy,' I urged. 'Surely you don't need to go to these lengths working on the *Guardian*? It's supposed to be a quality paper, not a tabloid.'

'You've no idea what lengths I need to go to,' she said in a low voice. 'I need this story.'

Something of her despair reached me. I clenched my fists until I could feel my fingernails cutting into my palms. Was I falling for the old damsel-in-distress routine yet again? It seemed that I was. Or it could have been that I was so disgusted with myself for accepting Arkwright's money that I needed to show an independent witness that I was really on the side of the angels? Whatever the reason, I shut her door and walked round to the driver's side and got in. Uppermost in my mind was the thought that if I let her tag along it might do no harm. Having another female on board if Melanie took a fit of the vapours could be a smart move, I told myself as I accelerated towards Rochdale Road.

'OK,' I said. 'I am going back to Meldrum Terrace. One of the inmates has asked me to help her to get away . . . escape . . . er, just leave, really. I don't know. I said I'd be there at nine thirty. More likely than not it'll be a no-show and that'll be the end of it. Dead boring really. You can come along if you promise to behave yourself and to keep our names out of your middle-class scandal sheet.'

'You've really got it in for the *Guardian*, haven't you?'

I shook my head. I dislike all the press, not just the *Guardian*. There was no need to tell her that.

'Cultwatch is trying to help victims of these cults to get out from under their influence. I'd never do anything to harm one of those poor souls, even if my editor was prepared to let me. Anything I discover will be for background only.'

There was silence for a while as I drove up Rochdale Road and found the turning that would lead me to Meldrum Terrace. I parked a few streets away and checked my watch. I was in good time. I intended to drive slowly down the street just once.

'Have this female's parents paid you to do this?' White asked eventually.

'No, it's a quixotic whim of my own,' I told her. I was already regretting it.

'It's just that the people in Cultwatch hear a lot about deprogramming . . . you know, locking these cult victims away while someone tries to reverse their brainwashing.'

'Does that work with *Guardian* readers?' I asked in a bored voice. 'Anyway, Melanie didn't sound as if she'd been brainwashed. She just wanted out and I said I'd help.'

I checked my watch again and drove off slowly. We reached the end of Meldrum Terrace in a moment. It was exactly nine thirty. I drove slowly past parked 4WD vehicles. Although I kept the speed down to a crawl the end of the street loomed swiftly enough. There was no sign of Melanie. I paused for a second or two outside number 79.

'It looks as if she changed her mind,' I said.

'Or had it changed for her,' Janine White added. She wound her window down and looked at the house. Nothing seemed to be stirring. A smell of old brickwork and damp wood wafted in with the night air.

Reluctantly, I put the car into gear.

A full-throated shriek conveying terror and pain made my hand slip from the gear lever.

'Oh God!' White gasped. 'Do something.' She was already on her way out of the car but I was in front of her. The shrieks went on and on, now punctuated by gruff male voices.

I tried the door and then banged on it. It was like pounding on a solid slab of stone. There was no give at all.

'Help her, you wimp!' Janine White urged.

I got the boot of my car open and attacked the double glazed window of number 79 with my wheel brace. It was one of those laminated glass affairs and fortunately the whole pane shattered. I dived through the Roman blinds in time to see Rufus, clad in T-shirt and jeans, dragging Melanie away. I gave him an elbow on the forehead and he lurched back, his mouth wide open in surprise. Recovering, he came at me like a tiger, his mouth open in a roar. What happened next was an accident. The heavy steel wheel brace was still in my hand and as he swung towards me and I dodged away it made contact with his face . . . heavy contact. There was a squelching sound and blood and teeth flew into the air. He reeled back, his roar changed to a high-pitched squeal. I dragged Melanie clear and, opening the door, shoved her into the front seat of the Mondeo.

'Oh look!' the *Guardian* journalist yelled in dismay.

I looked back over my shoulder. Where a second ago there'd just been a blank door facing on to an empty street there was now a seething mass of bodies surging forward to prevent our escape. It was like a speeded-up movie. Before you could blink an eye Melanie was out of the car again and being dragged back indoors.

I reversed the car and partly mounted the pavement, narrowly missing Janine. The scrum separated to reveal Melanie. Resisting with all her strength, she was being firmly gripped round the waist by a large individual in a green robe. I was round the car and on to the pavement again like a ferret after a rabbit. It was over in seconds. I struck the green-robed figure who was restraining Melanie. He went down with a bone-crunching thud; no one stepped forward to take his place and she dashed back into the front seat. My troubles weren't over. Janine White was now locked in the arms of another of Arkwright's pixies – Rufus's broad-shouldered partner, John. White was baying like a cornered bloodhound . . . 'I'm with the Press!' she bellowed. 'Get your filthy hands off me.'

The *Guardian* reporter was between me and her captor. I pulled her by the shoulders and as I tugged she kneed him in a vital spot. He yelped in agony but didn't let go. I tugged again and with a sound of ripping cloth she fell back into my arms. I bundled her into the back seat and sped away.

I say 'sped away' but in fact my progress was more like a switchback ride. Every street between Meldrum Terrace and the main road had suffered from 'traffic calming' measures. The jolting we received was worse than anything Aldous Arkwright's adherents had dished out. It got so bad that I pulled into a side street and stopped with the lights off for a moment. That was just as well. Two of Arkwright's 4WD vehicles bounced past the end of the street with all lights blazing.

'That's torn it,' I muttered. 'I expect Arkwright knows where I live.'

Beside me, Melanie released a sob.

I decided to stay where I was for a few minutes before doubling back along the way I'd come and going into town via Victoria Lane, Alan Turing Way and Oldham Road. There was a steady stream of cursing coming from the back seat where Janine White seemed to be having a tag-wrestling match with herself. She was turning this way and that, rocking the car on its suspension.

'Did you have to be so rough?' she asked. 'Thanks to you, that gorilla who had hold of me has ripped the dress right off my back.'

'That sounds interesting. Do you think I should have left you where you were and let Will Self come and rescue you?'

'He doesn't work for the *Guardian* and I won't either for much longer unless I file a story on Repeal 98,' she spluttered.

'Wrap your coat round you and I'll drop you off at the Midland or wherever you're staying.'

'The Midland? On my expenses? You must be joking, and if you think I'm getting out of this car before our young friend has told me what's being going on you've got another think coming.'

I drove off without another word. Janine White seemed to have forgotten her promise.

We passed through the desolation of Alan Turing and on to the ravages of Oldham Road before I turned my attention to Melanie. 'Where would you like me to drop you, Miss, or hadn't you got as far as thinking about that yet?' I asked.

She started crying noisily between gasps for breath, bowing her head into her lap and weeping buckets. I stopped again. She got out of the car and, removing her green robe, used it to dry her eyes. Ms White wound her window down so that she wouldn't miss anything. Melanie screwed up the cloak and pitched it into the gutter. It was a very dramatic performance and would have gone down well at RADA. I looked at her closely. My earlier judgement that she was pretty still stood but now she looked petulant and bedraggled.

'Is there someone we can phone?' I asked as gently as I dared. 'What's your surname? Perhaps I could phone for you and someone could come and pick you up? Going back to my flat doesn't seem a very good idea in the circumstances.'

Eventually, after much coaxing, Melanie disclosed that her last name was Varley and that she lived in Oundle, a small town in Northamptonshire.

'What about your father? Can he come for you?' I asked.

This set the torrents off again. 'He's dead, he died last

month. There's only my mother and she's crippled with arthritis.'

'Didn't you feel you should have been at home?' I asked bluntly. Calming hysterics is not my forte. I was brought up in the school where temper tantrums were met with hard slaps.

'The Master told me that I should separate myself from these earthly ties. You don't understand. There was a lot of trouble. My father wanted me at home. He's . . . he was used to getting his own way. He put a lot of pressure on me to go home . . .'

I wondered what had happened to revive her homing instinct.

Melanie's story didn't sound as strange to me as perhaps it would have to some people. I recalled my mother Eileen's stories about relatives who'd joined female religious orders and been refused permission to come home for final illnesses, funerals and suchlike. That was all a long time ago, though.

Melanie looked at me. I passed her a pile of tissues from the glove compartment and she did something about her appearance. Her mascara had run. She looked as if she was preparing for Hallowe'en.

'It was different when Daddy died. Staying with the Children seemed the right thing to do. Daddy was so nasty, saying he was going to cut me out of his will and everything.'

I could sense Janine White's interest rising.

'Everyone was so nice to me. The Director counselled me every day. I mean, on my own . . . apart from when I was in the common gathering.'

'Just what was involved in this private counselling?' White demanded. 'Was there anything intimate?'

'Well, we were on our own, but there was nothing physical if that's what you mean. The Director says we must leave physical relationships until we reach a higher plane of existence.'

'Are you sure?' the journalist asked.

'Oh yes, the Director punishes anyone who pesters a member in that way, and he'd never take advantage himself.

Getting away from that sort of thing was one of the reasons I joined.'

I was watching Melanie closely. To my unpractised eyes she didn't look like a natural recruit to a life of holy chastity. Under the strain of strong emotion her chest was heaving, and what a chest it was. Without exactly being a bimbo, she was a very attractive young woman in a 'page three' sort of way . . . wide eyed, innocent looking and above all vulnerable. A lot of men go for that kind of thing, and to be honest, I'm one of them.

'So what happened to upset this idyllic existence?' the voice of the intelligentsia enquired from the back seat.

Melanie turned to look at Janine.

'I'm sorry, but who are you?' she asked, as if taking the journalist in for the first time.

'Oh, I'm with Mr Cunane,' White mumbled vaguely, but truthfully enough.

'But I heard you yelling that you were with the press,' Melanie persisted.

'I only said that to make them let me go,' Janine said quickly.

Melanie looked at me, then showed me her hands. I switched on the interior lights. Each palm was marked by an ugly red weal.

'Since Daddy died I've seen things in a different light. I can't seem to do anything right for the Director. I've been punished several times. After you left today he caned me again. They call it self-correction. He enjoys it, but I don't. I decided that I've had enough.'

'Are you saying that they're using corporal punishment?' Janine White demanded. With the speed of a striking cobra she got out of the back of the car and, whipping out a small camera, photographed Melanie's hands and face. Melanie obliged by starting to wail again.

'Are there marks anywhere else?' Janine asked expectantly.

'I think we ought to get the police,' I said. This produced even louder wails from my passenger.

'No, no, it was all my own fault,' she protested. 'I won't tell the police anything.'

'In that case I'm going to take you home to Oundle,' I announced. 'There's no way you're going to be able to use public transport, the state you're in.'

'Oh yes, please,' Melanie agreed, offering me a grateful smile.

'What about you, ace?' I said to the reporter. 'Can I drop you somewhere?' Although I was being polite, if she'd asked me to drop her into the Ship Canal from the top of Barton Bridge I'd have complied happily enough. If she hadn't panicked me into smashing my way into Arkwright's house of correction I wouldn't be about to face a charge of GBH for pulping the unfortunate Rufus's face.

'No, I think I'll stick with you, Dave. I think this young lady might need a chaperon after her ordeal.'

I made no comment but headed for the M56, rapidly discovering that there were ruts in Oldham Road deep enough to bury a pig in. We made it to the intersection 19 on the M6 just after 10.30 and an hour later turned off the motorway on to the A5 towards Market Harborough, Corby and Oundle. Apart from an occasional grunt in reply to questions about which road to take there was little information from Melanie. Janine White tried to fish more information about the C of L out of her.

Accustomed as I am to the occasional feat of knight errantry, a three-hour drive across Middle England is a bit out of the ordinary even for me, particularly as no one was paying for my time. I put it down to 'labour deferred' for the £300 I'd been crazy enough to accept from Aldous Arkwright. Oundle turned out to be a curious stone-built little town so discreet and cared for that it was reluctant to announce its existence with anything so vulgar as a road sign. The high street was a single lane regulated by traffic lights. Quaint was hardly the word for it. It looked like the set for a Jane Austen movie. The contrast with Blackley couldn't have been greater.

However, the familiar surroundings worked wonders on Melanie. She began to speak without prodding.

'I was at school here. The boys public school decided to

admit girls. I was one of the first. Mummy and Daddy bought a house in the neighbourhood so that they wouldn't have to make long journeys to see me.'

Home turned out to be a large house set in its own grounds on the eastern side of Oundle. When I suggested that I see her safely to the entrance Melanie threw another wobbler.

'Mummy's not well. It's best if I slip in quietly.'

I glanced at the darkened house. It didn't look like another cult haven. Melanie was insistent that we leave, so we did. I wasn't convinced that we were doing the right thing, but Melanie wasn't a child.

The drive back to Manchester was punctuated only by the snores of my passenger from the press.

Political Assassination?

Charles Goodchild, the renegade MI5 official currently in hiding on the Continent, confirmed to this paper that the security service had extensive files on the Repeal 98 Movement and that 'termination with extreme prejudice' of Fred Travis had been considered as an option during his time with the agency.

Report in the *Sunday Times*

4

Sunday, 18 October

It was 3.30 a.m. on Sunday morning when I got back to Manchester. Janine White was staying in Whalley Range. A quick glance at the hotel's crudely hand-painted sign proclaiming that it was the 'Jewel in the Crown' confirmed that it wouldn't make a very big dent in her expenses sheet. The door was locked and barred and Janine hadn't got a key, but I felt no desire to offer the hospitality of my flat. I rattled and banged until eventually a turbaned Sikh pushed his head round the door and reluctantly admitted her.

All the activity had got my blood racing and, although I was tired enough, when I laid my head on my own pillow sleep was far away.

Was I a suspect in the Travis murder, or was I not? Would the police find my fingerprint on the business card and arrest me at dawn? Was my print even on the card? Why did Travis have the card in the first place? Was he really intending to get in touch with me? The questions churned round and round in my weary brain like a pile of soggy coloured socks in a washing machine.

Before I finally dropped off to sleep I was haunted by the vision of a cell door slamming and slamming and slamming.

I was still tired and tense when I woke up. My throat was dry and my eyes were bunged up. It was well past my usual waking time. The sun was streaming in at a high angle. In that first uneasy moment of consciousness my thoughts were about Travis, then I sat up with a start when I remembered what I'd done to Rufus. His face had been ugly enough to start with but smashing him across the mouth with a steel bar was hardly calculated to improve his looks. Just how urgently would the police pursue his complaint?

Very urgently, I decided. They'd do me for GBH, or aggravated burglary, or kidnapping sooner rather than later.

I got up nervously and looked down into the car park. There were no white vans there yet, just the familiar sight of Finbar Salway and his twin sister Fiona striding off to Sunday mass.

'Oh, for the joys of a well-regulated existence,' I said to myself as I watched the twins. Then I decided that as the existence I already had served me well enough I ought to enjoy it while I could. I trotted into the kitchen and made myself a major fry-up . . . full Sunday breakfast . . . egg, bacon, beans, sausages, tomatoes, mushrooms, fried bread – the whole cholesterol choir. I managed to hold back any further sad reflections about my plight until I finished wiping the egg yolk off my plate with a piece of bread.

Not many minutes later I was in the middle of what passes for an open space in Manchester and pounding my way along the banks of the Mersey. The old mountain bike I was riding on was creaking and groaning from the strain. I was still slightly on edge but the physical exertion was helping me to come off the boil.

Why was someone trying to involve me?

I mean, why stick that card in the dead man's hand? The best I could come up with was that the killer was someone I'd brushed against in the past. There were any number of those. Had some petty shoplifter I'd caused to be arrested graduated to contract killing? It didn't seem likely. I'd come across a few heavies, really bad guys in the local club scene, but why would any of them, assuming they were still alive and kicking, want to get even with me in this strange way? Their methods were usually far more direct.

I reached the old Barfoot railway bridge which carries the Metro trams across the river. There's a footbridge running alongside it and I crossed over, intending to return to Chorlton along the Sale bank. Looking at the swiftly flowing dark-brown waters of the river I asked myself for the hundredth time whether the decision to get out of private investigation had been the right one.

The sense of being a passenger trying to rearrange the deck chairs on the sinking Titanic was still strong. I was trying to generate the illusion that life might go on as normal. Worrying about my career in present circumstances was stupid but I couldn't help it.

I almost enjoyed some of the work at UNWIST. The lecturing and tutorials were bearable once I'd mastered the material. The trouble was, I'd got my foot on the academic ladder rather late in the day. I could see myself pottering round the Management Sciences department in twenty years' time . . . a licensed eccentric, someone who used to have his own business but who had failed and was now just about holding down an undemanding academic job. No, that wouldn't happen. It wasn't very wonderful being the low man on the totem pole but surely things would change.

What jerked me out of my self-induced reverie and almost brought me tumbling over the handle bars of the bike was the realization that I'd arranged to go to the Cornerhouse with Monica Withers last night. We'd arranged to see a continental film. Not my scene, but very much Monica's.

'Oh God!, being arrested for assault or even for the Travis murder is one thing, but standing up Monica Withers is another!' I thought. I raced back to the flat as if I was in contention for the Yellow Jersey.

Monica and I had been gently testing out our feelings for each other for some time. It was all part of my attempt to change my life-style. One of the discoveries I'd made in the grove of academe was that the area was as densely populated with followers of fashion, empty-headed careerists and general blockheads as anywhere else. Call me romantic if you like, but I'd had this idea at the back of my head that the scholarly pursuit is a search for truth. Maybe it is in some places, but the Management Sciences department at UNWIST isn't one of them. I'd been disappointed in my colleagues there but not in Monica Withers.

Monica was different. She seemed genuinely independent. Where others measured their words carefully for their effect on the academic hierarchy, she just let rip with whatever she was thinking. I admired that, though I wasn't yet securely seated enough to copy her. Anyway, the long and short of it was that over the months since my appointment we'd gradually drifted closer to each other. Over the last few weeks we'd got in the habit of seeing each other on a Saturday evening for a concert or a play and now I'd stood her up.

My eyes were full of salty sweat, and my vision was blurred as I slogged my way towards Thornleigh Court. I crossed the main road and reached the narrow path along the side of the garages only to find my final approach blocked by Finbar Salway. He was on his way back from his religious devotions.

'Hold on, Dave,' he shouted as I swerved to avoid him. 'Did you get the message from your friend?'

'What message? What friend?'

'He was waiting for you last night when I was coming back from the British Legion committee meeting, must have been about half ten or quarter to eleven. Course I didn't let him in your flat or anything but I did let him in the building. He said he'd push a note under your door. I saw him writing it.'

'Describe him,' I said. A familiar sensation of dismay was creeping over me. The fact that Finbar had let a stranger enter Thornleigh Court was an unusual event in itself.

'Well he was in a Discovery, had the damn big thing parked right up by the entrance. Cheery-looking cove, sort of ruddy face . . . looked like a farmer or something. He was very polite, nothing sinister about him. He just said he was supposed to be meeting you and could he leave a note to tell you that he'd turned up? Yes, I'd said he was in his mid-forties or perhaps a well-preserved fifty . . . quite fit, he sprinted up the stairs when I let him in. I had my work cut out to keep up with him.'

'And he went right up to my door?' I prompted.

'Yes, I'm sure I saw him pushing a note under your door.'

'I didn't find one. Was there anything else you remember about him?'

Finbar screwed his face up in the effort to remember. 'There was one thing. I thought his eyes and his smile were quite extraordinary. You know he fixed me with a look and stared at me for so long I wondered if the blighter wanted me to go up and kiss him.'

'I see,' I murmured.

'Did I do anything wrong?' the ageing military man asked anxiously.

'Not at all. Everything's fine,' I said as I pushed past him. I looked anxiously round the corner into the car park expecting to see a white van and a couple of burly coppers waiting for me.

It was clear and the relief must have shown on my face because Finbar picked it up at once.

'You're on a case,' he said excitedly.

'No, you know I'm a college lecturer now.' Finbar had filled in his time after retirement from the Army by rendering occasional assistance to Pimpernel Investigations. It had been a big disappointment to him when I chucked the towel in. He'd offered to help me out financially but I'd turned him down.

'I know that look, you can't fool me.'

'I was in a spot of bother yesterday,' I admitted. 'Fred Travis had one of my cards in his hand when the police found him.'

'But they don't suspect you, surely?'

'You know what they're like. They have to come up with answers.'

'But Travis? He never had anything to do with us when we were in Pimpernel Investigations.'

'You know that, I know that, but do the police know it?' I said. 'No, they don't.'

Finbar gripped the bike.

'You've got to let me help you. I was almost as involved as you were.'

'If I don't get under the shower in two minutes I'll get pneumonia,' I said.

'Here, I'll put this away,' he said, wheeling the bike towards my garage. 'Then I'll come up. Was the chap I let in last night a copper?'

'No, you might say he's a sort of a partner of Fred Travis in the fake religion business.'

'Oh, God! I should have known there was something wrong with him. Fiona would have spotted it right away,' Finbar said with a shudder.

I looked at him, almost expecting him to whip his rosary out but he didn't. Finbar is a very devout old-school Catholic and the last man in the world to be taken in by a shaman like Arkwright, yet he'd let him into Thornleigh Court without a qualm. He looked embarrassed now.

'There is something you could do for me,' I suggested. 'Get all the Sunday papers and bring them up to the flat. We'll see what we can glean about Travis and the Children of Light.'

Without another word, Finbar wheeled the bike away and I headed for the shower and the phone call to Monica.

The warm water washed away the mud and sweat and I decided that there was a limit to the number of things you can feel guilty about at any one time. The blow to Rufus had been an accident, though nobody was likely to believe that. Standing Monica up was also an accident and, as for Fred Travis or Aldous Arkwright, after today I was never going to let their names cross my lips again. The one thing I really did deserve a clogging for was giving Clint Lane's name to that sneaky Peterson. That was a bad mistake. I listened to the one o'clock news as I dried off. The Travis murder featured prominently but there was no mention of any suspects being arrested.

'Monica,' I said when I got through. 'What can I say . . .?'

'Where were you?' she snapped. 'I waited almost an hour for you.'

'I'm sorry, something came up and . . .'

'And you couldn't get near a phone.'

'I'm sorry.'

'So am I. I hope she was worth it. I know you think I'm just an old frumpy academic . . .'

'It was nothing like that, and for the record I find you very attractive. Hell, if you're an old frump what does that make me? We're almost the same age.'

'You're older than me.'

'Right. It was just something from my past,' I said

struggling for an explanation. I could hardly tell her that I was out assaulting muscle-bound Americans when I should have been escorting her to an Ingmar Bergman film.

'That's what I like about you, Dave,' she murmured. 'You're not the only one in the department with a disreputable past but you seem to trail yours about with you like a bad smell.'

'Thanks!' I gasped indignantly.

'Penetrated the Cunane defences, have I? I only meant that the others are better at putting a bold face on things than you are.'

'There's nothing disreputable about my past and I expect Professor Richardson would be less than delighted to hear that his department is as full of people trying to hide their pasts as a regiment in the French Foreign Legion.'

'Him! He's the worst of the lot,' she said with a laugh. 'I shall see you on Monday and I shall expect full reparations.'

When Finbar returned it took him about three minutes to get the whole story out of me.

'Why your card? Why was it put there?' he demanded. 'Why should someone want to implicate you?'

'I don't know. Maybe Travis was going to use me to start checking up on something. His enemies found out and left the card there to warn anyone with similar ideas what would happen.'

'Sounds pretty thin to me, mate. I mean, no one's actually suggested that Travis was a criminal.'

'But he was involved with Arkwright and he has some very dodgy friends.'

'That's another thing. Why haven't you been arrested for assaulting this Rufus yet?'

'I don't need more questions. I want some answers,' I said peevishly.

'Why don't you get your father to ask Assistant Chief Constable Sinclair what's going on?'

'You must be joking,' I said. 'Those two do each other favours but as for me . . .'

'You're his son . . . he's bound to help you.'

'It's easy to see that you're a bachelor.'

'So are you.'

'No, I'm not,' I said with a glance at the photo of my dead wife.

'Sorry,' Finbar muttered. Then, 'What do you make of Arkwright's visit, assuming it was him?'

'It was him. Presumably he was checking if I had the girl with me.'

'But what are you going to do about it?'

'What do you suggest?'

'Well, you can phone him and ask him what he's playing at.'

'Look Finbar, I'm a college lecturer now. All I want is to be left alone.'

Finbar gave me a look that was half-way between surprise and disgust. I couldn't really blame him, but there was nothing I could do that wouldn't make things worse. I was worried about how Arkwright had managed to get hold of my address so quickly.

We both lapsed into silence and began scanning the papers. There was plenty about Travis, a figure of interest to the press for years, but it was really his link with Arkwright that interested me.

Travis had paid for hundreds of Repeal 98 candidates in the recent election. None of them were elected but they were credited with drawing votes away from Government candidates. 'The biggest movement to come out of Manchester since the campaign to repeal the Corn Laws' it said in the *Observer*. But while the journalist writing the piece was happy enough to display his historical erudition by references to nineteenth-century politics, he made it very clear that Travis was regarded as a joke figure. His nuisance value was so insignificant that to suggest political assassination as a motive for his murder was downright silly. The previous Government was so unpopular that they'd have lost the election anyway.

There was a large double-page spread on Fred's life and achievements in the *Sunday Times* that included a picture of Aldous Arkwright, flanked by Rufus and John . . .

'At the time of his death Fred Travis was believed to be seeking an alliance with the mysterious Children of Light cult movement.

The cult, which has many branches in America and South Korea, is said to be anxious to gain recruits in the UK. Since its inception the cult has been at the centre of controversy. There have been claims that the cult is overzealous in helping terminally ill members into the next world and that the attitude towards sexual relationships is disruptive of family life. In America, several well-known Hollywood film stars claim membership but in Europe the cult has faced hostility and resistance to its attempts to claim religious status. The German Chancellor claimed that it is a conspiracy not a genuine religion. Cult leader Aldous Arkwright, seen here with his colleagues Rufus Jackson Polk and John Harrison Tyler, is believed to originate from Manchester . . .'

The article then detailed what was known about Arkwright, carefully blending fact and inference in a way that skirted round the laws of libel but discredited the 'spiritual director' as fully as the writer was able. When I studied the photo of Rufus I could feel my stomach tying itself in knots. He didn't look like a man who would let bygones be bygones.

Arkwright was born plain Clive Roper. Cult followers feel there's some mystical significance in the name Arkwright . . . it means 'shipbuilder', or so the Director says. Roper went to Oxford with the intention of becoming an Anglican clergyman but something went wrong and he left Oxford under a cloud. Those who know the reason are tight lipped but 'illegal substances' have been mentioned. Instead of being ordained, Arkwright headed off to San Francisco and joined a Satanist cult. It was just after the film **Rosemary's Baby** *came out in 1968. Polanski's film gave a tremendous boost to devil worshippers. Apparently Roper learnt that there was a great deal of money to be made in running your own religion. For a time the Church of Satan was actually recognized as an official religion by the US Armed Forces. Then came the Manson killings in August 1969 and the prospects for Satanists didn't seem so rosy any more. Roper ditched his own surname and took the name Aldous Arkwright at the same time as he bailed out of being a follower of the Prince of Darkness. He surfaced in New York in 1970 with two disciples, Polk and Tyler, to start the Children of Light. He was investigated but cleared by* *a grand jury in New York on charges of soliciting inheritances by promises of miracle cures. He is thought to have transferred the headquarters of the Children of Light to England in 1990 when there was a threat of further investigations by the US federal authorities. There was little heard of him until the attempted tie-up with Fred Travis's high-profile campaign for a return to traditional morality. Roper/Arkwright also claims to be a stalwart in defence of old-style morality. He now prefers to draw a veil over the Satanist period of his life. No mention of his Satanist past appears in the movement's official biography of him.*

'Sounds like the sort you'd need a very long spoon to sup with,' was Finbar's comment. 'I know what I'd like to do if he took a stick to a child of mine.'

Merseybeat Back?

Bernard Lester, the chairman of the Merseyside and Wirral Development Corporation, claimed that the booming club scene in Liverpool is attracting outside investment capital to the region for the first time in decades. 'Liverpool's throbbing at night and the vibrancy is being carried over into an increasingly optimistic scene in daylight hours,' the development corporation chief said at a press conference called to mark the agreement to open a giant car plant on Merseyside. Lester said 'there is increasing evidence that young people see Merseyside as an attractive place to live and work because of our highly successful night-club scene. We're buzzing.' Representatives of the rival Manchester-based NorWest Development Corporation were 'unavailable for comment'.

Sunday Times

5

Monday, 19 October

Next morning I was up early and felt as if a weight had been lifted. The police weren't waiting to slap handcuffs on me. Like waterlogged timbers sinking into an oily pond, the weekend's problems submerged one after another. There were a hundred and one domestic tasks to perform before I could launch myself back into my routine labours at the education mill. Shirts don't iron themselves and tackling my normal chores took my mind off my troubles.

Doing penance for yesterday's cholesterol excess, I breakfasted on a carton of Sainsbury's Authentic Greek Yoghurt. I spooned the last of the yoghurt down, struggling not to wince. Then I packed my notes in my executive briefcase, straightened my tie and hurried out to join the throng of commuters catching the Metrolink tram into town.

I prefer listening to Radio 2 rather than the local news these days. I suppose that's a sign of my present lack of engagement with the booming local crime scene. So when I caught the tram at Stretford after a brisk walk along Edge Lane I was still happily ignorant of the developments in the Travis murder. I soon found myself peering at the morning paper over someone's shoulder. 'Man Arrested in Travis Case' was the subheading that had caught my eye.

By the time we reached my stop I was unable to keep on kidding myself that I didn't care what the news was. I was desperate to know. There were no news stands near UNWIST and I ran up the steps of the tower block that housed Management Sciences into the department staffroom. It was liberally supplied with copies of the *Guardian* as well as the *Financial Times*. The article on the Travis case was by a reporter whose name I hadn't heard of. There was no mention of my name or of Janine White's either.

Details of the murder and of Travis's work with the Repealers were recounted, then came the following paragraph:

Fred Travis's murder is believed to be related to trouble in the club scene. Informed speculation is that the man assisting police with their enquiries into the death of the millionaire moral reformer is closely linked to a well-known Manchester club owner. Since the relative decline in attractiveness of Manchester's night-clubs and rave dens compared with those of nearby Liverpool there is believed to have been a tooth-and-claw struggle between club bosses to survive in a shrinking market. Travis's murder may well be related to this but police are releasing few details at the moment.

Breathing a sigh of relief, I laid the paper on the table and scanned it column by column, looking for any further mention of Janine or myself. There was nothing. I began quietly whistling. Then Monica Withers came in. She came straight over.

'You're looking sprightly, Dave,' she said. 'Interesting weekend?'

I realized that I was supposed to feel guilty.

I managed to smile. 'Yes, it was rather more active than I bargained for,' I said breezily.

'Oh, what did you get up to? Do tell.'

'It's highly complicated and very dull.'

'I see ... Like that, is it?'

'Honestly, Monica, my life is so boring I'm thinking of selling off bits of it as a non-pharmaceutical alternative to Mogadon.'

'Well, the film was great.'

'I thought I made you miss it?'

'I had the tickets, Dave. I waited so long, then I went in.'

'Sorry.'

'Yes, and after you phoned on Sunday I drove over to the Dales and had a nice stroll round Settle. You should have come. Malham Tarn's lovely at this time of year. Great for a solitary ramble.'

'Well, you didn't invite me.'

'No, of course I didn't.'

'As I remember, there was something said about me trailing a bad smell around.'

She laughed and looking at her I knew again why I liked her. Perhaps 'liked' is too weak a word. We hadn't reached the 'l' word yet but it could happen. There was this bittersweet, dry martini crispness about Monica that I always find appealing. Another thing was that Monica always looked just the way she acted ... there was no falseness. What you saw was what you got. I don't mean that she didn't wear make-up or anything. It was just that she was entirely herself, not some image consultant's creation. Her blonde hair was brushed back off the forehead. Her expression was open and confident. She liked to wear a plain but expensive blouse with the collar turned up and a white pleated skirt under a neat dark jacket.

'Look Monica, I'm sorry about standing you up. Forces outside my control, et cetera, et cetera. Too boring to go into. Anyway, I don't think I'd have been able to come to Settle with you, even if you could have coped with the smell. I had to go through my notes again. You know that if I give any wrong references someone's sure to complain.'

'I'd love to help you with those,' she enthused. 'You've only to ask.' Monica had a Ph.D. in management science. Her bail-out from industry into academia took place five years before my own. Looking into her brown eyes and studying that mildly mocking, tolerant expression I was aware of the repulsive forces that had so far restrained the attraction we felt for each other.

Monica was very much the captain of her own ship. The trouble is, I am too. However, she gave me the impression that she'd mapped out her life well in advance. I'm not like that. Too often my navigation has resulted in shipwreck. The compass doesn't seem to work well for me. If we were going to sail together it would take us a while to work out what direction we both wanted to go in. For the present we were content to be good friends.

I think the repulsion sprang from the fact that Monica was one of those lucky people for whom things had always worked out according to expectations. For her things *had* always gone according to plan. Life had taught her to expect success.

'Everything's more or less up to scratch now, Monica,' I lied. 'It's just that some of these Chinese students are so keen to find any error.'

She hid her disappointment with a shrug. 'What's so interesting about the *Guardian* then? I don't usually see you poring over the inside pages of a paper.'

'No,' I said hastily refolding the paper, 'there was just something I was checking.' As I replaced the paper she picked it up and homed in on the piece about Travis.

'It couldn't have happened to a nicer bloke,' she said. 'These Repealers must be crazy. They want to return women to the days of slavery.'

I murmured agreement.

'I'm not surprised that Travis was trying to link up with the Children of Light . . . like calls to like. If anything, they're even more backward-looking than his lot.'

'Really?'

'Did you know my poor sister Shannon got involved with these wretched Children of Light? She's ruined her life.'

'How's she done that?' I asked, steering her towards the coffee dispenser. I filled two cups and we sat together by a window with view over the London Road end of the

Mancunian Way. Traffic was gridlocked again.

'Poor Shannon, she joined the Children of Light in Peterborough right after she graduated from Cambridge.'

'So they're not just in Manchester? I knew they were well established in America but not here.'

'They keep a low profile here, or they did until recently, but they've got their nests up and down the country. There are well over a thousand members now. Just imagine it.'

From the way Monica spoke, it was clear that the analogy with some form of insect life was fully intended. I was intrigued. Unlike the Sunday papers she wasn't muzzled by libel laws.

'Has Shannon ever tried to get away from them?'

'Fat chance . . . She tries to recruit me from time to time. You know she has kids of her own now? Last time I saw her, she told me that if I came for instruction there'd be every chance that the Master would find me a suitable mate. Apparently he enjoys pairing up his followers, some of them anyway. The inner circle have to stay celibate, but the ordinary members are expected to produce children and work for the organization. According to what I can glean from Shannon, the inner circle try to get visions and insights by standing in pools of icy water for hours at a time and by eating magic mushrooms.'

'Sounds like fun,' I prompted.

'That's not the half of it. They run these communes like eighteenth-century men o' war, with punishment sessions for those who fail to reach targets for new recruits or fundraising.'

'What's Shannon like?' I asked.

'That's why it's such a dreadful shame . . . She got a First in Computer Science. We thought she was destined for higher things in the City of London but she fell for this boy and he was involved with the Children.'

'I suppose he's the father of her kids?'

'That's the fantastic thing . . . They don't believe in what they call impermanent earthly love, or in marriage. She's had children by different men she hardly knew. It's dreadful. There should be a law against these cults. They've no right to take people from their families. I don't think my mother's ever got over it. My father died not long after Shannon joined and she insisted on taking her share out of the family trust and cashing it in.'

'I suppose she was very impressionable.'

'Not really. My parents always used to say that of the two of us she was the more strong-willed. She certainly worked very hard to get herself into Cambridge and then get such a good degree. Shannon's always been deep, but then what do you expect when you name someone after an Irish river goddess? That used to be a family joke.'

As she sipped her coffee and thought of her sister, Monica's eyes began to fill with tears.

'I'm sorry. I shouldn't have upset you,' I said, passing her a handkerchief.

'It's not your fault. I must say I'm very glad to see that this Travis got his just deserts.'

I raised my eyebrows at this unusual display of fierceness.

'That's going a bit far, isn't it? I mean Travis was political. There was none of this supernatural mumbo-jumbo with him.'

'Yes, but he was linked to the Children. It says so here and it's time someone did something about them,' she explained. 'The Government should have acted years ago.'

People were moving out of the common room towards tutorial rooms and lecture theatres. Out of the corner of my eye I spotted Professor Richardson waving to me. Giving Monica an apologetic smile, I headed over to him.

'How are things?' he asked genially, without pausing for a reply. 'I've been meaning to speak to you. As you know, your contract comes up for renewal in two weeks' time. I must say everything's looking good. You seem to have settled in really well and I see you've developed good relations with the department's evergreen *femme fatale*, Dr Withers. Her heart's in the right place, but you mustn't let her bully you into becoming her toyboy, hey!' Alvin Richardson, a tall cadaverous-looking North American, chuckled at his own facetiousness. He gave my forearm a manly squeeze and trotted off. I guessed that he'd misunderstood the scene with the handkerchief.

I gawped at his rapidly receding figure. Richardson was a specialist on the culture of firms, enterprises, schools, etc.

Over the last few years he'd become a recognizable television personality usually called on to comment when something went wrong in any kind of institution. He'd devised an elaborate system of metaphors for describing the internal attitudes of these bodies. I knew what his attitude towards the one-man operation in which I'd worked for twenty years was. He told me that the institutional culture of one-man firms was either that of the Star, a person who worked in a tightly regulated framework and related to a planetary system of other specialists; or the Scavenger, a lone wolf prowling about in the wilderness looking for what he could devour.

Fortunately Richardson and his fancies did not occupy too much of my day. That was occupied by the usual academic grind of lectures, tutorials and marking.

By lunch-time my official duties for the day were over. I'd delivered a lecture on VAT to a group of third-year students and held a two-hour seminar on security measures with four M.Sc. students. Although there was no danger of my target audience ganging up and knocking nine bells out of me, both activities, but especially the seminar, left me more drained than when I was prowling supermarket warehouses tensed for a bunch of fives in the face whenever I turned a corner. There seemed to be so many theories, so many points of view that one had to keep up with, so many relevant and interesting books that one was supposed to have read that at times I felt quite hag-ridden and careworn. Anyway, I'd been advised that it could only get easier.

Before leaving, I checked at the departmental office to see if there were any messages. The departmental secretary was Lisa Lovegrove, a plump middle-aged woman who seemed to be quite partial to my charms; at least she always greeted me fondly enough.

'Oh, Mr Cunane,' she said, when I entered her inner sanctum, 'I was just talking about you. I was saying to Joyce that if I wasn't spoken for I'd definitely be interested in you.' Joyce, a secretary who shared Mrs Lovegrove's office greeted this sally with muffled laughter.

'If only I'd met you earlier,' I said, 'we could have got something going.'

'I don't know what Peter would say,' she replied with a laugh, 'but you're certainly an improvement on some of the fossils we've got in this department. Talk about management science, some of them couldn't manage their way to the toilet without assistance.'

Peter was her husband. His name was often invoked.

'Professor Richardson said he might want to see me. Has he left any messages?' I asked.

'Very businesslike today, aren't you? Who's the lady that you're going to see, then?'

'Now Lisa, you know I wouldn't meet anyone without telling you. The way I feel, I need a couple of hours' shuteye.'

'Heavy weekend?' she said with a leer.

I shook my head. 'Any messages?'

'There was one. He rang twice while you were in your seminar. I told him you couldn't be interrupted. Very impatient, he was. Left you his number and said would you ring right away.'

She passed me a scrap of paper with a Manchester number on.

'Can I use your phone?' I asked. 'My mobile needs recharging.' Since coming to work at UNWIST I'd avoided using my own phone as much as possible. My caller was probably a student asking for a postponement of an essay deadline. Using the department phone was one of the little economies I needed to make if I was to spin out a part-time lecturer's salary far enough to encompass my mortgage and car expenses. As it was, I was living like the proverbial church mouse . . . well, perhaps a cathedral mouse.

'Go on then,' she offered.

'Bob Lane here, is that you Dave?' my caller responded when I got through.

I must have looked surprised because Lisa Lovegrove spoke before I did. Hearing Bob's voice was a real blast from the past.

'Is it personal?' she asked with an expression of concern, 'I can transfer you to the prof's office if you like.'

I nodded. 'Hang on a minute, Bob.'

The few seconds it took to transfer myself to Alvin Richardson's office gave me the chance to get my wits together. Bob Lane, known as Popeye to his friends, is a tough club owner. Although he's not a beachcomber on the wilder shores of crime, he's dabbled in the past, as I suppose some might say that I have. I'd helped him on a couple of occasions and he'd returned the favours with interest. Nowadays he controlled at least four, if not more, fairly thriving clubs. He'd also recently moved into the expanding theme-pub scene.

'Dave,' he said huskily when I reconnected, 'they've arrested Clint. You've got to help me to clear him.'

'Of course,' I managed to say. My mouth felt dry. All the guilt I'd managed to suppress about Clint came rushing back.

It's difficult to say anything about Clint that doesn't sound condescending. He has a massive and powerful body but his mind has never developed beyond that of a five-year-old. The mental handicap hasn't prevented him from having a perfectly happy, contented and fulfilled life. Living in some small village in the past, Clint would have been a local prodigy, called on to use his giant strength where now we would summon mechanical aid. Life in a modern city presented a different set of challenges . . . not for Clint, who was perfectly happy wherever he was, but for his relatives.

It was difficult to imagine Clint harming a fly. He was about thirty-two years old, and he shared a house on the Langley estate in North Manchester with his mother and brother. I suspected that Clint was the reason why Bob had never married. Bob's the same age as me.

'They say he's killed someone . . .'

'Never,' I interrupted confidently. One of the last times I'd seen Clint he was holding back a predatory crowd of Irish tinkers by whirling a twelve-foot-long steel spar round his head like a cheerleader's baton and laughing happily, but he wasn't vicious. He did sometimes intimidate with his giant size and strength, but to my knowledge had never hurt anyone. That stood to reason; if he ever exerted himself, he could tear heads off shoulders.

'Listen. It's this Fred Travis, they say Clint killed him. You can guess what's coming next. I'm sure they're going to say I put him up to it.'

I gasped in surprise. Despite its boasts about being Britain's second city, Manchester's really just a big village as far as gossip and meeting people is concerned. I knew that Bob employed some rough types. He had to. But unlike some, he kept them in order. Predatory security firms still plague Manchester's club scene. They take over clubs by offering the services of 'doormen,' usually as a pretext for diverting the profits into their own pockets. The police do little to stop it or protect club owners, which is why the night-club scene is switching from Manchester to Liverpool. When I'd first met Bob he'd been in the process of leaving one of the more vicious security firms which didn't draw the line at occasional murder. He'd got his nickname because the body-building exercises necessary for his role as a club bouncer had resulted in grotesquely thickened forearms.

'What do you want me to do?' I asked as soon as my head stopped spinning.

'Could you come round here? I'm at Howl, my club near Stevenson Square.'

'Right, I'm on my way,' I said.

He broke the connection and I sat for a moment, trying to get my bearings. I'd said I'd go, but should I? Bob could hire all kinds of help. Why did he need me to volunteer? I remembered why: I haven't enough friends to start ignoring those who need help especially when I'm the one who gave the police their first clue. Whenever I'd turned to Bob in the past, usually for information, he'd come through and no questions asked. On my way out of the office my eye was caught by a file labelled 'Appointments Panel'. Old habits die hard. Almost without thinking I picked it up and leafed through. It was the minutes of a recent senior staff meeting. There were a list of new appointments and the names of those part-time staff whose contracts were to be renewed. My name was on the list.

I suppose that news resulted in the mixture of emotions in my face when I left the office.

'You look as if you'd just lost a pound and found sixpence,' Lisa Lovegrove said. She was intrusive but I'd encouraged her. Departmental secretaries have a lot more influence in the university world than temporary lecturers.

'You could say that,' I replied. 'Definitely a case of mixed news.'

'Anything I can do?' she offered, leaning over her desk to give me a full chance to inspect her well-formed upper body.

'I'll keep you posted,' I promised, allowing my gaze to linger.

'Don't forget you've bought two tickets for the departmental hot-pot supper next week. I shall expect the chance to share you with Dr Withers.'

Suppressing a shudder at the image of myself as the meat in the sandwich between the pair I gave her a knowing look and departed.

I decided that walking towards Stevenson Square was as quick as waiting for a taxi. I hurried across London Road, past Piccadilly Station into Dale Street, then round the corner into the Square. It was once the venue for Manchester's street orators but now is more famed for a very different type of noise-making. Bob's club certainly lived up to its name. It was in the basement of an old warehouse and getting to his office was quite a religious experience in itself. Everything was black or red. Frightening blasts of loud techno music accompanied my descent into the cellar.

'God, Bob!' I said when I finally reached his windowless office. 'How do you stick it down here? That noise is enough to strip bark off trees.'

'I've got some Cliff Richard or Slade tracks here, if you like them better,' he shouted.

'Sorry, I've not had your conditioning,' I replied.

He threw his hands up, revolved his chair to face a console behind him and turned the noise off. Suddenly we were merely sitting in a rather dingy office in a worn-out building rather than in the ante-room to the nether regions. Bob looked much the same as ever. The only change was his hair-style. He was having a little frontier trouble – locks had vanished from the front of his scalp and what he had left was now combed forward, Roman-emperor style, to provide coverage. Otherwise he looked fit. He was wearing well.

'Need it for the punters. They expect it. You get to ignore it after a while.'

'I suppose that says something about your sanity,' I commented. It was the wrong thing to say. Bob scowled and flexed his massive forearms. As usual, he was clad in an expensive suit that only fitted him in three places. His mother used to choose his clothes out of a catalogue and it looked as if she was still at it.

'It's not about me that I've asked you round. They got Clint banged up for this murder. The solicitor says they've got a video from Travis's flat showing him going there on Saturday morning. The time on the video coincides with the killing. It looks like an open-and-shut case, only I know that he was with me on Saturday morning. We only finished here at four and he came home with me like he always does.'

'Look Bob, before you go on I'd better tell you what happened to me on Saturday. I was questioned because Travis had my card . . .'

'I know . . .'

'I had to tell them that I gave Clint one.'

'I know, but they'd have arrested him anyway as soon as they saw that bloody video.'

'How are they questioning him?'

'Oh, they're bending over backwards to be what they call fair. They've got a representative from MENCAP there to help him as well as the solicitor, but that doesn't make a peck of difference. I know he wasn't at Travis's house. I know he wouldn't have done any harm to Travis, much as that bastard needed someone to harm him.'

I raised my eyebrows at this. 'Has Travis been a naughty boy then?' I asked.

'He got what was coming to him but our Clint had nothing to do with it.'

Bob seemed to regret having been so forthright. He shut his lips tightly and then reached into the bottom drawer of the filing cabinet behind him. He took out a bottle of whisky and poured us both a glass. There was a look of desperation in his eyes. I knew he'd long dreaded the day when his younger brother would get involved in something nasty.

'Bob, we both know that Clint could never do damage to anyone. If someone provokes him he just thinks they're playing a game. You know that. As for him cutting someone's throat, well, it's just daft.'

He nodded at this but I could see that he was still very shaken.

'What is it?' I pushed.

'Dave, he could have got out of the house and got down Didsbury where Travis's mansion was. I was that beat, it would have taken an earthquake to wake me, and mam sleeps very soundly too.'

'Are you still in the council house up in Langley?' I asked.

'Mam won't move. I bought this nice place in Prestbury in its own grounds but she wouldn't have any of it,' he said with a sigh. 'She came, stayed one night, and then moved back to Langley. Of course Clint went with her.'

'So you moved back too?'

He nodded. 'I'm paying a caretaker to look after the Prestbury house in case she changes her mind, but she won't.'

Knowing his mother, I understood his certainty. I was surprised she'd even entertained the idea of a move long enough to visit the exclusive Cheshire village.

'Do you think Clint is capable?'

'He isn't, not on his own anyway. But suppose someone got to him? Suppose someone said it's like a game . . . you creep into someone's house like hide and seek and then . . .'

Bob downed his drink and then poured himself another. I put my hand over my glass.

'Is that likely?'

'How the hell do I know? I'm that busy I can't keep an eye on him all the time. There's all sorts of people in and out of here the whole time.'

'What does Clint actually do while you're working?' I asked, trying to form a picture of the scene.

'Well, you know he's supposed to be educationally impaired, and I suppose he is in some ways, but he spends a lot of time doing these very intricate jigsaws. They've got some that are like three-dimensional models and he works at them for days. It's as if part of his mind's somewhere else.'

Bob got up from his desk and showed me into a side room. There were lockers round the walls but the main feature was a table with a partially completed model of a human head on it.

'That's the latest,' he said. 'He was doing that all last week.'

'Hmm, I should put it away if I were you,' I advised, pointing to the throat. 'You know how the minds of the fuzz work. It could be Exhibit A.'

'Damn!' he said. Bob was always rather mild in his cursing. His mother had seen to that. I helped him to dismantle the model and put it back in its box. 'He won't be pleased when he comes back,' he muttered doubtfully.

'What other evidence is there against Clint apart from the video and the card?' I asked.

'They say they've got footprints – footprints in the blood. From what the solicitor says, they think it's pretty conclusive. I don't know what will happen to him if he goes inside. He's never been very far from his mother or me before.' Under the glare of the strip lights it was impossible to be sure of Bob's pallor, but he sounded pretty close to the end of his rope to me.

'You know they can fake video evidence, don't you?' I suggested.

'What?' Bob demanded.

'If Clint had ever been in Travis's place before, it's possible that someone could have got the video, spliced a different date and time on to it and substituted it for the one in the CCTV system that Saturday morning.'

'Are you sure?' Bob said. For the first time there was a note of optimism in his voice.

'Yes, but has Clint been round there before?'

'You've heard of Melville Monckton?'

'Who hasn't?' I replied. Monckton had made his name as the leader of a pop group. His rendering of the song 'Moody Lady' had been used in a Hollywood film and had made his name.

Melville Monckton wasn't one of your run-of-the-mill nihilistic, sex, drugs and rock 'n' roll pop stars. Not at all. Monckton wasn't ever going to be one of the all-time greats of rock, not even if he committed suicide on stage. He must always have been astute enough to know that. His music was slick with a great deal of style and not an overabundance of substance. 'Melodic Mel makes another hit. Zzzzz,' they said in the *NME* and it was true. At his best his stuff was shiny and glittery, very streamlined, with not much to get hold of.

But if not the greatest rock star ever produced by Manchester, he was certainly the most financially successful. Unlike many of his ilk he'd always managed to ensure that a high proportion of the money that ran through his hands stuck to his fingers. What's more, he put it to work for him. He was admired for that and for keeping himself in the public eye and for holding his group together.

The guy really beavered away at his PR. Manchester people were fond of him. He hadn't cleared off to live in London or Florida. He was actually seen in the city streets from time to time, and not always coinciding with the release of an album, either. Certainly not many months went by without an article about him in one of the colour supplements and his movements were the staple fare of the diary feature in the evening paper. He liked to reminisce fondly about his childhood in north Manchester, the game of cricket in Heaton Park and the unsuccessful trial for Manchester City when he was sixteen. Yes, Mr Melville Monckton had very convincingly woven himself into the tapestry of local life. It was even rumoured that he was keeping Manchester's second-most-famous football team afloat with subsidies.

'Well, I've been working with Melville for some time. You know he's put some money into theme pubs. He's a great bloke.'

'Does that mean that he's your partner?'

Bob made a vague gesture which could have been taken as a nod of the head but said no more. Obviously his business arrangements were not up for discussion.

'Is he, or isn't he?'

'That has nothing to do with the trouble Clint's in.'

'How do you know?' I asked. 'Listen up, Bob, me old buddy. I can't help Clint unless you tell me everything.'

'Melville's a good mate. He's been round here a lot. He often takes Clint for a ride in his stretch limo. He makes a joke of it, says Clint's one of his minders.'

'And Melville might have taken Clint round to see Travis?'

'No, why would he? It doesn't make sense.'

'Then you must think Clint got himself down to Travis's house on his own.'

Bob sat in silence for a while. Sweat beaded his forehead. I couldn't understand what was going on.

'Come on Bob. I'll start calling you Popeye again if you don't give me an explanation. Melville takes Clint out for rides. Would he or wouldn't he have taken Clint to Travis's house?'

'Well, I know I haven't. What would I want with that nut?'

'Have you told the police this?'

'They thought I was joking. That Inspector Cullen as good as laughed in my face.'

'Cullen? You're sure it was Cullen?'

Bob made a tiny movement of his head that I took as assent. There was a look of impatience on his face as if these details were unimportant. He was wrong. Cullen was the one and only detective inspector in the GMP who might extend even a microscopic degree of tolerance to any theory I came up with. He owed his promotion to listening to something I'd said in a previous case – not that he'd think of it in that way.

'Look Bob, let's get this straight. The only time Clint's been away from you, he was with Melville Monckton?'

'Yep, that's about it.'

'What about your mother?'

'He's too much for her now. Anyway, she's getting really old. It's as much as she can do to make our meals.'

'Has Clint told you something?'

'You can never get a story out of Clint properly. He likes Melville and . . . honestly . . . getting him out of here for an hour or two gives me a bit of a break.'

'There must be some reason why you even mentioned Monckton,' I persisted.

'There was. Usually when you ask Clint where he's been he says feeding the ducks in Heaton Park, he loves that. About three weeks ago when he came back from his trip with Melville he seemed unusually excited, he was stammering and gabbling his words. I asked Melville what the matter was.

He just said that they'd been to the usual places, Heaton Park and so on. After that Clint shut up. I couldn't get another word out of him and frankly I had other things to worry about.'

'Maybe you should think of finding somewhere more permanent for Clint,' I suggested.

'Out of the question. It would kill his mother if he was institutionalized. She still thinks in terms of workhouses and insane asylums.'

'Bob, there are some wonderful places these days for people like Clint. It can't be much of a life for him sitting in that room doing jigsaws.'

'Yeah, but what kind of life will he have sitting in Broadmoor or Rampton with a crowd of psychos?' Bob said bitterly. 'I'm telling you, the only thing that's kept him so childlike and innocent all these years is that me or his mother has been with him all the time to shield him from the nastier side of life. Dave, I want him out. I want you to dig up the evidence that someone faked that video. We both know that Clint couldn't have killed Fred Travis.'

I looked at him, thinking carefully what to say next. Bob had stood up for me at a time when I needed him. I couldn't turn him down, yet . . .

'Bob, are you involved in anything I should know about?' I said slowly. It was in my mind that many of the homicides in this town are related to the profits of the drug trade.

'I run five clubs, three theme pubs and I own property all over town,' he said with a dry laugh, 'but I know what you mean. I've never had anything to do with the drug trade and if anyone tells you different they're a liar.'

'I believe you,' I said, holding up my hands.

Bob then looked at me for a long time.

'There have been one or two other little items,' he said eventually.

'Anything that might have got up someone's nose sufficiently for them to frame Clint?'

'I did a spot of fencing for a team up in north Manchester. I own a number of empty shops and we used them for our own version of a car-boot sale, but I jacked that in when the police began sniffing around. I've sold untaxed liquor and I've recycled stolen cash but I've done nothing that could have hurt anyone unless you count the Inland Revenue.'

'OK, my son,' I said. 'Confession over, but you're sure that no one wants to work you a nasty one?'

'Dave, you know what it's like in the club scene. Swimming in a pool full of piranhas with bleeding sores on your body is no comparison. I've knocked back a few guys who walked in here and thought they could take over my operation, but none of them are bright enough to stage something like this.'

'Are you sure?' I persisted. I didn't want to get involved and then find that I was taking on some gang or other.

With a weary sigh Bob leaned back in his executive-style chair. He stared at the ceiling for a moment.

'You know the game I'm in ... A few months ago some lads from Cheetham Hill way came down here. I was on my own, Clint was out with Melville. They suggested that I might like to employ their firm to provide bouncers for all my clubs and pubs. Rather pressing, they were. I decided to humour them a bit. They thought they were well hard ... shaved heads ... heavy rings on every finger ... home-made tattoos here, there and everywhere. Body piercing ... you know the type.'

I nodded.

'Well, it turned out that they were prepared to let me keep half my profits for the time being. "Very generous," I said, "now bugger off."'

'"But Mr Lane, you're on your own down here," pipes up one of them, all frightening like. I'm supposed to be wetting myself as they give me the hard look. Anyway ...'

Here Bob paused a moment and stroked the heavy modern statue that was the sole ornament on his desk. It vaguely resembled an assemblage of cubes and spheres. There was a barely audible click and an object emerged from the curiously shaped design. Bob pulled out a neat black automatic.

'"I'm not on my own," I said. "I've got Mr Heckler and Mr Koch with me." I squeezed one off into that wall over there. Christ! You should have seen it. They were up those stairs faster than fleas off a hot-plate.'

'Great, Bob,' I said, 'and that was the end of it?'

'I had to arrange for the two brothers who were in charge to have a little smacking, nothing too heavy of course, no broken bones, but they weren't bopping at the Ritz for a week or two. I've heard nothing from them since.'

'You might like to think about hiding that statue somewhere,' I said as he replaced the gun in its secret compartment. 'The fuzz are likely to pay you a visit.'

He nodded. 'Will you help us then?' he asked quietly.

'You know me, Bob. I can't keep my nose out of trouble for long.'

On my way out I glanced up at the deep hole in the brickwork where the bullet had struck. The music started up again.

Riot Fear

Manchester police bosses braced themselves for riots last night as members of Repeal 98 vowed vengeance for the death of their popular leader Fred Travis. Travis, revealed last year in this paper as the father of 42–34–38 starlet Dawn Aurore's two-year-old son Zipper, was brutally slain at the weekend. His death may be linked to his attempts to restore 'moral purity' in his home town through his Repeal 98 movement which demands abolition of page three pictures among other things. Readers will remember when Dawn (22) featured as this paper's 'Miss Teenage Centrefold' four years ago.

Mirror

6

Monday, 19 October

'Where to start?' I asked myself when I left Howl.

I made my way towards Piccadilly Gardens and the metro stop. If Pimpernel Investigations was to roll back into action I needed to go home to get my car. The briefcase in my hand weighed on me like a guilty conscience. I had essays to mark and I'd promised to look through an M.Sc. thesis. Well, college work would have to wait.

Bob had guts. He'd been alone in that office when I called, without even a secretary. Of course there'd be no money on the premises at midday on a Monday, but still. Others in his line of work employed more flexible forms of protection than an automatic hidden in the fixtures and fittings . . . such as a squad of heavies. What would have happened if Bob had been on the john or something when that gang came in? He'd have coped. Bob 'Popeye' Lane was one of the world's copers.

OK, he wanted me to help Clint and I would give it a whirl. Reading between the lines, it was clear enough that his difficulties with Clint were rapidly approaching the terminal phase. No one could blame him. He'd looked after his brother devotedly most of his life. Now he must be thinking about a life on his own. Must be – he was only human, and I'd heard something about a girlfriend. What was her name? I couldn't remember.

Nothing had been said about payment. That wasn't a problem. I had money in the bank, some anyway. Presumably Bob felt that he wouldn't insult me by discussing cash terms, not that I have ever felt insulted by being offered money for services rendered. With Aldous Arkwright it had been a different matter. He'd been playing some sort of mind game, using his money to gain control. There's no way anyone controls Dave Cunane, I told myself as I waited obediently for the green man to appear on the pedestrian lights across Piccadilly. Even as the thought formed I smiled. I guessed that if Alvin Richardson asked me to jump through hoops with a flaming torch in my mouth to illustrate his management theory, I'd do it quickly enough.

It was odd though.

On Saturday when I'd been let out of Bootle Street nick I'd thought I'd walked out into a benevolent world, a world of smiles and bright sunshine. Even the crowds had seemed cheerful, like those carefully posed wartime pictures of East-Enders after a raid by the *Luftwaffe*. Now, as I jostled among the scurrying office workers heading towards the fast-food bars of Piccadilly and Portland Street, everything had a much more sinister aspect. Walking towards the streaked, dirty concrete pile of the Piccadilly Hotel, I threaded my way through the crowds. Maybe it was the change in the weather but the faces that loomed in front of me seemed to be uniformly hostile, resentful, as if bordering on some private grief. It was like taking a trip through downtown Moscow at the height of the Stalin purges. What had happened to the famous northern sense of humour? Had it been liquidated along with the cotton mills?

I told myself it was the weather. My mother used to say that there were always more fights in the playground on windy days. That was it. The weather was on the turn from mild and cloying to wet and windy. Already little whirlpools of litter were being stirred into life by the playful breeze.

For once I reached my flat without meeting either of the Bobsey Twins returning from one of their religious services. I changed into a sweater and dug my old Burberry out of the back of the wardrobe. Proper kit for a private eye, I thought as I fastened the belt. I still hadn't come up with my next move in the Clint Lane saga but I knew where my thoughts were taking me.

Melville Monckton was an internationally renowned figure. Could he possibly have something to hide? Could a word from him clear Clint? It wasn't so simple. If my theory of a tampered video tape was correct, someone had gone to great lengths to put poor Clint in the frame. The trouble with VCRs is that few realize the many possibilities they provide for altering evidence.

Taking a deep breath, I phoned DI Cullen. As it turned out I needn't have been apprehensive. There was the usual protracted runaround before I was connected with him. It's amazing: the police spend millions on communications, but phone a police station and ask for a named officer and it takes them at least half an hour to find him.

'Dave Cunane, as I live and breathe, how are you, my old cocker?' he asked jocularly.

'Any chance we could meet?' I asked hopefully. I needed to soften him up a little before putting my theory to him.

'I'm heavily involved at the moment, Dave, although we seem to be on the downhill side of the current job. What's it about?' His tone was still genial.

'I'd rather not say, but it's something that's also serious and current and that you're involved in.'

'Dave, if you know something tell me now.' This time Cullen's voice had gone all hard and official.

'Look, I'm hungry. How do you fancy a nice steak down at Pier Six or the Salford Quays? . . . On me, that is.'

An appeal to Cullen's stomach was more likely to get results than a direct request for information.

'Hmm, you know how to push my buttons, don't you, Dave? Just what is this about?'

'I'd rather not say until I see you but it's important.'

There was a pause at the other end of the line. I hadn't spoken to Cullen in a long while. When I'd got to know him originally he was very much down on his luck, a detective sergeant then, whose career was going nowhere except to premature retirement on grounds of excessive elbow-lifting. God! It had to be excessive with a capital E to get you kicked out of the GMP . . . I think he'd been pally because he was basically a nice guy, but also because he could see himself looking for work as a private investigator before too long.

Those considerations didn't apply now. Mainly thanks to my unsung efforts, he'd got himself back on to the promotion track. I could almost hear him mentally tossing the dice while he worked out whether there was anything to be gained from seeing an old has-been like me.

'I heard you were out of the game, Dave,' he said cautiously.

'Still doing a bit of this and that,' was my equally cagey reply.

'OK, then. Pier Six in half an hour. Have a pint of Boddies waiting for me.'

Great, the throw of the dice had turned up a pair of sixes. Or had it? Cullen might decide to run me in for further questioning about the Travis job.

'Who are you acting for now, Dave? What was it last time? The Tombstone Press?'

'Headstone,' I corrected.

'I knew it was something to do with graveyards,' he chuckled, stuffing a piece of steak into his mouth. 'You must be on great expenses. You private lads have the best end of the bargain. Charge your clients what you like and then tell them you can't get a result because the police won't co-operate.'

We were seated in the first-floor restaurant looking out over the dock which had once been the terminus for shipments of cotton from such romantic places as New Orleans and Alexandria. There was no trace of any lingering sub-tropical connection now as the rain scoured the surface of the murky waters. Through the glass the blurred outlines of the ultra-modern flats and glass pyramids looked like a Cubist painting.

I decided to keep my mouth shut as long as DI Cullen was

in a pleasant mood. Cullen's first name was Brendan but he didn't like the name because when he'd joined the force an older colleague had mocked him by calling him Brenda. This preference for rank rather than personal name was a sign of the dehumanization which goes with being part of a hierarchy, I thought, then I mentally kicked myself for slipping into the pompous 'management science think' which dominated my waking hours these days. As we moved on to the second course Cullen started into his immense fund of dirty stories. Laughing obediently as required, I couldn't help observing that the genial, roly poly copper had really missed his vocation. As a travelling salesman he'd have done wonders for his firm and himself, but as a policeman in gloomy down-to-earth Manchester he was trying to irrigate the sea.

He must have noticed that I was slightly less than entranced by his flow.

'Come on then, cocker,' he said. 'What's so important that you can't tell me over the phone?'

Looking across the table at me now, he was a very different man from a moment ago. The gaze of his mild brown eyes was intensely serious, his expression reminded me of Pat O'Brien – the Irish–American film actor who specialized in sincere Catholic priests. DI Cullen was so honest and unaffected that you'd trust him with anything; that is, if you didn't know that he was actually an ambitious copper and not your father confessor. Despite my reservations, it was possible that Cullen would go far.

'I don't know, Brendan, perhaps you'd better have a brandy first,' I said cheekily.

'Like that is it? First names, eh? What have you done?'

'Not me, you,' I murmured. 'I'm sure that Clint Lane couldn't have murdered Fred Travis. You've got the wrong man.'

Cullen considered this gravely for several minutes. Then he got up and went to the loo. When he came back his expression was still very serious.

'We've not charged him yet. He's being assessed by a pair of trick-cyclists to see if he's capable. I have my own doubts but what makes you so certain?'

'I know him. I've known him and Bob for years. Clint's immensely strong and he's good with his hands. He can do small intricate tasks but he couldn't murder someone. He wouldn't connect cutting someone's throat with the idea of causing death and he'd never cut anyone because he'd know that would hurt them. He cries at the sight of blood. Ask his mother.'

'Even so, isn't it possible the brother could have put him up to it? They say this moral crusade of Travis's is eating into the club profits in town.'

'Are you saying that you take Travis seriously as a moral reformer?'

'Some people took him very seriously indeed, including my Chief Constable. Did you know that he had a hundred and twenty thousand paid up members in his Repeal Movement?'

'Oh come on, Cullen. You don't really see a booby like Travis as a genuine modern-day Savonarola?'

'Who?'

'Savonarola, the preacher who persuaded the women of Florence to chuck all their baubles on to a bonfire,' I said impatiently.

'Education's a wonderful thing, isn't it?' he said sarcastically. 'I thought you were talking about a Dutch serial killer. Christ, Dave, you've got really fancy since you started working at the university.'

'Don't change the subject. Bob Lane would as soon cut his own throat as send his brother to cut someone else's.'

'Maybe, maybe not. There's the awkward little fact that Clint's recorded on video going into the house at Didsbury at the relevant time. The poor guy had no explanation for that.'

'Of course he hasn't! He was at home in bed. Don't you realize that the same genius who stuck my business card into Travis's hand must have switched the videos? It's child's play to doctor a video, I've done it myself on the PC.'

'OK, OK, calm down. We haven't charged him yet. I was going to send that video to the national forensic lab in Birmingham anyway. They'll tell us if there was any funny business.'

'When will you know?'

'Could be the day after tomorrow,' he said.

'Do you know about Melville Monckton?'

'I know that Clint keeps talking about him. He gets all tongue-tied and confused.'

'Isn't it possible that Monckton took Clint round to Travis's place and . . .'

'And what? What possible reason could Monckton have for involving Clint in the murder of Fred Travis? Be careful what you're saying. You're shoving your head into a whole barrelful of worms there.'

'Worms, I'm sick of hearing about them . . . cans of them, barrels of them.'

'What are you on about?'

'Doesn't the fact that Monckton wants to trail a mentally handicapped young man about with him strike you as slightly suspicious?'

'No, why should it?'

'It does to me. There's all this sexual abuse of the mentally handicapped. Clint wouldn't have the words to explain what had happened to him if someone had been at it.'

'At what, Dave? Talking to you is dangerous.' He looked around at our fellow diners. None of them seemed interested in our conversation. 'In the space of two minutes you fling out accusations against respected figures. I don't know. You'd better get yourself a good lawyer if you're going to go round slandering people.'

'I didn't say that Monckton had done anything, just that it's a bit peculiar that he starts taking an interest in Clint and then soon after Clint turns up as the fall guy in a murder.'

'You watch too many American films. What happened to this Savonarola character, then?'

'Oh, him! He was burned at the stake. He was a friar, you know.'

'Wonderful, so he came to a sticky end just like Travis. What was his first name?'

'Girolamo, I think. Look, Cullen, he isn't in the police files. This all happened five hundred years ago.'

'Amazing.'

'Yes, some people took religion very seriously in those

days.'

'Talking about religion and politics, Mr Sinclair asked me to pass on a message to you.'

'Oh.'

'Yes, oh. Knowing your penchant for turning up unexpected bits of information he told me to tell you that if you find out anything about the Repealers or the Children of Light he wants to be the first to hear it.'

'They're of no interest to me, honestly. All I'm doing here is putting in a good word for Clint.'

'Well, me old fruit, I've got to go,' he said rising to his feet. 'Thanks for the meal, I'm not so sure about the chat.'

'You'll keep what I said in mind, though.'

'Yeah, I suppose so. By the way I liked your slogan; "Detection and Protection" eh? Just mind someone doesn't turn it into "Slander and Detraction".'

'I will.'

'All right, keep your nose clean then, cocker. Nice meal . . . Friar Girolamo Savonarola, I must tell the lads about him, most impressive. I used to go to mass at the Franciscan Friary up in Gorton. You learn something new every day in this job.'

A certain amount of nervous exhaustion was beginning to set in when I got back to the flat. Cullen was a decent enough copper. Would he be able to resist the temptation to close the book on Clint and leave it to the courts to sort out? That had happened before. The name of Stefan Kiszko sprang to mind. I hoped those days had gone but it was still possible to give Cullen's arm a little extra nudge in the right direction. He hadn't said anything about questioning Monckton but if he was as good a copper as I knew he was he'd be arranging that right now. I rummaged in the spare room for my old coffee flask, essential for stakeouts, and discovered that I hadn't emptied it from last time. The inside was now coated with green furry mould. I went into the kitchen and took a bottle of lemonade out of the fridge and made up a few sandwiches with honey-roast ham and cheese. What I had in mind might be an all-night job.

Part of the rock star's well publicized affection for his home town consisted of him living in a large house in Higher Blackley. Years as a private detective had conditioned me to expect the unexpected. I wanted to be in place to see what happened when Cullen rattled the bars on Monckton's cage and especially what happened after. I couldn't get rid of the tortured look on Bob Lane's face when I asked him about Monckton. Nobody could say that Bob was too trusting but the relief at having Clint off his hands for a few hours each week had blinded him to the possibilities. I thought it was significant that the gang from Cheetham Hill had called when Clint was out with Monckton.

Reaching Monckton's house and finding a discreet spot for observation proved to be much more difficult than I'd imagined. I turned off Victoria Avenue into a council estate and then through a modern private development of mock-Tudor houses cramped on to the side of a hill. They were huddled so closely together that not much could happen unobserved. The winding road through this development petered out into an unmade sunken lane surviving from when there had been farms in the area. One side of the lane fronted a rough meadow, on the other side four large individually designed houses, each set in a sizeable garden, slanted down towards the valley bottom. Monckton's house, second from the top, was the most secluded of the four, effectively screened by high hedges and even by an arch of yew over the entrance drive. I supposed that the place had been selected to make it difficult for his groupies to find on foot.

I made one pass, which was a mistake because the road was rutted with potholes. A quick glance through the arch of yews revealed a yellow Rolls standing in front of the house. The stretch limo was kept elsewhere. I backed uphill, up the bumpy lane to the very crest of the hill and parked. I was right up against the perimeter of Tudorville but sheltered behind the larch-lap fence. I hoped Neighbourhood Watch did not extend as far as the back lanes. My view of Monckton's house was less than satisfactory but at least I could see who entered and left without attracting attention.

I settled down for a protracted wait.

It was one of those afternoons we get so often up here after heavy rain. Optimists call it 'bracing' weather. A master water-colourist would have had his work cut out to catch all the tones which appeared in a completely cloud-choked sky. There were traces of orange and yellow where the sun was trying to break through, but above all, sharp-edged clouds in every shade of grey from fleecy off-white through to a dull slate. They jostled and tumbled against each other, providing a visual excitement which the dull sodden fields and rain-soaked roofs below lacked.

Observation is the most boring but often the most rewarding part of detection. When you see visitors arrive outside a supermarket manager's house at 4 a.m. with a van-load of goodies you know that it's not a visit from Father Christmas. I ruminated mildly on the events of the day. Shadows began lengthening in the fields opposite and that kind of grey, cold mist that penetrates to the bone began forming in little pockets and dips across the landscape. Lights began to come on in the houses. I had the binoculars in my hands, poised for close observation. So far there'd been nothing to see. Before long the half light of early evening began making it hard to see across the meadows. A few schoolchildren made their way home, none of them casting even an incurious glance in my direction. Magpies still wheeled about, searching for something to kill, otherwise the scenery was as quiet as an abandoned graveyard at midnight.

It was possible that the architect who design Monckton's home had Frank Lloyd Wright in mind, because the first floor, walled in glass, was supported on slender concrete pillars and jettied out from the hillside over the entrance below. On second thoughts maybe it wasn't Frank Lloyd Wright and Tumbling Waters that provided inspiration. It looked more like the Manchester matchbox school that had given us the wonders of the Arndale Centre. Venetian blinds screened that section of the glass-sided room that I could see through the hedges. From time to time the blinds shook, suggesting movement inside, but despite focusing intently I was none the wiser about who was present.

A girl of about thirteen came up the dusky lane, leading a pony. She went into the house below Monckton's on the hillside. I put the binoculars down and took out my camera. Quite swiftly it became dark, the last tints of colour disappearing from the sky. There was no moon, just a faint orange glow on the horizon from distant street lights. It began to look like a no-show by the boys in blue. Behind me on the housing estate I could hear car doors slamming as commuters arrived back from their daily stint for a night in front of the telly with the kids. I was just getting set to curse Cullen for his negligence when a car containing three men arrived, paused in the muddy lane and the hesitantly drove into Monckton's driveway. I couldn't see who got out but the venetian blinds on the first floor window parted briefly to reveal the shaggy head of Melville Monckton himself. I got a fleeting impression of him scowling at his visitors before the blinds clicked back into place. The car, a Ford Mondeo like mine, but newer, hadn't been in the drive more than a minute before it was backed out on to the narrow lane and awkwardly parked close to the hedge. This time I got a clear sighting of the driver. It was Detective Sergeant Peterson. It seemed that Mr Monckton was being difficult with the gentlemen from the constabulary and refusing them the use of his driveway. Peterson looked around briefly, but not in my direction, before passing back under the yew arch.

About twenty-five minutes later a cream-coloured Range Rover trundled up, went into the drive and was allowed to park inside. Using a low-light 800 ASA film and the long lens on my Nikon, I got a good shot of the driver, a tall Asian male in a navy blue turban and a dark pinstriped business suit, aided by the light set in the centre of the overarching yew hedge. By this time it was quite dark. I guessed that the Range Rover contained Monckton's solicitor because about ten minutes after its arrival the three coppers emerged with their heads down, got in their car, backed almost to where I was, turned round and drove away.

It was almost an hour later and my stomach was rumbling noisily before the cream Range Rover drove straight out and into Tudorville at a fair speed. The bump as it hit the rough track cause the rear wheels to jump into the air. I wondered what had upset the solicitor, if indeed he was one of the legal brotherhood. Perhaps he was just in a hurry for his evening meal.

I was now four hours into my surveillance and reaching that phase when it's difficult to keep awake and maintain vigilance. The trouble was, I had no partner to spell me for a few minutes. Bitterly regretting the lack of strong coffee, I took a swig of my lemonade even though I was getting desperate for a pee. I knew that it would go straight through me but felt I should be all right to take a leak against one of the fences round the back because no one was stirring. What I condemned in soccer fans I practised in necessity. I was working out just where to make my donation to the rural water table when another car rolled up to the entrance of Chateau Monckton.

This time it was a white Range Rover. For a second I dared to hope that the fuzz had returned to feel Mr Monckton's collar, but no such luck. Through the dim light from the lamp over Monckton's entrance I could see that the trio were all black men, all well over six feet tall and all neatly clad in identical blazers and ties. Two of them stretched their arms and stared about them in a bored sort of way and then all three went into the house.

There was nothing for it, I had to slip out of the car and pay a call of nature. Feeling rather shy, I made my way along the back fence a few yards from my car to where one garden fence overlapped another and there was an angle which afforded a slight amount of cover. I unzipped and no sooner had I done so than I heard voices on the road. The three-man protection squad were back out in the rutted lane. One of them had a mobile phone in his hand. He used it to point up the lane in the direction of my car. I crouched in the shadows down against the fence. If they came a yard past the car they couldn't help spotting me, yet if I made a move now they would be bound to see me in the glow of reflected light from the houses behind. I could feel my pulse racing as the pair sprinted up to my car with frighteningly athletic speed.

In the second before they reached the car a dozen different stories flashed through my mind ... I was a peeping tom, I was checking on the movements of an adulterous husband, I was out protecting badger sets . . . but it was no use. If they came a few steps further my goose would be well and truly cooked. I couldn't outrun them and I couldn't bluff them. I didn't even dare to zip up my flies in case the noise alerted them.

They stopped by the car.

'I don't know what the motherfucker's on about,' one said to the other as they paused to examine the interior of my car.

'Hey, man, as long as he comes up with the bread I ain't complaining,' his companion replied. 'You've got to take this seriously, Dwayne. It's work.'

'I suppose if you're pulling in a million a year for the type of crap music he dishes out you're entitled to be nervous, but why he should think the Dibbles are spying on him I don't know.' He put his hand on the bonnet of my car. 'This car's stone cold, man, and there ain't no Dibbles in it unless they're under the bonnet.' He humorously mimed looking under the car. I thanked my bladder for getting me out of it before they arrived.

The second man made no comment but turned and waved to their boss down the hillside. He beckoned them to join him and I allowed myself to breathe a sigh of relief as all three headed off down the lane with their backs to me. I found that I didn't need to pee any more. I stealthily crept along to the shelter of my car but didn't get in as I watched them efficiently search the lane, the adjoining field and even shine torches into the gardens of Monckton's immediate neighbours. Eventually, when they seemed to have exhausted all possible hiding places, the leader went into Monckton's house again. A moment later he re-emerged and all three departed as swiftly as they'd come.

My mouth and throat felt dry. Adrenalin levels plummeted back to normal, leaving me feeling strained and edgy. I got into the car and took another swig of the lemonade. It wasn't as powerful a restorative as coffee but it did relieve the dreadful ache in my throat. I felt as if my neck had increased about three sizes and although I wasn't wearing a collar and tie there was a feeling of constriction. I forced myself to try to breathe normally. It had been a while since I'd handled anything more dangerous than a mild argument in a tutorial.

I sat in the car for a long while, not even attempting to think. After a while my consciousness began to tune in with the very faint noises around me. It was quiet and I was still undetected.

By midnight I was deep into self-questioning. Should I go, should I stay? It was freezing. Occasional bursts of warmth from the car heater weren't enough to stop my toes losing all feeling. Every trace of common sense told me to go. I had lectures to deliver tomorrow. Yet years of experience warned me that if anything was going to happen it would be in the small hours. I hung on. People who have nothing to hide don't call on the services of a security agency to check the area for hidden policemen. At 1.30 precisely a large Korean 4WD vehicle containing two men arrived. It drove up so quietly and smoothly I had to rub my eyes to make sure that I wasn't dreaming. The 4WD was in through Monckton's drive so quickly that I was unable to use the camera. All senses were at full pitch as I gently shut the door without a sound and tiptoed down the lane to Monckton's archway.

I got there just in time to hear American voices and then the front door was slammed.

Risking a peek round the entrance I saw at once that Monckton hadn't stinted on passive security devices. There was a CCTV camera focused on the entrance and various infra-red devices were on the walls of the house. I crept swiftly away, back towards my car. Then, with the foolhardiness that has earned me a dozen beatings, I decided that I wouldn't wait until Monckton's visitors decided to leave to find out who they were. I ducked into the next property and, pulling my coat partly over my head in case the neighbour also had CCTV, ran the length of the drive and up the side of the house to the back fence. This turned out to be a low, green plastic chainlink barrier between concrete posts fronted by a struggling privet hedge. I vaulted over and landed in a mass of soaking wet tussock grass on the other side.

I lay where I was for five minutes, shivering and shaking. No one emerged from either house. Still keeping low and getting thoroughly drenched from the freezing wet grass, I made my way to the back of Monckton's property. His fences were far more formidable. There was a high hedge and plastic chainlink and then a razor-wire barrier set well inside his garden. Well, there are limits to what I'll do for my friends, I thought. Scaling this was out of the question. At the exact second that I was on the point of giving up, lights came on in a rear first-floor living room. This time the venetian blinds weren't drawn.

Monckton, a slightly built figure with a rat's nest of long hair and tangled locks, was showing two men into chairs round a low table. I could see it all like a movie projected on a screen because, with Monckton's house being built on a slope, the ground to the rear was higher than the front. Crouched as I was in the tangled grass at the foot of Monckton's hedge, I was level with his back living-room. Squinting through the lens of my camera I immediately recognized Rufus, Aldous Arkwright's battered apostle. Battered he certainly was. There was a large plaster across his nose and his jaw appeared to have been wired. Looking at him, I shivered again, but not from the cold this time. Such injuries would surely demand repayment with interest. The other man had his back to me.

I was taking photos as fast as I could when my mobile began to chirrup.

For a second I froze as the clear tones rang out across the sodden grass where I lay concealed. After a frenzy of fumbling I switched it off. What a stupid mistake, but who could be phoning at this time? To my horror all three men had come to the window and were cupping their hands over their eyes to peer out. I risked a last shot with the Nikon before taking to my toes. The third man was the broad-shouldered Tyler. I struggled through the grass with difficulty, turning my ankle on the twisting surface as I tried to run. I decided to veer round the buildings altogether and come to my car through the open ground backing on to the mock Tudor estate. It was a mistake. I hadn't been running more than a minute before I heard dogs barking. Not any old dogs either, it was that slightly insane, deep-throated yelling characteristic of Dobermanns.

My visit to Higher Blackley was rapidly turning from chiller to thriller, I thought. The barking was definitely coming nearer as I struggled through the grass. I ran headlong into a low wire fence and pitched right over it. The camera parted company with me and landed somewhere ahead. Cursing silently, I went down on all fours to feel for it. Possibly the heavy freezing dew made it difficult for the hounds to pick up my scent because I searched for what seemed like a full five minutes before my fingers made comforting contact with metal. I scooped up the camera and got to my feet ready for a final sprint. Expecting teeth to clamp into my backside at any moment, I dashed for the lane.

The dogs arrived snapping and snarling round the car just I turned the key and started the motor. I pulled my jacket over my face as I roared away toward the estate and back to the main road. I got the impression that there were more than three people standing under the light at the entrance of Monckton's house. They must have clocked the car if not the driver. When I reached Victoria Avenue for the turn towards Cheetham Hill and town I paused for a moment studying the rear-view mirror intently. There was no pursuit. I began to breathe normally. It was possible that Monckton would put my visit down to a prowling music lover or a burglar unsuccessfully scouting his property.

When I got to Cheetham Hill Road I pulled over and keyed the memory of my mobile to return the call that had nearly caused me to become dog food.

'It's you! Where were you?' an angry voice demanded. Stunned by cold and exhaustion, I didn't for a minute place who it was.

'Who is this?' I asked angrily.

'Janine White, formerly of the *Guardian*. Remember?'

'Oh you,' I said rudely. 'What's with the formerly?'

'Listen, Mr Cunane, while you're out swanning around the night-clubs some of us are trying to earn a living. Unless I can get Melanie Varley to verify my story I'm out on my ear.'

'Yes, yes, I'm weeping buckets here but why does your problem entitle you to ring me in the middle of the night?'

'Oh dear, did I catch you at an awkward moment? Give my apologies to your partner but I need you to confirm that we dropped Melanie off at her mother's house.'

'So?'

'So my dear man, I've had two staff reporters and half the Northamptonshire Constabulary round to that house but the mother adamantly denies that the daughter ever darkened her doorstep. So does your friend Aldous Arkwright. He's threatening to put an injunction on the paper if we even imply that Little Miss Melanie ever had her hands warmed.'

'Not my problem now, love. I've got other fish to fry.'

'I'm sure your lady friend can excuse you for a few minutes . . .'

'What lady friend?'

'Well, you're not at your flat. I went there first. I rang and rang until this old gentleman appeared. I thought he was going to brain me until I proved I was a journalist and not one of Arkwright's minions. Then he couldn't have been more polite. He even opened the door of your flat to check that you weren't in.'

'So that means I'm off pleasuring some desirable female?'

'One of your colleagues at UNWIST said you'd told her you were going be too busy marking and checking references all day.'

'What!' I spluttered. 'What gives you the right to go checking up on me?'

'I'm sorry. I've come at this all wrong. Forgive me but I'm really up the creek without a paddle unless I can find someone to back up my story about Repeal 98 and the C of L. You were my last hope.'

'Hope of what?'

'I thought if you came with me we might be able to make Melanie's mother tell the truth.'

'What did you have in mind? Thumbscrews?'

'Don't be sarcastic. I'm desperate. This job is my last chance to break into a permanent position with the *Guardian*. I might get a contract to produce so many pieces a year. You don't know what it means to me.'

'OK,' I said eventually, 'I might be able to see you tomorrow afternoon.'

'No,' she exploded, 'That'll be too late. I need to see you now, I need you to speak to my night editor and tell him that you at least saw this girl. They think I fabricated the whole thing.'

'Give me his number then.'

'That's no good, he'll want to speak to me as well.'

'Where are you then?'

'Same place as before, the Jewel in the Crown.'

'How appropriate. I can't guarantee being able to reach you tonight. I'm exhausted.'

'You need to start taking monkey glands or something if it affects you like that,' she snapped. I broke the connection.

Driving back down Cheetham Hill Road past churches and temples and synagogues and once grand Victorian buildings now turned into knitwear factories, I tried to concentrate my thoughts. Somehow I seemed to have lost the thread of what was going on. Why should Melanie disappear? There could only be one reason . . . she didn't want her story plastered over the *Guardian*. What was wrong with that? Nothing really, from my point of view. The more attention Saturday night's rescue raid at Meldrum Terrace received, the more likely I was to land up in the soup. I'd really made a mess of Rufus Polk's face. Thinking about it, I guessed that I had something to thank Janine for. Maybe it was her enquiries about the caning of Melanie that had persuaded Arkwright to make no fuss about what had happened to Rufus.

There was still traffic on Deansgate and it was 2.20 a.m. by the clock in Daisy and Tom's window. I drove to the end of Deansgate still undecided whether to go straight home or stop off at the crumbling hotel in Whalley Range. The heater was on full and there was steam rising from my clothes. In the end when I reached Brook's Bar, the old toll gate on the turnpike road, I turned towards Whalley Range, with its many mouldering mansions, rather than Chorlton.

I motored slowly into the dimly lit car park of the Jewel in the Crown, expecting to see White standing on the doorstep shaking her fist at me. I was disappointed. There was no sign of life at all.

After waiting a moment I got out of the car and rattled on the front door. Things then started happening in the usual disjointed sequence that these things happen to me.

Two turbaned Sikhs rushed from the darkened interior and,

grabbing me by the arms, they threw me bodily down the steps. I landed awkwardly on my rear end.

'Stinking bloody tramp! Stay away from here,' one of them yelled.

'You'll get a fucking good hiding next time,' the other snarled. 'This isn't a fucking doss house.'

'I've come to see Ms White,' I shouted.

At this, they both turned on their heels. I wasn't sure what he was saying but I distinctly heard one of them calling Janine a whore. They seemed to be in a frenzy of anger, the hotelier's equivalent of road rage. Seconds later, as I was picking myself up, a case came sailing out of the open door, rapidly followed by Janine herself. She landed at my feet like a parcel of old laundry.

'What the bloody hell!' I shouted but I was wasting my breath. I could hear heavy bars being slid across the front door.

'What's happening?' I asked in bewilderment.

'You mean what's happened to you? Do you do your lovemaking in a ditch?' White asked inconsequentially. 'You're soaking and covered in grass and sheep shit. I've heard of animal passion but this is hardly the season for rolling round in a field somewhere.'

'You first,' I almost shouted.

'Oh I tried to pay in advance with my credit card but it came up short. I owe them from last time I stayed. I told them a friend would turn up with cash but when they saw you they took my word processor as security and threw me out. It's all your fault for showing up like this. Now I won't be able to file my copy even if I get any.'

I took her by the arm and led her to my car. She offered no resistance. Having installed her luggage, I set off back along Withington Road towards my home.

'Whew! Open the windows,' she ordered. 'I'm all for nature but you're really ripe.'

It was after three before I managed to insert my body between the cool clean sheets of my bed. The night editor on the *Guardian* had sounded far from convinced by my support of Janine's story. Her account needed further research and verification, he said. I turned the light out but I couldn't sleep. I could hear Janine White noisily banging about in my kitchen. Eventually I dropped off.

MAD SLASHER CAUGHT

Full page headline, *Sun*

This paper demands sackings of the so-called health bosses who allowed suspected 'Mad Slasher' Clint Lane the freedom of the streets. There must be no more hiding behind official enquiries. This paper demands action now! The guilty officials must be removed. Lane's neighbour Mrs Maureen Cruttwell (37) has told our reporters that the suspect – seven-foot-tall Lane – was feared by the whole estate where he lived. Why was nothing done?

Editorial, *Sun*

7

Tuesday, 20 October

Surprisingly, I felt as full of bounce as a sprung-interior mattress when my radio alarm went off at seven. The pips of the Radio 2 time signal were like a challenge to me. I jumped out of bed before they finished and headed for the shower. Janine White was sprawled over the sofa in the living-room, sleeping on her stomach with her arms hanging out in an awkward position. I covered her with the duvet. She muttered something inaudible but didn't wake up. It sounded like 'No, not now Henry.'

I showered and then, clad in a dressing gown, went into the kitchen and ground some coffee. Unfortunately the machine makes a noise like a concrete-mixer gone wrong and a moment later Janine White slipped into the kitchen.

'Was that your signal that I should get up?' she asked, rubbing sleep out of her eyes. She had a waxy, half-dead look about her.

I shrugged my shoulders.

'Before you start, let me explain last night,' she volunteered. Her voice sounded apologetic but her expression hadn't altered.

'Who's Henry?' I asked, more to put her off her stroke than because I was interested.

This time there was a reaction. A faint glow of colour appeared in her face. For once she looked vulnerable and a lot younger. She looked at me questioningly.

'You were talking to him in your sleep,' I told her.

'He's my ex. If it wasn't for him I wouldn't be in the mess I'm in now.'

I said nothing. I didn't want to provoke a flood of matrimonial reminiscence. Janine fixed me with a look and set her jaw as if expecting to face a Force 10 gale. It was the old figure-head look. I could see that she was teetering on the brink of self-revelation. Would she, or wouldn't she . . .? She would.

'You might as well hear the story from the beginning. It's all his fault . . .'

The kettle boiled and I fixed the coffee. I carried the cafetiere and two breakfast cups over to the table. She followed.

'I can see you're not interested. You must have heard a lot of this in your job.'

'I never touched matrimonial cases unless faced with actual starvation,' I told her.

She managed a short half-strangled laugh. I suddenly found myself feeling more sympathetic.

'Go on, don't let me put you off,' I encouraged, but I could see that she was back in her hard shell. 'I'll be interested to know what it is about Henry that made you phone a complete stranger in the middle of the night.'

'I phoned you here at the flat nearly all evening. Then I remembered that I'd made a note of your mobile number. I'm sorry, but I was desperate to hear someone confirm that I really had seen Melanie. The way they went on you'd have thought I was making the whole thing up.'

'Is your credibility so low?'

'There have been one or two things . . . cases where I should have checked a little more, but this time I had the story and the pictures.'

I laughed. 'I should be flattered that you think my word

will corroborate your story. I seem to have a credibility gap myself . . . at least with the GMP.'

We drank our coffee in companionable silence for a few minutes. I waited for the question which I knew must come. Janine was able to restrain herself sufficiently to wait until the toast had popped up from the toaster.

'So what were you doing last night when I phoned?' she asked eventually.

'A bit of this and that,' I said.

'You weren't with a woman, were you?'

'Where have you got this idea that I'm at it like a buck rabbit all the time? I've been celibate for months . . .'

'So if you weren't with a woman, what were you up to . . . ? You were spying on the good old C of L, weren't you?'

'What me? I'm a college lecturer.'

She looked at me intently for a while. I returned her stare. There was something to be said for those old wooden warships. After all, they had served their purpose well.

'You know something about Melanie,' Janine said rapidly. 'I can tell. Where is she? Have they got her in some rural hideaway? That's what you were doing, isn't it? Has she asked you to help her again?'

'No, you're completely wrong. What I was doing last night had nothing to do with Melanie Varley.' Even as I spoke I could feel that my own words were false. There was *something* to do with Melanie. At least Tyler and Polk were. I felt mean at having to withhold information but Janine was the press. If I told her what I'd been up to, I might as well give Monckton a call myself.

Janine misread my expression. She read confusion as deceit.

'It has,' she stated, folding her arms and fixing me with that determined look. 'I can tell you're lying.'

'I'm not lying, just puzzled. There is a remote possibility of some connection with Little Miss Goody Two-Shoes. At least two of the same players were involved in last night's caper.'

'What was?' she persisted.

'None of your business,' I replied.

I went in my bedroom and began dressing for my day's toil

in the mills of academe. Janine followed me to the door and stood looking in.

'Do you mind?' I asked.

'I don't, if you don't, she said cheekily. 'I'm sure you got nothing I haven't seen before. Did I tell you I've got two children? A boy and a girl. They'll both be on the breadline unless I get to the bottom of this story. No husband, I'm afraid. The sad clown has cleared off for parts unknown.'

'My heart bleeds, but I don't see what that's got to do with me putting my trousers on.'

She retreated to the living-room but left the door open. I was reminded what it was like to have female company when I woke up. I told myself that human beings weren't meant to be on their own. Drawing back the bedroom curtains, I looked out on the world with a much more friendly disposition. Outside, though, nothing much had changed. A steady drip of rain seeped from a uniformly dark grey sky. A manic optimist looking for a silver lining would have been disappointed. Only the pearly brightness of the diffuse light suggested that it was morning. It was typical Manchester weather.

After several more rounds of negotiation I managed to usher Janine out of my flat. I'd promised to run her over to the Jewel in the Crown and bargain for the return of her Apple-Mac laptop. I was then intending to take the car into work and engage in the usual struggle for a parking space.

My Mondeo was in the centre of the parking area, not where I'd left it close to the garage. It looked as if a team of drunken navvies had worked it over with sledge-hammers. Roof, bonnet and doors were smashed. There wasn't one square inch of smooth metal on it. For a moment I wanted to puke, then my detective instinct, such as they were, kicked in. There was no broken glass near the vehicle. I walked round it and then out the main road. There was no glass there either.

It took the police twenty minutes to arrive, which wasn't bad considering that the rush hour was getting under way.

'You got someone who doesn't like you, sir?' the officer asked, scratching his head. 'It looks to me as if the car was towed in here in this state. I mean what vandal would go to the trouble of taking the car, smashing it up and then returning it?'

'I'm a college lecturer. Why would someone have it in for me?'

Janine looked at me sharply, as if to contradict, but I moved my fingers to my lips and she held her tongue.

The officer hummed sympathetically, promised to inform me in the unlikely event that he came by any information, took my details and gave me the crime number I was going to need for my insurance claim. Before leaving he asked me if I'd like a visit from Victim Support. I shook my head and kicked a tyre angrily. I arranged for a local garage to come and tow it away.

'That looks a write-off,' Finbar Salway said comfortingly when he emerged from the flats. 'What's up, Dave?'

'It's no good asking him. He'll only tell you that he's a college lecturer,' Janine interjected.

I shrugged my shoulders. I was getting good at that. 'Finbar, do you think you could hang on here for me?' I asked hurriedly. 'Tell the garage the loss adjuster will be round to confirm if it's a write-off.' I was too choked to go into any long-winded explanations. Finbar seemed to sense my mood because he nodded his head and retreated to his flat without further discussion.

'What about me?' Janine asked.

I bit back the obvious comment and looked at her. Once again she was the image of defiance. I could have just walked off and caught the metro at Stretford but something held me back. I took out my mobile phone and phoned for a taxi to take us to Whalley Range.

'We'll get the tools of your trade back for you. They've no right to hang on to your laptop because you owe a few quid.'

'I don't want to borrow money off you,' she said hastily.

'And I don't want to lend it,' I said equally quickly. 'You tell me what you think the laptop's worth and I'll buy it off you and you can buy it back at cost when the *Guardian* comes up trumps.'

We stood in silence for a few minutes waiting for the taxi. When it arrived I ushered her into the back. We were half-way to Whalley Range before she broke her silence.

'I don't accept gifts.'

I made no comment.

'You're a cool customer, aren't you? Do you know that your expression didn't change at all when you found that your car was smashed up?'

'It ought to have done. I felt sick enough.'

'About the money . . .'

'Look, we'll cross that bridge when we come to it. Those bozos at the Jewel in the Crown may be satisfied when I pay your bill . . .'

'I don't want you to pay it. We can persuade them to let me have it back. They'll understand that the only way I can earn the money to pay what I owe is by using that laptop.'

When we got to the Jewel the proprietor handed over the Apple-Mac without any difficulty but only after I had plonked my credit card down on his counter. There was no sign of the enraged pair from last night. Janine's entreaties cut no ice. In paying her bill I was aware that kind deeds have ruined more friendships than harsh words, but then did I want Janine White as a friend? She'd thrust herself into my life uninvited. Certainly what I did next seemed certain to ensure that I didn't see her again. Before dropping her in town I gave her all the cash I had on me – £200. She didn't speak, nor did I, but her eyes, almost brimming over with indignation and humiliation in equal parts, said more than words could have conveyed. She folded the notes up and put them away. The last I saw of her, she was striding purposefully in the direction of Piccadilly Station with her bag and laptop slung over her shoulder.

When I reached the Management Sciences floors at UNWIST my own concerns came to the forefront. Someone at the headquarters of the Children Of Light had sent me a very direct warning. I was brooding on the general injustice of life when I went into the common room. Cool and efficient as ever, Monica Withers was standing near the coffee machine. She pointedly turned her back on me as soon as she saw me. I hurried over.

'What have I done?' I asked.

She frowned and turned towards the door.

'Sorry, Monica, have I done something to upset you?' I persisted, blocking her route.

'Why didn't you tell me that you were working for the Children of Light when you pumped all that information out of me yesterday,' she said angrily. 'Should I expect a visit from one of their recruiting teams?'

'What are you talking about?'

'Don't come the injured innocent with me, Cunane!' she snapped in a fury. She pressed her lips together into a thin white line. Out of the corner of my eye I could see Professor Richardson pretending to have a conversation with a colleague in the far corner of the room but actually noting every word that passed between us.

'I still don't know what I've done to offend you,' I protested.

Monica seemed to gather herself up and for a moment I thought she was going to take a swing at me. Instead she extended her fingers. 'A,' she said, ticking her right index finger with her left, 'Mrs Lovegrove puts a call from some journalist through to me yesterday afternoon in which I learn that you've met this woman while on a visit to the local headquarters of the Children, and B, when I get home that same evening there's a fax from my dear sister Shannon requesting information about you. Now tell me that you're not involved with the Children right up to the top of your mucky little neck.'

'What happened to C, D and E?' I asked. 'Not to mention the rest of the alphabet?'

'Oh, mock if you like, but I know when someone's trying to take me for a fool,' she said. From her expression I could see that either blows or tears were still on the agenda.

'Look, Monica, nobody was more surprised than I was when you told me that your sister was a member of

Arkwright's barmy army. I didn't say anything at the time because, well . . . there was no time. I got involved in all this through no fault of my own. Can I explain?'

'Bah! Do you think I'm soft in the head? It's well known that the Children employ all kinds of investigators to harass their opponents.'

'First I've heard,' I said. 'No one's hired me.' I tried my hardest to exude charm and good feeling and her expression softened slightly but then Professor Richardson came over.

'What's this?' he asked breathily. 'We can't have off-the-ball disputes and heated words in here. I'm afraid I shall have to show you both the red card unless you moderate this discussion.'

Monica took that as an opportunity to stride out of the room. I tried to look relaxed and made no attempt to follow.

'I don't know what you've done to upset her,' Richardson said priggishly, 'but I find that extra-curricular activities are best discussed elsewhere.'

With that, he strode out after Monica, his face set in a glacial smile.

Hot words and hurt feelings were not what I was used to. I'd have preferred it if Monica had actually progressed as far as blows. I find that they clear the air much more quickly than amateur dramatics. As it was, I got through my morning's work feeling as if I'd been to the dentist and had my jaw anaesthetized. I had an hour's free time after my first tutorial and I spent it trying to write Monica a note of explanation. I started three times and each time scrapped what I'd written.

When lunch-time eventually came round I was waiting outside her door. The corridor was thronged with students of all nationalities, Greeks rubbing shoulders with Chinese and Africans. Monica opened her door and then backed out into the corridor like a crab with her key at the ready. I took a step towards her.

'Mr Cunane!' someone shouted behind me.

I turned. Framed in the angle of the stairs at the end of the corridor stood Alvin Richardson, Linda Lovegrove and Detective Sergeant Peterson, accompanied by a male colleague.

'Mr Cunane,' Richardson repeated. 'These gentlemen want an urgent word with you.'

Monica Withers emerged from her office to take the scene in and to my eyes seemed to exchange a knowing smile with Richardson.

'You can go in the staff office,' Richardson suggested grandly.

'Oh no, sir,' Peterson interjected. 'If Mr Cunane is free we'd prefer to have our chat down at Bootle Police Station.'

While all this discussion of my fate was going on it crossed my mind to take it on my toes among the crowd of students. As if reading my thoughts, Monica Withers stepped fully into the corridor to block my path.

'I'm free,' I said to Peterson. 'Do you mind telling me what this is about?'

'Yes, your mate Clint Lane has escaped and we want to pick your brains about where he might be.'

If he'd said that a UFO had landed in Albert Square and demanded my presence he couldn't have got my attention quicker. For once I couldn't think of anything even mildly amusing to say. I must have goggled at Peterson like a recently landed fish because he spoke again. 'Yeah, it took me rather like that. Apparently he bent back the metal screen round the exercise area at Bootle Street and scrambled up a drain pipe and out over the roof.'

'But Clint . . . he's handicapped,' I blurted.

'Apparently that's what the custody sergeant who left him on his own for five minutes thought. He'll have to explain his part to the official enquiry but you can tell us what you know now. Come on.'

'Hang on,' I said brushing his hand aside. 'Are you arresting me or something?'

'I can do if you want,' Peterson said with a wolf-like grin.

'Oh no you can't,' I said. By this time I was at the centre of an interesting piece of street theatre. Students were massed on the stairs and corridors with myself, Peterson and his colleague, Withers, Richardson and Lovegrove holding the stage.

'Trust the GMP. You allow a mentally handicapped man

with the mental age of a child of five to escape by your negligence and then in panic you try to haul in anyone who's ever spoken to him.'

'Come on, Cunane, cut the crap,' Peterson said. There was a note of unease in his voice. 'This is an interesting performance but if you want to be stroppy I can get a magistrate to sign an arrest warrant.'

'Well, perhaps we'd better wait until you do,' I said truculently. There was a brief round of applause from the assembled students at this display of defiance. Peterson's assistant pulled his personal radio out. Possibly he touched the panic button.

'Listen, sunshine,' Peterson said loudly, 'first Fred Travis is found clutching your business card in his fingers. Then you come up with this preposterous story that someone faked the video showing Clint Lane going into the flat. It sounds to me as if you've got a few questions to answer.'

'Yes indeed,' chimed in Professor Richardson, 'and Mr Cunane, I wish you'd go and answer them somewhere else. This display is most unseemly.'

'It's *unseemly* for a professor to hand over a member of his department to the police without a by-your-leave,' Monica exploded. 'This isn't Nazi Germany.'

'Dr Withers!' Richardson stuttered.

'Well, unseemly is as unseemly does. You shouldn't have led the police to his room like this.'

Richardson looked dumbfounded. An attack on his own political correctness was the last thing he'd expected. I seized the chance to put my oar in . . .

'Monica, whatever you may think I've had nothing to do with the Children of Light or your sister, would she have phoned you for information about me if I was working for them?'

Monica looked uncertain.

'Would you please conclude this discussion off university premises?' Richardson asked venomously.

'So much for academic freedom,' Monica Withers said from behind me. 'I'll come in with you if you like, Dave.' She shot Richardson a frosty look.

It's always nice to see how your friends line up when things are going against you.

'Could you?' I asked.

'For a couple of hours at least. I've not got anything on until 4.30.'

'It's just that if you could come with me it might deter our heavy-booted friends collumphing into here and pulling me in every time they feel in need of inspiration.'

'Fine, I'll get my coat,' she said, darting back into her room.

'You're making a lot of fuss about nothing,' Peterson said.

'No you are, bouncing into the university with your questions when you could just as well have phoned,' I replied. 'I'm not a private detective any more and I don't regard myself as being at your beck and call any longer.'

'We'll see about that,' the policeman mumbled vaguely.

The brief journey to Bootle Street was like the start of a bad dream. On arrival, I found myself being subjected to an in-depth interview by Peterson and Cullen. At least they didn't give me much time to feel uncomfortable about the fixtures and fittings. I hardly noticed the discomfort this time round. I waived the right to a solicitor.

'You're just helping with enquiries, Dave,' Cullen said reassuringly. Somehow I didn't feel reassured.

'What about the video? Have you proved it was faked?' I demanded.

''Fraid not, me old pal. The lab admits that it's possible to fake it by setting the date controls at a wrong date and substituting it for the video taped at the right time but there's no reason to believe that was done at this time.'

'Why not?'

'You're the one who's here to answer questions. Did Bob Lane give you any idea that he was going to spring his brother?'

'No he didn't. He knows that it's impossible for Clint to kill anyone, just as I do.'

'He could have done it without realizing,' Peterson interjected.

'How do you work that one out?' I demanded.

'Did you know that the lad had been doing these complicated anatomical jigsaws?' Cullen countered.

I drew breath while I thought that one out. A false statement risked landing me even deeper in the mire than I was already. 'What if he did? That doesn't mean that he cut Travis's throat.'

'Did you see the anatomical 3-D jigsaw?' Cullen insisted.

'Yes, it was in the room where Clint spends a lot of his time,' I admitted. 'I was the one who told Bob to take it apart and get rid of it because I know how your minds work.'

'Don't worry about our minds, Dave. Has it crossed your mind that Bob Lane is working an elaborate scam on you? That he's trying to involve you and leave you in the frame?'

'I know Bob too well for that,' I said.

'Have you seen Clint with a Swiss Army knife?' Peterson asked. They were working the old good cop–bad cop game very well, keeping me off balance with a stream of questions.

'I have, but so what? Lots of people have those.'

'Yeah, just like they have anatomical jigsaws when they're being trained to cut someone's throat,' Peterson growled.

'I've only ever seen Clint use his knife to do a little woodcarving. They have these little carvings he's done at his home, birds and elephants and things, made from bits of twigs he finds in Heaton Park.'

'If only he'd stuck to that,' Cullen said sympathetically.

'I'm telling you that Clint is incapable of violence.'

'As far as you know, Dave,' Cullen said with a sigh. 'You don't what's been going through the poor fellow's mind or his brother's either. Did you know that the clubs are in trouble? Bob's overextended his credit. He's either going to have to find a new partner or sell some of his business for a fraction of its value.'

This was news to me. I looked at Cullen and shook my head. I don't know what I intended to signify apart from my own confusion but he took it as some sort of signal. Turning to Peterson he said, 'Leave us for a moment, will you, Detective Sergeant?'

When Peterson had closed the door behind him, Cullen spoke in a more personal way. 'Listen, Dave, I wouldn't be doing this with everyone but I think you're being led up the garden path by that long twisted nose of yours. Bob's missing and so is Clint. There's no way that Clint could have stayed free on his own. Bob's into these killings right up to his neck.'

'Did you say killings?' I asked nervously. I allowed the slighting reference to my anatomy to pass me by.

'Oh yeah, didn't we tell you? I'm sure you can work out what sort of knife was found at the scene . . .'

'Swiss Army?'

'Right, only it hadn't been used to kill Fred Travis. The samples of dried blood found on it relate to the brutal killing of Marlon Westhead. You probably read about it . . . He was a pretty nasty thug up Cheetham Hill way?'

I nodded.

'He was found two months ago outside the Lamb and Flag on Cheetham Hill Road. He didn't have an easy death. Someone seems to have ripped the flesh off half of his face before stabbing him repeatedly with a short bladed knife. The pathologist said it was one of the nastiest killings he'd seen in years and that Westhead must have been screaming for several minutes before he died.'

'I heard about it,' I muttered, wondering what was coming next.

'Dave, Marlon was in the habit of going into clubs and pubs and threatening to smash them up unless he was bought off. He also had a sideline as a dealer. The interesting thing is that Marlon was considered to be exceptionally strong. The character who subdued him long enough to stab him more than twenty times also had to be exceptional . . .' Cullen looked at me with those candid brown eyes and paused for a moment. 'Of course, you know Bob Lane has a club in Cheetham Hill,' he continued.

I nodded. I could see the picture he was sketching. It was just that I didn't join up the dots in the same way he did.

'Bob wouldn't ever let Clint do anything wrong,' I said. 'He's kept him on the straight and narrow since childhood.'

'Things can change, Dave. It must be hell having to lug Clint around with him wherever he goes.'

'I've never heard him complain.'

'Maybe not, but don't you think he involved you as a last desperate attempt to throw a smoke-screen around what's been going on? He couldn't have known that Travis had CCTV in the entrance to his flat. When he realized that Clint was starring in his own version of Candid Camera he panicked. That's when he called in his friendly neighbourhood private detective to muddy the waters. You see, what you told us is perfectly possible, videos can be faked but with the other evidence, the footprints, the DNA . . .'

'What DNA?'

'Hairs were found at the scene. According to the lab there's only a one in forty million chance that someone else apart from Clint matches them.'

'It can't be him.'

'Dave, there's something else. I don't know whether you've thought of this, but isn't it possible that your old friend Bob actually told Clint to put your business card into Travis's fingers when he'd killed him?'

I shook my head again.

'Think about it. If Clint hadn't made more mess than Bob expected . . . bloody footprints, dropping one of his knives, et cetera, and there hadn't been that video to point us straight at Clint, this murder would have been down to you. We'd have thought that you were with Travis for some reason, perhaps touting for a job as a bodyguard . . . eh? *Protection and detection*, remember . . . and that you gave him your card and then killed him when he turned you down.'

'Would I be so stupid as to leave my visiting card at the scene of a killing?' I asked scornfully.

'Stranger things have happened. Anyway you'd have had a hell of a job wriggling off the hook. I reckon Bob wanted to fit you up, failed and then tried to involve you again.'

I put my head in my hands and leaned forward, examining the cigarette burns and scratched initials on the table top in great detail. I didn't know what to think.

'Where do you think he'll have gone, Dave?'

'You've tried his mother's?'

Cullen nodded.

'He has a place in Prestbury,' I said. As soon as the words were out of my mouth I felt like Judas. There was a flicker of triumph in Cullen's eyes.

'You don't say,' he muttered. 'I don't think we'll be needing you any longer, Dave.'

'What about Melville Monckton? Surely you're checking him out again?' I asked in desperation. Cullen was already on his feet.

'What do you mean "again"? . . . Not been up to your old tricks again, have you, Dave? Trying to keep one jump ahead of us?'

I shook my head earnestly . . . 'A slip of the tongue.'

'Monckton's contact with Clint was purely in connection with his work for a local charity and he'll sue anyone who says different. You, me or the Chief Constable, it doesn't matter to him. He'll sue and his pockets are quite deep enough to pay for years of legal harassment.'

With that he ushered me to the door and into the arms of Dr Monica Withers who was waiting anxiously on a bench outside.

'Is everything all right, Dave?' she asked.

'No,' I mumbled, 'it's all wrong. The police are certain that Clint killed Fred Travis and I'm certain that he didn't.'

This meant little to Monica. 'Well, where do we go from here? Do you want me to take you back to your flat?'

I studied her face for a moment, wondering exactly what she had in mind.

'Would it be too much to ask you to run me up to Blackley?' I asked.

'I thought your flat was in Chorlton,' she said.

'It is. I want to go and see Aldous Arkwright. I think he's the only one who knows what's going on.'

She looked shocked.

'It's not what you think. The last time I went to his headquarters I ended up knocking hell out of two of his underlings. I'm not one of his little puppets but I do want to know if he's pulling the strings in this Fred Travis killing.'

'Dave, it sounds dangerous. You don't know the lengths

that these people will go to. This cult the Children are involved in isn't just a game to them. They're capable of anything.'

'I'm beginning to realize that.'

Fascist Hyenas on the Prowl

Working-class people, especially young people without a sound ideological grounding in the Marxist–Socialist tradition, are being recruited by the pseudo-religious cult Children of Light movement and its dirty running dog, Repeal 98. All comrades should beware. Once these bloodsuckers take over they intend to imprint the brains of young people with hatred for all that we stand for.

Socialist Vanguard

8

Tuesday, 20 October

No amount of persuasion would coax Monica Withers to go any closer to Arkwright's Blackley headquarters than half a mile. She dropped me outside a pub at Boggart Hole Clough and promised to wait in the car park for me. If I hadn't returned in half an hour she was going to inform DI Cullen. I decided that the first thing I'd have to do when I found out what the spiritual director was up to would be to get myself a new set of wheels.

When I reached Meldrum Terrace the usual collection of 4WD vehicles had disappeared. The window I'd smashed had been replaced and there were now metal grilles in place over all the ground-floor windows facing the street. I went to the entrance door and banged the heavy knocker. In the quiet of the street it made a hollow sound like slamming the door of a crypt. This time there was no rapid opening. I banged again. I was about to turn on my heel and depart when the door was flung open by Aldous Arkwright himself.

'What's up?' I asked. 'Have all your servants taken the afternoon off?'

'I don't have any servants, Mr Cunane,' he replied evenly. 'We're a community of equals here.'

'Only some are more . . .'

'Don't say it,' he interrupted. 'It's quite untrue. We're an organic community in a way that a scoffer like you would never be able to understand.'

'I don't know, try explaining,' I suggested.

'Unless you have genuine interest, I think you ought to leave,' he said firmly.

'I might develop an interest if you could satisfy me on one or two points.'

Arkwright's serene lama-like expression faded for a second while he worked this one out.

'If you really are a genuine seeker after truth perhaps you'd better come in.'

'I am, in more ways than there are in your philosophy.'

We went into the small entrance vestibule where what seemed like an age ago I'd met Melanie Varley.

'Why don't you tell your followers that you were involved in Satanism?' I asked as he gestured me to sit on a high-backed wooden chair.

He gave a wry chuckle. 'My word, what I heard about you is true, you're a genuine sleuth, a sniffer-out of unconsidered trifles. However, my followers know about every aspect of my own spiritual journey because that is the path they themselves are seeking to follow.'

'What, the Manson murders and all?'

'That was an unfortunate episode . . . related to drug abuse. My followers eschew any unnatural substances. Only the aids so generously provided by Mother Nature are permissible. We're seeking enlightenment from within, but I don't propose to sit here and be insulted by you, Mr Cunane . . .'

'Wait a moment,' I insisted, laying my hand on his. His hand felt oddly hot and dry, like a snake's skin. I pulled my hand away as if I'd had an electric shock. 'Before you go I want you to tell me why your two American pixies are trying to frame Clint Lane for the Travis murder.'

'I would be interested to hear you justify your allegations against Mr Polk and Mr Tyler in front of a jury,' he said calmly.

'I might be doing exactly that soon enough. I'm sure they

told you about their nocturnal visit to Melville Monckton who happens to have all the resources to fake any amount of video evidence.'

'Monckton?' he said with genuine puzzlement. 'I'm not aware of any visit to Monckton. He's not one of our initiates. You must be getting confused.'

He picked up a large desk diary from the table in front of him.

'All arrivals and departures are logged in here,' he said. 'If you turn to Saturday afternoon you'll find every movement in and out of this building since your own visit on that occasion.'

I leafed through the pages. There was no reference to the 1.30 a.m. visit to Monckton nor to the departure of Melanie on the Saturday evening. The last entry read 'Communal Visit to Heaton Park'.

'This isn't accurate. You haven't got anything down about Melanie Varley,' I said handing him the book back. 'And I have photographic evidence that your two chief ghouls were definitely round at Monckton's house last night.'

For the first time since I'd met him, Arkwright showed something like a genuine human emotion. He stood up and clasped and unclasped his hands together several times and then put them behind his back. He struggled to achieve inner calm and eventually the mask of tranquillity slipped back over his features.

'I know you don't believe me, Mr Cunane, but when I first phoned you on Saturday I was genuinely seeking your help.'

'You were trying to find out what I knew.'

'No, there have been one or two troubling incidents lately that have disturbed life among my Children. Signs of stress that weren't there before. I don't believe things happen by accident. When your name came up on Saturday morning I thought cosmic forces were pointing me in your direction.'

'Just out of interest, which of your followers found Travis?'

'It was Brother Polk and Brother Tyler.'

'You do surprise me,' I said, getting up and turning to go.

Arkwright gripped the sleeve of my jacket. 'Stay a moment,' he commanded. 'I like you, Cunane. You've got a disrespect for authority that almost smacks of saintliness. I could use a man like you in this organization.'

'Sorry, Arkwright, my disrespect, as you call it, extends even to you.'

As I looked at Arkwright his expression underwent another transformation. A look of the keenest enthusiasm replaced the previous bland Buddha-like calm. The cult's gain was obviously the stage's loss.

'You may not realize it, Cunane, but we're standing at the edge of a new era . . .'

'Come on! I've heard all that bollocks from the politicians,' I said scornfully.

'Yes, no one senses change more keenly than those carrion hunters,' he said with intense seriousness. 'Don't you realize that the belief-system that sustained ordered life in this country for more than a thousand years has almost totally collapsed? All the symbols and signs that pointed people in a certain direction have been eroded from without or hollowed from within . . . family, patriotism, the monarchy, the church, the law, Parliament . . . everything. Others have rushed into the vacuum, the lawyers with their Bills of Rights . . . far more bill than rights in most cases . . . rationalists with their arid formulas for founding communities . . . none of them stand a chance. Spiritual power is the only thing the masses will respect apart from the lusts and hunger in their own bellies. I'm training an élite corps of followers with intense and concentrated spiritual power. You can be one of that élite.'

Arkwright was genuinely transfigured as he said this. His expression, his posture, his whole body seemed to radiate commitment to the extent that I felt churlish at not taking his hand and humbly asking for guidance. Unfortunately, I am churlish; churlish to the degree that I curled my lip at this offer of a place in his new order.

'Where did the late Fred Travis fit into your scheme of things?' I asked.

'What!' Arkwright muttered, reluctant to come down to earth.

'Travis was your partner. What role was he supposed to play in your intended take-over?'

'We're not intending to take over anything, the masses will

turn to us when they become convinced of our spiritual power. We offer the only viable alternative to the present chaos and Fred saw that. Although he didn't fully share our spiritual vision, he knew that we offered the only chance of establishing a decent, orderly and sane future.'

'Future! Fred was on an ego-trip back to the nineteen fifties, you mean. Talk about nostalgia, he was crazy for it.'

'It's natural that those who are revolted by the present drift into hedonistic chaos should look with longing to more orderly times. That's been the route that many converts to our way of enlightenment have initially followed. In time, as their understanding of the ultimate spiritual vacuum deepens, we hope to show them that it's only through the teaching of the Children of Light that a fresh order can be built.'

'So, according to you, Fred was out there trawling up potential converts for you, but I think he had different ideas about his role. Is that why he was killed?'

'How dare you associate that man's death with this movement!' Arkwright barked. 'The police have established that it was due to some squalid rivalry in the club scene.'

'That's what you'd like to believe but we both know it was nothing of the sort. Your chums with the phoney names are involved, aren't they?'

'Phoney names?'

'Polk and Tyler just happen to be the names of two American presidents.'

'Get out!' he screamed. 'I was a fool ever to think you had potential for our movement.'

'What, no bodyguards to march me out?' I taunted.

'I have no bodyguards. How dare you! My followers are elsewhere at the moment. If you are intending to do me violence, this is your chance.'

This was said with a certain amount of dignity but I didn't intend to allow him the last word.

I laughed in his face before going out.

'You were in there so long,' Monica said in relief when I joined her in the car. 'I was just screwing my nerve up to bang on the door and ask what they'd done with you.'

'That might have been interesting. Arkwright's there on his own. He was trying his best to recruit me to his cause – flashing eyes, waving hands, appeals to my finer feelings – you know the kind of thing.'

'Did he succeed?' she asked anxiously.

'He's just thrown me out. I suggested that his followers might have had something to do with the death of Fred Travis. He made a mistake with me, I have no finer feelings to appeal to.'

'Oh, Dave,' she said, leaning over and kissing me. 'I was a fool to think you could have been involved with them.' She went on kissing me hard on the lips.

'Steady on, Monica,' I cautioned. 'Haven't you got a lecture or something to get back to?'

She held up her mobile phone.

'I called in and cancelled. I'm free now until tomorrow.'

'Right, that's great,' I said. Too many signals were reaching my brain at once. First Arkwright and now Monica. Did she have plans on how she wanted to spend her spare time?

I looked at her blankly for a moment. She smiled.

'I was silly not to come to the door with you. I'm sure you can handle anything the Children throw at you.'

'Nice of you to be so confident. I wonder if you mind letting me drive the car for a little while. I'd dearly like to see if there are any developments at Meldrum Terrace.'

'What do you mean?' she said, pouting slightly. I got the impression that a single dose of detection per afternoon was sufficient for her.

'I'd just like to observe for a few minutes and see if Führer Arkwright goes anywhere interesting.'

'Dave, I didn't give up my lecture for this. I thought we might spend some time getting to know each other better.'

'We shall,' I promised, 'but there's a friend of mine about to be banged up for a murder he didn't commit and if I can find any evidence to clear him, I will.'

'You're so determined, Dave,' she said with a sigh, 'but you're not driving the car. It's only insured for me. I can handle whatever may be necessary.'

'Look Monica, I feel guilty about this. I'm using you.'

'Don't flatter yourself. I don't let myself be used by anyone.'

'You've done enough for me today. I'll get a taxi.'

'No, you won't. I said I'll drive for you, and I will.'

There was something about the determined set of her jaw that reminded me of how she'd put Richardson in his place.

'OK, lady,' I drawled. 'Now who's being determined?'

Her car was a brand spanking new Golf Gti, and as I'd already explained to her that mine had been pulverized her caution was reasonable. We parked the Golf close to the corner of Meldrum Terrace where we could discreetly observe any comings and goings. We didn't have long to wait for the Director to emerge. Arkwright's Land Rover Discovery swept round the corner only seconds after Monica had switched her engine off.

'Shall we follow him?' she asked excitedly.

'No, you follow him, see where he goes and then come back here for me. Whatever you do, don't tangle with him. If he spots you, just come back here.'

'I'd welcome the chance to give him a dressing down.'

'Monica, he's a rum bugger. For a moment when I was in there with him I thought he was trying to hypnotize me.'

'I'd like to see him try that on me.'

Ahead of the Discovery, a red Fiesta inched out of a parking space, and Arkwright slammed on the brakes. I turned to look at Monica.

'Humour me, Monica. Stay clear or go home.'

'But what are you going to do?'

'This is a golden opportunity to give his headquarters the once-over. Everyone's out communing with nature or whatever it is they do and I'll never get a better chance.'

'Ooooh! Dave! You'll get arrested and I'll be held as an accessory. I don't know what Professor Richardson will say.'

'We're only doing research. Get after Arkwright now,' I said, exiting from the car. 'See where he goes and then come back. I'll be in and out in no time. Meet me here. Give me a buzz on the mobile if Arkwright seems to be coming straight back here.'

Monica seemed inclined for further argument but as the Discovery was now turning into Rochdale Road it was make or break time for her. Reluctantly, she set off.

On my previous visits I hadn't noticed anything too elaborate in the way of security precautions. I ran round the back of the street to the small walled garden adjoining Arkwright's throne room. I scrambled over the wall and managed to force one of the windows open.

I don't know what I'd expected to find. In the large office area most of the staff had been working on the organization of a big joint Repeal 98/Children of Light rally to be held in the Nynex Arena. This was to announce a spiritual campaign to sweep new people and new measures into power. As the meeting was public I found nothing that I wouldn't have discovered eventually in the media. There were long printouts of names and addresses, each with a notation against it, R98 or C of L, presumably denoting which organization the individual was attached to. Monckton's name wasn't on any list, nor was Bob Lane's.

At one desk the monitor was still on. When I touched the mouse the screen lit up with another list of names. I scrolled back through the pages to the start. 'Membership Details – Most Confidential' the title page announced. This was too good an opportunity to miss. The file length was 1.2 megabytes so it would fit on to a floppy disc if I could find one. I looked through drawers and cupboards without success until I reached the supervisor's work station. I had to jimmy the lock before I could get the drawer open. There was an opened box of high-density floppies, but the number used was carefully marked off on the lid and each disc removed had been signed for.

I took a disc and scribbled an illegible signature in the signing-out column. It took a moment to format the disc and then get the computer into back-up mode.

While waiting for the download I looked round the room. It took me a moment to discover what was unusual. There were no telephones. Very curious. No telephones, no modems. The office wasn't secure against break-ins, as I'd proved, but it was secure against some snooper hacking into the system.

There had to be phones, though.

The computer had finished downloading. I extracted the floppy, and went exploring.

The telephone room was next to Arkwright's inner sanctum. It must have been the spot from which Polk and Tyler had emerged during my Saturday afternoon visit. Apart from the phones, including several mobiles, the only fixtures were two long sofas and a number of body-building devices including a large punch bag suspended from the ceiling. Presumably the pair worked off their less spiritual feelings by thumping it. I checked the last numbers phoned on all the receivers and jotted them down on an envelope. There was a note pad on the phone table with a flat sheet of glass next to it.

'Interesting,' I thought. Those scribbling down a message off the phone were supposed to use the glass sheet to rest their paper on to avoid leaving impressions on underlying sheets. Again, for a spiritual movement the Children of Light appeared to be well abreast of sophisticated security precautions. Even so, there was always the chance of carelessness particularly in a movement that thought its hour was about to come. I took the top sheet off the pad and delved in the waste bin for other blank sheets. As I carefully put the piece of blue note paper into an inside pocket I heard car doors slamming outside. I flew to the window by which I'd entered and made my getaway just as the front door was opened.

I was just dodging round the corner into the adjoining street in time to see Monica's car flying over the road bumps. The alleged traffic calming devices hadn't worked with her. She slammed to a halt and I'd barely got my behind on the passenger seat before she raced off again.

'Hold on. There's nobody after us,' I warned as the top of my head cannoned off the roof when we mounted another hump.

'Sorry. It's following that monster Arkwright. Can't you see I'm quaking with fright?'

'Did he spot you?'

'No, it's just that . . . You'll think I'm just a silly woman . . .'

'Tell me!'

'It's just that as I got closer I seemed to get more and more nervous. I can't explain it.'

'Oh,' I muttered.

'I knew he couldn't spot me but I felt that he was bound to be aware of me.'

'That's only natural . . . You were spooked.' She must have detected the disappointment in my voice because she turned and smiled.

'I'm not a total wimp. I followed him up into Higher Blackley. He went up Victoria Avenue, through a new housing estate and then into a big architect-designed house with a yew archway. I can take you there if you like.'

The breakneck speed slackened off and she pulled the car to a halt at the kerb.

'You did well,' I said, giving her hand a squeeze.

'Hold on to me for a minute,' she said. 'I feel cold.'

I held her. It was the first time we'd been so close and I suddenly realized that I did have feelings for her. I think she made the same discovery because she leant over and somehow we ended up in a passionate clinch.

'I've been a fool, Monica,' I said. 'You know that prig Alvin Richardson thinks we've been at it like knives for months . . .'

'We should have been,' she murmured. 'God knows why he thinks I cancelled my afternoon lecture. I think he's jealous of you, Dave. He's always fancied me himself.'

We both dissolved into giggles.

'I think we'd better be going,' I advised. 'We're a bit close to Chateau Arkwright here.'

She put the car into gear and drove off.

'Did you find anything that would get your friends off the hook?' she asked when we joined the traffic on Rochdale Road.

'Nothing, it's really just an office with some accommodations above. I don't know why they have to live in a converted street of terraced houses.'

'There must be some obscure reason,' she said, keeping her eyes on the traffic, but smiling to herself. 'There's never anything simple with that lot.'

'Well, they were getting the invitations out for this monster rally at the Nynex Arena.'

'Oh, that,' she said wearily. 'My sister's plagued me to go for months. The great leader is supposed to be commencing the conversion of Britain. He's going to give all his followers their mission statement. Each one is supposed to go out and find more followers until they run out of people.'

'Fat chance of success, I should imagine,' I said.

'I don't know. I think a lot of people are getting tired of an endless diet of soap operas . . . From the marketing point of view, this might be a very good time to start a new religion . . . a new millennium starting. I mean look at the waves of emotion that have swept over the country in the last few years.'

'You're not thinking of joining, are you?' I asked anxiously.

She laughed. The normality of that reassured me.

'There's something in it though. My sister's not exactly stupid. Arkwright's very clever. He's culled little bits of religion and philosophy from all over the shop and tailored them to suit himself. For instance, all this about evolution working to create a deeper consciousness in the universe. It appeals to a lot of scientific types.'

'Above my head, I'm afraid.'

'He thinks that every human being who's ever lived and every memory that's ever existed will be recreated in the future when the human race achieves full rapport with this consciousness of the universe . . . which he doesn't call God, by the way. I think Master Arkwright rather fancies himself in that role . . . It's about creating a perfect future by raising their level of spiritual awareness and as the most aware of them all he's bound to reach the very highest level.'

'You've got all this from your sister, have you? It sounds very deep.'

'Shannon's the only family I've got since my mother died. If I'd married and had kids it might have been different but I've always felt that I had to keep in touch with her in case she ever wanted to bail out from the C of L. I can give her a soft landing.'

'But you said she's got children.'

'Yes, that shows the lengths they'll go in binding people to them. They're evil, Dave. If you can do anything to put a spoke in Arkwright's wheel then I'm all for you.'

We drove in silence for a while.

'Do you feel hungry?' I asked eventually. 'There's a little Italian place opposite the Midland.'

'It's after five and I had no lunch thanks to your little drama with the police.'

'Then the least I can do is feed you.'

I directed her to park the car in the G-Mex car park and we crossed the road to Gio's Italian restaurant. When we got a table I must say that my appetite was keen enough to do justice to the menu. The tension of the last few days drained out of me as we tucked into course after course and the fact that I wasn't required to drive was an added bonus. Slipping back into the old private detective mode had another result. The part-time university lecturer who'd arrived at UNWIST that morning seemed to have thrown caution to the winds. By the time we were ready to leave Gio's, drink, food and renewed self confidence were all having their ruinous effect on my libido.

That's not fair. Monica was attractive in herself regardless of my internal workings.

Still, the excitements of the day helped me to look at her with a fresh eye and she returned my stare with a frank and open look. With her tall, rather slender figure Monica projected an aura of briskness and efficiency. Someone who didn't know that she was a university lecturer might have taken her for a successful businesswoman or perhaps even an army officer in civvies. She wore a navy blue blazer over a striped blouse with the collar turned up and a discreet gold chain round her throat. A Gucci bag slung over her shoulder added to the impression that here was a no-nonsense type ready for action.

'I don't fancy going home just yet, Dave,' she said huskily. 'Do you think we might give Professor Richardson something to worry about?'

'Do you mean . . . stop out late? Gosh, that would be naughty.'

'I was thinking about something a little more exciting than that.'

'Pubs? Clubs?' I suggested.

'Something more intimate than that.'

'Exactly what I was thinking,' I told her.

'Dave, I'm so sorry I doubted you this morning. I get really paranoid when I think about the Children of Light and the damage that they've done to my family.'

'No need for confessions. It's me that should be sorry. I still feel as if I exploited you by sending you chasing after our religious friend, but I felt certain that I knew where he was going. You confirmed it.'

'Dave, I've already told you. I don't let people exploit me. I'd have probably joined my sister in the Children of Light by now if I was that way inclined. I know what I want and I like to get it.'

'Right.'

'You'll have to tell me everything, but not here.'

A few minutes later we were back in the car heading towards my flat.

OK, we were a bit reckless, but you can reach a stage where elaborate preliminaries get tedious. I think we were both ready to push things a stage further.

Afterwards we lay together for a long time.

'Dave, we should have done this months ago,' she said eventually.

'I don't know Monica. Most of the females I get involved with seem to come to an unhappy end.'

'Don't be silly, Dave! You couldn't possibly have known that your wife would die of sickle cell anaemia.'

'How do you know what she died of?' I asked curiously.

'Dave, you're not the only one who can do a little checking-up on people.'

'So it seems,' I said.

'You're not annoyed, are you? It's common knowledge. You must have told Mrs Lovegrove.'

I racked my brains to remember. Lovegrove had pressed me for details of my private life but I couldn't recall providing her with much grist for her gossip mill. This little contretemps led to a slight cooling between us and I had to prove that my passion still ran deep and true by making love again. This time we both fell into a light doze afterwards. Maybe it started as a light doze but the exertions of the last few days and the heavy metal had taken their toll. When I woke up it was only because Monica was shaking me fiercely.

'Dave, the phone's ringing,' she said urgently.

I glanced at the alarm. It was 1.00 a.m. I must have still been groggy because I spoke without thinking . . . 'If it's that bloody Janine again, I'll go to London just to punch her silly head.'

I picked the phone up.

'Dave!' Bob Lane growled. 'You've got to help us.'

'What!' I gasped, alarm and guilt equally mingled in my tone.

'You know Clint's escaped . . . Very direct he is, just climbed out of the cop shop and ran all the way to my club right across Manchester without a single bluebottle stopping him. I thought he'd be safe at my house in Prestbury until I could get the solicitors and everything sorted but you know how restless he is at times. I took him for a walk to work off some of his energy and when I got back, what should I see but half the Cheshire Constabulary parked in my drive. They had my caretaker spread-eagled on the lawn with a machine-gun halfway up his ear. Some bastard must have told them the address. Anyway, to cut a long story short, Clint flung a couple of them over a hedge . . . all in a spirit of fun, like . . . and we legged it to where I'd hidden the car. Ever since then we've been driving round the side roads trying to keep out of their way. I need time to arrange a formal hand-over. I'm not going to let them arrest Clint . . . those armed police looked mean enough to shoot first and ask questions later.'

'Bob, I don't know what to say. . .'

'We need help, Dave. I've tried all my so-called friends and no one wants to know. You're our last chance.'

'Who is it?' Monica asked.

'It's Bob Lane,' I muttered, putting my hand over the mouthpiece. 'He and Clint are dodging round the back roads of Cheshire. He's terrified that the fuzz are going to shoot Clint and apologize later.' I was in a frenzy of embarrassment. Bob's predicament was my fault. If Clint was killed I'd never be able to forgive myself.

'Bob, they won't shoot if you tell them you're not armed,' I said hopefully.

'Grow up, Dave!' he snapped. 'They've already accused Clint of stabbing a man and cutting another one's throat. They'll shoot, all right, there's no way they could subdue Clint otherwise. He's all excited, like. Do you know anywhere we could lie low until he's more settled?'

By this time Monica had her ear pressed to the receiver.

'Ask him if he's anywhere near Marple,' she whispered.

I relayed this news.

'I can get there soon enough. We're just outside Wilmslow at the moment, that park place where they dug up the Lindlow Man.' He was referring to the two-thousand-year-old body recovered from a Druid ritual sacrifice. I was surprised Bob knew anything about that.

'Let me have the phone,' Monica demanded. In no time she was giving Bob detailed directions to her cottage.

'Come on, Dave. Wake up,' she said as she put the phone down. 'We'll have to get out there and help your friends. You still believe Clint's innocent, don't you?'

I nodded.

'Well, then,' she said, jumping out of bed and standing in front of me with her hands on her hips.

Being spurred into action by a naked woman felt strange. I'd lost the habits of domestication. Monica started pulling on clothes rapidly. . . 'I'll just duck into the bathroom for a minute,' she said, corralling her perky little breasts into her bra.

I was pulling my jeans on when she returned holding a pair of tights in her hand.

'Who would these belong to then?' she demanded, stretching them out in front of me. They were ripped. 'You don't wear women's tights, do you?'

'Of course not,' I said indignantly. 'That wretched journalist must have left them.'

'Oh, so you knew her well enough to get intimately acquainted,' Monica said angrily. 'I expect you ripped them getting them off her.' The expression on her face said it all. I was reminded of her angry suspicions at UNWIST that had led indirectly to our tryst. Passion and jealousy seemed to be close partners in her make-up.

Suddenly I found that I couldn't stand that knowing, accusing look for another second. 'Look, Monica,' I said angrily. 'Whatever I did or didn't do with Janine White is none of your business. As it happens, I can't stand the sight of her and if you think I slept with her you couldn't be more wrong. She dossed down on the sofa after they threw her out of her hotel.'

'I see,' Monica said coldly, making it quite clear that she didn't see at all.

'If someone's been telling you that I'm some sort of sexual athlete, they were lying.'

'Don't flatter yourself, Dave.'

'Perhaps you'd better reconsider what you're getting yourself into with the Lane brothers,' I told her. 'You know you can do time for harbouring a fugitive.'

'Of course I know that. I'm not stupid, but once I've given my word, that's it. I'm going to Marple. If you intend coming with me, lover boy, you'd better get your shirt over that athletic chest of yours.'

She punctuated her comment with a mocking laugh.

With a snarl I did as I was told. We rushed downstairs, banging our way out of the flats. As she was starting up the Golf I saw the light come on in Finbar Salway's living-room. The curtains twitched a second later. I knew my activities had been noted. There was little that I could hide from Finbar. I just had to hope that he wouldn't share his vicarious interest in my extra-mural activities with anyone else. In my present peevish mood I couldn't help thinking that he and his sister were the source of the information about me that was apparently the possession of half the population of Manchester.

Youth Market Saturated

New marketing opportunities in today's booming youth market appear to be in short supply, complained brewery chief, Steven Strongfellow. Since public pressure forced the industry to drop alcopops, the pressure is on to find new ways to reach the youth market.

Report in *Keg*, brewing industry trade journal

9

Wednesday, 21 October

My relations with Monica were still in the freezer when we reached Marple. I couldn't believe it when we parked in the drive of her home. I don't know what I'd expected. She'd always described the place in Marple as a 'cottage'. I suppose if you were an aristocrat or a wealthy industrialist it might amuse you to describe the sprawling, ranch-style bungalow as a cottage. To me, it looked more like some architect's attempt at a Southern plantation house with its pillared entrance and the magnolia-lined drive from the main road.

Things about Monica began to fit into place. What I'd taken for a belief that her life would run on tramlines was the expectation that her needs would always be catered for that you find in very rich people. I'd been fooled by her job into thinking that she needed to work for a living.

'Handy little chalet,' I said, indicating the double garage and colonnaded entrance.

Monica took no notice.

'They don't seem to be here yet,' she said.

'Bob won't show until he's sure we're on our own. He must have an inkling that I'm the one who told Cullen about his home at Prestbury,' I commented.

'Why did you do that, Dave?' she asked.

'It seemed harmless at the time. Anyway I can't hope to

have any influence with half-way decent coppers like Cullen unless I occasionally come up with the goods.'

'So you admit you're a grass?'

'It seemed like a good idea at the time. Anyway, it just slipped out and I'm sure that they'd have got round to investigating Bob's other properties before too long. I can't be the only one who knew he had a place at Prestbury.'

'No, I suppose not,' Monica agreed in that hard tone of voice that told me she thought I was contemptible. I sat quietly squirming in my seat. Bob Lane and Monica Withers were both capable of using me when they wanted to. Just as Monica had kept quiet about the millionaire's pad she called home, so there must be plenty about his relations with Melville Monckton that Bob Lane had kept his mouth shut about. I wished I was back at Thornleigh Court, tucked up in my lonely bachelor bed.

I spent an uncomfortable ten minutes sitting in silence in Monica's Golf GTi until the quiet crunching of wheels on deep gravel alerted me that Bob had arrived in his Toyota Land Cruiser. Watching him peering cautiously out of the bulky vehicle I marvelled that he'd been able to avoid the clutches of the law for as long as this, but then a lot of people in Cheshire drive that sort of massive chariot. Monica was quicker off the mark than I was. Leaping out of the Golf, she opened one of the garages and beckoned Bob to drive in. He did. There was a certain smoothness about the way that Monica closed the garage door, obscuring all trace of Bob and Clint's existence, that rang a little warning bell at the back of my mind. Had this innocent college lecturer had previous experience of hiding fugitives? She certainly knew what to do.

'Oh, do come inside, Dave, and stop eyeing me like a cod on a fishmonger's slab,' she said, opening the front door of her residence with an electronic key which she fished out of the Gucci bag.

'That's not the type of thing you were saying to me a couple of hours ago,' I said angrily.

'Oh, who's an angry old private detective?' she said with a laugh. 'That was then and this is now. I know you didn't like me finding out about your other affair but Bob's supposed to be your friend, not mine. You might try to put a bit of conviction into your rescue efforts.'

'There was no other affair,' I said vehemently.

'Ooooh, Dave Cunane, you naughty man! I swear that your nose has grown at least two inches,' she said with a not entirely affectionate grin.

'If I don't look totally enthusiastic about rescuing Bob it might be because I'm not absolutely sure about what's going on here. I've never understood why Fred Travis had my card in his hand months after I'd decided to give up being a private detective and why Bob Lane turned to me as his first port of call when he got into trouble. There's some connection that no one's told me about yet, but by God they will,' I vowed. 'And you might not be so keen to get mixed up with the law after you've seen the inside of a cell at Styal women's prison.'

Monica responded by laughing heartily. 'Don't get your CKs in a twist, Dave. I'm only teasing you. I think you're wonderful.' She laughed again, leaving me to wonder whether this was all a joke to a spoilt rich lady or whether she was serious.

She led me through the Swedish modern interior. It was all white pine and fantastically expensive-looking storage areas, with not a fitted carpet in sight. Applying the electronic key again, she led us into the garage space where Bob and Clint stood waiting for release.

Clint immediately began hugging and kissing me. I felt the breath whoosh out of my lungs as the affectionate giant gave me a squeeze.

'Where are you going, Dave?' he said. 'Can I come with you? Where are we going?'

'Now Clint, Uncle Dave's got other things to do,' Bob cautioned.

'Dave's my friend. Dave goes for walks with me,' Clint said. He was obviously in a highly overwrought state.

'We might go later,' I promised when he finally put me down. Looking at him, it was not hard to understand why a hostile copper like DS Peterson would think him capable of ripping a man to pieces with his bare hands. Clint's unnaturally broad face was suffused with colour and he was sweating with excitement. The gigantic shoulders were going up and down like pile drivers as he gulped air in and out of his massive chest. As I kept on looking at him, I told myself that this was a gentle giant.

'You've not got any smaller,' I said.

'Yes, Clint's big,' he agreed, the anxious expression on his face fading to a smile. I knew he lapped up praise like a small child.

'I've seen those jigsaws you were doing. You're really good at those, Clint.'

'I know, I love them,' he said in a shy voice. 'Those men wouldn't let me have the one I was working on, so I ran away from them.'

'He means the boys in blue,' his brother commented. 'As far as I can make out, he just climbed up a drainpipe, ripped the spiked barrier out of his way and came out over the roof. Then he headed straight to me like a homing pigeon.'

I was uncomfortable at discussion of Clint in his presence. Bob read my thoughts. 'He's all right. He hears me but he just thinks I'm saying what a good lad he is, don't you, big brother?' Bob slapped his brother on the arm at this like a trainer patting his favourite horse's flank and indeed Clint smiled as if he'd just worn first prize in a raffle. 'Aren't you going to introduce us to your lady friend, Dave?' Bob continued, giving Monica a very appreciative stare.

I introduced Monica.

'Dave's friend Monica,' Clint kept repeating as if worried that he was going to forget her name. Bob on the other hand couldn't take his eyes off my erstwhile sleeping partner.

'Bloody lucky for us you turned up,' he told her. 'I was getting to the end of my tether what with Clint being so excited and worrying what he'd do if the police laid a hand on him. I couldn't just turn him in. You've got to see that.'

I nodded without any great display of conviction at this but Monica more than made up for my less than wholehearted response.

'The police are hopeless,' she gushed. 'You were quite right not to trust them an inch. My father always said that most of them couldn't break their way out of a wet paper bag and now that they're armed to the teeth none of us are safe from their incompetence.'

I must have frowned slightly at this because Bob winked at me. Although never the first to praise the constabulary I couldn't help remembering that my father, for all his faults, had been a stalwart of the force.

'Hey miss, do you know Dave's dad was a high-ranking bluebottle?' Bob asked.

'Of course. I know all about Dave. We have no secrets, do we, Dave? But his father operated in the days before they were over-computerized, over-armed and overpaid, didn't he?'

I didn't know where to put myself. I didn't care to agree or disagree so I confined my response to the merest throat-clearing cough.

Monica again gave that rather horsy laugh that was becoming quite tiring to listen to.

'Let me show you round. I'll show you where you and Clint will be sleeping. I think you'd better stay here for a few days until we get something sorted, don't you?'

She led us from the entrance hall down a corridor. There were four guest bedrooms. Chuckling happily, Clint tried out the mattress springs in each one.

'Honestly, miss, we can kip on the settees,' Bob protested with a certain annoying Uriah Heep-like false humility.

'Nonsense,' Monica said briskly. 'I think this will suit you best,' she said indicating a twin-bedded room at the rear. 'There's no chance of anyone seeing you by accident here. There'll be no one working outside. My gardener doesn't come round during the winter months.' The rear of her garden was enclosed by a tall hedge of Leylandii and Himalayan balsam. Nothing less than aerial observation would breach her privacy.

'Bed's short,' Clint protested. He was clownishly measuring his length against the mattress. His legs projected at least twelve inches past the end of the bed.

'Don't worry, Clint, we'll put a chair there for you,' Bob said hastily. 'Look miss, I don't know if it's a good idea to keep Clint here for long. You can see how he is. It can be hard to keep him indoors for any length of time.'

'I haven't shown you everything yet,' Monica replied. She led us out of the bedroom wing through the central dining-room and lounge, to the other side of the house.

'Da-dah!' she said, opening a door with a flourish. Bob's eyebrows shot up, as well they might. The room that Monica now ushered us into was a fully equipped gymnasium and sauna. There were various exercise machines including a nautilus and a jogging/walking machine. She went straight over and switched on the walker. Clint hopped along beside her and jumped on the treadmill as soon as it started. His stride was so long that he strode off the end. Monica adjusted the controls until it was set at what would have been a fast trot for a normal sized person. With a beatific grin on his wide face Clint adjusted his pace and looked set for an hour or so.

'This is good, Bob,' he chortled. 'Dave, you can come and walk with me if you like.'

'I don't think we can get two of us on there,' I said.

'Why didn't I ever think of that?' Bob asked, striking his forehead with the palm of his hand. 'He'll not rest until I get him one. Mum will have to move from Langley now.' Then, looking at his brother contentedly pacing along, his face darkened as he suddenly remembered that his mother's housing problems were the least of his difficulties.

Watching that Herculean form pacing away I was suddenly aware just how surreal the whole situation was. Here I was, in the middle of the night, standing between Monica Withers and Bob Lane watching a fugitive from justice taking relaxing exercise. It was all crazy. I felt vaguely cheated by Monica Withers. She'd given me the impression or allowed me to gather the impression that she was a person of approximately equivalent status to myself. Now it turned out that she was rolling in the green stuff. Then there was Bob Lane. He must know that I was the one who'd grassed about his Prestbury pad yet when he phoned he claimed that I was his last resort. Just what was going on there?

'I need a word with you, Bob,' I said, turning to him.

'I thought you might,' he replied evenly.

'You're not going to start getting all heavy and official, are you, Dave?' Monica asked. Her eyes were sparkling and here in her own gym she looked fit enough to spar with Prince Naseem.

'Just one or two little wrinkles Bob and I need to iron out,' I said. 'Do you want to come into the lounge?'

'I'm involved too,' Monica insisted. 'I want to know what's going on and I don't think it's right to leave Clint on his own.'

'He's set for hours now, miss,' Bob told her. 'Why the hell I never bought one of these contraptions, I'll never know.'

'You were too busy with other things, Bob . . . such as whatever you were up with Melville Monckton.'

'Is that any of your business, Dave?' he countered.

'When it involves my business card being put into a dead man's hand and my car being pounded into a heap of scrap as a warning, I think it does.'

Bob gripped my forearm. He was almost as strong as his brother. 'You don't think I had anything to do with Travis's death?' he asked in a low voice.

'I honestly don't know. I think you haven't told me everything.'

This seemed to unlock some safety catch in Bob's mental equipment. He sighed, released my arm and headed for the door. Monica and I followed him. Clint kept on striding away delightedly, completely oblivious to his surroundings. Bob walked into the lounge and threw himself down on to one of the sofas there with an almost suicidal violence. I had little time to appreciate the ambience but did notice the expensive Bang and Olufsen telly and CD player. There were at least ten thousand pounds' worth of electronic kit in the room. There were also some delicate-looking Meissen figures in a display unit. I looked from Bob to Monica. She seemed to be entirely concerned with him.

'Melville wants to take over the business,' Bob said wearily. 'He wants me to front for him and manage more clubs and entertainment outlets. I'm practically bankrupt. I was on the point of doing a deal with him when all this blew up.'

'What do you mean by "entertainment outlets"?' I asked.

'Let's just say that Mel's a little less fastidious about how he makes his money than some of us,' Bob muttered disgustedly.

'Do tell!' Monica twittered excitedly. 'What are they . . . Brothels? Strip clubs?'

'I'd rather not say, miss,' Bob replied. 'It's a side of the market I've never cared to get into.'

'What's this got to do with Travis's death?'

'I can't say for certain but the only thing I can come up with is that they tried to fit Clint up as a way of taking me out of the scene and it seems to have worked too.'

'But why was I brought into it?' I demanded.

'I think that business card of yours was just another little pointer in Clint's direction. He's had one of your cards since that business two years ago. He takes it out and shows people and tells them that you're his friend. In fact he's taken it out so often that he wore away the original and I had to give him mine. Monckton must have known all about it.'

'Thanks a bunch,' I said, 'but why did I get the despairing phone call on Monday? You could have told the police all this. You must have hoped that by getting me involved they would put me back on their list of suspects. In fact, right at the top of their list.'

'Honest, Dave, it was nothing like that. Since when have the Manchester police given a club owner a fair shake? It might have been different if I was in Liverpool, but why do you think Monckton wanted someone to front for him . . . ? Admit it, Dave, you've had a certain success at unravelling one or two problems. I hoped that you'd find out what Monckton was up to.'

I looked at Bob. I was still undecided. Then he smiled and stuck his hand out and I shook it.

'Sorry mate,' he said. 'I should have realized that you were out of the detection game now.'

'But he isn't,' Monica said eagerly.

Bob looked up hopefully.

'I did find that Monckton is closely linked with two of Aldous Arkwright's heavies,' I admitted.

'Arkwright? Where's his club? I've never heard of him. Is he from over Leeds way?' Bob asked.

I had to smile at this. Monica laughed as well.

'What's the big secret?' Bob demanded. 'Who is this guy? Is

he from the smoke?'

'No, he's actually a cult leader who's on the point of launching a crusade to save the nation from its moral failings,' I said.

'Stop joking and tell me who the bastard is,' Bob said, smacking his fist into his hand, and getting even more annoyed with us.

'It's true,' Monica protested. 'Arkwright has a cult with members all over the country and he has this place up in Blackley . . . My sister . . .'

Bob shook his head in bewilderment.

'You're saying that some religious nut peddles muscle and that he was behind the move against Travis . . . ? I had nothing against Travis myself, by the way. He was a bloody nuisance at the time with his demos but my takings went up after every visit from him. The publicity was like a free gift and you should have seen the sour faces on the police shepherding his loonies out of the way so that my punters could get in . . . Talk about a month of rainy days, there was one inspector practically shitting himself. Ha! It makes me laugh even now to think of it.'

'Glad you can still see the funny side of things, Bob,' I murmured. 'The sad truth is that the police refused to believe a word against Monckton or Arkwright and that they're out there now scouring the highways and byways for you and Clint.'

'What have you told them, then?'

'I told Cullen that Monckton has all the contacts he needs to fake any amount of videos. I asked him what possible motive Monckton could have for seeking Clint's company . . . He told me that what I was suggesting was libellous . . .'

'What were you suggesting, for Christ's sake?' Bob interrupted angrily. He'd slipped the jacket of his green suit off and was now flexing the mighty forearms that had earned him his nickname. Monica didn't know I was watching her, but I could see she was examining Bob's muscular development with an approving eye. There was some sort of chemistry developing between those two. Oh well, better to have loved and lost than never to have loved at all, I thought wryly.

'What do you think I'm suggesting?' I snapped back at Bob. 'There's something bloody weird about someone wanting to cart Clint around night, noon and morning for weeks on end. He's hardly the world's wittiest conversationalist and now you tell us that Monckton was pressuring you for control of your clubs all the time. I can't understand what you were thinking . . .'

Bob slumped forward and put his head in his hands. All the aggression drained out of him. Monica left my side and put her arm round his shoulders.

'It wasn't like that,' Bob said in his deepest, gravelliest voice. 'I was flattered at first. Melville seemed genuinely interested in Clint. They had this joke . . . it involved you, Dave. Clint said he was giving protection like you used to . . . Melville went along with it. I thought it was just for laughs at first, then later it struck me that he was trying to use Clint against me. There was nothing I could do by that time. Clint loved going with him. You know how hard it is to dissuade Clint when he's made his mind up to do something.'

Bob began weeping quietly.

'Do you think they coached Clint to kill Travis?' I persisted. Monica shot me a resentful look.

'Never. I'll never believe that Clint could have done that.'

'Fair enough, but what about this Marlon Westhead business? You know they're trying to pin that on you and Clint as well?'

'That's rubbish! I was in the office at Stevenson Square when Westhead was killed. We had a top DJ booked at Howl and I was there all night. There's dozens of people will confirm that and Clint was at home with mam. You believe my mother, don't you? She'd never let Clint out on his own.'

'No, I suppose not,' I agreed. Mrs Lane was notoriously overprotective.

'If you ask me, Westhead got what he was asking for. There must have been dozens of people queuing up to slot that crazy bastard . . .'

'OK, then, Bob, lighten up. I'm not saying you did it. I just had to be sure. Hey, guess who found Travis's body?'

He shook his head.

'The same two heavies who went round to Monckton's place after I got Cullen to send police to interview him.'

'So?' Bob asked dispiritedly.

'It's got to be more than coincidence,' I said with a confidence I didn't entirely feel. 'Our problem is persuading Manchester's finest to give Melville Monckton the same degree of attention they're giving you and Clint. They seem to regard him as Mr Unimpeachable at the moment. You'll have to tell me all you know about him.'

'Such as what?' Bob said cautiously. He was still hiding something. 'Look, I know no more than you... He's a famous rock star and he's not short of a quid or two.'

'Have you been to his house in Higher Blackley?'

'No, he preferred to do his fraternizing in my club.'

'Well, has Clint been there?'

'It's possible,' Bob said with an angry shrug. 'Although Clint's handicapped he's entitled to a life of his own. I can't track him every minute of the day. I trusted Melville... maybe I shouldn't have but I don't think Clint would ever let anyone make him do something he didn't want to. You know what he's like... God almighty! You heard him tell you he bust out of the nick because they wouldn't let him do his puzzles.'

'Look Bob, the only reason I'm here is because I'm ruling you and Clint out of the frame for the killings. That leaves Monckton and Aldous Arkwright's two heavies... You must have some inkling about why they wanted Travis out of the way.'

'I haven't a clue.'

'Well, what was this... venture he wanted you to get involved in?'

Bob's face was a study as he worked out whether he ought to tell all.

'I'll only tell you if Miss Withers goes out.'

'Ha! Male bonding, eh?' Monica snapped. 'And it's Doctor Withers actually.' She withdrew the comforting arm from Bob's shoulder but made no move to depart.

'It looks like you're going to have to spill the beans in front of the lady,' I told Bob. I knew he had a curiously old-fashioned attitude at times. It had stood him in good stead when his previous employers on the club scene were anxious to follow the trail of profit through a deep mire of criminality.

Bob looked from me to Monica and back.

'I'm no bloody prude, you know that, Dave,' he said as if seeking reassurance.

'There aren't many chapel elders running night-clubs in Manchester,' I agreed.

'We might be making more money if there were. The bottom's dropped out of the club scene. There's coachloads of kids going to clubs in Liverpool and even Stoke on Trent of all places. It was different a few years ago. We had clubs like the Paloma which were pulling in punters from as far away as Japan. They lifted all the rest up, like.'

'Yeah, I suppose so,' I muttered. I had my own memories of the Paloma.

'Well, Melville reckons that there's only two ways to increase the turnover and pep the scene up a bit. He wants to go back to the old standbys . . . sex and drugs.'

'What's wrong with that?' Monica demanded. 'That's what you've always traded in.'

'Not me! I've never knowingly allowed tarts or dealers in my clubs,' Bob said indignantly.

'If he's thinking of introducing bonking for all, well he can forget it. He'd never get a licence to run a glorified knocking shop.'

'That's where you're wrong, Dave. His idea is for a kind of mega-entertainment centre where there'll be dancing, swimming-pools, hotel facilities. It'd be big on indoor sports too, not just the horizontal variety . . . like a sort of glassed-over Club Med for the eighteen to thirties . . . The staff will be trained to look the other way if the clients want to do what comes naturally in the mixed changing areas, etc. He's already had offers of support from a couple of the big entertainment conglomerates. The idea would be that the clients spent . . . say, the whole weekend on site. Hotel facilities would be on the rudimentary side to keep costs down . . . more like booths where they could crash out for a few hours . . . the idea being to keep them circulating round the bars and spending opportunities until they literally pass out from exhaustion.

They could get pissed legless or doped to the eyeballs and not have to worry about getting home. While they were sobering up they could be getting a tan in the solarium or a massage at the health spa. There'd be special offers for midweek. It would all be presented as completely above-board, healthy leisure. He wants me to handle the security angle. I've got a reputation for low tolerance of dealers that would be valuable, but really there'd be so many entrances and exits it would be impossible to prevent drugs getting in . . . not that I think Melville wants to. I think he'd be happy with a percentage. He'd probably franchise it.'

'Sounds a bit far-fetched to me,' I said dubiously. 'A leisurama in the middle of Manchester? Come on.'

'No, you're wrong. There's serious money involved. Melville's even talking of getting a soccer club involved. The club would sponsor it or the other way round. I wasn't quite clear about that.'

I laughed. Bob was a funny bugger. Why had he been so reluctant to reveal all this?

'You can laugh, Dave. I know you're all for the independent little man but that's the way everything's going. Look at retailing – first the Arndale Centre, which everyone thought was a monster when it opened – but now there's the Trafford Centre into which you could fit a dozen Arndales.'

'OK, so you turned Monckton's offer down. That still doesn't add up to him being anxious to frame you for murder.'

'Dave,' Monica interjected. 'Don't you remember Fred Travis vowing to fight tooth and nail against any expansion of night-club and entertainment facilities in Central Manchester? He said the nation's youth was being channelled into vice by big commercial interests.'

'Fred Travis vowed to fight so many things that they all cancel each other out,' I said. 'He wasn't above making money in dubious ways himself. I heard that a lot of those tractors he sold in Africa had turrets and guns on them.'

'Right, well all this reminiscence doesn't solve our immediate problem,' Monica said in her briskest tones. 'We've got to find some way of convincing the police that Clint wasn't involved and until then we've got to hide him.'

'Look, miss. It's not your problem. It was very kind of you to help us but you shouldn't get involved,' Bob said.

'No, really. I won't bore you with the story about what they've done to my sister, but if the Children of Light are involved I want to help you. Anything that puts a spoke in their wheel is all to the good.'

Bob looked at her as if she wasn't quite right in the head but then he seemed to accept what she'd said.

'I know nothing about the Children of Light – they sound like a right bunch of nancies – but if we can hide here until I can make some arrangements to get out of the country I'd be very grateful.'

'So you don't think I can do anything to help you?' I asked ruefully.

'Be honest, Dave. What chance have you got against the police and Melville Monckton? The man's practically worshipped in Manchester. People will lie down in muddy roads to save him getting his shoes dirty. If he's decided he wants me out of the way it's best if I shift myself before I end up doing time.'

'There's always a chance, Bob. These people have a habit of overreaching themselves. Then the media turn on them like hungry wolves and . . .'

'Yeah, I know, the bigger they are, the harder they fall. But that's not going to happen in this case, Dave. You've done enough. I was wrong to try to involve you. You've got yourself a life now and I'm going to butt out of it.'

'I am involved. I'm sure it was Polk and Tyler who pounded my car to scrap.'

'I can lend you a car, Dave,' Monica offered. 'You can keep it until your insurance comes through.'

I looked at her. There were so many things that I wanted to say. I wanted to tell her that my concern with Polk and Tyler and the car wasn't purely mercenary. In the end I decided to say nothing. Too much explanation was bound to come out like another set of excuses.

Maybe it was the late hour. Maybe it was because I was still not convinced that Bob Lane had told me everything, but part of me wanted to take him up on his offer. Heroics are all very well when you're a private investigator working off a grudge against an overbearing parent who also happens to be the most famous detective produced by the region for the last fifty years. That was over. I was a college lecturer now. My feeble efforts on Bob's behalf were the last flicker of a dying fire.

Infiltration Feared

In a lecture to the North of England Police Conference, Sir Cedric Baxendale, Her Majesty's Inspector of Constabulary, stated that while Masonic influence was on the wane, other dangers were increasing. He warned senior officers to be wary of the recent growth of a number of cults, some of whose members appeared to have an unusually strong interest in seeking positions of influence in the police service. The question to be asked, he said, was, 'Are these individuals motivated by the public interest or by the desire to spread the influence of their cults?'

Report in *The Times*

10

Wednesday, 21 October

When I left Marple I was seething with a mixture of emotions. Even the fact that Monica had led me to another garage behind the house and revealed that the car she was proposing to lend me was a 1961 Rolls Royce Silver Shadow did nothing to soothe. I told myself that it was because I didn't like being cast off like an old sock in the middle of an investigation. But as I sat behind the wheel of the venerable but perfectly preserved Roller and steered my way round the narrow lanes like a Mississippi river pilot navigating between sand bars, I knew that it was the sidelong looks that Bob and Monica had exchanged which had ruffled my feathers. She was definitely attracted to the tough-looking club owner and had hardly taken her eyes off him ever since they met. Well, who was I to complain? I'd had my chances with Monica and then left things until she was bound to imagine that I wasn't really interested. Still, we had slept together, even if belatedly, and I had been ready to . . . No, that was bollocks. She was entitled to shift her interest from a reluctant Romeo like me to someone such as Bob who was prepared to show proper gratitude. The transfer of affection was just a bit quick, that was all.

I got back to Thornleigh Court at 4.00 a.m. Evidence of the interrupted tryst with Monica didn't prevent me from setting the alarm and climbing back into my rumpled bed. Fortunately I didn't need to go into UNWIST until eleven so there was the chance of getting a bit of beauty sleep. I noticed that Monica had left her ear-rings on the bedside table. I shut my eyes and tried to sleep. I couldn't. Images of Arkwright and his confederates and the imagined scene of Fred Travis's gory death floated into my consciousness. Counting sheep did no good. In the end I got up and put the disc I'd taken from Meldrum Terrace into the computer. It was compatible with my software.

What I had on the disc was a long list of names and addresses. It did nothing for me except to produce mild surprise at the sheer number of Arkwright's adherents and my eyelids were beginning to droop by the time I'd got as far as the names beginning with P. Then I did hit something that caused a jolt. The name Anne M. Peterson stuck out like a sore thumb. It was attached to an address in Sale, so there was no way I could dismiss it as coincidence. I got that nasty old itch to meddle that had led me into so much trouble in the past. I was in a fever to find out more. Was she DS Peterson's wife, mother, relative? Where to find out at this time of night, though?

Then I remembered the scraps of blank paper I'd scavenged from Arkwright's memo pad. I took them into the kitchen and shaded the first with a soft pencil. There was nothing. I did the next. Bingo! It contained a jumbled palimpsest of written-over words and letters. I studied it for a while and then held it up to the light. There was at least one word I could make out clearly. It was my own name – Cunane. Whoever had written it had pressed down the pen with extra firmness.

So what had I got? A High Court judge or a QC would say that I had nothing at all. I knew that Arkwright had phoned me, so there was every chance that whoever had written my name had done it on Saturday . . . that was rubbish though. The careful attention to minor details of security shown in the C of L headquarters ruled it out. Possible incriminating bits of paper were removed daily. This scrap of paper contained yesterday's jottings, and anyway the name was written with such clarity that it must have come last, on top of the earlier writing. So someone had phoned Meldrum Terrace on Tuesday and mentioned my name at the time I was being grilled down at Bootle Street by Detective Sergeant Peterson who just happened to have the same name as a Sale resident who was a member of Arkwright's 'spiritual élite'.

I picked up the phone. I wanted to tell Monica what I'd found. I put the phone down again. Would I like it if I found that she was already in bed with Bob? God! It even sounded like a joke. Next I thought of DI Cullen, he'd certainly be interested, but only to tell me that of the seven hundred and twenty-five people named Peterson in the Greater Manchester area none were related to his Sergeant . . . Then he'd arrest me for breaking into Meldrum Terrace. I picked up the telephone directory and checked. There were few Petersons listed, none at all in Sale.

I slumped back into bed and fell asleep right away this time. Better ideas would come in the morning . . .

I woke just before ten. I was feeling benevolent. Last night's touch of spleen seemed to have disappeared. Monica Withers was nothing to me really, I told myself as I flung back the bedroom curtains. If I'd been interested, would our session on the connubial couch have been so long delayed? It was a bright clear day. Last night's rain clouds had all blown away over the Pennines. Down below in the courtyard Finbar Salway was admiring the Roller. It had been too wide to go into the garage so I'd left it near by. The good news was that it hadn't received any attention from sledge-hammer wielding intruders. Noticing me peering down, Finbar waved. I signalled him to come up.

'Are you busy today, Finbar?' I asked in as casual a tone I could manage when I'd finished explaining that the Rolls Royce was only a temporary acquisition. I was getting dressed and he was making us both a cup of coffee.

'Fiona wants me to push a trolley round Sainsbury's for her but I can get out of that easily enough,' he said eagerly.

'I wouldn't like to cause a rift between you,' I said.

'It's no problem. She always gets irritated with me anyway. She can go in a taxi, I'll give her the money.'

'You're sure?'

He nodded impatiently. 'Is it about those people who smashed up your car?'

'In a way, though there'll be no rough stuff involved. I just want an address checked out. I'd do it myself but I'm due to give a lecture on the operation of the price mechanism in small businesses at eleven.'

Finbar shook his head sadly at this. 'What a waste,' he murmured.

I laughed.

'There's this address in Sale,' I said, jotting down the details on a scrap of paper. 'I know that an Anne M. Peterson lives there. What I want to know is who comes in and out . . . physical descriptions, you know the type of thing. I don't want you to be spotted. If I'm right, her husband's Old Bill, so be careful. If you do see a short thin bloke with curly brown hair going in, give me a ring on the mobile and come home. I'll take it from there.'

'Is he at it?' Finbar said conspiratorially. 'I mean, do you think he's bent or something?'

'It could be something a bit worse even than that,' I said thoughtfully. 'A little bribery and corruption's one thing, but this, it could be more serious if I'm right.'

This impressed Finbar sufficiently for him to hurry downstairs to inform his twin of the change of programme. I lost no time in getting out before Fiona made her way up to my flat to protest. I didn't even think of driving the Rolls into town. At this time of the morning every parking space near UNWIST, even for a moped, would be taken up. I had the disc and paper from Meldrum Street in my briefcase. What I did with them would depend on what Finbar found.

I got into UNWIST just in time to give my lecture. This was no big deal, lots of lecturers only showed up in the department the minute before they were due to perform. We weren't required to clock on at eight thirty or anything. However, when I went into the lecture room – a large one on the ground floor – I noticed that a diffident young man wearing a massive pair of horn-rimmed glasses and clutching a sheaf of notes was hovering near the lectern. I went over in my usual brisk fashion, thinking this was some new student waiting to introduce himself . . .

'What can I do for you?' I asked jocularly. 'I haven't seen you in my lectures before.'

He gaped at me and then adjusted his specs. His prominent Adam's apple was doing a tango up and down his throat. 'Oh, Mr Cunane,' he croaked. 'Er . . . Professor . . . I must be in the wrong place.' Without another word, he turned on his heel and fled.

I got on and delivered my lecture. It was quite a good one, I'd spent many hours preparing it. I had every possible aid – flip charts and slides and computer diagrams. I first noticed that I was under observation when I darkened the lights to show these. First Mrs Lovegrove's face appeared framed in the window of the outer door. I gave her a little wave. She didn't respond with her usual come-to-bed smile. Shortly afterwards the long, lugubrious features of Professor Richardson appeared at the porthole. I continued with the lecture. Richardson peered down his aquiline nose at me for so long and with such fixed purpose that I didn't need to be a mind reader to guess what was coming next. The man was staring at me like a Sioux brave deciding just how to collect a scalp. I ignored him and went on with the lecture. It was going well. My preparation was paying dividends. Students were scribbling notes and I felt light-hearted enough to cast a smile in the direction of the window. Richardson was still there.

When the lecture eventually concluded there were students hanging around for some minutes, though the majority cleared off for their lunch at once. Richardson, however, waited until the very last one had departed before stepping into the lecture room. His eyes were now downcast so that he avoided looking at me directly as if catching a glimpse of my features might turn him into stone like one of the mythological victims of Medusa.

'A word, Mr Cunane,' he said magisterially, closing the door behind him. 'I wasn't expecting to see you today.'

I asked myself why it was that Americans in academic posts

on this side of the pond become more stuffy and 'British' than the British ever manage to. Richardson was looming up at me like some archdeacon in a Trollope novel.

'Why ever not?' I asked. 'Did you think the police were going to lock me up and throw away the key because I know Clint Lane?'

'Of course not, but there is the question of the incident.'

'What incident?'

'Your arrest in public.'

'I wasn't arrested. I merely accompanied DS Peterson of my own volition. When they established that I had no information I was immediately released. I'm sorry if it upset you but that's the way the police like to do things.'

'Well, I'm sorry too,' he said in a strangulated voice. 'I'm afraid I'll have to suspend you on full pay for the remaining two months that your current contract has to run . . .'

'But why?'

'Bringing the department into disrepute. We can't have these scenes where lecturers are apprehended by the police in public areas with half the student body cheering when resistance is offered.'

'But that isn't correct,' I protested.

'There's also the issue of your intimidating attitude. Mr Gormally, who I persuaded to replace you for this course at very short notice, thought you were going to hit him when you turned up to give the lecture.'

'Why on earth shouldn't I turn up? If this wimp thought I was intimidating, I'm sorry. I thought he was a student who'd lost his way. Your secretary doesn't find me intimidating . . .'

'I intended to forestall you and warn you not to attempt the lecture, and I would have done if you hadn't intentionally arrived at the very last moment. Your unwanted attention to the departmental secretary is another issue, Mr Cunane. You've introduced a note of predatory sexuality into the department that I find quite reprehensible. I've had to caution Mrs Lovegrove about her overfamiliarity with you and then there's your affair with Dr Withers. We simply can't permit anyone to conduct his lovemaking in public.'

'So you've suspended her as well?' I demanded.

'No, she's a permanent member of staff and there are other procedures. She will receive a letter of admonition when she arrives in the department. So far she's not turned up. I suppose you know something about that?'

'Nothing to do with me, guv!' I said, shovelling my papers back into my briefcase. 'With the greatest respect, I think you're making a mistake. There was nothing wrong with my work, was there?'

'I'll grant you that and I'll go so far as to say that if you leave without further fuss I'll be prepared to give you a reference for a job in another institution stating that your work was, well . . . satisfactory.' For the first time he looked me in the eye as he spoke and he may have caught a glint of my alleged intimidating attitude. 'Very well, better than satisfactory,' he added hastily.

'Thanks a bunch!' I muttered, snapping my briefcase shut and making for the door. 'You've got this all wrong, prof, and it will rebound on you. Please convey my best wishes to Mr Gormally-Normally or whatever he's called. I didn't mean to frighten him.'

I could almost hear Richardson give a shudder of relief when I stepped out into the corridor. I was puzzled. In the circles I usually moved in – that is, police and criminal circles – people were always telling me that I was soft to the point of sponginess, but here in the groves of academe, where I'd sought refuge from the hard life on the mean streets, I was regarded as a cross between a storm-trooper and Casanova. I walked out into the courtyard. Everything was normal, students were milling about as they headed for dining areas, lecture rooms and labs. No one ran screaming from the spectacle of a dismissed lecturer. Richardson was an old woman. Either that, or someone higher up the academic food chain had had a word in his shell-like. The only feeling I experienced was one of relief. It was as if a weight had been lifted off my shoulders. I was my own man again and I was to be paid for the next two months.

I took the metro to Stretford and walked the short distance to my flat. The sun was shining and a mild breeze was making it unreasonably warm for the time of year. Global warming? I had enough problems on my plate without worrying about that. For the time being the planet would have to take care of itself. My brief journey along the pot-hole-strewn footpath gave me time to think about my options. There was nothing to stop me digging into the affairs of the C of L now, but was it worth the bother? Someone in that crazed outfit knew the reason for the death of Fred Travis. I wasn't convinced that Arkwright himself was fully involved but then it would be in his best interest to be able to claim that his underlings had operated without his approval. What was it they called that . . . ? Full deniability.

Apart from continuing with my career as a snooper, my other options were limited. I could get the *Times Higher Education Supplement* and search for another job. I could even consult my union; after all, I'd paid the membership fee. Both prospects were less than enchanting. It seemed that I radiated the wrong vibrations for an educational setting. The hell with it! It was back to detection and protection. I had enough in the bank to survive for a few months and there were one or two assets I could cash in to provide the funds for setting up a new office. A grateful client had once given me a Lowry painting which now hung on the wall of my parents' cottage. That would provide enough to give me a start, although my mother wouldn't be pleased to part with the picture. I don't think Paddy had even noticed it was there. I began to ruminate about where to look for an office. I'd have to look for somewhere nearer to King Street and the lawyers' offices this time. Maybe that had been the reason why Pimpernel Investigations hadn't flourished last time. I'd been too far away from the legal district, secreted in my attic chamber. This time I'd think big.

Hope springs eternal, I thought to myself as I turned into the entrance of Thornleigh Court. As if my megalomaniac dreams were already becoming reality, the first thing I spotted was the gleaming bulk of the Rolls Royce. 'Well, why not?' I mused to myself, 'Start as you mean to go on.' I fished out the key, slung my briefcase in the back and set off for Sale.

I owed Peterson one.

The address of Anne M. Peterson turned out to be a large

semi in a cul-de-sac off Harboro Road, Sale. It was in a reasonably prosperous district but no one would have thought it was beyond the means of a detective sergeant so Finbar's concern that Peterson, if he did in fact live there, was 'at it' seemed to be ruled out. I couldn't spot Finbar until I rolled past the cul-de-sac for a second pass. He was coming out of the corner house. His car, an old Rover, was parked in the drive. I flashed my lights at him and parked further up the road. A moment later he pulled in behind me. I saw him examining the Roller with raised eyebrows.

'Bit conspicuous in this, aren't you, Dave?' he asked genially as he slipped into the well padded seat beside me.

'Oh I don't know. There's a church across the road. We probably look like a pair of undertakers.'

'Speak for yourself,' he said with a laugh. 'Anyway, what are you doing here? Taking a break from the university?'

'You might say that, only it's a permanent break.'

Finbar looked at me, still smiling. 'I never thought you were suited for a routine job, Dave, and I'm not just saying that because I enjoy helping you out from time to time. You're much better as a detective than a lecturer. What was the problem?'

I briefly sketched in the sequence of events involving Peterson without telling Finbar that I knew the present whereabouts of Clint Lane. My deception was intended to protect the old soldier if he was questioned. He was so honest that he'd be bound to tell all he knew, so the less I told him, the better. Finbar understood all these rules when operating with me.

'Well, nothing much has happened at this end,' he said. 'No small, brown-curly-haired coppers, but I did manage to log in with the neighbourhood gossip-monger. I saw the lady at the end house peering out of her window like a buckshee bulldog. She was clocking the comings and goings as much as I was. She saw me, so I waved and walked over before she decided to phone the police. I told her I was doing a credit check on someone who lives four doors down from her, not this Peterson. Anyway it wasn't long before she filled me in on all the neighbours. I think you were right about Anne M.

Peterson. At least, she is a former policewoman, so there's a connection. My gossip was a big vague about the husband but she doesn't half have it in for Anne.'

'Interesting,' I said.

'Anne has two children, a boy and a girl. According to Mrs Seaforth – that's the neighbourhood spy – Anne picked up expensive habits when she was in the force. They taught her to shoot and now she's obsessed with shotguns and goes to somewhere near Tarporley shooting clay pigeons and she's in some kind of grouse-shooting syndicate. Also she was in the mounted section so now she's into hunting as well. Mrs Seaforth was particularly disgusted with that. Apparently Anne regularly hires a horse and rides with the Cheshire Hunt. Oh, and she keeps two large German shepherd dogs in steel cages in her back garden. She takes them for walks and lets them crap against Mrs Seaforth's gatepost.'

'Sounds like quite a gal,' I commented, 'but was there anything about her being in a cult?'

'No, nothing about that, although she and her husband don't go to the church across the road. Mrs Seaforth's on the parish committee. They made a complaint about the bells.'

'You have been busy.'

'Don't thank me, thank Mrs Seaforth. If you like I could call on Anne and say I'm from the RSPCA investigating a complaint about cruelty to animals. I ought to be able to see something that would tell me if she's in the C of L.'

'No, I shouldn't try that. I should think we have enough to go on. If she's been in the force she'd probably have the cuffs on you before you sat down.'

I looked in frustration at the cul-de-sac that housed Anne M. Peterson and whoever her husband was. I still hadn't confirmed that it was Sergeant Peterson. I felt at a total loose end. In my regular detecting days I'd always had an office to retreat to. Going back to Thornleigh Court wasn't the same. Anyway Fiona Salway might be laying in wait for me there.

'There's a Japanese restaurant on Washway Road, do you fancy getting a bite and then coming back here for the afternoon and evening shift?' I suggested to Finbar.

'Japanese!' he exploded. 'There's no way I'd go to one of

their eateries! If you fancy raw fish slithering down your throat . . . I don't.'

'What's with the Japanese?'

'If you heard what some of my friends at the British Legion say about them you wouldn't need to ask.'

'Oh, come on, the war's been over a long while. This treat's on me. It won't only be raw fish. We've all got to adapt to survive.'

Finbar rewarded me with a sour look but made no further objections. I started the car.

In the end I drove past the restaurant and we went on to my flat. I made the old soldier scrambled egg on toast washed down with tea and a tumbler of whisky. This put him in a much better mood. I intended to spend the afternoon observing Harboro Road but Finbar insisted that there was no point in us both going.

'Dave, this is meat and drink for me. I don't want to spend all my retirement chauffeuring Fiona from one shop to another. I'll park the car up the side by the church this time. There were people waiting to pick up kids from ballet lessons or something in the church hall. Mrs Seaforth won't spot me again.'

'OK, if you put it like that, but you'd better take a mobile in case you run into any other inquisitive old ladies.'

I ran him back to Sale and he retrieved his car and drove it to the church car park. As I drove off I saw him in the rear-view mirror turning to face Peterson's cul-de-sac. With his white hair and benevolent expression the old soldier had perfect cover as an investigator. Unfortunately, providing him with a purpose in life left me without one. When I'd had an office, even as crumbling and decrepit an office as the one on the top floor of the Atwood Building, I could sit in there doing nothing for an afternoon but waiting for the phone to ring. At least that had given me the feeling that I was still gainfully employed.

There was no way of postponing a return to Thornleigh Court. Having to spend time there during working hours felt odd. I pulled into the car park and go no further than the entrance before I met Fiona Salway coming out.

'Have you won the lottery, Dave?' she asked.

'Someone's lent it me for a day or two.'

'Where's that brother of mine got himself to, then?' she demanded. She blocked my way up the stairs as no doubt she'd blocked the path of many tiny malefactors during her career as an infant-school teacher.

'He's just doing a little job for me,' I said guiltily. 'I thought he'd told you.'

She smiled and I breathed a sigh of relief. Her reactions were unpredictable. 'I don't know, you boys! I'm glad you've given Finbar something to do. He's been getting under my feet nearly ever day since you gave up detecting. I was so glad to read that you were back in business.'

'What!'

'There's an article in this morning's *Guardian*,' she explained.

Fiona was quite breathless by the time I'd bustled her back inside her flat.

'Dave, you're going to make me late,' she complained. 'I'm supposed to be in a meeting about the parish Christmas Fayre.'

'They'll mange without you for five minutes,' I told her.

'I only picked this paper up because they hadn't got the *Telegraph*. Of course, you know Finbar, he chucked it away unread. I spotted the piece about you after he'd gone out.'

She pushed the paper under my nose.

'Here, take it,' she said.

It was in the gossip section of the paper.

Cultwatch Irked

Members of the Cultwatch team assigned to watch the north Manchester headquarters of the Children of Light which is situated in the valley of the river Irk were feeling displeased with local private eye Dave Cunane. Cunane, back in business after a long spell 'resting' from his colourfully named Pimpernel Investigations agency, is believed to have had a hand in the 'lifting' of cult member Melanie Varley in an action that smacks more of the baronial politics of the

Middle Ages than of New Labour Britain. Melanie, 21, is heiress to the Varley Paints fortune and would have been a useful recruit for the cash-hungry cult, especially since the recent death of her father, Irvine Varley, aged 58.

Our reporter, Janine White, tells us that Cultwatch members feel aggrieved at Cunane because they specialize in the de-programming of cult victims and were themselves on the point of 'assisting' Ms Varley to make her exit from the corporal-punishment-addicted cult. Cultwatch founder, Everald Mallick, 39, told our reporter 'De-programming is too delicate a job for a guy with Cunane's skills. Basically, he's just a mercenary. We speculate that Melanie's mother must have paid this cowboy detective a nice fat fee to grab her daughter but Melanie would be better off getting help from professionals like ourselves or from any of the other responsible groups in the field.'

In the light of this latest round of semi-feudal heiress snatching, and it must be said that efforts by this paper and the Northamptonshire police to trace Ms Varley have been unavailing, the case for Government intervention in the activities of these cults and of the Lone Rangers who act against them has become overwhelming.

To say I felt hot and cold at the same time as I read this libellous piece of muckraking under the gentle eyes of Fiona Salway is an understatement. If she hadn't been there I'd have howled with rage and pulled out my hair in handfuls. One name from the collection of inaccuracies seemed to appear before my eyes in letters of flame – Everald Mallick! That bastard! I'd run across him when he was trying to make a dishonest living by whipping up racial resentment among the Afro-Caribbean community. Shite-hawk that he was, he'd been heading up a hate campaign against a local black police constable, Jay Anderson. Apparently blacks who joined the police were 'traitors' to their community. Jay had once been my assistant at Pimpernel Investigations . . . well, more like my apprentice really.

I looked at the article again. Every word was carefully chosen. Mallick's words especially . . . 'too delicate a job . . .

Cunane's skills . . . just a mercenary . . . nice fat fee . . . cowboy detective'.

'Dave, are you all right?' Fiona asked anxiously. 'You look as if you're going to have a seizure. It's only a piece in the gossip column, no one important will read it. Is it by that girl you had with you the other morning?'

I managed to nod my head. There was no point in taking it out on Fiona.

'You're wrong,' I muttered between clenched teeth, 'someone important has already read it and although it doesn't mention my job at UNWIST, I'm sure this is what Professor Richardson really meant when he accused me of bringing the department into disrepute . . . and as for the seizure, the only think I want to seize at the moment is the scrawny neck of Everald Mallick. He'll discover just what my skills are. I'll deprogramme the . . . so-and-so,' I trailed off lamely, searching for an inoffensive epithet.

Fiona looked at me with immense concern. Her eyes were almost brimming over with tears. She certainly hadn't intended to produce this effect. I explained to her that I'd been relieved of my educational duties by Professor Richardson.

' . . . Yeah, booted out of the department without ceremony,' I concluded. 'I expect someone higher up has pulled Richardson's chain for him.'

'Oh, Dave!' she exclaimed, taking my arm firmly and steering me back to her door, 'I can see you've had a very bad shock. You must let me make you a nice cup of hot, sweet tea. Father McDougall and the Christmas Fayre can wait.'

I looked at my elderly neighbour. Her eyes were darting here and there in consternation, her hands were fluttering in small bird-like movements. I decided that she was a lot more upset than I was.

'No, to hell with it, Fiona,' I said handing back the paper to her. 'Shove this in the bin. I've got to get on.'

'You won't do anything foolish?' she asked. 'I mean, about this Mallick?'

'The day I start letting dipsticks like him pull my strings is the day I'll take up bee-keeping.'

'I'm so glad,' she whispered, 'but I'm surprised at that

reporter being so spiteful. Finbar said she seemed such a nice polite person when he met her.'

At this I threw my head back and laughed almost to the point of tears. Fiona's warm-hearted comment made up for the resentment I felt against Richardson and Mallick and everyone else who'd conspired to spoil my day. Fiona looked at me doubtfully, shook her head and then scuttled off to her meeting with the other holy folk. I felt like volunteering to run the tombola stall for her.

I went back to my flat and poured myself a small whisky. I sipped it slowly and made the most of it. I couldn't afford to start looking at the world through the wrong end of a bottle again . . .

Despite what I'd said to Fiona, I don't think I'd have been able to control myself if that lying little git Mallick had appeared anywhere within my orbit. He was asking for it, but what did I expect from the likes of him? That was the way he operated . . . defamatory rumour, scurrilous misreading of other people's motives, all in a day's work for Everald. I ought to think myself lucky that he hadn't accused me of being a dyed-in-the-wool racist, which would have been par for the course with him. He must have been the one who'd clocked me up at Blackley on Saturday afternoon. I could just imagine what he'd told Janine White about me. Trust him to spend his Saturday afternoons lurking when most normal males were watching football matches or slumped on sofas. Still, his unmarked and undesired presence did leave me with a problem. Had he seen me bashing Rufus . . . ? Probably not, as that had occurred indoors. Worse still, though . . . had he seen me breaking and entering yesterday?

I thought that one through for a moment and then decided that he hadn't. Mallick was certainly peevish enough to have summoned the fuzz immediately if he'd seen me in a compromising situation.

So, what to do? An angry letter to the editor? It is a truth universally acknowledged that only nuts write letters to papers. No, I'd just have to smile gently to myself and count Mrs Varley's nice fat non-existent fee before I cried myself to sleep. Thankfully the phone in the flat was ex-directory and

Finbar had my mobile. There were bound to be people wanting to know what I'd done with the luscious Melanie.

Still, I owed Monica Withers a call. What was it that was winging her way . . . ? An admonitory letter? I phoned her home number. There was no reply.

A 10 Downing Street press briefing confirmed that Melville Monckton, the Manchester pop icon, has been asked to join a Government committee enquiring into youth culture. 'Melville is the kind of switched-on young guy with young people's best interests at heart that this Government is determined to encourage and listen to,' the spokesman added.

Report in the *Daily Telegraph*

11

Wednesday, 21 October

The way I felt at that moment, action, any kind of action, was better than moping about in my flat brooding on the injustices which were descending on me like an avalanche. I decided to motor over to Marple and check out the situation at Monica's bijou residence. If possible, I intended to return the car and cadge a lift back to Manchester. Maybe I could set about repairing our relationship if there still was a relationship. It had been a long time since I'd shared my bed and, to be honest, my self-esteem had been dented by the speed with which Monica appeared to have shifted her affections. There was nothing wrong with me, was there?

When I settled myself behind the wheel of the Roller for the second time that day, the weather had changed. There was a steady drizzle falling and the sky had turned to a uniform dull grey. It suited my mood. It must be hell having to be miserable in a place like Los Angeles or Miami where the sun shines relentlessly on sinners and just men alike. The evening rush had started and I soon found out how many of my fellow motorists were anxious to cut in front of a Rolls Royce or to refuse entry into a traffic stream. Talk about road rage and spite, you'd have thought I was an hereditary landowning peer travelling among a crowd of his recently evicted tenant farmers instead of an unemployed, 'mercenary' private detective.

Anyway, trembling but still in one piece, I eventually found myself threading my way to Monica's home along the quiet Cheshire lanes. I pulled into the deep gravel of her drive and gratefully jerked the Roller to a halt amid a shower of flying stones. There was no reply when I rang the door bell, but then if Bob and Clint were in on their own they wouldn't reply. I told myself that everything was normal. All I needed to do was to reassure Bob that it wasn't the police paying a visit. One advantage of the high hedges that surrounded Monica's home was that I was able to go round the back of the house without having to fear that some nosy neighbour was calling the police.

The ornamental metal side gate was fastened with a padlock so I climbed over and looked in through each of the rear windows in turn. The bedrooms and gym were unoccupied. On the off-chance that Bob and Clint were hiding in the toilets, I rattled the windows and shouted my name to let them know that it was safe to come out. My voice echoed hollowly from the damp trees and sodden walls. The place remained as silent as the grave. I was about to go when I noticed that I could see right into a corner of the living-room through an open bedroom door. I cupped my hands against the glass to shield out reflected glare. I could just make out a shape on one of the sofas. It was a woman and she was resting her head on a cushion. It had to be Monica, unless she had an identical twin.

Taking my chances with the local Neighbourhood Watch, I went back round to the front of the house. My view of the sleeper wasn't much better from there. I could see the back and side of her head. Unless the person shared Monica's exact shade of hair, it had to be her. I banged and rattled to wake her up.

She didn't stir.

I took a coin out of my pocket and rapped on the window as hard as I could without breaking the glass. Still there was no sign of life. Unless she was drugged, she would have woken. A nervy, energetic person like Monica didn't strike me as the sort who could sleep through the kind of racket I'd been making. I began to get frightened. All kinds of possibilities flashed through my mind. Had she received Richardson's admonition and taken it much, much more seriously than it deserved? Or was it something worse? I'd always secretly feared that Clint didn't know his own strength. Those hands could snap a neck like a twig, one reason I knew that he'd never need a knife to kill anyone. I paced up and down, shouted until I was hoarse, banged on the door ... all to no avail. The figure on the sofa remained as lifeless as a waxwork and there was no one else in the house.

In the end I phoned the police on my mobile.

When they arrived in the shape of a uniformed sergeant and constable, they went through the same motions of attempting to rouse the sleeper as I had done before proceeding to more active steps. Sadly, Monica's security arrangements soon baffled them. In fact, a well-trained housebreaker would have had his work cut out getting in there, never mind a pair of policemen without even a screwdriver between them. Doors and windows were too securely fixed for casual breaking and entering. The glass in the double-glazed windows was special armoured glass. God knows what sort of burglars Monica had been expecting. The front and back doors were as solid as bank vaults. Both coppers threw up their hands in frustration. However, the sergeant, who'd been content to let his junior bruise his shoulder on the solid doors, was made of stern stuff. He called in the fire brigade.

'When in doubt, do nowt,' he said calmly. He smiled at me. I smiled back at his thin wit as politely as I could but my mind was racing. It seemed as if besides living in a millionaire's pad, Monica Withers had taken every care to install as many security devices as money could buy her. No casual passer-by could have broken into her home. Was this just a neurosis of the wealthy, or something else, I wondered.

We had to wait half an hour before fire officers arrived and used a hydraulic opening device to force one of the armoured glass windows out of its frame. They chose a smaller frame beside the entrance which would just about allow someone to squeeze inside. As the glass tumbled forward I got a whiff of the all-too-familiar odour of decaying flesh and death. The central heating was on full and warm air gusted past us.

Once they'd done their job by providing an access point and checking for carbon monoxide, the fire-fighters cleared off, saying it was a police matter. With a grin, the sergeant volunteered the constable to go in. Stripping off his blouson and utility belt, the young man got his head and shoulders through the gap and then wriggled his way inside. A piercing security alarm went off simultaneously. Getting the front door open without the coded swipe-card proved to be a difficult job for the young PC. By the time he succeeded in working out the complex opening procedure I thought I was going to go deaf. The sergeant entered and motioned me to stay where I was.

A few minutes later I was called in to make an identification.

My mind wasn't ready for finality. There were things I had to say to Monica. It couldn't be true ... Alive and vital one minute ... a piece of lifeless meat the next. As I walked into the house the blood was pounding fiercely in my temples and my vision was affected. Everything was in sharper focus than normal.

The figure on the sofa was Monica and she was dead and she was wearing the same clothes as when I'd seen her last. There was no sign of violence, just a faint bluish tinge to her lips and cheeks. She was lying there on her side as peacefully as an old lady who'd slipped out of life in her own bed aged ninety-five. Her head was cradled on her hands which were joined as if in prayer and tucked under her cheek on the right side of her body. She looked like a sleeping infant in that pose. All age, maturity and managerial briskness had slid away from her. I felt a numbness spreading through my limbs and body. The incessant shrilling of the alarm made thought difficult. It was as if I was being pierced by a thousand dentist's drills at once.

Through the windows I could see neighbours gathering in the road and peering in at us.

The constable returned to the living area from a search of the other rooms.

'There's no one else in the house, sarge,' he said to his superior.

'Do you know the code for the alarm, sir?' the sergeant asked, obviously as put out by the ringing as I was.

I shook my head.

'We'd better go outside while I send for the FME,' he said indicating the door. 'This racket is getting on my wick.' The sergeant, whose name was Martin, took his cap off and ran his fingers over his smooth scalp. He led us out. After the cloying smells of that living-room the fresh air was a relief. I staggered to a wall and leaned on it for support. The first waves of an overwhelming feeling of guilt began to wash over me. My mind felt overburdened. I tried to concentrate on what was happening around me as an escape from my emotions.

Sergeant Martin took my arm and led me away from the house. Martin was sporting a vanity hair-do in which abundant hair from the side of his head was combed over his bald pate. When we reached the bottom of the front lawn where the howling of the alarms was slightly more bearable a gust of wind caught his hair and flicked it straight up like the spiky fingers of a hand sprouting from his head. Like a bird trying to make a nest in a gale, he tried to smooth the wayward locks into place; then gave up and irritably smacked his cap back on.

'Well, it looks like natural causes,' the young constable said, trying to make conversation during this sartorial hiatus. Neither man seemed to be affected by Monica's death.

'Got a degree in forensic medicine, have you son?' the older man said.

'I thought with the alarm going off like that . . .'

'Don't jump to conclusions, son,' he said, neatly snubbing his junior before turning to me. 'Do you know if the lady had heart trouble, or anything sir? Diabetes, epilepsy, brain tumour, anything like that?'

There was a certain lip-smacking relish in the way Martin listed the ills that flesh is heir to that I found repellent. It was as if putting a name to what had killed her added an unnecessary degree of finality to the proceedings. I shook my head.

'She was in the best of health last night. For God's sake, there's a fully equipped gym in the house which she used for working out every day,' I said. I think that I felt sticking up for Monica's physical fitness would benefit her in some obscure way.

'That's right,' the constable confirmed, 'the jogging machine was still switched on.'

'It's sometimes them that goes first,' the sergeant said philosophically. 'The fit ones . . . Did she use drugs or any kind of medication?'

'Did you see any?' I asked.

'She needn't have taken them where she died,' he said confidently. I knew that he was itching for me to challenge his death-scene expertise so I bit back hostile words.

'She never used drugs or medication in my presence,' I said in a low voice.

'Well, it's most peculiar in that case. Anyway, we'll have to see what the FME and the pathologist say.'

I don't pray much, not at all in fact; but I began praying then. I selfishly prayed that they'd find that Monica's death was due to natural causes and not to anything that I'd had a hand in. I think I had some sort of delayed shock reaction after that. I can't remember anything about the journey to the hospital.

Feeling still hadn't returned hours later when I sat in an office in Stockport Central Police station making a statement to the same uniformed sergeant, D. M. Martin. I never learned what the initials stood for but he'd managed to get his hair back under control before he took down my statement. Maybe it was something I'd said, but now he seemed unusually sympathetic.

'Do you mind me asking what your job is, sir?' he'd asked.

That threw me for a moment but what I came up with certainly met his approval a lot more than if I'd said I was a private detective. 'I've just been made redundant at

UNWIST,' I told him truthfully enough. 'I was lecturing in the Management Science department with Doctor Withers.'

'These things are sent to try us,' he said sorrowfully, before sending off for a cup of canteen tea. 'You seem to be having more than your share of bad luck.'

Hours before, at the hospital, Monica's sister had turned up to identify the body formally. She was very like Monica in appearance except that there was a hardness about her that I now realized was something her poor sister had lacked. Shannon Withers strode out of the identification suite like someone without a care in the world. That confident stride was frighteningly like her sister's. She certainly didn't look bereaved or even downcast. Sergeant Martin had introduced me as the person who'd discovered her sister's body.

'Cunane,' she said as if repeating a swear word. 'I've heard about you.'

Quite what she'd heard she didn't divulge because she left the hospital without another word or a change of expression.

'You realize that we have to ask you for a statement, sir,' the sergeant said to me later. 'You were the last one to see her alive. It's lucky that the pathologist was available for immediate autopsy. Anyway, he confirms that she died of heart failure . . . adult cot-death, he said. Sounds a bit strange. Was she doing something which caused her an unusual strain when she was with you? Besides the jogging machine, that is . . . we know about that. Rum time to be doing jogging in the middle of the night, if you ask me.'

He looked at me expectantly.

'Look sergeant,' I said wearily. 'I've put it in the statement. Monica and I made love at my flat before we came back here. There were things she needed for work. She gave no sign that she was under any physical or mental strain whatever.'

'I realize that, sir,' he replied in an apologetic tone. 'But sometimes people, er . . . lovers . . . er, use substances that might put a strain on the heart that might show up later, stimulants like.'

'There was nothing like that,' I said sharply.

'I appreciate that, sir,' the sergeant said gravely. 'The FME found no trace of substance abuse. It's just that I can't quite work out in my head why you needed to come back with her when you had no car of your own.'

'Do I look like the sort of man who lets his girlfriend drive across half of Cheshire in the middle of the night on her own?' I mumbled shamefacedly.

I knew he was angling for an admission that the shock of being taken to my bed had been too much for her, but I couldn't accept that. Monica had been no blushing virgin, not that I'd much experience of them. She'd been an enthusiastic and experienced lover who gave no sign of unusual stress.

Still, the sergeant's incorrect surmise that sex after long abstinence might have contributed to Monica's death set off an unpleasant train of thought.

Was I a jinx?

My last girlfriend was still in a psychiatric hospital . . . Well, she was an outpatient, at any rate, and the only other woman I'd tangled with recently . . . she almost didn't bear thinking about. That charming lady had conceived a child by me as a memorial to her own dead lover, a senior copper of all people, but while giving our child his name she hadn't neglected to pass my name on to the Child Support Agency.

On reflection, I realized that the attention Monica paid to Bob Lane was just a tease – her way of paying me back for finding Janine White's carelessly strewn hosiery in my bathroom. It was hell. There'd been nothing intense about my relationship with Monica. We'd both been too intent on laying the ground rules for that. Now nothing would ever happen. Her voice was stilled . . . a conversation halted in mid-sentence.

Perhaps, if I got through all of this, I ought to join an enclosed religious order. I wondered if the Trappists would have me. Besides being free from the opposite sex, they only have to speak to each other once a week.

'Yes, of course,' Martin said, bringing me back to earth. 'You'd have heard about this escaped loony from Manchester. Half the force was out searching for him and his brother last night.' Again I felt myself being searchingly inspected by those pale blue eyes.

Not trusting myself to speak this time, I nodded. There it was, out in the open. Martin had been in touch with someone in Manchester who'd told him of my connection. I dreaded what was going to happen next. He was going to call my bluff and tell me that Clint's fingerprints had been found all over the house. I was going to be arrested.

Instead, Sergeant Martin gave a wan smile.

'Well, you have my sincere condolences, sir. It's an awful thing to have happened, particularly as you'd been intimate with Miss Withers for such a short time . . .'

'Doctor Withers,' I interjected.

'Yes, it's very sad. I have heard of a similar case. Well, Mr Cunane, you're free to go now. Would you like an officer to drive you home?'

'No, I'll get a taxi.'

'Right then, Mr Cunane. Sorry about all this, but there's no alternative in the case of sudden unexplained death. I'll get in touch if we have any further information. I doubt if you'd learn anything from the sister. She took the death far better than you did. In fact, she hardly reacted at all.'

Call me odd or callous if you like, but brooding in my den isn't my way. Activity is my response to disaster. If I was ever shipwrecked in mid-ocean I'd swim for land until the sharks got me. Monica's death was shattering but I knew that if I stayed locked up in my flat alone with my thoughts there could only be one outcome. After the painful death of my young wife Elenki I'd gone off the rails for a while, trying to drink myself into oblivion. Clawing my way back to normal life, or what passes for normal life with me, had been an uphill job, but I'd done it and I had no desire to risk sliding back down the slope this time. I knew that the route between my present existence and sleeping in the gutter outside Chorlton Street bus station on Manchester's Skid Row was frighteningly short.

I had no desire for sleep. It was approaching dawn and I find it difficult enough to rest at that time even when there's nothing to cause me grief. So when I got into the flat, the first thing I did was to change into my cycling clothes. I padded downstairs past Finbar's landing without a trace of curiosity and took my bike out of the garage. Whatever Finbar had to tell me would keep. It all seemed rather trivial now. So what if Peterson's wife was a born-again Child of Light? It wouldn't bring Monica Withers back. I peddled down the cobbled road by Brookburn School and out towards the river bank.

A grey light was just breaking and the roar of traffic from the nearby motorway told me, even at this time of the morning, that I wasn't really in the countryside. It was a completely calm morning. Until I reached the river the only signs of life that I spotted were the twinkling lights of aircraft approaching the distant airport. I paused on the bridge at Jackson's Boat and looked down on the rushing brown waters of the Mersey. The river was high against its banks after the recent rain and pieces of plastic jetsam, branches and even tree trunks were rushing towards the estuary. Along the banks mallards were bravely swimming upstream against the flood. Maybe they were paddling furiously to keep themselves in the same place but I took their efforts as a sign that life had to go on in whatever circumstances. I then pounded along the Sale bank until exhaustion set in.

By the time I returned to Thornleigh Court weariness and adrenalin had temporarily blunted my despairing mood. Blaming myself until the cows come home wouldn't bring Monica back. Her death was a crippling blow. I had to understand that. I could have had a future with her. Oh yes, it had been a surprise to find that she was wealthy . . . That hurt my pride. However things might have developed, there was no way I'd have become an ageing toyboy even if Monica had wanted that. No, Monica Withers would have been a sustaining force . . . a woman as full of surprises and contradictory moods as the weather. I'd have done well with her.

Why had she died? I ran a range of possibilities through my mind. Had Bob and Clint had anything to do with her death? That was unlikely. It had to be natural causes. If there was even a shadow of a shadow of anything else, I'd never rest until I found out what it was.

As I opened the outer door of my block the sweat in my eyebrows was so persistent that no amount of wiping it away with the back of my glove would remove it. Blurred though my vision was, I could still make out the erect military figure of Finbar Salway guarding the foot of the stairs like Cerberus at the entrance to the Underworld. Did the man ever relax, I wondered?

'Are you all right?' he asked. 'Fiona told me that you'd had a nasty turn about some newspaper article yesterday.'

'That's the least of my troubles,' I said gloomily. 'Did you see me with Monica Withers? Well, she's dead. Died of heart failure some time in the early hours of yesterday morning.'

'Oh, God rest her soul,' he said piously. 'Is she the one who wrote the article about you?' He took my arm. I shook him off more roughly than I intended. Feeble after hours in the saddle I might be, but I was not yet in need of the attentions of a sexagenarian. Nor did I feel like giving him a timetable of the comings and goings in my apartment.

'No, she's the one who lent me the Roller,' I said abruptly.

Finbar made no reply. I could see he was confused and hurt. I'd been all over him like a rash yesterday.

'Sorry,' I muttered. With my friends dying off, or in hiding like Bob Lane, I didn't need to turn anyone else against me. 'Don't take any notice of me. I've just been shat upon from a great height and I'm feeling sorry for myself. Anyway, I think I've just about got the energy to get up to my flat, take a bath and then lie down on the bed.'

In his kindly and forgiving way, Finbar took this as an invitation to follow me upstairs and see I came to no harm. Nor did he show any sign of leaving until I began stripping off my sweat-soaked clothes and heading for the bath. He got up and blocked my way.

'I did see a policeman who looked like your Peterson arrive home in Sale tonight – but you won't want to think about that now. Now Dave, don't take this wrong, but I know you've had a lot of tragedy in your life . . . er . . . more than your share. Just take a bit of advice. When I was in the Army a lot of my fellow officers had come through the war and through the Malayan Emergency as well as the Suez, though that was a sideshow in comparison with Arnhem or anything like that. I asked them how they survived when their friends were being killed all the time. They told me that the secret is never to talk about the ones who've gone missing . . . To try and keep them out of your mind until the job in hand is finished. I've always found that to be the best thing.'

'Right,' I said, hoping that I didn't sound too unconvinced. 'Thanks.'

He gave my arm a comforting squeeze and left.

When I began to run the bath I found that despite my determination to be serious and gloomy I couldn't help smiling. Old Finbar was comparing the mortality rate among female companions of Dave Cunane with the casualty figures to be expected in a major battle. Things weren't quite that bad, were they?

Later, feeling as relaxed and purged as I was ever going to, I lay on the bed and fell into a deep sleep. It was five in the afternoon and fully dark before I woke. I was sunk into a kind of pleasant lethargy and felt as if I could stay where I was forever. Headlights of cars passing up and down the distant main road made intersecting patterns on the ceiling. I tried to follow Finbar's advice and not think about Monica Withers. Emptying my mind, I fixed my eyes on the shifting patterns of light. It was no use. A shape kept emerging from them. Whatever the pathologist and the police said, I couldn't remove the thought that Monica's death wasn't just one of those sad happenings that you read about. It was all part of a series of coincidences. She'd followed Arkwright – at my request. She'd welcomed two fugitives into her home – also down to me, and then, suddenly, despite appearing to be in perfect health, she died. Something didn't quite add up.

I must have lain there, paralysed, unable to make sense out of what was happening for at least an hour. My head was buzzing with possibilities which when I thought about them twice mostly turned into impossibilities. When my mobile rang it came as a relief from the profound introspection.

'Mr Cunane?' The voice was strong and confident.

I grunted.

'I don't know you, but my name's Melville Monckton.' He spoke more quickly now but the words 'Melville Monckton' came across with jarring clarity.

It took me a second to reply with the single word yes.

'I need to meet you, Mr Cunane. It seems that we have a mutual friend in common.' He spoke more quickly still, gabbling almost. I had to strain to catch the gist of what he was saying. However good a singer Monckton was, his telephone style was appalling.

'Sorry, could you say that again?' I asked, speaking slowly and distinctly.

'Yeah, man, well, I mean to say, you know a certain club owner, don't you?'

'So what?' I growled.

'Do you want to help him and help yourself at the same time?' Monckton said, and this time he made sure that I understood the message. 'You know who it is I'm talking about . . . the guy with the unusual relative.'

'Yes, but what's it to do with me?'

'That's the question we're all asking ourselves, Mr Cunane.'

'Who do you mean by "we", Monckton? Your charming American friends from the Children of Light?'

There was a pause before he spoke.

'It's true what they say about you, Cunane . . . You're a busy boy who gets his nose into places where it isn't meant to go, but it's not that that I'm worried about. You don't know nearly as much as you think you do. You claim to be a friend of Bob's and if you want to help him you'll meet me for a face-to-face chat. I'll make it very well worth your while.'

I didn't answer.

'Look Cunane, you think you know things about me. That cuts both ways. For instance, I know that you might be able to find a very good use for a few grand in your present circumstances . . . Follow me? Am I getting on to your wavelength?'

'OK,' I said slowly, wondering who'd told him I'd been fired.

'I'd like a private meeting. Do you know the cricket club near Heaton Park? I'm the honorary president.'

'Good for you,' I murmured.

'Don't get smart. If you come to the park there at midnight I can let us in and we can talk in comfort.'

'Come on, Monckton,' I said. 'Do you think I'm crazy? Do you think I'm going to drop into your lap while your hired help kick my liver and lights out?'

'It's not like that. I need to see you somewhere where I'm sure the police won't be around. I'm a friend of Bob and Clint. I want to help them. Surely you know if the police come across them they're likely to shoot first and ask questions later if Clint gets manky . . . which he will. I know him.'

'Yes, were you well enough acquainted to coach him to kill Fred Travis?'

'That's real stupid talk,' the rock star said angrily. 'You're talking through your arse now.'

'At least I don't try to sing through it.'

'Bastard! What was Travis to me?'

'You know something about his death.'

'Oh yes, Mr Private Dickhead. Why haven't the police asked me a single question about Travis's death?'

'That's something I've been asking myself.'

There's no way you can hear someone struggling to control their temper over the phone but that's what I sensed Monckton was doing.

'Listen, toe-rag, you've got the wrong idea about me,' he said, after a moment of heavy breathing. 'Christ, Cunane. I don't know how private eyes make a living but you couldn't be more wrong. That's why we need to talk. I know things that can help you to find where Bob's taken Clint and then you can help him to hand over Clint quietly. It'll be best for both of them and I'll make it well worth your while. I mean, like . . . if I meant them any harm . . . if Clint does have something to say that puts me in the frame . . . would I help you to surrender them to the police?'

Monckton's jerky, staccato delivery would have alerted a child of three that he was lying through his expensively capped teeth.

It was make-or-break time. If I was sensible I'd put the phone down and continue to lie on my bed wondering what had been going on for the last week or two. I'm not sensible though.

'All right, twelve o'clock,' I said. 'You'd best be on your own. If I spot your American friends within a mile of the place I'll be away.'

'Right, you can trust me,' he replied. 'I feel I want to make it up to Clint if I've put any wrong ideas in his head.' Then he broke the connection.

I knew that I couldn't trust a single molecule of him. He was like Aldous Arkwright. He went from chest-beating to breast-baring in the same slick way as the 'spiritual director'. The only difference was that Melville Monckton combined insincerity with a showman's sense of timing. Clint was on the loose. Was Melville getting nervous about what he might say or remember? Whatever the motive, this move was another little piece in a pattern that was unfolding. Quite what this impassioned invitation signified was a mystery. I didn't know what Melville was, but innocent wasn't it.

'Let me see if I've got this right,' Finbar Salway said slowly. 'You want me to drive you up to this cricket club and go in for a drink with you, claiming that we've come on the wrong night for a quiz game, and then clear off while you hide somewhere until this Monckton turns up.'

I nodded. An early arrival was the best precaution I could come up with. In these piping days of peace no one is allowed to carry a gun or even a baseball bat for legitimate protection.

'Sounds pretty risky to me, Dave. I mean, if he's the honorary president of this club, what's to stop him having it packed to the doors with his friends? They might recognize you as soon as we go in.'

'It's the best I can come up with.'

'Don't you think we ought to tell the police? I mean this Inspector Cullen, he sounds like a pretty reasonable type.'

'He is, but I doubt if he'll suspend Peterson just because we've found out that his wife is a keen member of the C of L.

Until we know exactly what the connection between Peterson, Monckton and the Children of Light is, we can't take the chance that everything we tell the police will be relayed straight back to Arkwright.'

Finbar looked at me very dubiously for a long while, then he nodded his head.

'All right, I'll come with you, but only on condition that I phone the police if you're not out of there in ten minutes.'

'Ten minutes or ten hours, time doesn't make any difference. Get the fuzz if you hear any shots or screams.'

Finbar went back to his flat to get his coat and I went out to wait beside his car. I felt excited and in a way glad that things seemed to be reaching some kind of resolution. Finbar emerged wearing his MCC tie. I carefully said nothing.

When we got to the cricket club it turned out to be a pretty ramshackle affair. Melville Monckton's presidency hadn't produced any benefactions in the shape of a new clubhouse. It was a whitewashed wooden building that consisted mainly of annexes accumulated over the years and now leaning against each other for support. We went round to the front of the building which faced the cricket pitch. There was a sort of glassed-in veranda where members could shelter from the equinoctial gales while watching our national summer game. At one side of the veranda there was a toilet, at the other the door to the clubhouse. A notice beside the door read, 'Non-members must be signed in'.

Finbar pressed the buzzer on the intercom.

A squawk came out of it, barely recognizable as a human voice.

'Can we come in?' Finbar demanded.

More squawks were emitted.

'We're here for the quiz,' Finbar shouted.

Eventually an inner door was opened and a burly man in a short-sleeved cricket sweater came and opened the door.

'There's no quiz tonight, mate,' he said to Finbar. 'You from Burnage?'

'There, I told you,' Finbar said turning to me. 'I told you it was the wrong night.'

'Bloody hell, I was sure,' I mumbled defensively. 'We seem

to have been driving for hours.'

'You should check the fixture list,' Finbar scolded.

'Look lads,' the member said pleasantly, 'it's all right if you want to come in for a drink but you're in for a long wait if you want to see the quiz team. They'll not be here until next week.'

'I'll buy you a pint,' I volunteered.

'That's the least you can do to apologize,' Finbar grumbled. We followed the man into a small bar. He made no move to sign us in but gestured towards the bar before going to sit down with his friends. At one side of the room there seemed to be some kind of committee meeting going on. I breathed a sigh of relief when I saw that Monckton wasn't among them.

I bought two pints from a young barmaid who had a distinctly underemployed look about her. There were only twelve people in the clubhouse, all men. Some were wearing track suits embroidered with the three lions of English cricket.

We sat in a shady corner. I drank my pint in two or three swallows.

'You were thirsty,' the blonde barmaid said.

'Yes. Have you got a loo in here? Then I must go. The wife will play hell with me if she finds that I'm sat here drinking without even the excuse of a quiz.'

'Talk about hag-ridden,' Finbar said with a conspiratorial smile for the barmaid's benefit. She grinned at me sympathetically.

'It's just on the way out, next to the visitors' changing-room. Surely you don't need to hurry off, I won't tell her.' She gave me an encouraging wink.

'Oh, let him go,' Finbar said. 'I'll never hear the last of it if he doesn't get home in time to tuck the kiddies up.'

'It's just that it's so quiet in here. Apart from the committee and the quiz teams I never see a different face during the off-season months,' the barmaid explained. 'This place is usually empty by eleven.'

I gave her a smile and left. We'd arranged that I would hide and then after a few minutes Finbar would return to his car which was parked in a nearby side-street. I went in to the loo and, remembering my previous experience of staking out Monckton, I used the facilities. There was nowhere to hide in the toilet, which was a bare functional room. A connecting door leading to the visitors' changing-room was locked but it only took me a moment to open it with a pick lock. The changing-room offered many more opportunities to hide for an hour or two. They seemed to be using it as a temporary store. Nets were draped in one corner and empty beer kegs stacked up behind the outer door as a barricade.

I spent a boring two hours perched on a narrow bench behind the door. The committee meeting finished not long after ten thirty and by eleven the clubhouse was locked up and empty apart from myself. At about twenty to twelve I heard the sound of a car drawing up outside. A door slammed and then several other doors. So much for trust, I thought, as I heard voices outside on the veranda. There were at least two men with Monckton, possibly more.

'Just check the place out and then lie low,' Monckton ordered whoever it was who was accompanying him. 'And for Chrissakes stay down until I call. We don't want to frighten our little bird away.'

If they replied I couldn't hear what was said as Monckton and his friends went into the bar. Still it was nice to know that this was definitely a set-up. The only question in my mind was whether his assistants were the two Americans from the C of L or the squad of Afro-Caribbean security men he'd employed at his home in Higher Blackley. For a moment or two I could hear noises of people moving around in the adjoining bar. I was only separated from it by a thin wooden wall. Then everything went quiet again. I thought I could hear the sound of my own heart beating.

Midnight came and with it the sound of murmuring from within.

'Get back in your places,' I heard Monckton say in a stage whisper.

'You're bad, man. Real ba-a-ad,' came the audible reply. So it was the Afro-Caribbeans.

I crept through the changing-room, which as it opened to the outside hadn't been checked by Monckton's squad, into the toilet, which had been, and then very quietly opened the door which led to the members' veranda. There, sitting on an old leather armchair with his back to me, was Melville himself. He was alone. The outer door was open to await my arrival.

I clamped my hand over Monckton's mouth and jerked him to his feet. Despite the volume of sound he was capable of creating, he was a small man. Lifting him out of the seat was like lifting a child. I put my hand on his painfully thin wrist and jerked his arm up his back. Apart from a muffled choking sound he made no attempt at resistance. He was wearing an expensive brown leather coat with a fur collar that was probably worth more than I made in six months. I dragged him through the open door and straight out across the darkened cricket pitch. The moon was behind clouds but there was sufficient light for me to spot a score box on the opposite side of the pitch.

Monckton's feet hardly touched the ground until we reached the box. I pulled him to one side and pressed him against the wall, face first.

I took my hand off his mouth for a second.

'Don't kill me,' he gasped.

'That's your game, not mine,' I said.

At that moment all the lights came on in the clubhouse, then three individuals waving powerful torches emerged from the front entrance. They shone their torches across the pitch and all round the building. With a thrill of horror I realized that my journey across the dew-soaked grass had left a trail right to where I was now standing. However, whether our tracks were only visible at an oblique angle or for whatever reason, Monckton's men didn't spot us. The torches receded towards the car park and a moment later there was a squeal of tyres. I guessed it was the same blazer-clad trio I'd seen at Monckton's home.

'Whatever you're paying that lot, it's too much,' I said sarcastically.

Monckton ground his teeth.

'Get on with it, you bastard,' he grunted.

'Charming. I come for a face-to-face meeting only to find

that you've brought three heavies with you and then you call me a bastard.'

'I was frightened you'd try to beat me up,' he said over his shoulder.

I turned him to face me and rested my arms against the brick wall on either side of his head. An unpleasant odour of warm urine reached me as I did so. A glance down confirmed that Manchester's Mr Melody had wet himself.

'You wanted a face-to-face meeting, so here we are,' I said not wishing to disabuse him of the impression that I intended to do him violence.

'You won't hit me, will you?' he pleaded. 'You made a hell of a mess of Rufus Polk's face. I've got a gig next week.'

'Shit happens,' I said calmly, then I could have bitten my tongue as I felt a shiver pass through Monckton. I didn't need further proof of his lack of intestinal fortitude. At such close quarters it could get rather messy.

'Listen, Monckton,' I said quickly. 'I've no intention of doing you any harm. I just want to know why you and the so-called Children of Light tried to frame Clint Lane for the Travis murder and why you tried to drag me into it.'

'I had nothing to do with that. I'd no idea that was going to happen,' he said desperately. It had a ring of truth.

'Well, what have you been up to with our morally uplifting friends?'

'Polk and Tyler were coming in with me on a business deal, that's all.'

'What, to build this leisurama? Your effort to make Manchester into Sin City.'

'So you have been talking to Bob Lane. I knew you had. I'll give you ten grand if you tell me where he is.'

As he spoke we both heard the distant wail of a police siren. Someone must have noticed the lights in the clubhouse. I released my grip on him.

'Twenty grand, then. No one will ever know. Just tell me. I've got it on me.' He pulled a thick wad out of his pocket and waved it in my face.

The sirens were getting closer. I pushed Monckton away and sprinted across the pitch as if I was trying to stop a boundary. Despite my recent exploits on the bike I was short of breath by the time I reached the car park. 'That's the academic life for you,' I told myself as I reached Finbar's car. It was just as well that Monckton's super-fit security men hadn't had the chance to chase me.

'Cutting it a bit fine, aren't you, old chap?' the ex-military man asked as we turned out on to the road. When our car reached the end of the short road where the Cricket Club stood I looked back. Two police cars and a stretch limo turned into the other end of the street.

Hidden Danger?

Environmental health chiefs reported that the Beaufort Fault and the North Atlantic may not have been the only places used to dispose of chemical and biological warfare agents (CBW) at the end of the last war. In the haste to get rid of these unwanted materials disused quarries and old coal mines in the Mersey Valley area were also used.

East Cheshire Observer

12

Thursday, 22 October – Friday, 23 October

That night I slept the sleep of the just. I felt fairly secure at Thornleigh Court. Of course, Polk and Tyler and presumably Monckton knew where I lived but the residents were pretty canny about letting strangers into the block. They had to be with the numbers of sneak thieves and smackheads prowling the streets of Chorlton these days. It was a tribute to Aldous Arkwright's mesmeric powers that he'd persuaded Finbar to let him in a few days previously. That was very unusual. Often gas and electric officials were kept waiting for hours by suspicious residents until identities were verified. In any case, in my detective days I'd heard the menacing formula 'We know where you live' so often that I'd had a reinforced-steel security door installed in the flat. No one was going to get past it without using explosive charges.

I got up and showered, feeling slightly guilty that I didn't have to set off for UNWIST. It helped to hold the much bigger guilt about Monica at bay.

As I sat in my kitchen waiting for the coffee grounds to settle, feelings of discomfort grew. Last night's caper was nothing to be proud of. I'd tackled Monckton expecting to find a criminal mastermind only to discover a frightened little man who wet his pants at the first brush with danger. It was horrible. I always think celebs are larger than life, but they're not. I hated the feeling I'd got when my fingers clamped round that stick-like wrist of his. Maybe I'm a masochist, prefer being on the receiving end to dishing it out. Still, in Monckton's book I was probably down as an irredeemable sadist, what with the damage to Polk's face not to mention the pop idol's designer jeans. He'd called me a bastard and he was right.

The trouble was, I had no one I could discuss things with. I needed a sounding board. But who? There were very definite limits to what I could discuss with Finbar. Despite his keenness to play detective I knew that he was upright enough to draw the line at any action verging on the criminal. What he'd done last night was about as far as he would ever go. Anyway, I had enough on my plate without worrying about Finbar passing his declining years slopping-out in one of Her Majesty's mephitic jails.

Troubled, I took a scouring pad out of the kitchen cupboard and approached my cooker hob. Usually I find that a careful scrubbing of the work surfaces induces some kind of mental as well as physical reflection. This time, though, no light dawned.

I gave up shortly after nine o'clock.

Then something did strike me. I hadn't told the department that Monica was dead. Dear old Professor Richardson might still be composing his sharp note of reprimand. I'd better save him the trouble.

'Terrible news, wasn't it?' Lisa Lovegrove said when I called. 'We heard yesterday. Monica seemed so healthy and full of life. She never had a day off all the time she was here. The professor's quite shocked, poor thing. He's not come in today.'

I thought about this for a moment. Perhaps I wasn't the only one with guilt to nurse.

'What have you heard?' I asked, pleased that Lisa felt able to communicate with me again.

'Well, not much really. Some kind of heart failure, they say, but nothing definite. Dead's dead, I suppose. They don't always know the causes even today. The university medical centre has asked for clarification. She had a full medical only three months ago at the Well Woman centre and there wasn't a trace of any cardiac trouble.'

'No, she was so fit.'

'Will you be at the funeral? The department's had to arrange it, apparently she didn't have much to do with her sister. It's set for 10 a.m. on Tuesday at Southern Cemetery Crematorium.'

'Of course,' I murmured. 'Thanks for telling me.'

'Mr Cunane . . . Dave,' she said in a sort of embarrassed half strangled voice. 'There's such a lot I need to say to you, and not just about poor Dr Withers.'

Lisa seemed unwilling to put the phone down and as I had no pressing engagements any more I carried on listening.

'I don't know what Cousin Jonathan said to you,' she continued.

'Who?'

'Old Fuddy-duddy Richardson. He warned me about what he calls libidinous conversations with members of staff. Honestly, I didn't know where to put myself. It isn't as if I haven't spotted him trying to get an eyeful down my blouse often enough but to hear him talk you'd think I'd propositioned half the department. I don't know what you said to him but he was breathing fire against you. I thought I'd get my union in to talk to him but then I don't want any more scandal, especially now.'

'No, of course not,' I sympathized.

'I wondered if you'd be doing anything this afternoon. I'm getting off early.'

'I don't know,' I said awkwardly. An empty day yawned before me.

'It's just that we could talk over what Richardson's been saying. After all it concerns me as much as you.'

'I haven't got the car at the moment,' I said hesitantly.

'Don't worry. I have one. I could pop out to Chorlton on my way home. You're still at the flat, aren't you? Thornleigh Court is it? I often pass on my way home.'

'Number 23,' I muttered, as if she didn't know.

'All right, well I'll see you at about one. Perhaps we could go to one of those new restaurants on Wilbraham Road. It'll be my treat, Dave, as you're now among the unemployed thanks to that stuck-up American bastard. Do you know he has his hair permed?'

Lisa certainly knew how to express herself in a forthright way but her indignation on my behalf was unnecessary. I now understood that I ought to be grateful to Richardson for sending me back to detection. Though, without a car, I wouldn't be able to do any detecting. I got dressed, choosing the nubuck jacket and cord trousers with a dark shirt. Then before I left Thornleigh Court I make a quick return call to the number Melville Monckton had left on my mobile.

'Who is this?' a female voice enquired.

'I want to speak to Melville.'

'You'll have to call him at his Florida number. He took a night flight to his home in Florida.' She sounded more than slightly peeved.

'Are you Mrs Monckton?'

'I am not!' she said sharply. 'I'm Mr Monckton's administrative assistant. Look, who is this? I'm expecting a call from Mr Monckton's PR advisers.'

'I'm a friend of Melville's,' I said in my most dulcet tones. 'I was with him last night before he left. He got very upset about something and I just wanted to reassure him that I still have his best interests at heart.'

'What's your name?' she pressed. She sounded less impatient than before.

'It's Dave Cunane. Melville knows me well. In fact, I'm a business partner of your boss. When you get in touch, tell him I sent my best wishes.'

'Wait a moment,' she rapped back. 'I don't know who you are but if you were with him perhaps you can tell me why he left for America in such a hurry. All he left me was a note on my desk and there were masses of things that he was supposed to be doing. I've documents here for him to sign. The phone's not stopped ringing for him since I got in.'

'I'm sorry, miss, but I can't really discuss it with you. Melville's had a little upset in one of his business deals . . . you know, with Mr Polk and Mr Tyler.'

'Oh, that! That's what he's supposed to be doing today, signing letters of intent for the banks.'

'All I can tell you is that there's been a problem . . . maybe you've heard of Mr Lane?' I said coyly.

'I thought all that had been sorted.'

'Apparently not. That's what I was helping Melville with and that's why he's so upset.'

'This is awful. I've got the transfer forms for the deeds of acquisition here. Nothing can go ahead without Mr Lane's signature on them.'

'Can't you stall on that?' I enquired helpfully.

'Stall? I've done nothing but stall for the last three weeks. I've had three banks and a brewery breathing down my neck to remind me that completion date was last month.' She sounded tearful now, but perhaps she was beginning to realize she'd already said too much because she put the phone down abruptly.

I'd really called to see if Melville had his hounds out on my trail but the call had paid unexpected dividends. I walked out of the block after giving the neighbourhood a fairly cursory survey from my kitchen and bedroom windows. There didn't seem to be any blazer-clad Afro-Caribbeans or muscle-bound Americans in the neighbourhood, so I set off up Wilbraham Road towards the bank. On the way I passed several travel agencies.

Miss Molly's was advertising a two-week break in Barbados . . . £259, travel only. It crossed my mind that taking an out-of-season holiday would be the streetwise, smart thing for me to do at this stage of my fortunes. Why not? No one was employing me and when I came back I would get stuck into rebuilding my business. Why shouldn't I do a 'Melville' and pop across the Atlantic to toast my toes for a week or two?

Then the ancestral voices of generations of Cunane coppers and schoolmarms recalled me to my day-to-day world of senseless drudgery in the cause of I knew not what . . . Revenge for the slaughtered Fred Travis? Scientific proof that Monica's death was not natural? Discovery of whatever dirty dealing Monckton had been involved in? I was thinking along these lines when I joined the queue at the bank. My usual cashier, Gudrun, looked at me oddly when I reached her counter.

'Are you all right, Mr Cunane?' she enquired. 'You look as if somebody has been walking over your grave.'

'Sorry,' I said quickly, handing over the slip for a £2000 withdrawal. I replaced the savage expression on my face with my usual bland smile, sliding my hand over my face like a comedian.

'Tens or twenties?' she asked after tapping the keys on her terminal. 'How would you like it?' I could have sworn that she gave me the very smallest, barely detectable trace of a wink as she smiled at me from behind her glass screen.

Coming out of the bank, I caught a glimpse of my reflection in the glass door. With the leather jacket and the open-necked shirt all I lacked was a big medallion and a chest wig. That image wouldn't do at all. No wonder Gudrun had been hard put to suppress a laugh. I walked back to Thornleigh Court and changed into a business suit before knocking on Finbar's door to see if he was willing to give me a lift to the garage to which my battered Mondeo had been delivered. Detection without transportation being an impossibility, I'd decided to blow my hard-earned savings on a decent set of wheels.

'What's on the agenda?' Finbar asked eagerly.

'Nothing much today,' I said and he immediately pulled his face and stepped out into the corridor before partially closing the door behind him.

'I was counting on you to save me. Fiona has all sorts of plans for me.'

'I didn't know I was running a rescue service for beleaguered bachelors.'

'Just give me something to do,' he pleaded.

'OK, you can drive me to the garage and then to the insurance office and then if you like you can go back to watching Mrs Peterson.'

'Great! What am I looking for?'

I laughed.

'Finbar, I honestly don't know. Mrs Peterson's a member of the C of L and her husband is a copper investigating a murder in which the C of L may be involved, but whether that amounts to the proverbial hill of beans is anyone's guess. Just sit outside the house like you did yesterday, see who comes and goes . . . come home when you get tired. It's all low-key stuff.'

When we got to the garage, situated in a converted farm in the oldest part of Chorlton, we found that the car was a write-off as expected and that the insurance assessor had been. My next call, at the insurers, brought the news that my claim was being processed.

I then went to the main Ford dealers on Chester Road and put a deposit down on a new 2.5 litre V6 Mondeo. After much cajolery they agreed to lend me a battered, fawn-coloured Escort until the paperwork on the Mondeo had gone through. It wasn't much but at least I had my own wheels again. Finbar and I parted company. He headed off towards Sale and I decided on impulse to pay a visit to the Hulme home of Everald Mallick, the 'professional' de-programmer. Perhaps he could sort out one or two of the little bugs in my own programming.

Everald lived in one of the new housing association and private homes which had replaced the eyesore flats erected as a social-engineering experiment in the late sixties and early seventies. I knew where to find him from previous contact though I'd never actually entered his home before. In everything except scale it was a Georgian villa; the effect only spoiled because instead of standing in its own grounds in front of a green sward of manicured lawn, it stood shoulder to shoulder with a regiment of other Georgian villas. Whatever the aesthetics, the new face of Hulme represented a vast improvement on what had gone before. I noted that there were still houses and flats for sale.

I rang the doorbell and after an interval in which various banging sounds emerged from the house a mixed-race teenage girl opened the door. She was neatly dressed in school uniform.

'I'm a friend of your dad's,' I said cheekily. 'Is he in?'

'He's in bed,' she said. 'What's your name?'

I smiled. 'Your dad calls me Cowboy Dave.'

She grinned, went to the foot of the stairs and bawled, 'Dad, Cowboy Dave's here to see you,' before exiting through the front door with her Reebok bag full of books slung over her shoulder. She ushered me into the house before departing towards the bus stop, almost bent double under her burden. A wave of tropical heat almost felled me when I put my foot over the threshold. I don't know what the maximum setting for domestic central heating is, but Everald's place was on or above it.

A second later, as I loosened my tie, I was rewarded with the sight of Everald peeping round the top of the stairs like a shy little elf. His quaint granny glasses glinted in the light. He didn't speak and made no sign of recognition. His face was shiny with sweat. Then he disappeared, for all the world like one of the 'wee folk' tiptoeing back to Fairyland.

I listened for a moment. Various stealthy scraping sounds came through the ceiling. There was the noise of a window being opened.

'Oh, hell,' I thought, 'in for a penny, in for a pound.' I dashed down the narrow corridor into the kitchen and out of the back door. Sure enough, Everald was emerging through the back bedroom window, skinny rump first. He was clad only in vest and pants and was attempting to swing out on to the roof of the small garden utility shed.

'Do you want a hand, partner?' I shouted.

He almost lost his grip, but then scrambled back into the bedroom.

'I only want a word,' I said soothingly.

'No way, man. I know your "words". I'm not going to end up picking my teeth out of the toilet pan.'

'Come on, old buddy, just have a little chat with your old partner Cowboy Dave.'

'Clear off, you racist bastard!' he shouted before slamming the window shut.

I went up to the back bedroom. I didn't try the door but there was the sound of furniture being piled against it.

'Everald, I only want a word,' I pleaded. His reaction to my casual visit was extreme even for him. I knew he was no coward. He'd been a boxer, quite a useful lightweight, for many years before taking up the cause of the oppressed.

'Go away,' he moaned. 'I've already had one beating. I don't want another.'

'What are you on about?'

'Your friends up at Meldrum Terrace, the big guy's enforcers, they beat nine shades of shit out of me for . . .' his voice faltered into silence.

'For what?' I prompted. 'I've no friends at Meldrum Terrace.'

His only reply was an inaudible curse.

'Tell me and I'll go,' I promised.

'That rich bitch who you were paid to hijack. They wanted to know where she was.'

'How come they expected you to know that?'

'That's what I told them but they wouldn't listen, two great big ugly white Southern racist rednecks, just like you.'

'I'm not an American!' I said.

'But you are a racist and a redneck.'

'I married a black woman, which is more than you did,' I shouted through the door.

That shot hit home. Everald's wife was white, an Irish nurse.

'—Your mother, you filthy racist pig!' he screamed.

I was starting to get annoyed. I tried to get a grip on my emotions. I told myself that Everald's scatter-gun approach with the racist accusation was just his way of being friendly. I gave the door an admonitory rattle.

'Look, Everald, I don't care what you think about me but for your information I wasn't paid to help Melanie Varley and all I want to know is why they thought you would know anything about her.'

'It's not her, you fool. They made me tell them the journalist's address. That fancy bitch Janine White.'

'Which is what?'

'Look it up in the phone directory like I did, fool!'

I left Hulme little the wiser, but not before I turned the central-heating thermostat in Everald's house down to zero.

The poor guy was definitely overheated. Actually being pummelled by two genuine racists: it must have been one of his worst nightmares come true. It must have come as a profound shock to meet red-blooded specimens instead of the creatures of his own imagination. No wonder he'd taken to his bed. I consoled myself with the thought that he was still capable of motion as his acrobatic escape attempt showed.

So, Aldous Arkwright was interested in locating the luscious Melanie, or at least his henchmen were. So what? It wasn't my problem.

From Hulme I drove into town and spent the rest of the day at the Central Reference Library reading about cults, not that it left me much the wiser. I read about the early history of the Quakers, and of the Shakers, both of which originated in England but flourished in America. I read about the Mormons and Moonies and the Perfectionists and about the founding of New Harmony: a socialist Utopia started by a man who'd made his money in Manchester textile mills. Interesting stuff, but I felt that Arkwright was in a different league.

Next day I got an early start. I drove to Stockport police station and asked at the enquiry desk for Sergeant Martin.

'They've held a second autopsy,' Martin told me when I eventually met him after a half-hour wait, 'but I'm afraid it doesn't really shed much more light on your friend's unfortunate death than the first. I must say I didn't realize I was going to be landed with all this work when I answered your phone call.'

'Can you tell me anything?' I asked with suitable humility.

'I shouldn't really as you're not a relative, but I just happened to mention your name to my inspector and he said you're the son of Paddy Cunane. He was the big cheese at Bootle Street when I started on the beat in Manchester.'

'Yes, I am his son,' I said defensively, wondering what was coming next. I concentrated on studying his ridiculous hair-do . . . The side hair was carefully plaited over his bald dome today.

'He was like a terrier, that man, never let go once he got his teeth into a case. Last of a dying breed.'

I still wasn't sure whether this was said in praise or blame. Martin looked me in the eye.

'Are you like that? Persistent, like?'

'I do want to know what happened to Monica.'

'Yes, that's more than her sister does. She put the phone down on me when I rang to give the results of the second autopsy.'

'Oh?' I mumbled questioningly.

'The long and short of it is that the pathologist who did the second autopsy, Dr Jeremy Matthews, found that her cardiovascular system was healthy. He next suspected an intermittent gas leak might have been responsible. We've had the gas people out to the house, but they say all appliances are up to specification. Anyway, Dr Matthews has examined the body for carboxyhaemoglobin and carboxymyoglobin – you know, the stuff that makes people who top themselves with car exhaust go all cherry-pink. There was no trace. So now they're sending samples from her basal ganglia, that's in the brain, to a specialist lab in Birmingham. They've ruled out poison in her food or drugs, you'll be glad to hear.'

I nodded.

'The coroner has ordered that the funeral be postponed until everything is sorted,' he continued loquaciously. I could have sworn he was licking his lips as he went on.

'You see, the result of the first autopsy . . . adult cot-death, or some kind of unspecified "insult" to the system isn't really a scientific finding. Environmental-protection people are taking it all very seriously. They're worried about seepage from land-fill sites of which there are quite a number in the Marple area. They're checking if there's been any dumping of nerve gas by the military or powerful chemical agents by civilian firms. I shouldn't be surprised if they haven't got half of Marple dug up by now.'

I sat with eyes downcast. None of this was what I'd expected to hear. The truth is, not being a doctor, I didn't quite know what I expected to hear. I just couldn't take it in. Martin mistook my confusion for grief.

'Cheer up, son,' he said genially. 'You've nothing to reproach yourself for. It sounds like some kind of freak accident that they'll never get to the bottom of. If it was nerve gas or something like that she got a whiff of, you can count yourself lucky that you escaped.'

'Yes,' I muttered, 'there is that.'

I got up to go.

'By the way, son. The environmental people might want to check your flat. I mean, they know what Miss Withers . . .'

'Dr Withers,' I corrected.

'That's right, Dr Withers,' he agreed with a condescending chuckle. 'They know what you and she were doing before she died, but they'll be discreet, I'm sure.'

As I left the police station I couldn't help being offended by Martin. He probably meant no harm but I didn't like the relish with which he'd relayed the details and the way he kept harping on about the fact that Monica and I had had sex before she died. My heart was in my boots when I retrieved the Escort from the multi-storey park near Debenhams and set off back to Chorlton. With Sergeant Martin on the case it couldn't be long before the story became national news. He'd certainly rehearsed telling it several times. By tomorrow the readers of the *Sun* and *Mirror* might be reading about what had happened at Flat 23, Thornleigh Court, Chorlton.

'You know that new restaurant on Wilbraham Road? Oh, what's it called?' my visitor asked shortly after she arrived at 1 p.m.

'Actually Lisa, I don't feel much like eating. I've just been told that they don't know what poor Monica died of and that they're postponing the funeral.'

'Yes, I was told. I've spent part of the morning phoning round her colleagues and Joyce was still at it when I came out,' Lisa said, putting a suitably lugubrious expression on her face. That wasn't the only thing she'd put on. She definitely wasn't dressed in her work clothes. I guessed that she'd gone home to her flat in Brooklands before calling on me. She was wearing a loose blouse over tights. The blouse was in a filmy purple material and I could clearly see her bra. It was the sort of thing which would have looked marvellous on a twenty-year-old model but was rather more problematical on a mature gal like Lisa.

'How's Peter?' I said by way of discouragement.

'Oh, he's fine . . . you know . . . husbands. He spends more time in the garage tinkering with his motorbike than he does with me. It's really him I wanted to have a chat with you about.'

'You don't say,' I said, raising my eyebrows. It certainly looked as if a spot of tinkering was on Lisa's menu, but was it on mine?

'If Richardson's going to go round saying I indulge in lewd conversations with the management science staff, I don't know what might happen. Peter can be very jealous.'

Visions of an enraged biker taking his place in the lengthening queue of those who wished to rearrange my features flashed across my mind.

'I shouldn't think Richardson will go into any further detail,' I said dismissively. 'After all, he achieved his object of removing me from his department.'

Lisa gave me a coy look, then she sat on the sofa and folded her legs underneath her well-padded rear.

'I *could* find out more about why he dumped you,' she said tantalizingly. She wet her lips with her tongue and showed me her teeth.

I was beginning to get worried about exactly what was on her programme for the afternoon. I decided to offer her food if her inclinations were really tending towards cannibalism.

'I can make you some cheese and pasta if you like. I might even have a nibble myself,' I offered, 'but I don't feel like going out. That restaurant you were thinking of is very noisy. It's full of people using mobile phones. I think they come down from the TV studios, or maybe they just want us to believe that they do.'

'Dave Cunane! It's interesting what you find out about people. From the way you carried on in the department I'd never have guessed that you have such delicate feelings . . . Of course, I'd love to see how you perform in the kitchen. I don't think Peter even knows how to open a tin.'

There was a roguish twinkle in her eyes. I shut my mouth firmly and headed for the culinary part of the Cunane establishment. Lisa uncoiled from the sofa and followed me.

The next few minutes were occupied as I took out fresh pasta from the fridge and quickly prepared a snack with a carbonara sauce.

'Have you anything to go with this?' she asked as I served her. I followed her glance to the wine rack by the window. I took out a bottle of excellent Chianti I'd been saving for a rainy day and offered it to her.

'How about this, madam?' I asked, entering into the spirit of the occasion.

'Lovely,' she said, getting two wine goblets from the cupboard behind her. 'Richardson was on the phone to someone for a very long time that morning before he fired you,' she said after taking a mouthful of wine. 'If you like I can find out the number from our itemized telephone bill. I know the time.'

'He was probably telling the Vice Chancellor that he'd done the deed,' I said.

'Of course I do have to observe confidentiality. I mean I can't just divulge information about the department to any Tom, Dick or Harry.' There was an interesting gleam in her eye as she said this.

'I'm not any Tom, Dick or Harry,' I said encouragingly.

We ate in silence for a while. Lisa appeared to relish her food and because she was enjoying the food and drink so much I began to feel more relaxed myself. When we finished Lisa leapt from her chair and stacked the plates and pans on the draining board.

'I'll wash up,' she said.

'Don't bother. We can take our wine into the living-room.'

She obeyed, holding the door open for me. She paused for a moment in the doorway.

'Has all this been dreadful for you? I didn't realize that you and Monica were such an item. I mean, I knew she was interested. After all, apart from spotty Ph.D. students there isn't much wearing trousers under forty in Management Sciences – unattached, that is.'

I shrugged my shoulders.

'I expect she took you out to her cottage for bonding sessions.'

'She didn't. I only went there once and you could hardly call that mansion a cottage.'

Lisa gave me a puzzled frown at this but she didn't let whatever I'd said put her off her stroke. 'You must have been getting on very well with her though. I mean I was surprised at the way she stuck up for you when Richardson got huffy about the police coming for you,' she persisted. 'Like a mother hen with her chick, she was.'

'I was a bit taken aback myself,' I admitted. I pressed on into the room and she let me pass but not before I was forced to brush closely against her. I got a strong whiff of her perfume. That was the moment I should have suggested a nice long afternoon walk on the Meadows. Instead I asked her what her perfume was.

'Champs Elysées by Guerlain,' she replied.

'Powerful stuff,' I muttered.

She resumed her place on the sofa. I poured more wine for us.

'Did you know that Professor Richardson was separated from his wife?' she asked.

'Fat chance he'd have had.'

''Course, I don't hold with divorce.'

'You're religious then?' I suggested.

'Not likely,' she said with a laugh. 'It's as much as Peter can do to drag me down to church once a year at Christmas. He's a Methodist, you know. They're very regular. I think he often has a silent prayer session in the garage – just him and his motorbike. He certainly doesn't commune with me very much these days.'

I smiled at her and she leaned across the sofa towards me. She ensured that I got a full view of the charms she was careful to withhold from old Richardson. I decided it was time to beat a rapid retreat.

'Do you think I'm awful for criticizing my husband?'

'Well, actually, I can't stand disloyalty,' I said, scrambling for the moral high ground with a straight face.

Lisa's over-friendly expression froze but she recovered quickly.

'Present company excepted,' I added.

'No, you're right. I think Richardson should have stood up to that policeman for you. Poor Monica had so much more about her than he does.'

'Lisa, you know I've always got on well with you. You made such a pleasant contrast to some of those desiccated types down at UNWIST, but I think you should be careful what you say about Richardson. You don't want anything getting back to him.'

'I suppose not. I only came to see you because of what he said about me, but getting back to Monica . . . You said something odd – you know, when you were talking about Monica before?'

'What?'

'You said you could hardly call her mansion a cottage. I didn't understand that. It's only three rooms. I know because I've been there.'

'It's like a young stately home,' I countered.

'You mean the house in Marple. She often called that her cottage but that was just her little joke. She had a small cottage not very far from Eyam in Derbyshire in a secluded valley. She liked to keep it quiet but I stayed there for a weekend. I think she wanted to have somewhere private, of her own.'

'Have you got the address?'

She nodded and, going to the hall table, wrote it down on the pad by the phone.

'Why do you want this?' she asked, holding the paper close to her chest.

'There's such a lot I didn't know about Monica's life. I'd like to have a look at it if I'm passing that way.'

'OK, but it's so much off the beaten track that you won't find it without these directions.'

She handed me the paper.

'You and Monica being an item, that's what got Richardson's goat, I'm sure.'

'We might have been but we didn't have enough time,' I said sadly.

'We never know how much time we've got left,' she said, giving me a chaste peck on the cheek. 'Make the most of what you've got, that's my philosophy.'

As I ushered her out I didn't let my determination to get to the Eyam cottage show. It was better if she thought my interest was purely casual. I hurried over to the living-room window to make sure she'd gone. I saw her walking across the car park and then she turned and hurried back to the entrance. A second later the intercom buzzed.

'Dave, you know what I said about never having enough time?'

'Yes,' I said cautiously.

'Well, you'd better get down here right away. The garages are on fire.'

I hurtled down to the car park and one glance was enough to confirm her warning. I broke the glass on the fire alarm immediately. It was the quickest way to summon the brigade.

Mafia Repulsed?

The Commissioner of the Metropolitan Police was questioned by the House of Commons Home Affairs Select Committee about Mafia penetration of the British crime scene. He claimed that since the determined efforts in the 1960s by New York crime families to move into the London club and casino scene there had been little evidence of Mafia involvement. Manfred Gauntlet MP (Lab, Croal Valley), chair of the committee, expressed scepticism about this.

Parliamentary Review

13

Friday, 23 October – Saturday, 24 October

The bad news about the fire was that it destroyed my garage and the whole adjoining row. The good news was that I'd parked the Escort in the street – and all the fuss and action didn't give me time to brood about the information supplied by Lisa.

I found the drive to Eyam relaxing after the stress of the fire. I've never much liked the drive into Derbyshire, especially late in the afternoon in winter. The light has a very gloomy quality and some of those valley bottoms look as if they've never been reached by sunlight. Today, however, the encircling gloom was just what I needed. All that raw grey stone showing through its overburden of wind-seared grassland matched my own scarred mood. I felt that I was on the edge of finding out just what was going on.

That only goes to show how wrong you can be.

The fire in the garages seemed straightforward enough. Someone, and you could take your choice from several candidates not excluding Everald Mallick, had gone up the narrow access alley at the back of Thornleigh Court and pushed combustible material into one of the garages and then set fire to it. It wasn't paranoia that made me certain it was my garage which was the target. However, the Fire Brigade weren't sure. What concerned them more than the cause, which they assumed to be simple vandalism, was the fact that one of the residents had been storing petrol in his garage and when the flames reached that, it exploded, taking out the whole row and almost Thornleigh Court itself. They were lucky not to lose a fire-fighter. The residents had to stand around on the road inhaling smoke and a fine spray of water. When some of them got around to grumbling about the cause of the fire I decided it was time to keep my suspicions to myself. It all pointed to Polk and Tyler . . . a smashed car, a burnt garage. What was coming next, a fiery cross on the lawn with a bunch of hooded spooks baying for my blood?

Neither Fiona nor Finbar was on hand to risk hypothermia mooching around outside so I had no responsibilities for anyone but myself and I took off in pursuit of dear Bob Lane and his brother. I was sure that I'd find them in Derbyshire. It was the only place they could be.

At last I drove down the narrow lane to Eyam, a village doomed by plague in the seventeenth century. My own feelings about doom were enhanced. I followed Lisa's careful directions out of the village and soon found the cottage. It was remote and secluded right enough, at the end of a track and backing on to a dark woodland. I imagined it had originally been built as a gamekeeper's cottage. It looked a bit like the cottage in the children's story of Goldilocks and the Three Bears, a tall narrow building, basically just one room below and one above. There was a light on in the downstairs room. Even though it still wasn't fully dark the curtains were drawn.

I drove straight up and banged on the front door and was rewarded by an immediate twitch of the curtains. The massive features that peered out didn't belong to Goldilocks though they were large enough for a bear.

'It's Dave!' boomed the unmistakable voice of Clint Lane.

A second later the door was opened with a great deal of slamming back of bolts and turning of keys in locks.

'Wait, Clint,' Bob cautioned before admitting me. He shoved his head out of the door and gave the area a careful scan.

'I'm on my own, though I don't know why,' I said ungraciously.

'Has anyone seen you come?' Bob asked. His brows, always on the beetling side, now appeared to have set into a permanent frown.

'No, I wasn't followed,' I said.

'Have you brought it?' he demanded angrily. 'We're starving. I don't know what took you so long but you'd better have a good explanation.' Clint was hopping up and down in excitement as Bob spoke. He looked rather more gaunt than usual.

'Got what?' I asked nastily. The only thing I had with me was a burning need for explanations.

'Christ man! Food!' he exploded. 'What else? I'm almost on the point of boiling up shoe leather here. There's nothing in the house to eat and Clint can't understand why I'm not feeding him. Didn't she tell you what to do?'

'Didn't who tell me?'

'Monica, of course. She said she'd send you out with some grub as soon as the coast was clear. I'd have called but the battery on my mobile's flat and I've no charger.'

'Bob,' I said, as gently as I could, 'Monica's dead. She died two days ago just after I left her with you.'

Bob's face paled from an angry beet-red to a deathly shade of white in about three seconds. The pupils of his eyes dilated and then he grabbed his throat and started struggling to breathe. He stumbled to a sofa and began choking.

'Bob's asthma,' Clint said, like a frightened five-year-old. He stood shaking like a leaf, his eyes as big as Chinese lanterns. Obviously his mother must have had to cope with these emergencies on her own.

By this time Bob's face was changing from white to almost blue or black. I was as frightened as Clint. So much for my theory that Bob might have some answers about poor Monica's death. If he was faking this attack it was an Oscar-winning performance.

'What does mam do when Bob's like this?' I asked the baffled giant, who by this time was kneeling on the floor beside his prostrate brother.

'Inhaler,' he sobbed.

'Where is it?'

He shook his huge shaggy head. God, that man was big! Being penned up with him in that narrow room was like sharing space with a fair-sized pony or even a cart-horse. In the event, Clint might as well have been a quadruped for all the sense I could get out of him.

Searching the downstairs room didn't take long. There was no inhaler there. Praying that a potential asthma victim wouldn't have travelled without his medicine, I dashed up the narrow stairs to the bedrooms. A small spartanly furnished box-room contained a bed, a bare mattress, chest of drawers and little else. Next to it the main room was lavishly furnished in what I guessed was Monica's taste for Scandinavian design. It was definitely a notch or two above IKEA. Like a ship in full sail, the large and splendid double bed had a canopy matching the duvet covers. It wasn't hard to guess why Monica had wanted to keep this cottage secret. This was her retreat. The downstairs room was furnished with old but serviceable stuff that no passing thief would covet overmuch but she'd spared no expense in here. That thought was comforting in a way. I hoped she'd been happy sharing this room with a kinder lover than I'd been but after a glance round I applied myself to the task in hand. Bob had pulled up a chair to the end of the bed where Clint's feet protruded and among the blankets draped over this was the jacket of the suit he'd been wearing. The inhaler was in the inside pocket.

With little help from the weeping Clint, I was able to get Bob into an upright position with the inhaler in his mouth. He began sucking noisily on it. After what seemed like an age his breathing became easier but he was only just clinging on to consciousness. I was on the point of summoning an ambulance with my mobile when he spoke.

'Nebulizer – in car,' he gasped.

Clint took me out to the car which Bob had off-roaded right into the edge of the small wood behind the house. It was concealed from casual glances by a large rhododendron bush.

With the aid of the nebulizer Bob began to make some kind of recovery but it was obvious that he wouldn't be coherent for some time. My vengeful feelings towards him had well and truly subsided. Clint, meanwhile, was making a pathetic attempt to convey his hunger to me.

'Feed – him,' Bob said with a voice like a tomb door creaking. The effort of speaking set him off again. I was almost at my wits' end. I tried to arrange him in the position that would best favour his labouring lungs. Then I took out the mobile. There was no reception. Bob's eyes tracked me as I stood up.

It was like a scene in a play about a nineteenth-century workhouse. I looked from Bob to his giant brother, now whimpering and holding his belly. I had to do something. I felt desperate. Was I going to have two more corpses on my hands? I had a tin of boiled sweets in the glove compartment of my car. I turned to the door and began tackling the elaborate series of locks and bolts.

It was a mistake. Bob's gasping immediately worsened as he battled to get a word out.

'Don't,' he pleaded. He pointed to Clint.

I got the message. 'I'm not turning you in,' I said quickly, all thought of ambulances gone. 'I've got some sweets in the car that Clint can have.'

Bob flopped back with a helpless shake of his head. Tears added to his distress.

Clint fell on the sweets like the proverbial starving man, gobbling them until his mouth was full.

'Food,' Bob croaked.

'Don't speak. I'll go,' I said abruptly. 'You need a hospital.'

The wheezing redoubled. He shook his head. I passed him the nebulizer and after a few minutes he became calmer. Arguing with him was clearly out. I decided that Clint's predicament wasn't doing Bob any good.

'All right, no hospital, no police. I'll go to a supermarket.'

With an immense effort, Bob indicated his trouser pocket. I pulled out a thick wad of notes. I shrugged and started to push it back. He shook his head and insisted that I take it. Whether he intended it as a bribe or to pay for the groceries remained a moot point because he slumped back exhausted. He was past caring what I did.

I checked that he was still breathing. He was. I set off.

I soon discovered that finding groceries entailed a long drive to Chesterfield. It would take me a long while. I realized that I didn't mind that as I settled behind the wheel again. As the car headlights followed the twists and turns of the moorland road the panic caused by Bob's attack subsided. Reason and caution began to return. There were too many twists and turns in Bob's story for me to completely trust him, but there was no doubting that news of Monica's death had come as a shock to him.

Eventually I reached Chesterfield and stocked up at two separate supermarkets, the Late Saver and Safeway, just in case anyone got curious about a single man buying such a massive load of groceries. I fairly ran round the aisles, chucking stuff into the trolley almost at random. Even so it was a ninety minutes before I got back to the cottage.

I had to smile. The 4WD was in front of the cottage. Clint was holding Bob propped up ready for a racing start if I returned with the constabulary. The tough little club owner looked more dead than alive. As a getaway driver he'd have been a total loss.

I made no comment as I helped him out of the high-sided vehicle. I passed the wad of notes to him as Clint picked him up like a mother with a small child. Later Clint helped me to unload the groceries, then I put the Toyota back in its hiding place. When we got into the single room Clint started eating an uncooked family-sized pizza while Bob sorted out a pile of frozen chips, sausages and steaklets.

'Let me do that,' I said, snatching the frying pan off him.

I watched thankfully as Bob made his way to the sofa under his own steam. He seemed to be on the mend.

'That should hold him for a while,' I said dubiously as Clint demolished the cold pizza.

'Don't you believe it. That's just the starter,' Bob replied before relapsing back into weary silence.

It took me the best part of an hour to stuff sufficient food down Clint's whale-sized maw to make him stop demanding more. Then I faced Bob across the small table while Clint in his turn stretched out on the sofa with his legs draped over the end and a contented dreamy expression on his face.

'Is he all right?' I asked.

'He'll be like this for hours now. You'll not hear a cheep out of him until morning.'

Bob listened in silence while I filled him in about Monica's death. When I'd finished he took another few pulls on his inhaler.

'Right after you left Monica was on the phone to her sister . . .'

'What, at that time in the morning?' I said sceptically.

'There was a message on the answerphone saying that it was vital that Monica call her, whatever the time,' Bob explained patiently. 'Monica thought one of Shannon's brats might be sick so she phoned. Instead Shannon said she was thinking about leaving the Children of Light and could she come and stay? Monica was over the moon. She didn't want us to frighten Shannon away so she gave me the directions to get here and the keys and she said she'd send you out with some provisions. I drove straight here, there were no road blocks or nothing, and Monica said that the locals wouldn't think it strange to see lights on in here. She often comes herself, either alone or with a friend.'

It took me a few minutes to take all this in. At least Monica had intended to continue some sort of a relationship with me. I don't know what I'd thought before. I must have been mad to think that she was intending to take up with Bob.

'So Shannon was the last one to see Monica alive?' I said at last. There must have been a note of doubt in my voice because Bob looked at me angrily.

'I suppose so,' he said with a shrug and a grimace. 'I hope you don't think I had something to do with what happened.'

'Nobody knows what happened. There just seem to be one or two coincidences too many. Monica comes to help me check out the Children of Light because she hates what they've done to her sister. Then, lo and behold, the sister turns up out of the blue and Monica snuffs it.'

'Are you saying I made it up about the sister?'

'No, how could you have? But it just seems so odd her turning up at that hour in the morning.'

'I didn't make it up. I had a hell of a job tearing Clint away from that exercise machine as it was. I'd have much rather stayed, believe me. Monica phoned Shannon and she must have been alive when Shannon arrived at the house.'

'It doesn't add up, Bob. If Shannon was ever at the house, why didn't she report Monica's death?'

'I don't know, ask her.'

'This whole thing's a mess and these damned Children of Light seem to be involved right up to the top of their pointy little heads.'

'Great, so they're the suspects, not me and Clint.'

'There are no suspects. We don't know that Monica's death was anything but an accident.'

'Fred Travis's death was no accident and I can see the way your mind's working. The only link is me.'

'If you hadn't let Clint play with my business card I'd never have been involved at all.'

'Oh, poor you.'

I started to reply but he waved his arms and cut me off, 'All right, don't go on. You've no idea how bloody irritating you can be when you start looking down your nose at people. I imagine you take after your dad, a smart-arsed copper if ever there was one.'

'Well, what do you want, an apology from the Cunane family because we don't like being lied to?' I couldn't lose my temper with him, he still looked very ill.

'Shut up! Isn't it bad enough that Monica's dead?'

'Not really, there's been a hell of a lot more than that happening,' I said. I told him about Monckton's flight to Florida and points west and about the various fires, wreckings and sackings I'd been involved in.

He listened with an expression of ever-deepening gloom on his round face. Previously I'd have described Bob's features as inexpressive. His mug was like a turnip that someone had poked two eyes in, but now he was the picture of misery.

'I always knew bloody Melville was a wimp. It's all his fault,' he muttered. Then he bit the knuckle joint of the index finger of his right hand and shut up. I winced as I watched him draw blood.

'I'm waiting with bated breath,' I prompted.

He looked at me. His eyes were as flat and dead as those of a stunned mullet waiting for the gutting knife. The silence lengthened. After a moment he looked at Clint. 'Promise me you'll see nothing bad happens to him,' he said at last.

I made no reply.

'I liked Monica, you know,' he said with a deep sigh. 'She was really nice to Clint.'

'Yes. Now tell me why Monckton offered me twenty grand to tell him where you are.'

'The business was bust. About six weeks ago Melville, who'd been sniffing round for a while, came along and offered to buy 51 per cent of the business for one pound. "Look at it this way, Bob," the lying little toad said, "you'll have 49 per cent of a viable business because I'll take care of the debts, put money in and turn things round. What do you want? A hundred per cent of nothing or a share in a good business?" I was fool enough to believe him.' He lapsed into silence again, as if contemplating his own stupidity.

'Go on then.'

'Of course, I should have realized that he only wanted to use me to break into the club scene. It's not so easy to start up from scratch . . . you need licences and there's always a lot of opposition to granting new club licences.'

'So what happened?'

'Didn't want to put up any of his own money, did he? Careful with his pennies is our Melville. He's got a little friend in Miami, bugger with an Italian name. This friend is willing to put money into the business, only it's got to be a bigger, grander business, something that's going to make the Commonwealth Games or whatever it is they're always agitating to bring to Manchester look like a kiddies' tea party.'

I nearly fell off my chair. 'You're not telling me the Mafia are involved, are you?' I demanded.

Bob waved his hand dismissively. 'Americans are into everything else in this country. Why shouldn't they be? They're businessmen with money to invest.'

'A little more than businessmen, aren't they? Their ideas on free-market competition are a bit strong, or hadn't you heard?'

'Dave, you don't understand this sort of thing. It's business, not bouncing people off walls.'

'Try me,' I said indignantly. 'Bloody hell, I was a lecturer in the Management Sciences department at UNWIST until this week.'

'So that means you know all about running a business?' he asked with a sneer.

'I've got to know.'

'The friends in Miami have got lots of money. Those wop geezers are really wadded, they've got so much money that they don't know what to do with it. Do you know what I'm talking about?'

'Laundering drug money.'

'Yeah, and quite a bit of it is in good old pounds sterling since Florida became one of the major holiday destinations for the UK. So they get Melville to put up a package deal to the banks and other legitimate businesses in Britain. He's popular, he's got a good name for financial acumen. He can build a great success on the wreckage of my clubs. Meanwhile he pumps money into my business, cash supplied by his American friends in large brown paper parcels once a week, making it look as if the profits are enough to finance his share in the new venture. The boys in Miami own him, he owns me, and everything's hunky-dory for a huge expansion in the club, music and drugs scene here in England. Only it doesn't happen . . .'

'Why not?'

'Because I wouldn't sign. I'd rather go bankrupt and shut the clubs. Do you think I want to become some kind of glove puppet for the Mafia?'

'No, I suppose not.'

'It just took me a while to catch up with what Monckton was up to, then I thought I might as well cut my own throat as let those cold-hearted bastards do it for me. Did I ever tell you that Clint and me had a sister?'

I looked at him sharply.

'No, she wasn't handicapped or anything. Just that living up at Langley got too much for her. She got a habit, a really bad habit, and then one day she OD-ed. I swore that I'd never lift a hand to help a drug dealer.'

'All right, you threw a spanner in the works and they fitted up Clint to blackmail you, but what part did Fred Travis have in all this? Was he in with Monckton?'

'Honestly Dave, I don't know anything about Travis. Monckton never mentioned his name. He wasn't in the deal.'

Now it was my turn to sit in silence for a while. Was the whole saga with Travis and the Children of Light a gigantic red herring to cover up the involvement of the Mafia? I couldn't take it in.

'Listen Bob,' I said urgently. 'Did Monckton ever mention Polk and Tyler, two American heavies who work for Aldous Arkwright?'

'Oh, are you on about them again? I never heard of them until you told me about them at Monica's place. If they're fucking Yanks I expect they're all in it together.'

'Come on, not all Americans are involved in drugs.'

'Aren't they? The whole fucking country was started to grow tobacco. Did you know that my dad died of lung cancer and what did it say on every packet? . . . Virginia tobacco. Where the hell do you think all this drug taking started? It wasn't Germany or France, you know.'

'Shut it, Bob, I've got lots of American relatives,' I growled.

'Good for you,' he said peevishly.

He didn't speak for some time and I didn't want to quarrel. I'd reached this point before with people who I'd thought were friends. You can agree on everything under the sun and then you suddenly find that they hate blacks, or the Irish or the English. There's no point in further argument. It's like a nasty scab on a wound . . . once picked, it just leaks out more venom.

I got up and made coffee in the small kitchen. I passed a cup over to Bob. Clint had fallen into a deep sleep and the whole room was being rattled by his stentorian snores. Bob looked at him sourly. I was aware of the strong brotherly bond but there must be times when affection wore thin, even for Bob.

'Give us a hand with the big bugger, will you?' he said wearily.

I looked at him. He looked as if getting out of his own chair would be a struggle. There was no way he was going to shift Clint.

'What are you going to do?' I asked. 'I won't turn you in and you don't need to try to bribe me. I know Clint could no more have cut someone's throat than he could have written a sonnet.'

'I don't know about sonnets but at least he knows when somebody is on his side, unlike his thick brother,' Bob said with a wry smile. 'Give us a hand getting him into bed, mate.'

'Stand clear,' I advised. 'Get the doors open.'

Even when I got Clint on to his feet it took all my strength to get him up the narrow staircase. As I laid him on the bed, Bob said, 'If you ever wonder why I took up weightlifting, here's your answer. He was big even as a kid.'

'When all this is over you've got to think about yourself. You can't look after him for ever.'

'Don't start that, Dave. I've heard it all a thousand times before. I'd never have amounted to anything if I hadn't had to take care of Clint. It's given me an aim in life. I can't just ditch him.'

'Well, I shouldn't think you can stop here too long if you were thinking of hiding until the heat dies down. The locals will start getting curious once the news about Monica reaches here.'

'It isn't just that. Clint needs to be out in the fresh air. I can't keep him cooped up.'

'So what will you do?'

'If I could get to Hull, I could reach Holland. I've got friends there who would hide us on their farm. Clint would love it. He's been before.'

'I'll help you,' I said impulsively.

'No, you've done enough, Dave. There is one thing though,' he said hesitantly. 'You know the club?'

I nodded.

'Of course it's all locked up now but there's something in there I need.'

'Not the gun.'

'No, I wasn't thinking of hijacking the North Sea ferry,' he said with a grin. 'You can have the gun if it's still there. It sounds like you'll have more use for it than I will. There's a small suitcase in a hole in the wall behind the lockers in the doormen's room. You'd have to unscrew the lockers from the wall to get at it but if I had that I could get out of the country with no trouble.'

I looked at him curiously.

'It's only travel documents, false number plates, money and one or two other things,' he said with a very innocent expression on his face.

'So you've been planning to skip for some time,' I said.

'A good businessman's got to plan for all eventualities, matey.'

'There's no question of this or any other British government tolerating the formation of any kind of citizens militia to patrol the streets of our big cities.'

'But surely, Home Secretary, people are entitled to defend their neighbourhoods. Isn't active citizenship something this government's trying to foster?'

Extract from an interview on the BBC Radio 4 *Today* programme

14

Saturday, 24 October

The stench of burnt rubber still clung heavily to Thornleigh Court when I returned in the small hours. A swathe of destruction had scorched the trees and one side of the building, not my side fortunately. All the car park and garage area was sealed off by police tapes so presumably the morning would bring some kind of investigation. I found a parking space on the main road with some difficulty and crept into the building stealthily and not without a certain sensation of guilt. Whatever was said about vandals, I knew what was behind the sudden incendiary outbreak.

I slept late because the clouds of dense smoke had left a deposit of carbon on the windows which filtered out the bright, fresh sunlight. When I eventually managed to get a look at the outside world through my kitchen window I saw squirrels running along the broken wall that was all that remained of the garage block. A fireman was poking among the ruins while a uniformed police officer and a couple of the residents looked on. It was a weekend and I felt entitled to a solid breakfast so I fried bacon and eggs and settled at my kitchen table to eat them slowly with lots of fresh bread and butter.

I was in an odd mood, light-hearted yet with an ominous awareness that I appeared to have bitten off considerably more than I could chew. I'd got involved in the affairs of the Children of Light who now seemed to have their dirty fingers in every local pie. I'd agreed to help Clint Lane only to find that his brother was mixed up with Monckton and his Miami friends. Yesterday morning I'd considered hopping on a plane to Barbados but that was out of the question now. Besides promising to help Bob Lane to escape, I had to know more about the death of Monica Withers.

The doorbell rang and, wiping the melted butter off my chin, I went to open it.

'Well, where did you get yourself to?' were Finbar's first words. 'You've missed all the excitement round here.'

'I don't think so,' I said with a grin. 'Come in, I've just put the coffee on.'

'It took four appliances to save the block,' Finbar insisted, not to be cheated out of his story. 'Another few minutes and we'd all have been homeless. They're talking about arrests.'

'Arresting who?' I said, leading the excitable veteran into the kitchen.

'Your next-but-one neighbour on this floor had at least fifty gallons of petrol in drums in his garage. He's some kind of car salesman and it seems he's done a bit of fiddling by stealing petrol which he kept in the garage. You wouldn't believe what people get up to, would you? Imagine, the meanness of the man! If the place had caught fire in the night we might have all been burnt in our beds.'

'The rotten swine,' I said jokingly, pouring out the coffee.

'I don't see anything funny about this, Dave. It amounts to nothing less than sabotage. The only good thing is that I had my car with me in Sale and Fiona was round at the church hall when it happened, but I can tell you it was a pretty nasty shock for both of us.'

'Yeah, they should put the petrol-hoarder up against a wall along with the charmer who started the fire, and shoot the pair of them.'

'I can see you're in one of those moods, Dave. Be serious. They *would* have shot them at one time.'

'Sorry, Finbar, it's just that sometimes I come up against things that alter my sense of proportion.' I told him about my suspicion that the Children of Light were linked to the Mafia, or at least that two of them were.

'I don't know,' he said when I'd finished. 'What did people expect? I've never liked them, you know.'

'Who?'

'The Americans. They pulled the plug on us at Suez.'

'Finbar, first the Japs, now the Yanks. Is there anyone you do like?'

'Not the Mafia, certainly. Very corrupt that lot. I was really glad when they chose a non-Italian as Pope . . .'

'Finbar!'

'Oh, yes, well . . . I stayed outside the Peterson house until five, you know. There was a lot of coming and going. At about two thirty a couple of men came. Mrs Peterson gave them something from her garage and then they left.'

'You didn't follow them?'

He shook his head.

'They might just have been your arsonists,' I said. 'What did they look like?'

'They were both small and skinny, one was black.'

I took a long swallow of my coffee.

'Dave, if they are connected with the Children of Light, don't you think it's time we told the police? After all, if they keep coming here to sort you out, you won't be the only one to get hurt.'

'How do you propose I tell the police? It looks as though Peterson's involved and do you fancy telling them that you've been mounting a surveillance operation against a police officer? The Chief Constable might not be too pleased.'

'There must be some way that we can get the authorities involved. What about your journalist friend? Can't you give her the story?'

'What friend?' I asked forgetfully.

'Janine White.'

'Oh, her!'

'I thought she was very pleasant.'

'That was because she wanted something.'

'Not at all. I know an attractive young woman when I see one. Not a skinny beanpole like most of these modern girls either.'

'Restrain yourself.'

'Can't you give her this story? She seemed interested enough in your doings.'

'I don't think the press work like that.'

'You've got to do something, Dave!'

'What do you propose, then?' I asked.

'Get her to do one of those pieces full of hints like that one she did about you. She could say that there are rumours that a police officer is enjoying a very close relationship with a brainwashing cult. You know . . . hint, hint, and so on.'

'You think it's that easy?'

'Dave, you've got to do something. I can't stand idly by while these Americans incinerate my sister.'

'Where've you got the idea that the Children of Light are all Americans? Everyone seems to have a down on our transatlantic cousins these days.'

'Everyone knows that all these cults start in California and didn't you say that two of them were Americans?'

'Polk and Tyler were the *only* Americans involved, apart from the Miami Mafia and as far as we know none of them are over here. Mrs Peterson isn't American, nor is Aldous Arkwright.'

'Hmmph!'

'OK, so you want me to get Janine to whip up a crusade against cults and Americans, implying at the same time that there are bent policemen involved?'

'You can be an irritating bastard at times, Dave, with all due respect to your parents; but yes. Why not? It might get some attention paid to what's really been going on around here.'

'You've convinced me,' I said with a laugh. 'I'll send a copy of the floppy disc I pinched from Meldrum Terrace to Assistant Chief Constable Sinclair. That at least should put him wise to Peterson and any other coppers whose names appear on it and I'll whisper a word or two in Janine White's shell-like, not that she seems to need much grist for her mill before firing off on all cylinders.'

'Good man! But you're mixing up your metaphors a bit there.'

'There's just one thing, Finbar. Are you still ready to help me?'

'Of course, I only called you a bastard out of a sense of righteous indignation. I'll do anything apart from breaking into houses or hitting old ladies.' I hadn't told Finbar in so many words that I was intending to assist Bob and Clint's escape, but he'd have to have been pretty dense not to know what I was up to.

'Right, well, I promised Bob Lane that I'd let his mother know that he's safe. How do you feel about delivering a message? I expect the police will have the house under observation in case he and Clint turn up.'

'You've only to say the word,' he said happily.

'I'd go myself except that they may be on the look-out for me and I don't want to spoil your fun.'

Getting Finbar suitably equipped to call on Old Mother Lane took up most of the rest of the morning. Using my office equipment, we printed up a pile of spurious fliers for a car boot sale. The plan was that Finbar would deliver these down the street where Mrs Lane lived and slip the note that Bob had given me into her letterbox. This was just the type of activity that appealed to Finbar's schoolboy sense of fun. He was in the best of spirits when he reached Langley just before eleven. On the way there we dropped off the floppy disc for Sinclair at Chester House, headquarters of the GMP.

As we turned off the M62 at the interchange for Middleton and the Langley Estate I felt a good deal less carefree than I had earlier. Finbar was whistling 'Colonel Bogey' to himself. I wondered if he knew the chances he was taking in just walking down a street on the Langley Estate.

For once, the plan I'd laid worked well. Finbar was up and down both sides of the street in no time.

'I think they were observing from the bedroom of the house opposite,' he said when he rejoined me. 'I caught the flash of a reflection that could only have come from a pair of binoculars. They ought to have them shielded at this time of the day when the sun is shining right at them.'

Finbar had dressed for his role in a long dirty coat and a bobble hat. Even if they'd photographed him they would hardly be able to recognize him in that get-up. Having succeeded in one part of the task, I decided to push my luck by trying to complete the other. On leaving Langley I didn't turn back towards the motorway but went into Manchester city centre. Bob's main club, Howl, occupies a prominent spot in Stevenson Square and I had considered entering it during the night but I guessed that going now, when there were lots of people about, might be less difficult than later. I had the keys and the code for the security alarm so it was just a matter of getting in there without being seen.

I managed to park near Affleck's Palace on Church Street, a kind of twilight zone of Manchester's shopping district. There were street traders, shops selling accessories for the pop industry and fabric emporia.

'You'll have to sit this one out in the car, Finbar,' I warned. 'If I'm not back in half an hour, go home on the metro because it'll mean that I've been arrested for aiding an escaped fugitive.'

'Is that all? I knew you were helping Bob Lane,' he said getting out of the car. 'He isn't the fugitive, it's his brother and I think they might have a hard time proving that you know that Bob has his brother with him. Clint escaped from police custody on his own, don't forget, and no one's seen him since. For all you, I or the police know, he could be at the bottom of the Manchester Ship Canal.'

I stared at Finbar in surprise, then scratched my head. 'When you put it like that it sounds very straightforward. All right then, come along.'

We walked along Tib Street until we reached the turning for Stevenson Square where we split up. I went along the back street while Finbar took his time in strolling around the grandly named square that had come down in the world since it was the focus for political unrest in Manchester. It's more of a widening in the road than a square. I quickly came to the side door of the club and let myself in. I had some trouble in orienting myself in the gloom but had time to switch the alarm off. Then, groping in the semi-dark, lit only by the occasional shaft of light, I made my way down the stairs into the doormen's rest room. I realized now why Bob played loud music night, noon and morning. This place was gloomy enough to be haunted.

There was still a stink of embrocation and cheap after-shave in the air, along with the smell of stale sweat from the piles of discarded trainers in the corners. I found a main power box and switched on. For a frightening moment there was a burst of sound from the music system. I flicked the switch off again, wondering whether I'd advertised my presence by turning on the flashing neon sign outside. More cautiously this time, I checked the array of switches. They were all in the off position except for the outside lights and the stereo system. I cursed Bob for not warning me.

I turned everything off except the house lights and settled down to locating Bob's little cache of escape equipment. The lockers came away from the walls easily enough and revealed a small blocked-up fireplace containing a medium-sized Samsonite suitcase. It was securely bound with several leather straps. I picked it up to test for weight. It was heavy enough to be full of bricks, not number plates or fake passports. I replaced the lockers. Wondering whether Bob had decided that he couldn't be parted from his dumbbells in any circumstances, I hefted the case out of the room and when passing the door of Bob's office threw it open just to check. The enigmatic table ornament containing his automatic was still there.

I went over and ran my hand over it expecting to hear it click as the secret compartment opened. It didn't. Impatiently I scooped the ornament up in my left hand and left the club. As I was securing the outer door I became aware that I was under observation. A neatly dressed young black man was speaking into a mobile phone. I don't know how he caught my attention, but there was something about the sharp way he looked at me. He was dressed in a Crombie overcoat and a neat bowler hat, apparently the latest fashion in headgear. I stared back at him and he turned away. I grabbed my burdens and fled towards the Square. As I turned the corner I bumped into Finbar.

'Here, take this,' I said shoving the suitcase at him. 'I'm being followed. Go home on the metro.' It would have been nice if he could have disappeared into the crowds but it was the Jewish Sabbath and all the garment businesses in the area had the shutters up so there were no people. However, having more sense than me, Finbar made no effort to carry the case. Instead he lowered it on to its wheel, and rapidly pulled it by the handle into a side street.

I had no time to worry about Finbar because I was almost vacuumed up by a street sweeping machine which helicoptered along the pavement behind me. Barely keeping ahead of its powerful brushes I retreated down Hilton Street. When I broke cover to turn into Tib Street the bowler-hatted black man sprinted in my direction, one hand on the bowler, the other clutching his phone.

I dashed past the market stalls and nearly fell under a bus as I crossed Church Street. The car park was on my left and Affleck's Palace on my right. The huge former department store has been transformed into a warren of small shops like an oriental souk. It attracts seekers of style. Now I ran panting into its cavernous interior seeking refuge.

My oddly shaped burden attracted no attention. I paused inside a shop on the first floor to get my breath while contemplating the combat trousers on offer and keeping one eye on the stairs via a mirror. Bowler-man was baffled by the labyrinth of shops. I spied on him through the balusters. He seemed to be on his own. I waited a moment. He spoke on his phone again and then went on up to the next landing. I left by a narrow side stairway and a rear exit and ran to the car.

Seated behind the wheel, I was facing the wrong way for direct observation but I was able to see him emerge from the same door I'd used. He surveyed the area and then spotted the side entrance of the Coliseum across the car park. I breathed a sigh of relief as he quickly ran in there. Since the centre of Manchester was blown away in the cause of Irish nationalism, dozens of small shops formerly in the Corn Exchange have migrated to the Coliseum. It would take the detective with the strange chapeau, if detective he was, quite a while to discover that I wasn't in there.

I checked Bob's ornament again. Somehow it seemed to be the wrong way round from when Bob had had it. I checked for buttons and secret switches. There was nothing. I sat in the car park for twenty minutes. There was no scream of sirens or arrival of car-borne reinforcements so I was unable to confirm if the young man was from the police or some more menacing organization before driving home to Chorlton.

When I was safe behind my own steel door I put the puzzling sculpture down on a coffee table before calling Finbar to check that he'd arrived.

'He's not back yet, I thought he was with you,' Fiona said.

With my heart in my mouth, I took up a position where I could observe the main road that leads to Stretford, where Finbar would have got off the metro. I was rewarded after fifteen minutes by the sight of his weary figure trudging along, pulling the suitcase behind him. I started to my feet but then settled down again. If he was being followed or the building was under surveillance it would do no good at all to draw attention by rushing out to help him. I could see no one on the lane behind Finbar and no one watching, but that didn't mean they weren't there.

He finally arrived at my door in an advanced state of exhaustion.

'God, I'm sorry, Finbar,' I said. 'I'd have given you the ornament if I'd known no one could get it open.'

'What are you talking about?' he said angrily. I could see that I'd really offended him now. 'I'm as fit as ever I was. I could have shifted two of those cases.'

'I just meant that I'm sorry I put you in danger.'

'Look lad, I've been under artillery fire more than once,' he flared up, all his natural truculence to the fore.

'Right, right, forget I spoke. Would you like a drink?'

He nodded. While I was pouring him a whisky I discreetly observed him remove his tie and mop his forehead with the large coloured handkerchief he always wore tucked into his breast pocket. His face was purple. I still felt nervous about his health.

'What's this effort then?' he said pointing at my new decorative acquisition. 'It's one of those what's-its, isn't it? They make them in Thailand or somewhere round there. They certainly don't run them off for their beauty.'

He gestured at the sculpture and I handed it over.

Within a moment I heard the familiar click and the Heckler and Koch slid out. Finbar put the sculpture down and worked the slide on the gun.

'Handy little thing. There's one up the spout, you shouldn't leave it like that, you know. The safety was off as well.'

He handed me the gun after ejecting the round and removing the magazine.

'I can see now why you took the ornament and not the case. I was cursing you all the way through town and along the lane. I thought you were putting me through some kind of test.'

'I'd never do that to you, Finbar,' I said. 'I think Bob kept the gun for immediate use, like a quick draw. Do you want to look after it?'

A bright eyed, boyish expression appeared on his face, softening the strain lines.

'Sorry, old lad, I would if it wasn't illegal but the first thing the boys in blue do if they know that you're an ex-regular officer is check you out for illegal firearms. They always think you might be concealing a machine-gun or have an 81 millimetre mortar under your bed. A friend of mine got nicked because of that. All he had was a derringer that he'd picked up as a souvenir.'

'Fine, I'll dispose of it then,' I said.

Finbar smiled broadly and then rubbed his finger on the side of his nose.

'I must go and have a shower and let my twin know that I'm still in the land of the living,' he said before knocking back his drink.

That was the last I saw of him that day. When I enquired later, Fiona sternly informed me that he'd gone for a little nap. I made myself a ham sandwich for lunch. I was half-expecting to hear something from Sinclair. I'd left an unsigned printed note with the floppy disc explaining that it held information on membership of the cult, but now I was anxious. Was it possible that Peterson had intercepted it? Although I hadn't left my name on it, I expected Sinclair to guess it had come from me. There couldn't be that many people willing to supply him with information.

After lunch I began to feel drowsy myself. I'd promised Finbar that I'd enlist the services of Janine White and the *Guardian* but since Monica had died I was superstitious about involving another female. I decided to go for a run along the Meadows. My bike had been destroyed along with the garage but I still had a track suit. The first part of my run towards the Mersey banks seemed to consist mainly of trying to avoid the large pools of water that had gathered in the path. This meant zigzagging off the direct route and cutting through marshy grassland. After a while I gave up bothering. My legs and feet were soaked in mud and icy water and a chill feeling began to creep up my body. A bitter wind was sweeping through the river valley and despite an increase in pace I began to cool down. There's nothing I like less than to have sweat trickling down my back while my front is freezing.

I rang along the reed beds of the nature reserve, hoping that the high vegetation would provide shelter, but it didn't. So when I came in sight of the bird watcher's hide I was more than happy to go inside. The two occupants weren't so pleased.

'This place is provided for bird watchers, mate,' an elderly man, clad in a Barbour jacket that was so new that the wax was practically dripping off it, informed me.

'Yes, I am one. I've come to see the cormorants and I've heard that jays have been seen,' I said glibly even though my teeth were chattering.

The complainant clutched his expensive binoculars as if to say that I wasn't equipped for twitching but he made no effort to eject me. Perhaps he mistook the half-frozen, teeth-clenched set of my face for desperation or savagery. Whatever it was, he turned his back, clamped the binoculars on to his eyes and got on with eyeballing the feathered friends.

I pressed forward and took my place at one of the hatches. Sure enough, there were a pair of cormorants fishing in the deep pools. I watched them until feeling returned to my lower body. Gradually my strength came back. I felt warm all over. I left without a word. I'd got my second wind and on the run to the flat I didn't experience the same sense of discomfort as on the outward leg.

I took a shower and a brown stream of peaty liquid ran off me for at least a minute. As I watched the filth drain away it came to me that I'd not been approaching the case from the right angle. By luck or judgement, I'd got some idea of what two of the Children of Light were up to but the whole picture was as blurred as ever. I needed to focus on them. In fact, a spot of genuine detective work was called for.

But where to begin? That was the hard part. What could one man do? When Bob Lane had involved me in the Travis Case my first move had been to call on DI Cullen. That was out of the question now. I knew too much about the whereabouts of Clint to be able to meet Cullen again. He was a good copper. He'd soon sniff that I was concealing something.

There had to be another avenue, but what? Money always tells a story. If I could find out how the Children of Light were financed, light might dawn, but I'd already broken into their headquarters once. A second attempt would be suicidal. There was literature about the cult available in public libraries and on the Internet. I could try that. I had all the time in the world, after all. The Children weren't going anywhere except upward and onward according to Arkwright.

Another way might be to approach Monica's sister. Had she visited Monica before I found her? There was a similar chance with Mrs Anne M. Peterson. She must be aware of what her husband was doing. Maybe I could get her to crack.

That was as far as I got. I guessed that there was as much chance of either of those women cracking as there was of Aldous Arkwright dancing naked round Albert Square. The thought was depressing. My exertions, both mental and physical, were inducing a feeling of torpor and I was ready to collapse in front of the television for the rest of the afternoon and evening before making a night run out to Bob Lane. I still had to deliver the escape kit which remained in the spot where Finbar had dumped it. I'd scrupulously avoided trying to open the Samsonite case so far. It was heavy enough for anything. It's strange how a wrong idea can get lodged in your head. The idea of dumbbells was still in the forefront of my mind.

I towelled off and slipped on a bath robe. When I came back into the living-room the first thing that caught my eye was the Heckler & Koch automatic sitting on the coffee table. It was as obvious and unconcealed as a nude in a nuns' convention. I picked it up and started looking around for a secure hiding place. There was nowhere – the safe was the first place anyone would look – but somehow I was reluctant to just chuck it away. That illegal piece of ironmongery might prove as vital in preserving my health as it had Bob Lane's. Then my eye landed on Bob's meaningless 'sculpture'. The secret compartment was still open. It worked for Bob and Finbar, why not for me? I replaced the gun and it fitted as snugly as a key in a lock. Then I pushed against the hidden spring and with the faintest of clicks the compartment closed.

I tried to open it again. It wouldn't. Whatever the trick was, I didn't have it. As a piece of modern art the work did nothing for me. It was all intersecting spheres and cubes and triangles. I think I'd have preferred a dissected lamb suspended in formalin but then it wouldn't have filled its true function as a means of concealment. Annoyed at my own stupidity, I removed the precious *objet d'art* to the window-ledge, then on second thoughts I shifted it to the corner almost hidden behind the curtain.

Feeling fussed and foolish, I switched the telly on. As usual there was little to divert me. I'd never had Sky or cable installed and after switching channels restlessly for a few minutes I turned it off. Then almost on cue the phone gently cheeped.

'Mr Cunane?' an official, educated female voice I didn't know enunciated with precision. 'This is the almoner's department at the Manchester Royal Infirmary. We have a little problem that we wonder if you could help us with.'

I felt as if a hand was squeezing my heart. Was one of my parents ill? But surely they'd have gone to a hospital in Bolton? It couldn't be Finbar, I'd have heard the ambulance.

'Yes,' I said nervously.

'This may sound curious but can I just confirm your identity? Are you known as David Cunane?'

'Yes,' I murmured, 'but my friends usually call me Dave.'

'That's precisely what I wanted you to confirm. Now, have you got anyone who could sit with you? I'm afraid I've got some news that might come as a shock to you.'

'I'm on my own here,' I said, mystification deepening.

'Well, if you think you'll be all right . . . a young woman who might be your wife . . .'

'Hold on,' I said, 'my wife died more than ten years ago.'

'I'm so sorry, our patient is wearing a wedding ring and we assumed that you were her husband when she kept calling for Dave. She kept calling "Dave" over and over again. It's the only thing that's assured the neurosurgeon that there isn't any permanent brain damage. We found your name and address in her purse. Is there any chance . . .'

'Describe her,' I said curtly. I could feel the hairs standing up on the back of my neck.

'She's a white woman aged about twenty-five or twenty-six, five foot five in height. Rather on the stockily built side, she has light-brown hair and grey-blue eyes. She's in rather a bad way, I'm afraid.'

'That sounds as if it could be someone I know, a woman called Janine White, a journalist.'

'Is she your partner or close friend?' my interrogator prompted.

'No, but I do know her,' I said after a second's hesitation.

'If it isn't too much trouble, could you come into ward 3C and identify her? It would be so kind if you could.'

'I'm on my way.'

'Sorry, Mr Cunane, there's more. You must think we're dreadful bureaucrats but could we trouble you to bring some proof of your own identity . . . like a passport, driving licence or something? There have been so many mix-ups lately.'

'Right,' I said crisply. 'Ward 3C, I'll be there in twenty minutes.'

'That's marvellous. Ask for Marie Croft, that's me.'

I'm prepared to admit that I was in a lather by the time I reached the hospital. Twenty minutes was a wild underestimate of the amount of time it took me to get to ward 3C. It wasn't the journey through Chorlton and Moss Side. That only took ten or twelve minutes along Lloyd Street and Moss Lane East. The delay was in finding somewhere to park in the confusing maze of car parks at the huge hospital complex. Eventually I reached ward 3C, out of breath and out of patience with myself.

When I dashed to the admin station at the end of the ward the sister in charge gaped at me, open-mouthed. I must have looked somewhat dishevelled.

'Marie Croft?' I said.

'Oh, you must be here for our unidentified lady. Sit down and get your breath while I go and find Mrs Croft. I'm afraid all this might be a shock for you.'

I felt like screaming at her solicitude but she was just being professional. There must have been unpleasant cases of wrong identification of accident victims, or so I told myself. The other possibility that occurred was that the unidentified woman was on the point of death and maybe the hospital had an alternative set of relatives lined up for some other unidentified victim.

The sister returned with a rather elderly, grey-haired lady who introduced herself as Marie Croft. She scrutinized my passport and driving licence carefully before returning them.

'It's so awkward identifying someone over the phone,' she said. 'You'll appreciate that we have to be careful.'

I nodded feverishly.

'You must calm yourself, Mr Cunane. I can see that Janine White, if this is her, means more to you than you were prepared to admit on the phone. Now, she's in the ICU, it's still early days but we think she's off the critical list. Her vital signs are all steady but she's still not regained consciousness. Unfortunately there's always the danger of a relapse with a brain injury. It won't do her any good if you have hysterics when you see her. Her head's swathed in dressings. The surgeon has had to relieve pressure on the brain.'

'Please, can I see her?' I begged.

I was then led by the almoner and the ward sister to the ICU.

The sister drew me forward. She removed a dressing from the victim's face but it didn't help. For a moment I thought there had been a mistake and that I was looking at a piece of swollen, purple meat. Then gradually I began to make the outlines of Janine's face beneath the mass of cuts and bruises. From her eyebrows up, her head was swathed in gauze dressings. There was no sign of any hair. I recognized the eyebrows, the prominent cheek-bones, the determined jut of her jaw and even the incipient double chin. It was her all right. I felt ill and I felt like crying and I felt like smacking someone's head very, very hard.

Both almoner and sister were watching me anxiously. I couldn't avoid emotion but I was determined not to come up to Mrs Croft's worst expectations. Speechless, I nodded my head emphatically several times.

'Are you sure?' Croft asked, gently drawing me away from the bedside. 'It can be very difficult in a case like this.'

'It's Janine White.'

'Could you come to the admin station now?' the sister asked. 'We'd like to get some information.'

There wasn't all that much I could tell them. Janine was divorced and didn't know where her husband was. She worked as a freelance journalist and she had two children. I did have the telephone number of her home, so that was something. The almoner left, promising to get social services to go round and see how the children were coping.

'What happened?' I asked.

'We don't actually know. She was found at the side of Rochdale Road in Blackley early this morning. It's possible that she was struck by a vehicle or dragged some distance. There was no report of any RTA on Rochdale Road this morning, however, and there were no marks on the road. It's something of a mystery. The police are treating it as an unreported RTA at the moment. Could you tell us why you are involved with Ms White and why she should be so anxious to see you?'

I scratched my head. I was in a quandary, saying too much or too little could be equally dangerous for both Janine and myself in the circumstances. In a vast organization like the MRI there had to be at least one member of Arkwright's infernal band on the loose.

'Ms White's an investigative journalist, or at least she wants to be,' I said carefully. 'She came to me for help with a project she was on. I'm a private detective. I helped her but I was unable to do as much for her as she'd have liked. The last I saw of her was when I dropped her at Piccadilly Station on Tuesday morning. I thought she was going back to London. Apparently she didn't.'

'The police will want a word with you, but as she was so anxious to meet you, do you think you could sit by her bedside and talk to her? Hearing your voice may help her out of her coma.'

'Of course.'

'I'm afraid, in the circumstances, we'll also have a hospital security man present until the police get here. That's because the cause of her injuries hasn't yet been established.'

It was only now that the shock of seeing Janine's horrifically battered face hit me, now that the sister had as good as told me that I was a suspect. Unreported road traffic accident, be damned! They obviously believed that someone had beaten Janine to within an inch of her life.

Speaking to a person who makes no response is a lot harder than it sounds, especially when there's a beady-eyed security man present jumping out of his seat every time you lean forward or cross your legs. I didn't know what to talk about. I talked about the delights of the Jewel in the Crown Hotel in Whalley Range. I talked about the weather. I talked about the fire at Thornleigh Court and about the Government. I recited snatches of poetry. I mentioned everything, in fact, except the Children of Light, Melanie Varley, or Fred Travis. There was no response. I was getting desperate for something else to say when a grim-faced uniformed female police sergeant approached and asked for a word.

I was conducted to a small room off the ward. It had the usual mystifying medical devices attached to the walls. A heavy-set middle-aged constable accompanied us. He reeked of tobacco.

'Sit down, Mr Cunane,' the sergeant said. There was no trace of sympathy in her long bony face. 'I believe you claim to be a private detective?' she lisped disapprovingly.

'I don't claim to be, I am one,' I replied.

'Ex-job?' was the next question, as ever.

I shook my head.

This produced a deepening frown.

'You identify the woman as Janine White? . . . Is that correct? Is that woman in there really Janine White?'

From the way the officer spoke I understood that she was accusing me of concealing the true identify of the victim. I racked my brains to think why she might think I would do that. Perhaps she thought I was trying to play for time or that Janine was a prostitute and I was a violent pimp.

'Miss White stayed with you when she was working? Is that right?'

'Just one night on my sofa.'

'Well, is that usual practice for your clients?'

'I don't know, it was late. She couldn't get in to her hotel.'

'Which was?'

'The Jewel in the Crown, Whalley Range.'

The sergeant carefully noted this and nodded to the constable who left the room to check. He returned after a few minutes and whispered something to the sergeant who'd passed the time by writing up her notebook.

She then turned to me, 'Mr Cunane, I must caution you . . .'

'Save it, I've heard it all before,' I snapped.

'Can I see your hands?' she asked.

I extended them, knuckles upwards. Fortunately, I'd used my elbows and a blunt instrument in the affray at Meldrum Terrace on Saturday so there were no incriminating bruises.

'That proves nothing,' the sergeant said as I breathed a sigh of relief. 'This woman's injuries are consistent with being beaten with a baseball bat. Where were you at three a.m. this morning?'

'In bed, on my own, and I've no one to verify that.'

'Very well. As the woman hasn't regained consciousness and the only clue as to her probable attacker is that she repeated your name over and over again, I must hold you on suspicion . . .' Was there an expression of relish on the sergeant's face or was I just feeling very jaundiced and bitter? Before she could complete the arrest formalities there was a soft tap on the door. The ward sister poked her head into the room.

'Janine's come round. She's asking for Mr Cunane.'

The two police officers looked at each other and the sergeant reluctantly put her handcuffs back in their pouch.

When I got to her bedside, still flanked by the pair of officers, a nurse was adjusting some sort of drip into Janine's arm. Janine's eyes were open.

'Dave,' she moaned in a low voice when she saw me. Her voice was almost inaudible. I leaned over her. 'Dave, it was awful,' she whispered then lapsed into silence. I stood upright after straining to listen. There didn't seem to be any more words forthcoming. I could see the sergeant getting herself wired-up again as she looked at Janine's injuries. I wasn't off the hook.

Then Janine stirred again. Whether she'd taken in the situation with myself and the officers I don't know but I was very grateful for what she said next in an audible voice . . . 'Dave, kiss me, darling.'

I responded with the faintest possible pressure on her battered lips.

Greater Manchester Police appealed for information about the missing men but warned the public to exercise extreme caution in approaching the pair who may be armed and are certainly dangerous.

Radio and TV announcement

15

Saturday, 24 October – Sunday, 25 October

I stayed at the hospital until nine o'clock. Janine wafted in and out of consciousness. My would-be arresting officers hung around for a while in the hope that she'd say more but although Janine made it clear that she definitely wanted me to be close by, she didn't answer any direct questions from the sergeant. Slamming her notebook shut and baring her teeth, which I noticed were rather crooked, the sergeant left.

'I'll be back,' she said with a menace that owed nothing to Arnold Schwarzenegger.

By nine, the staff on the ward had changed and so had my status. I was now a concerned friend of the victim, not a suspect. I sat by the bedside listening to the steady cadence of Janine's breathing. Janine was tough, I decided. She'd pull round. I also thought she had something to tell me that she didn't want the police to hear. I guessed that was the reason for her display of affection at the crucial moment.

'Mr Cunane.' A nursing auxiliary tugged at my sleeve and pried me away from my post. 'Would you like another cup of tea?' I shook my head, there was enough hospital tea sloshing around in my innards to fill an urn. 'Sister thinks you ought to go home and get some rest. You can come back first thing in the morning but your partner seems to be on the mend. She's young and she's strong. Her heart's going like the clappers, although it was a different story when they brought her in. The best thing you can do is to go home. You look shattered, if you don't mind me saying so.'

I nodded and made my way back to the visitors' car park. It took me almost as long to get out of it as it had to get in. I had no change for the unmanned barrier and had to wait until someone came along who could give me some. It was cold in the car park and I took my outer jacket from the back of the car where I'd thrown it the night before. I patted the pockets on the off-chance that there was some change. To my surprise the thick wad that Bob had given me was still there. He must have slipped it back into the pocket before I left Eyam.

That discovery reminded me of what I had to do next. I'd left Bob's case in the boot of the Escort before racing off to the hospital. I now felt a compulsion to hand it over to its rightful owner so that one element in the tangled mess would be sorted. There was little traffic as I drove through Stockport and took the Chesterfield road. I'd struck that interval between nine and midnight when the population density in pubs and clubs nears maximum and the roads were deserted.

This time I approached Bob's hideaway more cautiously than previously, although unless they were using some kind of remote tracking device fixed to the car there was no surveillance of my movements. On those long deserted country lanes anyone following, even five miles away, would have been very visible. I swept through Derbyshire, each little village like an oasis with its gleaming pub signs promising life and liquid refreshment in the wilderness.

Then I went to the door of the cottage I discovered that Bob had booby-trapped the path by stringing up empty tins. Alerted by the clangs, a face appeared at the window and a torch shone into my eyes.

'Let me in,' I snapped. I wasn't in the mood for games.

'OK, don't lose your rag, old buddy,' Bob said in much more genial tones than he'd been using last night.

'Dave, Dave,' crowed Clint, coming out to hug me as if he'd been starved of affection all his life.

'Put him down, put him down,' Bob warned on a rising note, as Clint threatened to smash my head, as well as his own, against the limestone lintel above the door.

'Christ, Dave, you look as if you've been through the wars,'

Bob commented as soon as I arrived in the cosy light and warmth of the narrow little room.

'I don't know if this has anything to do with you whatsoever, Bob, but another person who was interfering with the Children of Light has just had her head beaten in. She was following the Fred Travis story. I've come straight from the hospital.'

'Oh shit! That tears it,' Bob said when I told him exactly what had happened. 'I can get some of the lads together and go into that ayatollah's place mob-handed. Just give me a couple of hours back in Manchester. We'll tear the fucking place apart.'

'No you won't,' I shouted angrily, slamming the Samsonite case down. 'You'll take this case that's so important and get the hell out of the country while you still can. It's obvious to me that it isn't the police that you and Clint need to be afraid of but these holy rollers from Blackley. If they get one sniff of where you are they'll probably shoot you as soon as look at you.'

I must have made an impression because Clint went and stood behind Bob, as if sheltering from my anger. He clutched his brother's hand nervously. I came off the boil.

'Bob you've got to go, if only for Clint's sake. I've got a feeling that something's going to break one way or another soon.'

'Right. It won't take me long to get ready. I've just got to change the plates on the Toyota. I can be in Hull in a few hours.'

'Thank God for that. Don't take this the wrong way, but I'll be glad to see the back of you. And by the way you can take this with you,' I said, fishing the bundle of notes out of my pocket. 'You'll need money more than I will.'

'Get real, Dave,' Bob said with a grin, pushing my hand away. 'What the hell do you think I've got in this case? It's me holiday money.'

'Oooh! Bob's holiday money!' Clint echoed gleefully. He picked up the heavy case as if it was a child's piggy bank and shook it.

'Is it in pennies and ha'pennies?' I asked stupidly.

'Gold, Swiss francs, marks and dollars, you fool,' he said with a laugh.

I looked down at the thick bundle of currency in my hand.

'Keep that, it's a lot less than I owe you, and if you've an ounce of sense in your head, you'll stay here for a few days. There's plenty of food and a week out of the limelight might do wonders for your own life expectancy.'

I didn't feel inclined to argue about the money or the suggestion. I headed for the door, leaving the brothers to make their preparations.

'At least take a set of keys with you,' Bob said as I went to the car.

I shook my head and left.

Normal feelings began to return when I was on the road home – relief and hunger, mainly. Relief that the Lanes were out of my hair. Hunger because I hadn't eaten for hours. Whether it was delayed shock or some kind of innate cunning I don't know, but though I passed several chip shops, and even pubs and restaurants, I found that I couldn't summon the resolution to park the car and buy food. Following a homing instinct, I drove straight into Manchester and down the Oxford Road 'Curry Mile'. That was only a stone's throw from the MRI and somehow it felt right.

It wasn't a very clever decision but I made my way into the Star of Kathmandu restaurant and devoured a chicken balti then, hunger satisfied, made my way to the MRI.

'You shouldn't have come back,' the night sister said. 'There's been no change except that her breathing's a little less laboured. She needs sleep now. Just take a little peek.'

She led me through the darkened ward to the bay where Janine lay. Her hand was out of the bedclothes and I gave it a squeeze. She murmured something. I don't know exactly what had impelled me to come back. It wasn't love or affection. I think that since Monica's death my own sanity was being tested. If another female of my acquaintance came down with anything more serious than a stubbed toe I'd be in hospital myself. I needed to reassure myself that Janine White was going to make it. I wanted to be there when she explained what had happened.

'I'll stay sister, if you don't mind. She may wake up and I'd like to be near.' I couldn't tell her that on my long drive from Derbyshire the vision of Monica Withers lying so peacefully on that sofa had recurred at every bend in the road. This time I wasn't prepared to leave things to chance. I realized that I'd put the night sister in an awkward spot. If she made a fuss and insisted that I leave she'd disturb her other sleeping patients.

'Get yourself an armchair out of the day room, then,' she said imperturbably. Dealing with awkward customers was probably all in the night's work for her. She pulled the screens partly round the bed.

I settled into the armchair. From time to time nurses came and checked on Janine. Hospital staff moved through the ward on unexplained errands. Patients stirred and cried out. Although quiet and darkened it was a busier place than I'd anticipated. I fell into a kind of waking doze. My eyes were open but my mind was elsewhere. At about 4 a.m. Janine stirred.

'Where am I?' she asked. 'Is that you, Henry?'

'No, it's not Henry, it's Dave Cunane,' I muttered.

There was no reply but her eyes filled with tears as she remembered what had happened. For a moment she shuddered as if reliving the beating, then she lapsed back into sleep.

Jarring noises of hospital routine started well before six and I felt able to relax my vigilance enough to close my eyes. No unknown killer had approached Janine to administer some subtle poison or nerve gas. Clattering sounds of dropped metal trays, trolleys banging into doors and noisy whistling on the corridors didn't prevent me from nodding off to sleep.

It was almost nine before I woke to a stiff neck. Someone was shaking my arm really hard. I forced open my gummed-up eyes and tried to focus. The person rousing me so roughly was none other than my father's old friend Assistant Chief Constable Archie Sinclair himself. He must have received the C of L membership list. Trust him to guess that I'd sent it. I could see why he'd never married. The sight of his purple wattles flapping around first thing in the morning was too much for anyone.

'All right, all right!' I exclaimed. 'Are you trying to break my arm?'

Janine reminded me of her existence by emitting a deep groan that came all the way from whatever level of consciousness she was in.

'Come outside!' Sinclair hissed, leading me to the day room.

'So you've succeeded in making a public exhibition of yourself again,' he said angrily as soon as we were on our own.

'What are you on about?' I asked.

My puzzlement was genuine. Apart from knowing that I must have done something to get up his nose, I wasn't aware of exactly what indictment I faced this time.

'Ach! Why do I bother?' he asked himself rhetorically. Then he poked me in the shoulder with his long bony forefinger. 'A car is destroyed at a block of flats. Who does it belong to? . . . You.' He punctuated his comment with another aggressive finger stab. 'A woman is found dead in her own home. Causes unknown. Who discovered her? . . .You.' The finger jabbed again. 'Arson is suspected. Whose garage did the fire start in? . . .Yours.' Again his accusing finger struck painfully. 'Now we have a woman beaten almost to death and who is she calling for? . . .You. I want some answers and I want them quick, laddie.'

This time I intercepted the descending fingers before they could make their emphatic point on my bruised shoulder. I pushed his hand down and stood glaring at him from a far closer distance than either of us was comfortable with. I could see the tiny bloodshot veins in his watery blue eyes.

'Yes, I'd like some answers too,' I said incautiously. 'I'd like to know why Sergeant Peterson is investigating the Travis case while his wife is making daily reports to the likely culprits.'

'So that was you!' he said stepping back from me in triumph. 'I knew you were the only person in the whole of Europe, let alone Manchester, who could think of wrapping important information in a brown paper envelope and dropping it off at Force HQ so casually.'

'Spare me the Scottish hyperbole,' I said dismissively. 'What are you doing about Peterson?'

He looked at me through his hooded, bird-of-prey eyes. It was clear he didn't like what he saw.

'Well?' I pressed.

Instead of reacting angrily he sat down in a battered armchair and gestured me to sit opposite. I slumped into my seat. I should have known there was as much chance of him discussing police business with me as there was of him flying to the moon.

'I'd rather talk to you here than at HQ,' he said confidentially. 'My, but laddie, you've given me a sleepless night.'

'Sorry to hear it,' I said, dripping as much sarcasm into my words as I could.

'In view of the importance of the information I'm prepared to overlook the no doubt illegal methods you used to obtain it,' he said, as if awarding me the brass clock at the annual coppers' raffle. 'How many people know about the floppy disc?'

'No one knows,' I said with a shrug.

'Good, good,' he replied, rubbing his hands. 'How unlike you to be discreet.'

'That's not fair,' I mumbled. I felt too tired and generally ropy to engage in a battle of wits with Sinclair.

'So?' he said looking at me expectantly. 'I'm waiting for the words from the oracle.'

'What words?' I muttered stupidly.

'I'd like an explanation of what links vandalism and arson in Chorlton, a near-fatal beating on Rochdale Road and a death in Marple.'

It was my turn to be amused. I grinned until Sinclair turned away.

'If only I knew myself,' I said truthfully.

'If you're hiding something you should know that I won't hesitate to have you arrested for obstructing police enquiries,' he threatened. 'The young woman in that ward is the one who wrote that you were involved in abducting one of Arkwright's followers. Is she helping you to de-programme Miss Varley?'

'Of course not!' I said angrily. 'That stuff in the paper was garbage.'

'Davie, come clean,' Sinclair appealed. 'It's obvious that you're hiding this girl somewhere and that these cult people are trying to get her back. Hand her over to us and we can ascertain if any charges should be served on them.'

'I haven't got her, and I wasn't paid by her mother,' I said. 'My involvement was purely spur of the moment.'

'Only somebody who's known you since childhood would be prepared to accept that.'

'So you do believe me?'

'I suppose so.' His eyes were hooded. Obviously doubt remained.

'What about Clint Lane? Is he still wanted?'

'Despite the unprofessional behaviour of Sergeant Peterson there's a cast-iron case against Lane, so don't try to bargain with me, Davie. That lad's fate is out of police hands now unless some startling new evidence turns up. If you know anything about him, tell me now. I'm told he's not quite *compos mentis.*'

'Oh, so that makes it all right to bang him up for a murder he couldn't possibly have done?'

'Unlike you, we operate according to the rules of evidence, and the forensic evidence against Lane is overwhelming. Give me something to set against that and I'll act immediately.'

'Listen, Mr Sinclair, we both know there's something extremely dodgy about the Children of Light . . .'

'I can't investigate without specific instances of wrongdoing. I need probative material . . .'

I gaped at him.

'Proof, laddie. Give me proof and I'll feel Mr Arkwright's collar for him.'

'He doesn't wear a collar and tie but there is something going on . . . Did Cullen tell you about Monckton?'

He nodded.

'Well I've reason to believe that dear old Melville's tied up with the Miami Mafia. In fact, he's in Miami right now.'

'He lives there, along with millions of other innocent people,' Sinclair said with his usual dry chuckle. 'Bring me some evidence against him and I'll act.'

I looked at him for a long while. It would be a relief to turn everything over to the police but what I'd found out about Polk and Tyler, their connections with Monckton and the Miami godfathers might only serve to strengthen the case against Bob as well as Clint. Sinclair had never seen the tender way Bob cared for Clint. It was impossible to make him understand that, lacking in charm as Bob was on occasion, he could no more involve Clint in a killing than he could walk on water. Once again, I was banging my head against that old solid brick wall of police procedure. Despite any assurances Sinclair might give, Bob wouldn't surrender voluntarily. That would mean a violent arrest in which the police would almost certainly be armed. In view of Clint's unnatural strength they'd have to shoot him before they could get cuffs on his wrists. He'd never go willingly a second time. They just weren't equipped to shoot anaesthetic darts into him as if he were some rogue elephant in need of sedation.

Sinclair knew I wasn't going to give him anything else. He stood up to go but he had a parting shot ready for me. 'The membership list was very useful for me, Davie, and I'm duly grateful, which is why we're having this conversation here and not in an interview room. But I wonder if you've considered that it may only be the fact that these criminals, whoever they are, know that you have links to me and the GMP that's preserved you from the sort of treatment meted out to Ms White and possibly to Dr Withers? It might not be healthy to be a friend of yours at the moment, Davie.'

I remained in my seat as he departed. That wasn't just due to weariness. Sinclair's words were like a kick in the stomach, crystallizing my own fears as they did. Was someone even now descending on Chorlton to batter Finbar and Fiona into a similar or worse condition than Janine? That wasn't right. Janine had brought about her own troubles. Monica had only been with me for a few hours. Surely there was no criminal gang on the planet so ruthless that it exacted death for such a brief encounter? Even the most savage Chechnyian gang in Moscow or Jamaican Yardies would have acted with more deliberation and weren't the Mafia supposed to be almost a by-word for the careful planning of their 'hits'?

As I walked back into the ward I tried to convince myself

that Sinclair was only trying to rattle me. I knew he'd succeeded when I returned to the day room and phoned Finbar.

'Is the word retreat in your vocabulary?' I cautiously asked the old soldier.

'Oh, so that's the way the wind's blowing, is it?' he replied. 'We call it tactical withdrawal. I knew there was something the matter when you weren't in your flat. Where are you calling from?'

'The MRI, but I'm not hurt. Someone's given Janine White a hammering and frankly I'd be happier if you and Fiona were about a hundred miles away from Manchester.'

'Mother of God! Is she badly hurt?' He sounded deeply shocked.

'Quite badly and I need to be here.'

'Ah, I see. Sure that I can't do anything to help?'

'The best thing you can do is to keep Fiona safe.'

'Yes, there is that, but are you sure?'

'Finbar . . .' I growled.

'OK, fine,' he said. 'Our ninety-year-old Auntie Lily, who lives in Cockermouth, is always asking us to come and stay. Our cousin has a farm there near Beckermet and he can put us up with no bother, so that's where we'll go, but are you absolutely . . . ?'

'Finbar, there's one thing you can do for me besides getting out of town. You can tell me how that blessed statue thing works.'

'Is it that bad? Look, I can leave Fiona up there and come back if things are so hairy.'

'No, you won't,' I said firmly. He could be stubborn but the last thing I wanted was to see him here in intensive care.

'Right, never let it be said that I don't know how to take orders. The trick with the statue is that there are two places which you have to press simultaneously. You press where the gun comes out and there's a concealed stud in the extreme left-hand corner of the base.'

'Thanks,' I replied, grateful that he hadn't turned the meeting into a counselling session.

'Is Janine in danger of death? We can get prayers said at church,' he concluded.

'She's off the critical list but not out of the woods yet. I'm sure she needs your prayers, but look out for yourself.'

When I reached Janine's bed the ward sister I'd met yesterday was helping a nurse to change her dressings. The sister was smiling.

'What a tremendous improvement in a single day!' she was saying. It took me a second to realize that she was speaking directly to Janine and not to me. 'My goodness, dear, we almost thought we were going to lose you yesterday. Do you know that your boyfriend stayed at your bedside all night and now he claims that he isn't even involved with you.'

The nurse at the other side of Janine gave me a warm smile. She wiped Janine's face with a sponge. Janine's eyes tracked from the sister, to the nurse and then to me. She held out her hand and I gave it a squeeze.

'Now, my love,' the sister said briskly, 'if you're up to it I'm going to have to get the police to come and see you so we can establish exactly what's been done to you.'

'Can I speak to Dave first?' Janine asked in a weak voice.

'Of course, love,' Sister agreed. 'You must have plenty to say to him but don't tire yourself. The pair of you will have the whole of the rest of your lives to talk to each other.'

Janine held my hand while we waited for the nurse and sister to depart.

'Dave,' she said in a voice that was barely a whisper. 'I had to pretend that you were my lover. I couldn't tell them the truth. Getting you involved again was the only thing I could think of. It was that man you hit, that man Rufus.' She broke off and started crying. Tears streamed down her face. 'I had a source called Everald Mallick . . .'

'I know, I read all about it,' I said grimly.

'I'm sorry, Dave, they got that story all twisted,' she said tearfully. 'I'm afraid private detectives aren't flavour of the month at the *Guardian* offices.'

'Don't worry, all publicity's good publicity,' I told her smoothly.

'Everald said if I went up to Blackley yesterday evening . . .'

'It was the day before yesterday,' I said. 'You've lost a day.'

'He said that he had an informant who would tell me why Fred Travis was killed.'

'And had he?' I asked, marvelling that a grown woman, mother of two children, could exhibit trust in such an unreliable character. Brave, Janine might be, but streetwise she wasn't. She was acting like a character in a soap opera whose script-writer was ingeniously involving her in one improbable catastrophe after another.

'No.'

'I could have told you that. They must have put the frighteners on Mallick to make him set you up. Who was there?'

'It was that horrible man. He hit me in the mouth. He wanted me to tell them where Melanie was. I wouldn't and he hit me again and again.'

'That bastard, I wish I'd killed him,' I said.

'He said he'd get my children,' Janine said desperately. 'He said he'd have them taken off me by a member of the Children of Light who was far better qualified to bring them up than I was.'

'There's no chance of that,' I said to reassure her.

'You don't understand. When I still wouldn't talk he began hitting me with a rounder's bat. He said if I told the police what had happened he'd personally kill the children. He knew my mother's address. That's where they're staying. He says he has an undetectable method of killing people.'

Her voice faltered and I looked round for the nurse but Janine wouldn't let my hand go.

'Dave, you're the only one I could think of,' she said. Her voice grew stronger and more determined. That strong chin of hers was firmly set. 'You've got to get my children and take them to somewhere where they'll be safe. Melanie's with them. You've got to help her too.'

'Melanie! I've just been asked by a high-ranking copper where I'm hiding her. Everyone thinks I was paid a fortune to abduct her.'

'I'm sorry, they twisted what I wrote.'

'How did Melanie end up with you?'

'Later, Dave. You've got to get the children somewhere safe.'

'I've not got to do anything. You work for a national newspaper,' I reminded her as gently as I could. 'Won't it be better to get them involved? They could hire ex-SAS men as guards, a whole platoon of them. That would be better than a broken-down private eye like me.'

'I don't work for the *Guardian*, I only sold them occasional pieces and they say they don't want any more of those. It has to be you,' her eyes were so desperate and inflamed as she pleaded with me that I felt frightened to look directly at her. 'You're the only one who can help me now. Pull the phone trolley over and I'll call Mum and tell her that you'll be coming.'

I did as she asked, feeling that I was being press-ganged into total madness. Yet there was sense in what she said, too. So Rufus had claimed that he had an undetectable method of murder. Poor Monica!

Janine spoke to her mother at length, repeating over and over that the children weren't safe and then insisted that I speak to her as well.

The woman sounded as frightened as her daughter. 'There are two men in a car outside in the street,' she said. 'I've got to get the police.'

'Janine thinks not,' I told her. 'Describe them.'

'They're both big but one's got plasters all over his face as though he's had an accident.'

I put my hand over the receiver, 'Janine, I'm sorry but this has gone far enough. You'll have to tell the police. It sounds as if Polk and Tyler are sitting right outside your mother's house.'

'No,' she said with iron determination, 'I know a lot more about what's been going on than you do. They're not joking. They'll kill Jenny and Lloyd. They've done it before.'

I felt as if an iron band, which someone was slowly tightening, had been fastened round my head.

'Listen,' I said. 'Tell her she's got to get out of the house. Tell her to use the back way and to go somewhere public like a restaurant or a fast-food place and sit tight until I get to her. I'll recognize Melanie.'

'Dave, it'll take you hours to get to London. They can't sit in McDonald's or Burger King all day.'

'Yes, they can,' I insisted. 'Some people even enjoy it.'

Proving that despite having been battered about the head she was far more practical than I was, Janine gave her mother careful instructions to keep the children in the McDonald's at King Street in Twickenham just around the corner from their home. I would arrive about one.

Just as she put the phone down the ward sister returned. She looked me up and down. 'Are you going to go home now?' she asked cheerfully but in a way that implied she didn't expect me to refuse. 'Janine seems to be on the mend and the police are on their way to take a statement.'

'Right,' I said.

'Well, I can't let you go like this. With those poached-egg eyes, you look as if you'll drive right into the back of a lorry as soon as you get on the street. Go and take a quick shower in the staff toilet...Here's the key,' she ordered, pressing the key into my unresisting fingers. 'Go on, the water won't hurt you but if you drive in the state you're in you'll end up in a bed next to your girlfriend.'

Janine looked at me as if imploring me to agree. I went.

Twelve minutes later, showered and refreshed, I stepped into the hospital corridor. The snaggle-toothed sergeant was waiting to sink her fangs into me. I mentally christened her Jenny Greenteeth, after the river monster.

'Tell me, Mr Cunane,' she asked poisonously. 'Is your girlfriend always like this?'

'I don't know what you mean.'

'For an alleged member of the press she's the most unobservant person I've ever met. She saw nothing and heard nothing of the men who attacked her. She says it was a mugging.'

The sergeant stared at me with narrowed eyes. She was itching to slap the cuffs back on me. Clearly as far as she was concerned I was as guilty as sin.

'We can't do anything if a victim of brutal violence won't make a complaint against her attacker, but tell me, Mr Private Detective, have you ever heard of a mugging where the victim not only still has her purse, but has more than a hundred and fifty pounds in it?'

'And have you ever heard of amnesia caused by head injuries?'

Sparks were jumping out of her eyes. 'Selective amnesia,' she barked. 'I won't tell you everything I'd like to do to men who use violence against women,' she hissed, 'but castration with a blunt knife would only be the start of it . . .'

I was on my way to London before she finished the sentence.

'I couldn't agree with you more,' I shouted over my shoulder.

'Families are a thing of the past. They belong to a lower stage of human development. In our movement we're pioneering new ways of living and new ways of bringing children into the world. People have got to break free from these hampering ties if they are to achieve full self-realization and move on to the next phase of human development.'

Extract from a Children of Light manual believed
to have been written by Aldous Arkwright

16

Sunday, 25 October

Sunday's never the best day to head down the M6 towards London. Endless columns of Scottish and northern heavy vehicles are on their way south to position themselves for their work on Monday. Their names were like a lesson in Scottish geography. There are also lots of Sunday drivers. Saturday's far quieter usually. Driving a clapped-out Escort didn't help either. I could only just about match the speed of the fastest lorries and frequently had to pull over when impatient drivers flashed from behind. My thoughts weren't on my driving. I was going over the instructions on how to get into the centre of Twickenham and pick up two unknown children as well as the elusive Melanie Varley. I could only hope that Janine's mother wouldn't want to come along as well.

As it happened, the choice of the McDonald's in Twickenham couldn't have been improved on. I left the Escort in a side lane that led to Eel Pie Island and the Thames. By luck or good judgement the first person I saw was Melanie, who was sitting in a window seat, scanning the street with longing eyes. She had a baby boy aged about one on her knee and beside her was an older woman who was helping a three-year-old girl to consume some fries. Melanie was on her feet and out of the door with the child as soon as she saw me, closely followed by the older woman. The main thing that struck me was that the children were almost aggressively Anglo-Saxon, each with a shock of startlingly white hair and wide-set blue eyes.

My heart sank when I saw Rufus and his sidekick. They began struggling to their feet, scattering fries and burgers. They'd been waiting for their prey to bolt but rapid movement was a mistake. The chairs in McDonald's are screwed to the ground. Rufus sprawled forward and went down on to his hands and knees in his haste to get out of his seat. For an enforcer the guy was definitely on the clumsy side. I strode forward and when he recognized me he slipped his hand into his pocket. I hoped that he wasn't reaching for a gun. Whatever he was reaching for, neither of us got a chance to display our prowess because Janine's mother stepped between us . . .

'Are you the one we're waiting for? *Dive K'nine?*' she asked in a strong Cockney accent. She was a solidly built woman in her middle years. There was no mistaking where Janine got her determined expression from.

I hardly had time to agree before she pushed the little girl into my hands, turned round and with her arms flailing like a windmill in a hurricane laced into the semi-prone Tyler and Polk. She had a fold-up umbrella in her hand which she made efficient use of.

'You dirty buggers,' she screamed. 'You tried to feel me up. You've been making eyes at my au pair all the time we've been in here. They're trying to rape us.' This was shouted at a volume sufficient to shake the rafters in the Royal Albert Hall. She got her hand round Rufus's collar and clung on for dear life, screaming and battering him all the while. Rufus struggled to disentangle himself but his efforts only added veracity to Mrs White's accusations. Staff began converging on the luckless pair from all corners. An athletic Afro-Caribbean youth in McDonald's uniform actually vaulted over the counter.

Other people joined in the struggle on the floor. One woman threw a large milkshake which impacted on Rufus's already battered head.

I must have been gaping at this sudden and completely

unexpected display of violence when I was pulled fiercely from behind. I unfroze and turned.

'Come on!' Melanie shrieked, 'Can't you see she's giving us a chance to get away?' She tugged me out of the fast-food shop and we dashed round the corner into the little car park. Melanie fairly flung herself and the infant she was clutching into the back seat.

'Come with me, Jenny,' she said stretching her arms out to take the little girl off me.

Jenny threw back her head and howled with fright as I pushed her into Melanie's arms.

I jumped in the front and drove out of the little pay-and-display car park with frantic speed. There was a one-way street system so we didn't pass McDonald's again but I did hear a deafening wail of sirens as the Metropolitan police converged on the eatery. We raced away from the scene.

'Slow down,' Melanie yelled, having to roar to make herself heard above the noise of her two charges, both of whom were in the process of proving that they'd inherited their admirable granny's lung power. 'You don't want to get arrested for speeding after all this.'

I slowed down.

'I've got a problem, Melanie,' I told her. 'How come you happen to be looking after Janine White's kids?'

'It's complicated.'

'Try me, we've got lots of time.'

'I can't make myself heard with these crying children.'

'Shout then,' I insisted, 'but I've got to know.'

'Honestly!' she said angrily. Jenny was trying to snuggle in her arms and avoid looking at me. 'Janine left me her mobile number when you dropped me at Oundle. You didn't see. She'd written it on a piece of paper. I phoned her on Tuesday and she said I could stay with her mother. That's all there is to it.'

'You do know she's a journalist?'

'I figured that before I got out of your car. I think people ought to be told the truth about Aldous Arkwright and Janine's at least making an effort, unlike some.'

'All right, that'll do for now,' I conceded.

'Have you any idea what you're going to do?' Melanie demanded. Somehow her voice had lost the magical bell-like quality of our first encounter as she struggled to be heard above the wailing. I've faced a lot of things; thugs armed with baseball bats, knives and even guns. I've fallen out of moving vehicles, and even survived a helicopter crash, but that eldritch, high-pitched wailing had an effect on me. I found that I was incapable of thinking further than was necessary to steer the car and change gears.

It didn't take long to discover that Melanie had little more idea of how to care for infants than I did. However, we decided it was safer for me to go into shops to buy disposable nappies, baby food, rubber dummies and a child's car seat among other assorted odds and ends than it was for her. The children seemed to relate slightly better to her than they did to me.

I chose to head north. Despite all considerations to the contrary there was only one possible destination – my parents' home in a sheltered fold of the West Pennine Moors north of Bolton. It crossed my mind that we might stop at Melanie's mother's home in Oundle. I was desperate to find an alternative to Paddy and Eileen's hospitality.

'Forget that,' Melanie said when I suggested it. 'My mother had her hands full coping with me, and that was with the help of a full-time Norland nanny and a nursery maid. She only relates to animals. If we turn up on her doorstep with two howling kiddies who aren't even related she'll have a breakdown. She just retreats into a private world of her own.'

By this time we were well north of London. I wasn't on a motorway because it occurred to me that if Rufus had managed to dislodge Mrs White (Janine used her maiden name) from round his neck and escape the police, he might be scouring the motorways for us. By the time I'd reached the Midlands, travelling at a snail's pace behind Sunday drivers on A roads, this argument had lost its force and I turned on to the M6 at the first sign I saw. We'd have been driving until midnight otherwise. We hadn't been on the motorway long before both children were sick over Melanie. I pulled into a service area when I reached one north of Birmingham and Melanie spent ages in the mother and baby room getting herself and the children clean. I hovered about outside, feeling more useless than ever.

'There, Jenny, sit on Uncle Dave's knee while I get Lloyd changed,' Melanie said when she emerged to dump the little girl on my knee. She shot me a resentful stare as if to ask what disqualified me from changing a nappy, but I gave her a stony look. I then spent an awkward few minutes trying to divert Jenny with a little book about the Gingerbread Man until Melanie re-emerged.

'So, what's with these two?' I asked, indicating our charges who were both now showing signs of exhaustion. That was hardly surprising as they'd produced more sound in the last two hours than the London Symphony Orchestra and the Three Tenors combined.

'What do you mean? They're Janine's children,' Melanie snapped. She was on edge. The delicate quality that had attracted me had disappeared. I could see that she wasn't so different from her mother when it came to the rigours of child care.

'Any sign of their daddy?' I asked hopefully. If she'd said he lived in Inverness or the Irish Republic I'd have been prepared to make the trip. 'Do we know where he is?'

'Oh, from what I can gather, their father, Henry Talbot, who's some kind of TV producer, cleared off with his production assistant before Lloyd was born. Janine thinks he's in the States, Hollywood probably. She's had to cope on her own. She leaves them with her mother while she's trying to break into journalism.'

'The Gingerbread Man was on the fox's nose,' I told Jenny, who was demanding an explanation of why the little two-legged piece of confectionery had ended up as carnivore fodder.

'What are we going to do, Dave?' Melanie asked. I could see she was on the point of tears.

'But why didn't he swim?' the child demanded with impeccable logic. The news about Henry hit me with the same force that the poor Gingerbread Man must have felt when he realized that it was the fox's tail or an early bath.

I tried to divert Jenny by turning the pages and pointing to the pictures but she was just like her mother. 'Tell me,' she shrieked, 'why didn't he swim when he knew the fox was going to eat him?'

Melanie gave me a helpless look.

'He thought that he might dissolve,' I explained desperately. 'He was only made of gingerbread.' If Rufus had turned up at that moment with a whole gang of Mafia heavies, I think I'd have given them a run for their money if that had been the alternative to looking after the little girl.

There was nothing else for it. I took out my mobile and keyed my parents' number.

'Hello,' answered Paddy in his familiar combative tones. This was a disappointment. I'd hoped to break the news that I was intending to arrive with two strange infants to my mother first so that she could soften the blow for the old curmudgeon. Paddy must have been waiting for the phone to ring.

'He could have crossed. It was only a small stream,' Jenny insisted in a piercing voice.

'Who is that?'

'Dad, it's me, Dave. I was wondering if I could call on you this afternoon?'

'You do pick your moments. I'm in the middle of re-tiling the kitchen floor.'

'He could have crossed,' Jenny insisted again.

'Who is that with you? Is there a crossed line?'

'Dad, I've got one or two friends with me. I just thought a country trip might be good for their health.'

'What? . . . Oh, it's like that, is it? Why is it that we only hear from you when you're in trouble?'

'That's not true . . .' I started angrily, then bit my lip. I refrained from saying that they'd hear a great deal more of me if only he'd phone me as often as he seemed to phone Sinclair.

'Dave, why did the fox swallow the Gingerbread Man?' Jenny asked. She pronounced the word Dave as '*Dive*', like her granny.

I struggled not to laugh and tried to block her out by stuffing a finger in my ear but remorseless Paddy had picked up the word fox.

'What's that about foxes?' Paddy demanded. 'They're not

some of these hunt saboteurs, are they?'

'No Dad, actually they're quite young.'

'How young?'

'Three and one, I think. There's also a young lady with us as well. Honestly, we'd be no trouble.'

'Yes, yes,' he barked impatiently. 'Come one, come all. You know your mother and me are running Liberty Hall here.'

'Right, well, we'll be a couple of hours.'

'Funny time for an afternoon visit,' he grumbled. 'I expect I shall get on with the tiles. I'll tell your mother the glad tidings when she comes in. She's over with one of the neighbours.'

When I put the phone in my pocket Jenny pushed the book into my hand. I found the situation hard to take in. The child looked at me wide-eyed, 'Why do foxes eat gingerbread men?' she enquired patiently.

'I don't know. There are some naughty men about, like the men who frightened Granny. I think the story's meant to warn children to beware of strangers,' I said self-consciously, sweeping the little girl up and carrying her out to the car. Melanie hitched the baby on to her hip and followed. We must have looked like a lovely couple, perhaps ill-matched by age but certainly well blessed.

The remainder of the journey was uneventful as both children slept most of the way. Being inexperienced in these things, I didn't understand that that would mean they would be as lively as crickets when we arrived.

It had been some time since I'd paid a visit to the old homestead in the hills . . . it was actually a former weaver's cottage that was part of an old fold; that is, an eighteenth-century weaving business in which there were several cottages attached to a farm. The farmer kept sheep in his 'fold' and the weavers wove the wool in the upper rooms of their homes which had long wide windows so that they could toil without wasting a minute of daylight. Through some weird process of transference the spirit of those toiling weavers lived on in my father. Only his endless toil was not directed to producing cloth. He was a builder who laboured, long and hard, ant-like and tirelessly, to add extensions to his home. Since he'd been at it ever since moving from Manchester, the original weaver's cottage now made up only the core of an extensive development. It made me shake with exhaustion just to catalogue the list of Paddy's improvements, all done to the highest professional standards.

It was driving my mother Eileen crazy. She'd bargained on a peaceful retirement from teaching, not taking up a new life as a navvy's mate.

When the man wasn't engaged in domestic improvements he directed his energies to the fields. Already he'd landscaped the small paddock beside his house in a way that would have made Capability Brown come out in heat lumps of jealousy.

As well as all this, he found time to wage ceaseless war on his neighbours. The farm family, appropriately named Corless, degenerate descendants of those long-departed entrepreneurs, had been happy to sell off the cottages around their crumbling old spread to butchers and bakers and candlestick makers from the city, even to senior policemen. What they hadn't been prepared to do was mend their ways. These were people to whom the word 'ecology' was just a seven letter swear word and 'environment' a worse one. It was their practice to let broken-down machines rust into the ground wherever they conked out. They allowed their foul-smelling dogs to roam as the fancy took them, and still seemed to have proprietorial feelings towards the various bits of land and gardens they'd sold off. Their hounds tried to improve the fertility of the area by endlessly crapping over lawns and terraces.

Perhaps the original idea was that they'd sicken the incomers by sheer slovenly mess. Then they might buy back the improved cottages for a song. If so, they hadn't bargained on Paddy Cunane.

Paddy had made himself the bane of their lives. Every time he drove down the narrow lane to his home he tried to run over one of the farm dogs that came barking up at the car. So far, his score was dogs – nil, crumpled wings – three, which hadn't improved the old goat's temper.

All this flashed through my mind with the vividness of a recurrent nightmare as I turned the car into the little port Paddy had developed outside his cottage.

'What's happened to your own car?' he demanded as soon as my foot trod on his ground. I could see him eyeing my passengers carefully.

'Slight accident,' I muttered, opening the door for Melanie. She passed me the sleeping Lloyd and then took him back as he began to wake.

'This is a bit above and beyond, even for you, Dave,' my parent said glumly, looking at the two disoriented children. A sheep behind the dry-stone wall that separated the Corless lands from the narrow lane let out an anguished bawl by way of reply. Knowing the Corless family, it was probably suffering from some dreadful untreated disease. As if on cue, both children started crying loudly. Jenny clutched me in fear as the sheep favoured her with a look.

'What do you mean?' I said angrily to Paddy.

'Oh stop it, you two,' my mother said sharply. 'Can't you see that you're frightening the children?' she bent down and offered Jenny the shelter of her arms. Jenny went to her and was led inside. Melanie followed with Lloyd. I was left face to face with Paddy.

'Well, what's the score?' he rapped out grumpily.

'I should think "The Hills are Alive with the Sound of Music" would be appropriate,' I said cheekily. The nearby sheep was working itself up into a frenzy.

'Don't be flippant, Dave. Are these two more of your by-blows? We've heard all about your efforts to put population decline into reverse. It was as much as I could do to stop your mother setting off to see that woman you're paying child support to.'

This came as a rather unpleasant surprise until I worked out that the lady in question's former employer was the Greater Manchester Police. Dear old Mr Sinclair must have lost no time in filling my father in about my little mishap when news of his forensic psychologist's pregnancy percolated round the Force.

'Look, Dad, they're not mine. Their mother's in hospital and I think she was beaten up by members of a cult that Sinclair's keen to learn more about . . . The girl might have information for him.'

'Oh, that puts a slightly different complexion on things, but where's the kids' father?'

'Apparently he's in Hollywood, USA, or some other remote spot where the Child Support Agency can't get at him.'

Paddy took this in gravely, examining me speculatively with his bright blue eyes. If Sinclair was a bird of prey, then being under Paddy's gaze was like being on the receiving end of a scanning electron microscope. I felt that he missed nothing. His features, which I'd inherited, were slightly more regular than my own. He could be an irritating pillock at times, but usually he knew when to stop. This looked like being one of his off days.

'Dave, lad,' he said wearily. 'Your heart's in the right place, but when are you going to stop falling for everyone and anyone who has a convincing sob-story and start looking after yourself? Your mother and I are getting no younger, and we'd both like to see some regular grandchildren of our own before we pop our clogs.'

'You weren't so happy when I married Elenki,' I muttered, disheartened to have the same old complaint thrown in my face again. 'As I remember it, you weren't too keen to have black or coffee-coloured grandchildren.'

Paddy's face darkened in anger. Then I could see him making a strenuous effort to restrain himself.

'That was more than ten years ago. Times were different then and anyway both Eileen and I would have come round to it. I'm sorry if I ever said anything out of turn. No one was more upset than me and your mother when that lovely girl died.'

'OK, spare me the violins,' I said ungraciously. What he said was true but it hadn't felt that way at the time. I didn't like raking over that episode in my life.

He shrugged his shoulders. 'I suppose what can't be cured must be endured,' he stated calmly enough. His constant resort to folksy proverbs was just one of the aspects of him that needled me. 'This girl, she's a pretty little thing. Are you sleeping with her?'

That was it. I felt my cheeks reddening. I ground my fingernails into the palms of my hands.

'If you must know, she's another refugee from cult violence and this is only the third time I've met her.'

'Sorry,' he said in a way that showed he wasn't sorry at all. 'She gave you such a warm smile when you let her out of the car. I was just speaking so as to warn you that you won't be sharing a bed with her under my roof.'

'Chill out, Mr Barrett of Wimpole Street,' I growled. 'I should think the poor girl was smiling because she feels safe for the first time in days and as for sleeping with me . . . Oh, bugger off!'

'You shouldn't be so touchy, lad,' he said, giving me a complacent smile. 'It's a compliment to you if the lass fancies you, but happen her wits are addled enough if she was one of these blasted Children of Light. Lord alone knows, Jock Sinclair's in a right state about what they're up to with this bloody rally they're planning. I think he should have arrested that Arkwright bugger when he had the chance instead of sucking up to him, but there you are. He was always a devious one, was Jock.'

I was grateful that he'd changed the topic of conversation to something that I could agree with . . . 'You don't know the half of it,' I said. 'Do you know that one of the sergeants who claimed to be investigating the Travis murder has a wife in the cult who's probably reporting everything straight back to Arkwright?'

I could see that Paddy was reluctant to hear any criticism of a serving officer from a civilian even if that civilian was his own son. There were times when I felt like dragging a stone out of the wall and bashing him on the head with it.

'Just because she's in the C of L, it doesn't mean she's told them anything,' he said grudgingly. 'You shouldn't go leaping to conclusions.'

'Yes, I should,' I bellowed. 'I have documentary evidence that she was relaying information that only her husband could have supplied her with.'

I told him about the break-in and the message pad and the computer discs. He gave me a crooked grin. 'Maybe you are a chip off the old block after all, Dave. Come in before you freeze,' he invited genially.

I was met by the familiar smell of my mother's baking. It almost made me wish that I was ten years old again and living under their roof. Then I shuddered as I recollected what life with Paddy had been like. It hadn't all been up hill and down dale. Perhaps there'd even been slightly more ups than downs if I was honest, but the downs had been bad enough to make me anxious never to repeat the experience.

'Come in, Dave, and sit down,' Eileen said, beckoning me to join her at the large kitchen table which had been re-erected in the living-room, making the whole place look much smaller. She noticed me observing the arrangements.

'He won't stop, you know. I told him that the old tiles weren't worn. He only laid them three years ago. Now we're all in here until he grouts the new ones.'

'When has he ever stopped grouting?' I asked.

She gave a sympathetic, if slightly wan, smile. 'I'm just getting to know Lloyd and Jenny and Melanie,' she said. A huge mound of sandwiches occupied the centre of the table. Jennie was sitting up at the table eating a ham sandwich. There was a box on her chair so that she could reach. Melanie still had Lloyd with her. She was feeding him spaghetti hoops from a bowl. All three of them seemed to have begun to thaw out. The children were chattering to each other, at least, rather than howling.

Paddy and I joined the party. To his credit, Paddy did his best to amuse Jenny with all sorts of stories and little jokes, some of which rang a chord in the dim recesses of my own memory. As I warmed up, I remembered the happier occasions of my childhood. It certainly hadn't all been bad. It was only after my eccentric career choice that the most grinding friction had occurred. Jenny seemed to be taken with his silly jokes and snatches of song, which were just about on her level. The baby boy watched his sister and had a sort of guarded look of amusement on his little face. Perhaps I had been wrong to deny my aged parents grandchildren, legitimate ones anyway, but who can judge these things?

We finished the meal with one of Eileen's apple pies and for the first time in a week I began to relax. After the meal Eileen set about organizing the sleeping arrangements. It was assumed that we were all stopping. You couldn't fault either Paddy or Eileen for generosity in a crisis. I knew that despite all my resentment at his irritating ways Paddy wouldn't have turned me away from his door when I needed him.

I settled into a comfortable chair beside the large stone-built fireplace which Paddy had 'improved' by re-opening the original eighteenth-century inglenook which had been bricked up. Although I'd resolved to keep awake, the day had taken its toll. I fell asleep.

When I came to someone had covered me with a blanket. I'd been wakened by my mother. She was walking up and down gently crooning to herself. The room was darkened and it took me a moment to realize that the bundle on her shoulder was Lloyd. She noticed that I was awake and came over.

'I used to do this for you often enough, Dave,' she said with a smile. 'He's just got a touch of wind. He'll drop off again in a minute. That girl Melanie is utterly exhausted. I don't know what you've been up to, Dave, but despite your odd little ways I like it when you drop in on us unexpectedly. It makes me feel young again.'

Without waiting for a reply, she set off on another circuit of the room, stroking and patting the child and gently singing to him.

'I wish you wouldn't quarrel so fiercely with your father,' she said softly when she passed me again. 'He gets very anxious for you. He knows only too well what some of these criminals are capable of and you've not got the protection of the Force behind you.'

'No, the Force isn't with me,' I quipped.

'There you go,' she said, shifting the infant from one shoulder to the other. 'You know, you two are so alike, it's no wonder that you quarrel.'

'I haven't felt any desire to rebuild Thornleigh Court,' I said.

'From what I hear, your tendencies there are in the other direction. It was in the paper about the fire, you know.'

'Oh,' I murmured.

'Dave, do you care for this baby's mother?' she asked unexpectedly. 'I think you must do or you'd have found some other solution for these poor children, but promise me that they won't be hurt any more than they already have been. It took me hours to get little Jenny to sleep.'

'It isn't like that, mother,' I said.

'Well just you make sure that they're all treated right or I shan't be putting apple pies in front of you again, David Cunane.'

I got a few more hours' sleep before dawn and the next person to wake me was Paddy. He always got up early, it was a holdover from his days in the Army. Born in 1926, he'd just been in time to see action in the Second World War. 'From the Belgian border to Luneburg heath' was how he described his campaigning days in the infantry. Watching him stride towards the kitchen to examine his tiles, you wouldn't have taken him for a man who'd passed his seventieth year. There was a youthfulness and firmness in the way he moved that was quite intimidating. He clattered around in the kitchen for a few minutes before coming out and putting a mug of tea into my hands.

'If you're wanting to stay again tonight I'll have the back bedroom ready for you,' he said in a matter-of-fact way. 'I wasn't expecting to have this tribe descend on me, but if I put the spare bed in there you can have that rather than sleeping in this chair.'

'Don't worry, Dad. The chair was fine,' I said, getting up and stretching. I felt as if I'd spent the night being passed back and forward through an old fashioned clothes-mangle.

'Right then, you'd better tell me what the hell's been going on, and I don't want the edited version either.'

'Look Dad, you know I can't tell you everything. There are one or two details where . . .'

'. . . the law's been honoured more in the breach than the observance thereof. Dave, lad, don't try to teach your grandmother to suck eggs.'

'But Sinclair . . .'

'Won't get to hear more than is good for him. You don't think I'd shop my own son, do you?'

'Well, actually . . .'

'You haven't murdered anyone, have you?'

I shook my head.

'Was it just your usual tricks of poking and prying and putting yourself where you weren't supposed to be?'

'There was a little bit more . . . I've helped Bob Lane to get his brother out of the country.'

Paddy looked at me gravely for a moment.

'What have I told you about your heart being bigger than your head? You'll end up doing time one of these days. Tell me the whole story and without any of your old varnish, either.'

I spoke for the best part of an hour with Paddy asking the occasional question and nodding sagely from time to time.

'Dave, lad, you do get yourself into it . . . I suppose the next thing we'll be hearing is that this feminist sergeant has arrested you for assaulting Ms White?'

'I don't think so.'

'That's because you never expect the unexpected. Your best way out of all this is to get the White woman to make a formal complaint in which she identifies Polk and Tyler as the men who assaulted her. Once they're in custody you can be sure that Jock will want to know every little detail about how they just happened to come across Fred Travis with his throat cut. You're lucky there's two of them. I don't think it'll take Jock long to persuade one that it'd be in his best interest to shop the other. Then you'll be in the clear about helping Lane.'

'That simple, is it?'

'Bitter experience has taught me that nothing's simple where you're concerned, Dave, but persuading this woman to get those scum banged up shouldn't be too difficult, even for you.'

He gave me a rather crooked smile that didn't suit him.

'Come on, Dave, a lad with your ability at charming the ladies shouldn't find this too hard. Get yourself to the hospital and take her a bunch of flowers. Your mum and me will keep these kiddies and Miss Melanie safe until you get things sorted.'

I could hear the children stirring upstairs even as he spoke.

'What if the cult has traced me to here? Arkwright knows you're my father. He even mentioned your reputation when he was trying to flatter me into working for him.'

'Dave, have I shown you my new shotgun?' Paddy said genially. 'I got it to keep the rabbits down, and between you, me and the gatepost I've still got that old Webley & Scott mark VI revolver with plenty of ammo.'

I raised my eyebrows in mock surprise. Actually, the surprise would be if a shotgun and an illegal war souvenir comprised the full extent of the old guy's arsenal. He'd served with Special Branch as a volunteer during the Cyprus Emergency in the 1950s and it would be a very clever Child of Light who succeeded where EOKA had failed and managed to creep up behind him. He had the happy look of a man who has a mission that he likes.

I could only shrug and wish I felt the same.

'While we may raise £100,000 in a nationwide collection the main source of our funds, as that of most other charitable bodies, is the money people leave us in their wills. We have to keep the possibility of a charitable bequest fresh in the minds of the public. When is it better to remind them than in the hour of grief?'

Professional fundraiser explaining an advert in the undertaker's magazine *Grave News* to the Charity Commissioners

17

Monday, 26 October

I drove up the narrow lane between the dry-stone walls and took the road to Manchester. It was with an odd feeling of *déjà vu* that I took my departure from the rural scene. My mother had insisted that I 'get a good breakfast down me' and I felt like a schoolboy again. However she didn't insist on inspecting the back of my neck for tidemarks and I was quickly away from the order and neatness that my father had wrought and into the rustic squalor of the hillbilly farm. As I drove past the yapping Corless dogs I was reminded of the constant moans about the 'inner city' and its alleged deprivation. I caught a glimpse of one of the older Corless males staggering towards his milking parlour. His unshaven jaw was open and I'd be prepared to testify in any court in the land that the man was actually drooling; not that anyone would believe me. Everyone knows that slums and slum-dwellers are features of our cities and not of our lovely English countryside.

It didn't take me too long to thread my way through Bolton but I hit the slows when I reached the M61. I found myself crawling over the Barton Bridge. Listening to Terry Wogan's amusing inanities perched two hundred feet above the Ship Canal, while the odours from the Davyhulme sewage farm wafted over me, is not my idea of the best way to spend a

Monday morning. The fine bright weather of the last few days continued to hold. From the top of the bridge I could see miles in all directions.

'You mustn't tire her,' the ward sister insisted when I took my place at Janine's bedside. 'Her condition's still extremely serious. She'll be on anti-coagulants for days.' There was already a bunch of flowers in a vase on the table beside her and I looked around for somewhere to put mine. I was embarrassed really. I was here under false pretences. The ward staff thought that I was Janine's partner and now that they, at least, believed that the journalist wasn't a victim of domestic violence they were prepared to put out the welcome mat for me.

'We're still very shaky, aren't we, my dear?' the sister said to Janine in that caring but mildly condescending tone that seems to be unavoidable in the nurse–patient relationship. Turning to me, she said, 'Janine's had a good night and as you can see we've taken the I/V drip away but it'll be several more days before you can take her home with you. Doctor's still a bit concerned that there might be fluid on the brain. These things take a few days to settle back to normal even when you're as fit and strong as Janine.'

We both looked at the patient. She was propped up by at least six pillows and while it was still frightening to look at her face at least she didn't look on the point of imminent death as she had done on Saturday. The purple bruises were less livid.

'The children?' Janine said, extending her hand to me.

'They're safe and well, they're with . . .' then I looked at the smiling ward sister. Was it conceivable that she was a member of the Children of Light . . .? It was. 'They're being looked after,' I said.

Janine began to cry.

'Come with me and I'll get you a vase,' the sister ordered, whether to cover her embarrassment or mine I couldn't say. She led me to the small room near the ward station where I'd been interviewed. It seemed as if I'd never left it.

'Come in and take a seat,' she said. 'Janine's very tearful

and easily upset at the moment. We often find this with victims of serious violence, of course. It'll take her a while to get back to normal emotionally, but I should tell you that the doctors are quite concerned. She's had a CAT scan, and they think there may be a clot on the brain. Now if she stays here very quietly for the next few days and continues with the medication we're giving her there's every chance that it will dissolve and go away of its own accord. She's young and she was fit before someone did this awful thing to her. You should be prepared, though. We may have to operate and I'm afraid that there's a very high risk . . . It's deep in the basal layer. She's been asking about the children and she seems anxious. If she's going to pull through you'll have to calm her and do whatever she wants . . . or at least, give her that impression.'

'Why haven't you told her?'

'She's very stressed about the children.'

'They're with my parents,' I said hurriedly.

'Good. Well, Doctor thought it might be better if you found an opportunity to break it to her gently. It'll be some time before she goes home.'

Having delivered this message, the sister pressed a cut-glass vase into my hands and briskly went on her way. Life and death were routine to her, but not yet to me.

Back at the bedside it was my turn to be anxious. I put water in the vase and arranged the flowers as best I could. They'd put a sort of cap on Janine's head and she looked like an illustration of Whistler's mother. I tried to smile and look reassuring.

'Dave, whatever they've told you, don't look at me like that. You're frightening me,' she said with a smile. 'They won't let me move out of this bed or see a paper so I know that everything's not quite as rosy as they'd like me to think. Where have you left my children?'

'They're in a large comfortable cottage with my parents and Melanie. It's quite a long way from here and I don't think I should give you the exact address but they're quite safe.'

'Is your father also a private detective?' she asked.

'I don't think he'd be pleased to hear himself described as

that,' I laughed. 'He's one of the country's leading experts on personal security, a retired high-ranking copper. One of his last jobs for the police was in Northern Ireland. He led an inquiry into security leaks in the RUC which had led to several informers being killed. If anyone's aware of the need for discretion, it's him. I don't think you could find a safer place for Jenny and Lloyd in the whole country.'

Janine lay back and seemed to relax. Then some thought disturbed her. 'Dave, you don't mind if the nurses get the wrong impression about us, do you? I know I'm the last woman on earth that you'd look at. You must think I'm so stupid . . .'

'I don't care what they think as long as it helps you.'

'Proper old-fashioned hero, aren't you?'

'Not really, I can run quite quickly when I have to.'

'I had to give that nosy almoner the impression that you're the father of Lloyd and Jenny. It seemed the easiest thing to do. She was fussing about getting the Social Services in Twickenham to take them into care . . . It's only until I'm well.'

I felt an involuntary movement in my throat as my Adam's apple bobbed up and down like a yo-yo. 'No, no . . . that's all right,' I said, perhaps a little more weakly than my previous protestation. I looked at her, trying to remove any trace of nervousness from my expression. This was a woman I'd known for not much more than a week and already I was being saddled with a family. If I wasn't careful the Child Support Agency would soon be nominating me as Renegade Dad of the Year.

She smiled. 'I'll be out of here soon,' she said confidently.

'Right, just concentrate on getting better,' I advised. Then, guiltily, I remembered my father's instructions. 'Janine, has it crossed your mind that the best way to make everything safe and sound is to give a statement to the police identifying the men who attacked you?'

As soon as the words were out of my mouth I knew it was a mistake. Janine shuddered. I looked round for a nurse, more frightened about what might happen to her than concerned about personal liability. Her colour seemed to have gone several shades lighter. I hardly dared to breathe.

'Dave, do you see those flowers?' she said eventually.

I nodded. The bunch at her bedside was considerably larger and more expensive than those I'd brought.

'Read the note that came with them.'

I did as I was told.

Dear Janine,
Get well soon. We're thinking about you and we're specially thinking about poor little Jenny and Lloyd. They must be missing their mom. Make sure you look after yourself and don't do too much chattering. We're looking forward to seeing you and young Melanie up here again as soon as you're well.
  Love from your friends in Meldrum Terrace.
  XX

The writing was done in black ink in an old-fashioned copperplate script. I felt sick but struggled not to give away my feelings. I put the note in my pocket.

'They're as good as telling me to keep my mouth shut, aren't they?'

'It looks that way,' I said laconically.

'My mum phoned me about what happened at the McDonald's in Twickenham . . .'

'She's a quick-witted woman. Was she all right?'

'Mum's indestructible but those creeps were released almost as soon as they were taken to the police station. What do you make of that?'

I shrugged my shoulders. I didn't know what to make of it, except that there were plenty of names from the London area on the computer list that I'd supplied to Sinclair.

'We've got to do something. I can't just sit around waiting for the axe to fall,' I said incautiously.

'I think it's me that's having to wait for that,' Janine said grimly. 'This all started with Melanie. She found my address from the *Guardian* and I was following up something she said . . .'

'What?'

'She doesn't think her father died from natural causes, although the coroner put the death down to heart failure. She says he was a healthy outdoor type who lived for golf.'

I was spared further paranoid thoughts by the arrival of the ward sister.

'I think you ought to go now, Mr Cunane. You can come back tonight but I think Janine needs her rest,' she said, looking at me meaningfully. 'We don't want to have to sedate her, do we?'

'Who brought these flowers?' I asked casually.

'Oh, it was a skinny black man. Janine was asleep and he said he wouldn't disturb her, so he left them and went.'

'Had he a thin face, granny glasses and a little round, leather hat?'

'That's him. Is he a friend of yours and Janine's?'

'You could say that,' I commented with a smile.

Everald Mallick was in when I arrived at his home. This time he made no attempt to evade me. He seemed to have lapsed into some sort of suicidal fatalism.

'I been expecting you, man,' he said glumly. He seemed tensed for a blow.

'What's with the flowers? I thought you hated these cult people but now you're acting like Interflora for them.'

'Oh God, man! That Rufus told me he was going to kill my kid unless I did exactly what I was told.'

'So you'll be on the phone to him as soon as I'm out of the house?'

'You don't understand, Cunane. They want to frighten you. They know where you live anyway.'

'Was it you set my garage on fire?'

'I had no choice.'

'You had a choice about setting Janine up.'

'You don't know what these cults are like. My cousin got involved with those Branch Dravidians over in Waco, Texas. He was lucky to escape with his life. There was a lot of people from round here didn't.'

'Davidians,' I said.

'Yeah, Dravidians,' he agreed.

'You'll tell all this to the police, will you? Like the concerned member of Cultwatch that you are?'

'Man, Cultwatch was mainly me. These boys don't play by the same rules they got down at the *Guardian* newspaper. They're real heavy. They'd squash me like a bug if they thought I was a threat to them.'

I looked at him and realized that I was wasting my time. He was expecting me to beat him up so I decided to disappoint him and left.

Angst isn't my scene. I like to be up and doing, but I must have been dazed because when I set off from Hulme I drove into town and was on the point of leaving the car near where the Atwood Building had once stood before I remembered that I no longer had an office. I felt as if each of my problems – the C of L, the Lanes, Janine – was a rat sealed in its own separate crevice in my skull. Each was gnawing and squeaking and squealing its way through the fabric of my brain.

When I found myself where I didn't want to be, I turned the car round and headed back to the leafy suburb of Chorlton like a starving orphan reaching for a comfort blanket. Even there, things were bad. Recent events had left their scars. Sharp-edged black shadows were everywhere.

The only sign of activity when I got to Thornleigh Court was a builder's skip occupying part of the parking area. Tarpaulin had been lashed over the side of the building that had been seared by the petrol flames. I collected my mail and went up to the flat. The place seemed bleaker without the expectation that Finbar might come scuttling in, frothing with demands for employment. It was as if someone had turned down the intensity of light. I looked across towards the Meadows for reassurance that the prevailing dimness was something internal, peculiar to my mood. There, the harsh, bright oblique sunlight of northern winter was highlighting each manmade defect – a broken wall, ugly graffiti, branches ripped off ornamental trees, drifts of windblown debris at the base of hedges. Trees were shaking in the breeze, leaves and empty crisp packets skittering along the pavements.

If all trace of human existence could have been wiped away I knew that nature's alternative was hardly less bleak. The natural winter scenery of this area was grim; the stuff of dark legends – sombre bare branches of shrunken trees, yellowing wind-whipped sedge set amid unpleasantly green swamp grass – home to boggarts and jack o'lanterns. This place was never a paradise.

There must be softer, cleaner places to live. Places where the people didn't feel the need to decorate the streets with fast-food wrappings and broken beer bottles. Places where disorder and violence weren't always simmering just below the surface. I had to face it, though, I'd go mad from boredom in a month if I settled in Berne or Bournemouth or Buxton. It wasn't just the people who tied me here. As I looked out of the window of my flat the light was constantly changing as angry clouds, bilious with rain, were rapidly driven across the sky. I was part of the scene here. I could no more uproot myself and clear off than the trees or the river bed could. I was stuck and I had to find a way out.

I was getting gloomy enough to bash my head into the wall when the phone rang. I picked it up expecting to hear from my esteemed parent, but it was the Ford main dealer to say that my new car was ready to be collected. A wave of relief washed over me. Something positive was happening. I took the stairs three at a time. I was behind the wheel of the Escort and heading for Chester Road almost before my caller had finished speaking. It was great to be doing something.

When I got to the showroom I spent a pleasant half-hour having the various technicalities explained to me then I found myself on the road in a new car with a full tank of petrol. The open road beckoned. Somehow those serried ranks of heavy goods vehicles weren't so menacing when I could sail past with a touch on the accelerator. I was almost half-way to Birmingham before I allowed myself to think about what I was doing. Janine believed that her little 'accident' was due to her enquiries about Melanie's father. She must have trodden on an exposed nerve. The Children of Light, or at least the enforcement division – Polk and Tyler – must have something they wished to hide . . . something relating to the unexplained deaths of Irvine Varley and Monica Withers and, yes, Fred Travis, because I didn't accept the police explanation for that, did I?

Mrs Varley must have some of the answers if only I knew what the right questions were. The drive from the M6 to her home in Oundle took much longer than I expected: there were immense jams on the A6 – Watling Street approaching Walsall and Tamworth. Ghosts of Roman legionaries marching along the old imperial main road could have forged ahead of the crawling traffic, but if there were any ghosts present they stayed stubbornly inside my head. After I reached Oundle with its neat stone houses it took me some time to retrace my route to the house where I'd dropped Melanie so casually just over a week previously. It was mid afternoon before I arrived at the end of the lane leading to the house.

I took my time and as I was rounding a bend a car passed me going in the opposite direction. It was something small and red, a Fiesta or a Metro. I caught the driver's eye for a brief instant just long enough for a flash of recognition to explode in my brain. It was Shannon Withers. I slammed to a halt on the verge and looked up the road after her but she was gone. For a moment I almost thought paranoia was taking over. How could it be her? But it was her, I wasn't so far gone as to mistake a woman I'd seen only last week and one moreover who looked very like her sister. She had that same air of efficiency and of leaning forward to press on with the job in hand, just like Monica. I knew for a certainty that she'd seen and recognized me just as much as I had her.

I drove on very slowly towards Mrs Varley's house. I stopped the car on the main road and looked over the hedge towards the house. A fairly new neo-Georgian construction, it had everything that Everald Mallick's home lacked to lend it authenticity. It stood in at least an acre of its own grounds with a spacious lawn and wide carriage drive to the pillared front door. Even the pale off-white paint used for the windows and doors looked like a genuine early nineteenth-century shade. Only the unweathered red tiles of the roof jarred and weakened the historical illusion. Sitting on the gravel drive, there were two more intrusions from the twentieth century – an ambulance and a medium-sized furniture van. Two men were loading chairs and boxes into the van. I reversed my car up the road and pulled it into a side lane and then went forward again on foot.

There was a field with a hedge that would have given me the chance to approach the house under cover but I wasn't dressed for prowling about in the undergrowth. I was wearing a Hugo Boss navy blue business suit and black shoes. After hesitating a moment at the entrance to the drive I decided to just walk up to the house and ring the door bell. The ambulance and van might be there for perfectly legitimate reasons. It was only seeing Shannon Withers that had inflamed my ever-suspicious mind. On the other hand if you prowl about in the footsteps of murderers there's a chance that you'll come across them on the job, as it were.

I managed to get half-way along the drive without being seen, as the two men had their backs to me. They looked like perfectly normal removal men, clad in jeans and sweaters with long brown aprons. I hadn't come across either of them before, certainly not at Meldrum Terrace. At that point, though, my courage failed me, or common sense kicked in; whichever explanation seems most plausible. You have to trust your instincts. If there were people going round killing by undetectable methods they wouldn't have flashing signs on their heads saying 'murderer'. As the pair of workers returned to the main door, I dodged to the side and dashed across the lawn to the side of the house. I took out my mobile and keyed in my parents' number. There was no reply. Wherever she was, Melanie was unavailable to confirm whether her mother was moving out or not.

I crept round the back of the house. Everything looked normal from the outside. Then I spotted something that definitely wasn't kosher. The wires on the telephone fixture running from the back of the house had been cut.

I phoned the police . . . 'There seems to be a robbery in progress, they've got a van at the front door and they're loading the woman's furniture . . .' I reported breathlessly. The female officer I was speaking to seemed to be determined to deny that such things happened in Northamptonshire.

'Are you sure that Mrs Varley isn't supposed to be moving?'

'Of course she isn't. Is it normal to cut the phone lines before you move? Check, call her yourself.'

'She could still be moving. There might have been a change of phone company.'

'Don't you think she'd have mentioned it to her daughter if she was intending to do a flit? I saw her daughter yesterday and she knew nothing about a move,' I stated with a confidence I didn't feel.

'Well, it'll be at least ten to fifteen minutes before we can have a car with you . . .'

'OK, one of the delights of country living, I suppose,' I said, breaking the connection.

Keeping clear of the windows, I scrambled towards the hedge. The business suit would have to take care of itself, I remember thinking as I clawed my way between the hawthorns. Running to the road, squelching through cowpats, I managed to reach the car without being detected. I looked over my shoulder. The two furniture shifters were coming out with another load. They didn't seem to be in any particular hurry.

Composing myself, I drove into the carriage drive and parked bumper to bumper against the ambulance. Jumping out and boldly striding forward, I took a look inside it. It was empty. The two workmen put down their load, a large chest of drawers, on the gravel and started towards me but I was on the front doorstep ahead of them.

'Excuse me,' one of them shouted. 'You can't go in there. There's no one in the house.'

I ignored him, rapped on the door and entered. One of the men laid a hand on my arm.

'You can't go in there,' he repeated, in a Birmingham accent. He was a tall, thin young man with a prominent Adam's apple protruding from his spotty neck and a shock of uncombed blond hair hanging over his face.

'Oh yes, I can,' I said, twisting free from his grip. 'I'm Mrs Varley's doctor.' I waved my mobile in his face. 'Nobody's told me that she's to be taken for any treatment. What's the ambulance here for?'

'Sorry mate, they mustn't have told you but she's been

booked into a private residential clinic. We're moving her and her stuff.'

I continued into the house with the two men trailing behind me. There was a sound of raised female voices from behind a pair of doors. I opened them with a flourish. A wild-eyed woman of about sixty, whom I took to be Mrs Varley, was being strapped into a wheelchair. Her hair was in rollers.

'What's going on?' I snapped. 'I'm this woman's doctor.'

Mrs Varley gaped at me, open-mouthed. She was white faced and seemed to be in shock.

'You've no business here, Doctor. We're from Social Services and we've been authorized to move this woman into sheltered accommodation for her own good,' one of the three young women attending to Mrs Varley said smoothly. None of the three was wearing any kind of uniform or ID. They were fastening straps round Mrs Varley's legs. They'd already attended to her shoulders and waist. She was trussed up like a turkey ready for basting.

'When was this arranged?' I demanded. I went forward and bent down in front of Mrs Varley and took her wrist as if to check her pulse. 'This woman's in shock. She needs to be in bed.'

Mrs Varley wasn't so far gone that she couldn't speak.

'Don't let them take me, Doctor. I don't want to go in a home,' she wailed.

I pushed forward and brushed the woman holding the chair aside. This produced a reaction. The three women began struggling with me to keep hold of the handles of the chair. My elbows were harder than theirs and I shoved them to one side.

'She's coming with us,' one of them shrieked, sinking her fingernails into the back of my hand. I propelled Mrs Varley forwards towards a corner and let her go. I turned round and pushed the female who'd scratched me, a dark-haired short woman in her early twenties.

'Look what you've done,' I shouted, displaying the bloody evidence. 'I demand to see your identity cards.'

'And what about you?' the tall youth who'd challenged me at the door shouted back.

'Mrs Varley's already identified me,' I said. 'I'm her doctor.' This seemed to flummox them. I could see that they'd not been expecting any opposition to their plan. All five now retreated to the double doors, blocking any chance of a quick exit even if I could have moved Mrs Varley. They'd cleared the room of most of its furniture, apart from the phone which sat on a low table in the corner.

I stood in front of Mrs Varley while the five held a quick huddled conference.

'Listen, Doctor,' the tall man said in a conciliatory tone. 'This is just a mix up. Why don't you phone Northampton Social Services?' he suggested, indicating the phone in the corner and proffering a scrap of paper. 'They're on this number. The director will sort out any problems you may have.' He detached himself from the group and came forward as if to usher me to the phone and at the same time separate me from Mrs Varley. I took a stride in the direction of the phone with him just behind me, then I swung my elbow round with all my strength and caught him in the face. He went down with a groan. As expected, the other four had moved forward to pounce on Mrs Varley. I intercepted them and we all ended up on the floor in a tangled struggle.

I clung on to the wheelchair with one arm while trying to defend myself with the other.

'There goes Hugo,' I thought as I felt and heard the right sleeve of my jacket part company with the rest of my ensemble. Two of the women were trying to bind my legs with one of the same fabric belts with which they'd lashed up poor Mrs Varley. I was kicking and cursing, trying to punch the woman who was attempting to smother me by pushing her ample rear into my face. The second furniture man was trying to pinion my free arm. The man I'd thumped was on the point of jumping on top of me. He had rather a nasty expression on his face, and blood was pouring from his nose.

Instead of jumping, he paused. 'Oh, fucking hell!' he muttered. 'You tosser!' In the distance I could hear the wail of police sirens.

It was over in seconds. All five were out of the house and into their vehicles. I followed, slightly winded by the contact with the counterfeit social worker's ample derriere. Her butt end was anything but bogus. I felt as if an elephant had mistaken me for a trampoline. When I reached the door, I was just in time to see the ambulance scrape along the side of my new car. Then the furniture van cut a deep swathe into the gravel and departed with Mrs Varley's furniture and clothing spewing out of the back. I went in to undo the intended victim. The police arrived as I was fumbling with the straps.

There followed one of those frustrating episodes which seem to happen to me so often but perhaps are just the natural hazards of my profession... I had to repeat the story to officer after officer, climbing up through the ranks, until a sharp-eyed detective chief inspector arrived. His name was Ritchie. Tall, and immaculately dressed in what looked like a Savile Row suit in a rather nice worsted material, with a thin face and receding brown hair neatly combed across a prominent forehead, he didn't look the sort who let much get past him. My rendition of the story wasn't improved by the fact that Mrs Varley insisted on clinging to me and referring to me as 'Doctor' despite all attempts on my part to explain that my use of the medical handle was just a ruse. I couldn't blame the police for finding it hard to understand why I'd turned up in the way I had. I'd no intention of telling them all the goings-on of the last few days but long experience has taught me that any attempt to cover up the fact that I'm a private investigator always rouses intense suspicion in the 'official' detective service.

'Look, Mr Ritchie, I was with Melanie yesterday. I just happened to call on her mother...'

'... just at the moment that someone else apparently decides to kidnap her,' Ritchie said, completing the sentence for me. 'You are aware, aren't you, *Mr* Cunane, that Mrs Varley is a very wealthy woman indeed?'

'Are you saying I was trying to help those people? Look at the state of me... they've ripped a five hundred quid suit off my back and wrecked my car.'

He looked at me very closely as if inspecting a strange new breed of bug that had swum into his soup. 'I do read the papers, Mr Cunane. I have heard about your remarkable efforts at . . . how did they describe it . . . "heiress snatching"? should imagine you got paid more for that little jaunt than I get in two years.'

'That was rubbish!' I said fiercely. 'The article was completely untrue.'

Ritchie merely gave a knowing smile.

'And now you've come to collect your payment, and who knows what else? Did you get a little greedy and decide that there was more to be gained by staging this mock kidnapping than there was from your heiress?'

'I didn't help Miss Varley for money . . .' I said indignantly, realizing that I was miring myself deeper with every word.

'Perhaps, then, all the more reason why you should be involved in these curious events. There have been stranger confidence tricks, and meanwhile, until Miss Varley can be reached to vouch for you, you'll have to stay here,' he said in a tone of deep satisfaction.

I could hardly blame him. Everybody knows that what they print in the papers must be true.

A curious feature of this incident was that Mrs Varley continued to smile warmly at me throughout. She obviously didn't read the papers and had no idea what Ritchie was talking about. When Ritchie had finished with me she came over and asked me to prescribe something for her nerves.

Ritchie left, 'to pursue his enquiries', shaking his head.

After many agonizing delays and further bouts of close questioning, my story of an off-chance visit was more or less accepted but it only raised further questions in Ritchie's mind.

'Do you know that a national newspaper asked us to trace Miss Varley last week?' he asked.

'The *Guardian*, wasn't it?' I asked.

'Look, are you going to tell me what's been going on?' he asked wearily.

'I wish I knew that myself,' I said in an equally exhausted tone.

'Miss Varley now turns up, and she's staying with your

parents. Surprise, surprise! As your father's a widely respected former policeman whom we've even heard of here in the backwoods of Northamptonshire, I suppose I've got to go along with your story but I want to get to the bottom of this.'

Meanwhile Mrs Varley's own doctor had arrived and he'd prescribed bed rest for his patient. I was facing Ritchie in the other downstairs reception room, as I supposed it was called in estate agent's parlance. My whole flat would have fitted comfortably into a corner in either room. There was a curious sort of hospital smell of strong disinfectant about the place. I wrinkled my nose to try and identify it and I caught Ritchie doing the same.

'She's a very odd lady is Mrs Varley,' he said, 'in case you don't already know. She and her late husband Irvine used to occupy separate wings of the house. This is Mrs Varley's drawing-room. You see those holes in the windows?'

He pointed to three circular holes which had been cut into the glass in three of the large casement windows and covered with removable perspex discs.

'She feeds the birds through those.'

I went over for a look. Sure enough, the window-sills and paved areas outside each casement were encrusted with birdseed.

'They aren't the only thing she feeds. This place is overrun with mice and rodents. I don't know how the late Irvine managed to stick it.'

At this point a uniformed constable came in. His radio was on and it was loud enough to echo round the room. Neither he, nor Ritchie, seemed to be aware of this or pay the slightest heed to the messages floating on the ether.

'We've found the van and the ambulance sir,' he announced. 'They're on a disused airfield about five miles away. A local farmer saw the suspects escaping in a helicopter. Headquarters is trying to contact Air Traffic Control and the RAF to get some idea of where it went but the witness says it was flying low and in a northerly direction.'

'What about the vehicles, where were they from?' I interjected.

The constable looked at his superior who inclined his head almost imperceptibly.

'Stolen at the weekend near Cambridge,' he said.

'Well, you seem to have foiled a well-planned attempt,' Ritchie said as soon as the uniformed man had left the room. 'But I can't let you go until I'm satisfied.'

'Where, though?' I asked. 'Where am I supposed to stay?'

'Either here or in a cell at Oundle police station. There are a number of things I still need to check.' The glint in his eye told me that it was pointless to argue. Having delivered his decision, he left. I wasn't exactly alone. I could hear numerous officers outside, and vehicles coming and going. I decided to test the waters.

I walked out of the room and went out to examine my car. Almost immediately I was collared by a uniformed WPC.

'It's all right. I'm not making a break for it,' I told her. 'I'm just checking my car.'

'Made a right mess of it, haven't they?' she said in a not particularly sad tone of voice.

I grunted agreement. Actually it wasn't as bad as I'd expected. There were two deep parallel scratches down one side but the lights weren't smashed and the door still worked. I checked it with the WPC at my heels, poised to restrain me. I needed time to think. Everything was getting out of hand. A mad drive back to Manchester with half the police in the East Midlands in hot pursuit wouldn't do me, or anyone else, any good, I decided. I slammed the door shut.

I looked back at the house. Mrs Varley was in the doorway beckoning to me. She was wearing a purple silk dressing gown. Her hair was still in rollers.

'Do come in, Doctor, I haven't had the chance to thank you,' she gushed.

'I only said I was a doctor so I could have an excuse to come in,' I told her for what must have been the twelfth time.

'I know that, but I prefer to think of you as a doctor,' she said calmly. 'Do come in and tell me all about what my naughty girl's been up to.' She extended her arm and when I took it she firmly clamped me to her side and led me back into her drawing-room.

I was offered sherry and a small piece of cake. My stomach rumbled to remind me that I hadn't eaten since breakfast.

'So lucky you turning up,' she warbled.

'I didn't just turn up, Mrs Varley . . .'

'Oh do call me Jean, Doctor. I feel as if I've known you all my life.'

I looked at her carefully. She wasn't trying to take the mick, or anything. As Ritchie had said, she wasn't playing with a full deck.

'OK, Jean,' I said after a deep breath, 'you know a week on Saturday I left your daughter in the drive of this house?'

She nodded.

'. . .yet you told the police that you hadn't seen her. Why was that?'

'She's such a naughty girl is my Melanie. I expect she slept in the summer-house round the back.'

'You're saying you never saw her at all?' I asked incredulously.

'That's right. Melanie has plenty of friends round here, perhaps she stayed with one of them, or maybe she was out scouring the fields for fungi. That's one of her obsessions.'

'What?'

'Since she joined these Children of Light she's spent a lot of time researching fungi.'

'Why?'

'It's one of the things they do. Didn't you know that?' she said with a bemused look.

I shook my head. This interview was getting nowhere fast.

'So you don't get on with Melanie?' I probed.

'Not since before the Dad died, Doctor. She hates animals does Melanie.'

On cue there was a rapping on the window. A pigeon was perched on the window-sill peering into the room. Jean Varley stood up and went over. She took a packet out of a drawer, slid back the perspex covers and began pouring seed out of her windows. Almost instantly a whole flock of pigeons descended.

'Do you love birds, Doctor?' she asked over her shoulder.

'Oh yes,' I said quickly. 'I was bird-watching only this

weekend. I saw a lovely pair of cormorants on the banks of the Mersey in Manchester.'

This got her full attention. She turned and gave me a warm smile.

I knew you'd be a friend to animals, Doctor. You've such a kind face.' She came away from the frenzied pigeons and settled into the armchair opposite me.

'The Dad was very upset when she ran off to join those people . . . the Children of Light. He kept trying to get in touch with her but they wouldn't let him speak to her. She was the apple of his eye, was Melanie. She never got on well with me, a difficult girl. You know she says I'm a hypochondriac, Doctor?'

I nodded my head and glanced at the sideboard which was piled with enough medication to stock a small pharmacy.

'Oh, that!' she said. 'I get the medicine I'm entitled to but I never use it.'

I must have looked rather sceptical at this.

'It's true, Doctor,' she said. 'Look . . . all unopened.' She swept up several packets and displayed them to me. 'The National Health doctor came with a little yellow sack last year and collected up all my medicines.'

'Why do you get them?' I asked, genuinely interested.

'I like going to the surgery a couple of times a week. It gives me something to do,' she admitted with a wistful sigh.

'Was your husband ill for long?'

'Irvine? . . . The Dad never had a day's illness in his life. He was out on the golf course in all weathers since he sold the business.'

'If it isn't too painful for you, do you mind telling me exactly what he died of?'

'There, I knew you were a doctor after all,' she said triumphantly. She went over to the sideboard, opened a drawer and took out a piece of paper.

'Here you are, Doctor. The poor Dad's death certificate, and didn't it take them long enough to issue it?'

'What do you mean?' I asked as I unfolded the certificate.

'They had a coroner's inquest and two post-mortems before they decided that he died of simple heart failure. I think some of these doctors don't know their job.'

'Gross insult to the cardio-vascular system associated with extreme emotional stress,' was listed as the cause of death of Irvine Samuel Varley. He was fifty-eight years of age when he died.

'What emotional stress was your husband under?' I asked.

'You ought to ask Melanie that,' she said bitterly. 'That little madam really put the Dad through it. He died of a broken heart, that's what they told me.'

I must have looked at her oddly because she went on . . . 'The Dad had been in touch with that Aldous Arkwright, who seemed to think that he owned Melanie, body and soul. He sent him a solicitor's letter stating that unless he heard from Melanie by the end of the week he was stopping her allowance and cutting her out of his will . . . threatened to leave the whole lot to the People's League for Sick Animals, he did. He wasn't one to mess about once he made his mind up was the Dad. That letter was posted on the Monday and he was dead on the Thursday.'

Jean didn't look too upset by all this. I imagined they'd been leading separate lives for a long time.

'So he wasn't broken-hearted?'

'The Dad thought she'd soon come to her senses when he cut off the cash. Worked hard all his life did the Dad. All he expected was proper respect in return.'

'Fair enough,' I agreed. 'Did Melanie get in touch to tell Irvine, er . . . I mean the Dad, that she wasn't going to play ball?'

Jean looked at me as if I was the one who hadn't got all his chairs at home.

'What do you mean?' she asked blankly.

'The Dad was all set to cut Melanie out of his life or to get her back. It was one or the other, right? Something must have happened to tell him that she wasn't coming back . . . a phone call? . . . A visit? . . . A letter? There must have been something that broke his heart.'

'Nothing like that happened before I went out and the post is always here before eight. I was shopping in Peterborough all morning and when I got back the Dad was sat up at his window watching me get out of the taxi. I waved but he didn't move. I wanted him to come out and help me with the bags but he just stayed there. I thought he was thinking but when I went in I could see he was dead. Just sitting there in his chair, peaceful as a sleeping cherub.'

Proposals to replace England's archaic system of local coroner's courts with a national organization of medical examiners on the pattern of some American states were said to be premature in a submission to an enquiry organized by the Lord Chancellor. It was claimed that Coroners, whether medically qualified or not, have a detailed knowledge of local conditions and that few unexplained deaths go without further explanation.

Bulletin of the English Law Review Panel

18

Tuesday, 27 October

Convincing Detective Chief Inspector Ritchie that he ought to treat the death of the Dad as a possible murder was an uphill job. I had help from an unexpected source . . . Sinclair. The connection was Shannon Withers. It turned out that poor Jean had left the bit about Shannon's visit out of her statement to Ritchie because she felt guilty about hoarding piles of unused NHS medicines. Even when Jean 'remembered' that Shannon, complete with stethoscope and white coat, had turned up just before the snatch squad, Ritchie remained sceptical.

He was certain I was involved in some obscure scam. It was only when he phoned Sergeant Martin at Stockport and confirmed that Shannon's sister had been found dead in similar circumstances to Mr Varley that he gave me more credence. Then he phoned Mr Sinclair who urged prompt action. His own Chief Constable agreed and a Home Office exhumation order was applied for and granted.

The result was that I found myself shivering in Oundle Churchyard at 7 a.m.

'You'd better be right about this,' Sergeant Martin of the Stockport police said to me in a whispered aside as we stood in Oundle churchyard watching a small mechanical digger slowly approach the grave of Irvine Samuel Varley. I stood in a small group with Martin and Dr Jeremy Matthews, the pathologist from Stockport. Matthews had admitted that he'd be delighted to find evidence of murder because the Health and Safety Executive had already excavated half of Marple without finding a convincing reason for Monica Withers' death.

Matthews turned out to be a dapper little fellow in rimless glasses, bow tie, crew cut and designer beard who looked as if he'd been born to wear a white coat, if not born in one. He was friendly enough. The Northamptonshire police took a rather different line. They risked being accused of botching the investigation of Irvine Varley's death and now they stood in a small group round Ritchie directing hostile stares at me. At this time of the morning, though, I was fairly impervious. As far as they were concerned my efforts over Irvine had not dispelled the impression created by the *Guardian* article. I was here on very limited sufferance.

I'd slept in Irvine's bed last night, or rather I'd lain on it listening to rats scraping about under the floorboards. The whole house was infested.

'They're all God's creatures,' Jean had explained when I complained. Eventually, I went downstairs to await the dawn fully dressed and with a blanket over my shoulders. I don't know what it is but there's something about the idea of rats and mice crawling over my sleeping body which gives me the horrors. I'd rather face Polk and Tyler with my hands tied behind my back than go through that again.

The battery on my mobile was flat and Jean's telephone hadn't been repaired so I was out of touch with Manchester. My imagination had gone into high gear for a few moments during the small hours of the morning but I told myself that Janine was safe enough in the MRI. If the Children of Light had intended to eliminate her, they'd already had sufficient chances . . .

Still, I shivered as the digger's claw began scraping the dirt off Irvine Varley's grave and it wasn't due to the cold. I was wearing my heavy coat. I knew too much and I'd said too little. I had the uncomfortable feeling that very soon the law would be squeezing me for information like a miser with an almost empty tube of toothpaste.

A few moments later the undertaker stepped forward to identify the coffin and pathologists began taking soil samples.

'We've got to get samples from above, below and on both sides of the coffin to eliminate poisons that might be in the soil,' Matthews explained *sotto voce* to Martin and myself. 'Though I shouldn't have thought the body's been in the ground long enough for much material to have leached into the coffin. According to the undertaker, the body wasn't embalmed so there's a much better chance of any evidence being preserved.'

Martin responded to this unsolicited information with a toothy grin.

We all lapsed into silence again as the grave-diggers jumped down and hauled the coffin out. The varnish on its surface was still fresh enough to gleam under the headlights.

'It's been cold and fairly dry here for the last couple of months so the cadaver should still be in prime condition,' Matthews volunteered. Then the coffin was loaded into the back of a police Land Rover and we all drove off to Northampton for the autopsy.

I parked my battered two-day-old Mondeo in the car park with the rest but as I was getting out one of the Northampton detectives approached . . . 'Nice car,' he said, idly kicking the tyre. 'Even with the scratches it's more than I can afford.'

'Yeah,' I murmured, waiting for him to ask how much Mrs Varley had paid me, but he didn't.

'Sorry mate, DCI Ritchie says you can't come in. Police, doctors and relatives only.'

'But I'm representing a relative, Melanie Varley . . . the deceased's daughter.'

'Yeah, but she's not here to confirm that, is she? Sorry, but the Guv'nor says you've to go.'

I felt angry enough to go and make a scene but I realized that that would only give Ritchie the opportunity to arrest me for obstruction and send me to cool my heels in a cell for a few hours. So I said nothing. I drove out of the hospital grounds and went in search of food. I'd passed a Happy Eater on the outskirts of Northampton and now I made my way back to it for a distinctly unhappy breakfast. I was feeling more than slightly light-headed when I finally located it. I ate a double order of breakfast, having subsisted since Eileen's provisioning yesterday morning on a little seed cake and a few dry biscuits that had escaped the rats at the Varley mansion. Thank God I hadn't attempted to start yesterday morning on my usual yoghurt. Sometimes Mum really does know best.

As my blood-sugar level rose following the sustained cholesterol intake, the day took on a slightly rosier hue. Some things were slotting into place. Assuming that Irvine and Monica had both been murdered by the same hand, the police would have to start taking a serious interest in the activities of the Children of Light. On the other hand, knowing the constabulary as I do, it was quite conceivable that they might start making enquiries in another direction entirely. They might come up with some sort of tenuous link between Bob Lane, Monica Withers and Irvine Varley. God knows how, but anything was possible. I was desperate to know the results of the autopsy.

I drove back into Northampton and parked in a lay-by on the busy dual-carriageway near the hospital. I could see the back door of the crumbling mortuary block where the pathologists were at their grisly work. I looked at my watch. The autopsy had been under-way for an hour and a half. I settled to wait. Surely it couldn't be much longer. An hour later, I spotted Sergeant Martin emerging from the back door for a quick fag. I decided to take my chances. Risking life and limb crossing the road, I dashed through the car park and caught his attention just as he was going back in.

'Oh, it's you,' he said dismissively. 'They don't seem to like you much round here.'

'What's going on? Why is it taking so long?' I demanded, braced for another discussion of journalistic accuracy.

'That's for me to know and you to find out,' he said with a sly grin.

'You don't work for Ritchie. Tell me what they've found.'

'Nothing much yet. I've been bored rigid, I can tell you.

They keep taking samples and sending them for tests. It might be weeks yet before they come up with a conclusion.'

'Why didn't they do all these tests before?' I groaned.

'Foul play wasn't suspected.'

'Varley threatened to scrap a will which would have brought millions to the Children of Light. He snuffs it three days later . . . before he can change the will . . . and nobody suspects a thing.'

'Don't take it so hard,' Martin said more sympathetically. 'You never know, they might come up with something. I can tell you that we're definitely looking for Shannon Withers. She gave me a false address.'

'I'm going to wait until they find something,' I said firmly. 'There must be something that one of these highly paid experts will spot.'

'Up to you, but don't blame me if you're here all day.'

I returned to my vigil. Two hours later all involved suddenly dispersed from the hospital car park. Risking a U-turn on the dual carriageway, I set off after Martin and managed to flash him down just before he turned on to the M1.

'Well?' I asked. 'Any news?'

'You've got a bloody cheek, haven't you?' he asked. The ground shook as heavy lorries rumbled past us in low gear towards the motorway interchange.

'There wouldn't have been any autopsy if it hadn't been for me,' I said angrily.

Martin looked at me as if weighing up whether to risk his stripes.

'You're a regular nuisance, aren't you? . . . They think there may be bruises on the back of Irvine Varley's wrists. They showed up under ultraviolet light. Jeremy Matthews is going back to Stockport to check out your friend's wrists.'

'But what does that mean? Was there some kind of gas?'

'They don't know yet, it's merely a suspicious circumstance. Eh, though, before we go our separate ways, there was one thing. It's one for the scrap-book really . . .' he said tantalizingly. He took his cap off and smoothed his meagre strands over his bald pate.

'What?' I said angrily.

'I don't know if I should tell you. It's a bit confidential really.' He was really enjoying this. I felt ready to smash him in the face. He must have seen my face darken. 'All right, don't get your rag out. You know that old Varley was buried from his home?'

'What do you mean?'

'His wife insisted on having him back at home the night before the funeral.'

'OK,' I said, still mystified.

'Well she must have had the lid off the coffin because when we opened it this morning they found a dead rat in there. It hadn't done much damage except to the face but I can tell you they had to pass the sick bags round.' Martin laughed loudly as he studied my reaction to this news. 'The point is, Mr Cunane, the rat died of lack of oxygen, not poisoning. So work that one out.' Still chuckling at his own marvellous sense of humour, he got in his car and drove off. I was certain at that moment that he was lying but then as I drove back towards Oundle it came to me that he wouldn't have had the imagination to make up something like that. What the hell did he mean? My brain felt weary from constantly trying to permute the possible combinations of skulduggery involved.

When I met up with Jean Varley again she was dressed and in the process of packing. She looked none the worse for her little brush with the Children of Light, if it was them. There was a police car parked in her drive with the same WPC I'd met yesterday behind the wheel.

'What happened helped me to make my mind up, Doctor,' Jean said. 'I've decided to sell up here and pay a visit to my sister in Australia. No one bothers about how much medicine you like to have by you out there. They call it the Lucky Country, you know.'

'Jean, don't you realize that that woman who said you had to go into hospital for tests was lying? You're not really in trouble with the NHS,' I explained. I'd already given up trying to persuade her that I wasn't a doctor but it stuck in my throat that the old bat still believed Shannon Withers was genuine.

She looked at me as if she was surveying distant hills, or maybe it was like Captain Cook on first sighting Botany Bay. She was definitely spaced out but not on drugs. 'I don't know about that, Doctor,' she murmured and her lips set in a cunning smile. 'They say there's no smoke without fire. I think it was a warning to me.'

'What about Melanie?'

'She'll be well looked after. She's got her trust fund. The poor Dad never did have the chance to disinherit her, did he?'

'You know she's run away from the Children of Light. Surely Irvine, er . . . the Dad, would have been pleased to hear that.'

'She's changeable is Melanie. You don't think that was the first time she's run away from them, do you? She ran away from the Dad and me and from school. She likes nothing better than legging it for a while does Melanie. The Dad always said she was a drama queen.'

On the drive north I had plenty of time to ponder her words. Either she was nuts or I was. I'd gone leaping into that room at Blackley and bashed Rufus on the face to liberate Melanie from a ruthless sect, or so I thought. Now, according to her mother, Melanie made a habit of these little escapades. If it was all so innocent, though, why were people dying? Why had Janine been beaten? Nothing added up any more, yet only this morning I'd thought I was on the verge of a solution.

My first port of call in Manchester was at the MRI. I got a shock when I went to ward C3. Janine wasn't there. My heart pumped painfully in my chest as I walked to the nursing station and asked the nurse on duty where she was. I forced myself not to panic.

'Janine White? She's been moved to a side ward. First door on your left,' the nurse said, oblivious to the noisy sigh of relief issuing from me. When I reached the room my visit was an anticlimax. I'd thought I'd be able to discuss what I'd found with the journalist but she was drugged to the eyeballs. She recognized me and murmured a few words but it was obvious I wasn't going to get much conversation from her.

'We thought it better to be safe than sorry. She was fretting about the children and the consultant decided to sedate her,' the ward sister explained.

My next visit was to the farm on the moors beyond Bolton. I got an even worse shock there. Paddy's little car parking bay and the lane beyond were jammed with cars – police cars. I slotted my car into a field entrance down the track and rushed to the front door to be met by Detective Inspector Cullen.

'Oh look who it is . . . Dauntless Dave,' he said with a laugh. 'How's Girolamo Savonarola doing?'

'What's going on?' I snapped. I had a taste in my mouth as if I'd been sucking broken hacksaw blades. The day's events hadn't put me in the mood for banter.

'You might well ask,' he said, turning off the humour like a tap. 'There's a few people here waiting to ask you the same thing.'

I pushed past him into the living-room. It seemed to be crammed with men. The large kitchen table had been pushed into the centre of the room and maps were spread out over it. Assistant Chief Constable Sinclair, looking like a model in a suit catalogue as always, was poring over the map while Paddy indicated locations. The biggest shock came when I looked in the corner. Detective Sergeant Peterson stood there, scribbling something in a notebook.

I felt a sudden constriction in my throat. After days of being on the receiving end of violence from the Children of Light, here one stood, bold as brass, in my parents' living-room. I lost it completely.

With a formless roar of rage I launched myself across the room at him. The next few minutes were confused to say the least. I think I made contact with his smug and treacherous features but I couldn't be sure as so many men pinned me to the floor that it was impossible to be certain where my blows were landing. Plenty came in my direction.

It was my mother who broke the spell. I was pinned to the floor with my face grinding into the carpet as I roared and struggled to get up. Then I heard her yelling into my ear above the din . . . 'David Cunane,' she shouted in the commanding tones that had brought obedience in a hundred classrooms. Mum hadn't ended up as head of a primary school in inner-city Manchester without learning how to use her larynx. 'David Cunane, this is disgraceful! You're upsetting the children. Stop this at once.'

Like the naughty boy I once was, I desisted in the face of superior authority. Strong hands hauled me to my feet. I was delighted to see Peterson pressing his handkerchief to a swollen lip. He snarled at me and threw himself forward and I struggled to land another blow. Cullen got between us.

Then my father joined in. 'What the hell do you think you're playing at?' he demanded. His face was so red and swollen with rage that I immediately felt chastened when I guessed he might be developing angina. The madness that had struck at the sight of Peterson left me as quickly as it had arrived. I must have gone limp because the men holding me relaxed their grips.

Paddy calmed down as well. 'Come here, you fool,' he said dragging me into the kitchen. I couldn't help noticing that the grouting of the tiles had been completed as he poured me a glass of water and mopped my face with a flannel. 'Hell and damnation!' he exclaimed. 'Maybe it's just as well you never joined the Force if that's your level of self-control.'

'Sinclair knows Peterson is a rotten little spy,' I grunted.

'Yes but Peterson doesn't know he's suspected, unless you've given the game away like a soft fool.'

'He'll think I hit him because I lost the UNWIST job.'

'Say nothing else; knowing and proving are two different things,' he cautioned quickly, rubbing his nose with two fingers. 'Look at the state of you.' He cast an eye over my clothing. It was lamentable to say the least. I was wearing the suit trousers which were now adorned with mud splashes as far as the knees. My shoes were so covered in grass and cow-muck that it was impossible to tell what colour they were meant to be and of course, what remained of my suit jacket was in the back of my car.

'Get those shoes off,' he ordered. 'You're not trekking that muck into my living-room.'

I pulled the shoes off and threw them under the sink.

'Wash yourself,' he commanded. 'It won't do much for the

stink but it might lessen it.'

I did as I was told. Then he pulled me back into the living-room.

Sinclair was just in the process of ordering his men out for a search. As I arrived they departed, leaving only Paddy, Sinclair, Cullen, Peterson and myself. My mother must have been upstairs getting the children to bed.

'Davie, I really enjoyed that,' Sinclair said sarcastically. 'I think you've had more dramatic entrances than Kevin Costner's had hot dinners.'

'All right, all right,' I shouted, my anger flaring again. 'I'll say it once . . . I'm sorry. There, I've no intention of repeating that.'

'Aye well,' Sinclair said complacently. 'We're all here together like a nice happy family, eh? And what's a family without a few blows struck in fun?'

'He's a dangerous maniac,' Peterson protested. 'He'd have killed me if there hadn't been people here to stop him.'

'I don't know about that, Detective Sergeant. I didn't really see much rough stuff at all, just a few cross words. How about you, Detective Inspector Cullen? Did you see much?'

'There was a bit of a draught in here,' Cullen said blandly. 'We've been having some very rough weather.'

'Aye, it's been a blowy old day, right enough,' the enigmatic Scot lisped. He looked at Peterson with a raised eyebrow. Peterson kept his mouth shut this time. 'Now, Davie, suppose you tell us where Clint and Bob Lane are hiding.'

'What?' I said looking angrily across at Paddy. He returned a bland smile and a shrug of the shoulders.

'Come now, we found the cottage in Derbyshire where you had them hidden. Don't deny that you persuaded the unfortunate Miss Withers to hide them.'

'It's Doctor Withers,' I said.

'Whatever her title, you somehow wheedled your way into her confidence and persuaded her to lend you her cottage.'

'I don't know what you're talking about.'

'Yes, you do,' Peterson chipped in. 'That Tuesday morning when I came to question you, you said something or did something that made Doctor Withers completely change her attitude. I've interviewed Professor Richardson, he says that she was bitterly hostile to you before, then she suddenly changed her mind. What was it? . . . A neat bit of blackmail? . . . What did you have on her?'

'Nothing, it wasn't like that,' I stammered.

'What was it like?' Cullen asked with a sneer on his face. 'You seem to have a way of getting lonely women to change their mind about you, Dave.'

'That's not true.'

'Well, what is true is this,' Sinclair concluded, 'I shall expect a full written statement from you about the part you played in Clint Lane's escape. That statement will be submitted to the Crown Prosecution Service to see if a charge of aiding and abetting can be laid against you. I'm afraid you're looking at a substantial spell in jail unless you decide to be helpful.'

'Clint Lane had nothing to do with Fred Travis's murder,' I said flatly.

'You may be able to ignore cast-iron evidence but we can't,' Peterson said.

'All right,' Cullen said sharply. 'We don't need to go into that now. What I'm interested in knowing is what part Dave's played in Miss Varley's latest vanishing act.'

'I don't know what you're talking about.' My heart sank. So this was why Cullen's attitude was so hostile. They still thought I was the cowboy detective who abducted cult members for cash.

'Sorry, lad,' Paddy said, 'but I had to tell them. Melanie went out for a walk with your mother and the two young ones this afternoon. They went up to Bluebell Woods, Melanie wanted to pick mushrooms. She wandered off and she hasn't come back yet. I had to get in touch with Jock.'

'Perhaps your son can speak for himself, ex-Detective Chief Superintendent,' Peterson said acidly. 'He's seems to be old enough to charm half the women in Greater Manchester into his bed, particularly wealthy ones like Doctor Withers. Maybe he can tell us what he's done with this other heiress, or has he forgotten that he was paid to snatch her from a perfectly respectable religious group?'

I looked at the four men gathered round the table. My father kept his eyes averted, but Sinclair, Cullen and Peterson were studying me for reaction.

'As you're so clever, Mr Peterson, perhaps you can tell me how I'd have time to get here from Northampton to do this second snatch?'

'You had ample time,' Peterson said. 'Detective Sergeant Robertshaw of Northampton CID confirms that he ordered you out of the car park at Northampton General Hospital shortly before nine a.m.'

'Well, Davie?' Sinclair chimed in. The wily Scot looked like a cat that had just lapped up a whole dishful of cream. I was sure in that moment that he knew that I'd spoken to Sergeant Martin well after nine o'clock. However, I was saved from the need to drop Martin in it by Peterson, who was unable to disguise his eagerness to slam a cell door in my face.

'With all due respect to you, sir, and to Mr Cunane senior, I think this interrogation should be taking place on official premises. We've plenty of grounds to charge David Cunane with abduction as well as aiding an escaped prisoner. I also feel he should be under arrest now for an assault on an officer.'

'Don't take it so personal, Peterson,' Cullen said. 'By the time we've finished with Dave here, he'll be facing so many charges he'll think all his Christmases have arrived at once. Right sir?' he commented, looking at Sinclair.

'If you think I'm going to let you fit . . .'

'Hold on a minute, Davie,' Sinclair cautioned. 'I think I hear something.'

I'd often thought that the old vulture had unnaturally keen senses but now here was the proof because a moment after Sinclair spoke there was a loud banging on the door and a uniformed officer opened the door to admit Melanie Varley. She looked slightly dishevelled and was carrying a large basket full of mushrooms under her arm.

'Wandered off in the direction of Dimble, sir. I spotted her at a bus-stop,' the officer explained. 'She says she didn't know how to get back to here.'

Melanie looked tired and sulky but Sinclair didn't spare her

... 'Perhaps you'd like to wash and change, Miss,' he said, putting on all his olde worlde charm, 'then if you could come down, there are some questions I'd like you to answer.'

Paddy leaped out of his seat and tried to relieve her of the mushrooms but she wasn't having any of it. She clung to the basket. 'I'll take this to my room and sort it. I need to check some of them in the fungi book.' Then she departed up the winding metal staircase that Paddy had installed to give access to one of his extensions.

'Well, am I still going to be charged with her abduction?' I demanded as soon as she'd disappeared.

'You took money from her mother to kidnap her before,' Peterson muttered angrily but Cullen shook his head. 'There's still the question of Clint Lane's escape.'

'Are you saying I helped him to escape from Bootle Street police station?'

'Maybe not, but we'd have had him by now if it hadn't been for you.'

'What evidence have you got that I helped him?'

'Circumstantial, but strong enough for a jury, I should think,' Cullen replied. 'You admit you slept with Dr Withers . . . that she was at your flat . . . and then the Lane brothers turn up at her cottage . . . the cottage of a total stranger. I don't think there's anyone who wouldn't think that you induced the woman to give you the keys of her cottage. Also, Dave old lad, you went to the trouble of buying me a meal to tell me how innocent Clint was and to try to throw suspicion on Melville Monckton.'

'OK then, arrest me,' I said with a weary sigh. 'I'll be out on bail in no time . . .'

'Not if we state that you're likely to continue helping an escaped fugitive,' Peterson interjected. 'That's what all this is about, isn't it? Ever since Fred Travis was killed you've been doing everything you can to deflect the blame from your friend's brother and put it on to anyone you can plausibly suggest . . . Monckton, the Children of Light and now Shannon Withers.'

'And of course the GMP have never arrested an innocent man before?' I said scornfully.

'It's up to the Courts to find them guilty or innocent, Davie,' Sinclair said. 'We just collect the evidence.' His tone was much less vitriolic than his subordinates'. 'You know there was an American president who said he would much rather have a well-known nuisance inside his tent and pissing out, than the other way round. Sometimes I feel that way about you, Davie . . .' He gave me a wan smile. 'And then again, sometimes not.'

My face may have reddened slightly at this back-handed Caledonian compliment. I made no reply. Whatever I said, I would only dig myself into deeper trouble. I didn't think that they had much evidence that I'd helped anyone other than Bob Lane who, after all, was not guilty of any crime. Or if he was they weren't saying so.

'Right,' Sinclair said decisively. 'I'd like a word on my own with Cunane Senior and Junior, so if you two can go and wait in the car . . . I'd like DI Cullen to accompany Davie to his home in Chorlton and to see that he stays there, so . . .'

Cullen and Peterson left in the direction indicated and my mother appeared at the foot of the stairs. 'That girl's in no fit state to be questioned by you or anyone else, Jock,' she said.

'Very well, Eileen, I defer to your judgement. I'll send for her in the morning.'

Eileen went back upstairs.

'Now, what am I going to do with you?' he said turning to me.

'You've seen Peterson's wife's name on that list, haven't you?' I said hotly.

'That's your trouble, Davie, you're too impatient. I can't dismiss the man just because he sleeps with a member of the Children of Light. God knows what would have happened to you by now if you'd been held responsible for all your . . .'

'OK, OK,' I growled, 'point taken. But what are you doing?'

'If you weren't such a bull in a china shop, Dave,' Paddy said, 'we'd have told you by now. The young lady is going to be bait. Peterson knows where she is and if his friends in the C of L try to liberate her tonight, then we'll know that he's leaking information.'

'What? You're proposing to hold them off by yourself?

Don't you know they've already killed several people?'

'Hold on, Davie,' Sinclair ordered, holding up his hand. 'There are armed officers observing this house from several directions but friend Peterson doesn't know about that. As for the alleged murders of your friend Dr Withers, and of Melanie Varley's father, it's not yet been established that any crimes have been committed. There's considerable dispute among the pathologists.'

'What's the matter with you, sourpuss?' DI Cullen asked. I was driving along the aptly named St Peter's Way, an urban freeway that permits rapid access and egress from Bolton, a town which had lost some of its 'heavenly' appeal in the last hour. Acting on Sinclair's orders, I'd agreed to what virtually amounted to house arrest. I was to stay in my flat for the next few days 'to keep out of Sinclair's hair' . . . a typical self-deprecatory joke from him as he was on the verge of baldness.

'You talking to me?' I asked.

'Yeah, you, Mr Grumpy. It's no fun for me, you know, acting as child-minder for a forty-year-old school truant.'

'I'm still a long way off forty.'

'Not really. Old age creeps up on us all.'

'Thanks a bunch.'

'Oh come on, Moody Blues. What did you expect . . . ? Did you really think old Sinclair is going to start a major scandal with the Children of Light two weeks before they hold a massive rally?'

'I thought he was opposed to them.'

'In case you hadn't noticed, we're not living in Nazi Germany. The police can't stop people holding rallies just because we don't like them. If we catch your friends Polk and Tyler heading out to your parents' cottage then we can do something, but until then, keep your nose out of police business.'

'Right,' I mumbled.

'You can count yourself lucky that you're not behind bars . . . Attacking Peterson like that. Are you mad? It's just as well for you that he thinks it's because he made you lose your job.'

'With friends like you . . .'

'You may not believe it, but I am your friend. The trouble with you is, you keep coming up with crazy ideas like trying to blame Melville Monckton . . .'

'I could tell you things about him that would make your hair curl.'

'Stow it, Dave.'

> **'If it was the manifest destiny of the United States to seize all the finest territories of the Mexican Republic, will someone tell me how that was morally superior to the evil British Empire occupying Ireland or the late Adolf Hitler taking over Poland?'**
>
> Part of a speech by a Chicano delegate to the 'Free our Mexican territories' congress in Chihuahua, Mexico

19

Friday, 30 October

For the next few days I was in a kind of limbo, confined to my flat, unable to find out anything except by reading the papers. I deduced that there'd been no attempt to 'lift' Melanie because when I repeatedly asked Cullen, who'd been detailed to phone me at odd hours, he became very irritable. That's the police for you. They'd wait weeks for the Peterson–C of L connection to be revealed. I was inclined to more hasty methods.

After two days sitting on my hands at Thornleigh Court I was ready to beg for mercy. That, however, did not come 'dropping like gentle rain' from Mr Sinclair but from Janine White. She was recovering and was demanding to see her children. For some reason she also wanted to see me. The delicate state of her brain must have lent weight to her wishes because suddenly it was all happening. At midday on Friday, my parents arrived at my flat while Melanie, Jenny and Lloyd waited down below in Paddy's large Vauxhall.

'So this means that any plans to smoke out Peterson have been abandoned?'

'How do you work that one out?' Paddy asked genially.

'Well if you're seen in the company of Melanie the whole police force will know where she's staying.'

'Yes, that's why we're going to stay here while you take her and the children to see Janine.'

'Can't Melanie stay here as well?'

'No,' my mother said sharply. 'It's bad enough for those children being dumped on strangers. If you take them on their own they'll only start howling. At least they're getting used to Melanie.'

'Lovely,' I muttered, heading for my bedroom to change.

'You know what I mean,' Eileen explained. 'You're hardly at your best with small children.' She went into the lounge and Paddy followed me as if to check that I didn't make a break for it through the window.

'Come on, shape yourself, lad,' Paddy ordered when I was slow about selecting my wardrobe. 'Those kiddies are getting to be a right handful for Eileen. That one does nothing . . .'

'You mean Melanie, I suppose.'

'Proper "lady" she is . . . Sits on her backside all day long waiting for your mother to put food in her mouth.'

'Getting a bit browned off with Mr Sinclair's little ploy, are you?' I asked.

'You shouldn't sneer. If it comes off it'll probably help you and the Lane brothers off the hook.'

'I'm not counting on it. Why haven't there been raids on Children of Light premises? Why hasn't Shannon Withers been arrested? Those people at Oundle must have come from the Peterborough group.'

He shrugged. It was obviously a waste of time for him ever to attempt an explanation of the labyrinthine machinations involved.

'Get a move on,' he snapped. 'They'll have my car wrecked. That girl's a freak, you know.'

'Jenny?' I asked, while carefully choosing a tie to match my shirt and jacket.

'No, though she can do her share. I've read stories to her until my jaw's ached. I mean the other one, the beauty queen. When she's not polishing her toe-nails, she's constantly wandering off to pick mushrooms. I've never known anything like it. She's got them in the garage drying out. Night, noon and morning, she's at it.'

'Well, at least she's trying to feed herself,' I commented.

'She doesn't seem to be eating them. Just sorting and picking.'

'In that case she's like Mr Sinclair, he just sorts and picks the evidence he responds to.'

'Give it a rest, Dave. You know he's worried stiff that the Children of Light are going to send the Repealers out on some sort of vigilante campaign. If he can stop them, he will, but it'll be by legal methods not your cowboy tricks.'

I kept quiet for the sake of peace. It seemed that I was saddled with the cowboy label now that my own parent was using it. Maybe I ought to start wearing a broad brimmed hat and humming country and western tunes.

As it happened, I needed all my sense of humour when I got to the MRI. Someone at Bootle Street police station had gone to the trouble of informing the sergeant who'd wanted to arrest me for beating up Janine that I'd be in attendance. She was waiting at the door of Janine's room.

'Mr Cunane, can I have a word?' she asked politely enough as Melanie was ushering the children in. 'We're still not clear about how Ms White came by her injuries.'

'So?' I asked cautiously.

'I've been speaking to Janine's mother . . . It seems that Janine contributed to an article in the *Guardian* that you might have taken exception to.'

She looked at me with an air of grim expectancy. I wondered what I was meant to do.

'My back's broad enough to bear a little criticism,' I said as pleasantly as I could manage.

'But if you were hoping to get started in business again, this allegation that you're some sort of professional kidnapper would be the last thing you'd welcome,' she persisted.

'Look, Sergeant . . .'

'Culpepper,' she snapped, white-lipped.

'Sergeant Culpepper . . . Janine White's a journalist but she doesn't have control over every word that goes into her paper. There are editors and sub-editors. Maybe you ought to see if I've tried to beat them up . . .'

'That may be true but Miss White thrust herself into your life, didn't she? And according to Professor Richardson at UNWIST the comments in the paper had a material effect on your career prospects.'

'Great, Sergeant Culpepper, that's just dandy!' I said angrily. 'For your information, the reason Richardson decided not to renew my contract was because your colleague Detective Sergeant Peterson thought it might be a whole bunch of laughs to come and collect me on a corridor at the university and drag me off to Bootle Street for a stream of unnecessary questions about the Clint Lane fiasco in which the Force allowed a mentally handicapped man to climb out of the cells. Since then I've been hearing about nothing else but the efforts that you and all the other Keystone Cops down there are making to find someone to put the blame on!'

'Professor Richardson said your activities were bringing UNWIST into disrepute.'

'He never mentioned anything about the *Guardian* when he gave me the old heave-ho and I'm going to bring a legal action against him for unfair dismissal and I shall cite this interview as an example of the sort of persecution I've been subjected to.'

'Oh dear!' she mocked. 'Your feathers do seem to be ruffled. I think men who go around beating up women should be persecuted, and as for legal action, sue away! I'll see you in court one way or another.'

Having made her point, Culpepper strolled off along the corridor, seeming well pleased with herself. She thought she was chipping away at the armour of a serious criminal. I was left to regret that I hadn't brought the Union in on my dismissal immediately. Now there was no one except Lisa Lovegrove to confirm my account of the proceedings.

Trying to hide my anger with a smile, I went into the room. Melanie took my belated arrival as a sign that she could depart. She passed Lloyd over to me . . . 'I'll wait in the corridor,' she said. 'Don't worry, I won't try to run off. You'll be able to see me all the time.'

Janine raised her eyebrows as Melanie dashed out. 'I hope it wasn't something I said,' she murmured with a laugh. 'Coping with young children doesn't seem to be Miss Melanie's scene, does it? Have I lumbered you with them now?'

I looked at her carefully. The swelling that had so disfigured her had now almost gone. It was now nearly a week since the beating. Though her face was still bruised, it was recognizable as the face of the determined young journalist who cornered me at Thornleigh Court. She smiled. I felt something. I don't know what it was, and I didn't know whether I liked it or not, but there was definitely a twinge of emotion there.

'Was that Sergeant Culpepper I heard?' she asked, her smile fading to a more anxious look.

I nodded.

'She's been on and on at me to make me admit that you've been having an affair with me and that you beat me up because I walked out on you and did the dirt on you in the paper. The woman's obsessed. I told her that I didn't even like you . . . that we only met for professional reasons, but everything I've done . . . I mean, letting the staff here think you were my partner . . . it's all rebounded on me. Every time I say the beating was nothing to do with you she ties me up in knots. Why did I call your name? Why did I kiss you when she wanted to arrest you? She's so certain she's right.'

'We both know the answer to that. All you have to do is tell the truth about Polk and Tyler.'

'But I'm scared . . . You know what they said . . . They'll harm my children.'

'So you're another one who doesn't trust the police,' I said in a poor attempt at humour.

'I'm sure they're very good at sorting things out in the long run, but in the short run . . .' She clutched Jenny, who'd been sorting through the contents of her mother's bedside table.

'So what are we going to do? None of this would have happened if you'd taken that money I gave you and gone back to London.'

'Don't you see, Dave? I know you meant that kindly but it could be seen as a pay-off to drop the story. It only made me more determined to find something out on my own.'

'I see. You still half-believe that I was working for hire when I went charging off to rescue Melanie.'

'No, no,' she protested.

'Look at her. She doesn't look much like a damsel in distress, does she?'

We both looked at Melanie who gave us a bored grimace in return when she saw we were talking about her.

'Dave, I know you're not a cowboy detective or anything. You wouldn't have helped my children if you were.' She laid her hand on my sleeve. Both children looked up at us expectantly. Melanie, still seated in the corridor, favoured us with a glum look. She was well out of earshot.

'I got the impression there was something you wanted to tell me.'

Janine looked at her children. The expression on her face was of acute fear.

'Don't upset yourself. Are you ready to tell me how you ended up in here?'

'You already know that.'

'Not really. When I last saw you, you were heading for Piccadilly Station with enough money for the fare to Euston.'

Her eyes filled with tears and she looked at the children again.

'I'm a fool, Dave. I couldn't face going back to London without the inside story about Travis and the Children of Light. It could have been bigger than Watergate or cash for questions. I went all over Manchester trying to find someone who'd give me a story about the Children of Light. Most of the ones who knew something were too scared to open up. Then I remembered Everald Mallick.'

'I went to see him after that piece in the paper.'

'I know. He hates you, I realize that now. He said you'd been to threaten him but that you aren't as hard as you think you are. I should have realized that meant some real heavies had terrified him.'

'Yes, you should. If you'd phoned me I could have told you that he'd already given your address to Polk and Tyler.'

'Oh no!' she gasped.

'When you went back to him, Everald must have got in touch with Polk right away.'

'I don't know that it was like that. Cultwatch was genuinely interested in finding out more about the Children. Those thugs must have got him to . . . what is it they call it in spy stories?'

'You mean they turned him . . . made him into a double agent? That's more or less what he told me.'

'You've seen him again?'

'If he's going to deliver bunches of flowers with threatening messages I thought it was only fair to let him know what the risks are,' I said.

Janine lay back on her pillow for a while.

'You didn't hit him? I mean, like you did Rufus.'

'That was more of an accident than anything. I know that according to you I'm supposed to be a cowboy but I don't make a habit of hitting people.'

'Dave, I've already told you I'm sorry about the paper calling you a cowboy. I just reported Everald's phrase. I'm sure he's a good man at heart but perhaps he gets frightened more easily than you do. He has a family and he's terrified of racists.'

She looked so pale and brave lying there on the bed, sticking up for Everald, that I hadn't the heart to argue.

'So what happened next?'

'Everald said he'd let me see the Cultwatch files but I'd have to pay. I gave him £100 of your money. He has an office in a back bedroom. It's part of an information exchange he set up.'

'What the hell! Easy come, easy go,' I said with a feigned laugh.

'He had the names of several C of L members who'd broken away from the group. He told me that some of them claimed that their relatives had died in unusual circumstances.'

'Where was he when you were studying the files?'

'He was downstairs.'

'On the phone to Polk and Tyler, no doubt.'

'Before I left Everald, he claimed that he knew a disgruntled member who was still with the Children of Light up at Meldrum Terrace . . . someone who'd back up the story. You know my editor . . . I thought . . .'

'You thought you'd see this person without any back-up.'

'Dave, I had to take the chance. I checked out all the names Everald gave me before I went. It was true, all the relatives had died.'

'How many?' I asked. My heart was pounding like a hammer.

'When you become a full initiate in the Children of Light you have to transfer all your money to the group. There are at least seven who said that relatives who'd objected died soon after.'

'Janine, didn't that warn you that it might not be a good idea to quiz Everald Mallick's alleged turncoat on your own?'

'I'm not totally crazy. I checked. All the premature deaths were put down to stress or heart failure or suicide. There was nothing about murder.'

'Where are the names?' I asked.

'That's just it,' Janine said helplessly. 'The only thing that was missing from my bag when I was brought in here was my notebook with the names in.'

'You're certain it was Polk and Tyler who assaulted you?'

'Tyler held me while Polk worked me over. He enjoyed it.'

I put my head in my hands and tried to think.

'Can you remember any of the names?' I asked eventually.

She nodded. I spent the next ten minutes writing down names and addresses.

'I'm sure some of those are mixed up . . . They might not even be genuine,' she said anxiously when we'd finished.

'If there's even one, it might give us a lead,' I said hopefully.

I told her about what had been uncovered by Dr Matthews at Northampton.

'Dave, I hope this makes you see why I can't take a chance with the children,' she said.

I sat on the bedside and sighed. Lloyd stretched out and ferreted his way into his mother's arms in that way small children have. I looked at the three of them. They were totally vulnerable.

'Your mother and father have been very kind, they say my mum can stop with them in their cottage until I get out of here.'

'Yes, they're kind, if a little set in their ways,' I agreed.

The ward sister came in then.

'I'm afraid we'll have to bring this little family get-together to a close,' she said.

Janine looked upset at this but before she could object the sister whipped her thermometer out and popped it under her tongue. She took Janine's wrist in her hand and began taking her pulse.

'Now you know what Doctor said about getting excited. Your partner will have to take these lovely children home with him now. I think if they stay here a moment longer I shall eat them both up, they're so beautiful.'

While the children looked at the sister with eyes like saucers, I gave Janine a rather strained stare. The pretence that I was Janine's partner was wearing a bit thin. I picked Lloyd up. He made no protest at being parted from his mother. Jenny said, 'Will that old man read me another story?' as I took her hand.

'I'm sure Paddy will,' I said happily enough.

'Knick-knack paddy-whack, give a dog a bone,' the little girl chanted.

The sister leaned back to admire this comment and I suddenly understood that she was waiting until I kissed my partner farewell. What had seemed to be an acceptable subterfuge a few days ago now felt wrong. I lifted up the children for a kiss from their mother, but just bobbed my head in her direction briefly. It seemed to be enough to fill the sister's expectations.

On the way out she put her hand on my arm.

'Janine's much better. The clot seems to have dispersed. You'll be able to take her home in a day or two,' she told me.

Melanie maintained a surly silence during the journey to Chorlton. I could sense that child-minding wasn't her scene. However, Lloyd and Jenny were happy enough to see my parents, as they were to see them. Was that scheme called 'Rent a Granny' or something? As there were no genuine grandchildren for 'hands on' experience of grandparenting, maybe surrogates would do. Whatever the arrangements, though, the five of them set off back to the moors leaving me feeling oddly bereft. I wandered slowly up to the flat, trying to work out what was wrong.

It was only when I picked up the whisky bottle that I realized what it was.

I gave enough sighs to out-sympathize a whole convocation of undertakers. I really was in the soup. I recalled Janine saying that she'd told Sergeant Snaggletooth that she didn't even like me. I now knew that I wanted her to like me. I'd fallen for her, hook, line and sinker. I put the bottle down.

I needed to get air. Sinclair thought he was entitled to hold me under virtual house arrest. Well, he could stuff it. Let him arrest me if he wanted. I left the flat and began walking along the main road.

I must have been deep in thought because I didn't notice the car sounding its horn at me until the third blast almost startled me out of my scattered wits. It was DI Cullen, he wound down his window. 'Hi-de-hi!' he shouted. 'Are you on something, cocker? You just walked across the main road without looking in either direction.'

I shrugged my shoulders and carried on. The sudden arrival of Cullen confirmed my suspicion that they had me under surveillance as well.

'Cold shoulder, eh?' Cullen shouted. He cruised forward in the car. 'Jump in, Dave. I'm taking you out for lunch . . . my treat.'

I turned and looked at him. There was a charming and open smile on his face. He looked as honest an altar-boy as ever walked off the sanctuary at St Francis Monastery.

'To look at you, no one would guess that you're so good at back-stabbing,' I said bitterly.

'Oh come on, Death-Defying Dave,' he said in a silly voice, pulling a sad face. 'I think I liked you better when you were making a flying tackle on that prat Peterson. I'll swear you were off the ground for a full ten feet. It was the best entrance to a conference that I've seen in years. It's worth knowing you just for the sheer drama . . .'

'That's all I am to you, isn't it? A chance to crack a few jokes about daft old Dave.'

'Stop feeling sorry for yourself and get in. You'll have me weeping buckets.'

I did as I was told. It felt comfortable to sit down. The car was a Mondeo, but not the 2.5 litre executive model.

'Well?' I mumbled ungraciously.

'This isn't like you, Dave,' Cullen said with a chuckle. 'What's up? Haven't you been getting your oats lately? I noticed you eyeing up Little Miss Melanie the other day. You could help her with her mushroom sorting,' he cackled. 'It would almost be worth risking my rank to have a crack at her myself.'

'Do you think so?' I asked coldly.

Cullen shut up then for a few minutes and concentrated on his driving. I couldn't help feeling patronized. It wasn't so long ago that Cullen had been a broken-down sergeant in the Vice Squad, looking at the premature end of his career because of a drink problem. Now here he was, dressed to the nines in his C&A suit.

'Seriously, Dave,' he said when the car was stuck in a jam under the railway arch opposite the G-Mex. 'Things haven't been going too well. We're having to pull the men off surveillance up at your dad's place.'

'I see. And you want me to go up there as an unpaid replacement?'

'God, you are bitter,' he said turning to me with a frown. 'Who's been rattling your cage?'

'No one,' I snapped. He was getting too close to the truth.

'Well, we don't want you acting as an unpaid police officer so I can put your mind, such as it is, at rest about that. I just wanted to fill you in on the state of play as a courtesy, like.'

'Did Sinclair suggest this?' I asked.

Cullen lapsed into silence again. He parked the car in the underground section of the G-Mex car park. He didn't speak until we got into the street opposite the new Bridgewater Concert Hall.

'What's it to be, mate? We'll go this way,' he said, indicating the Midland Hotel, 'and have a nice meal in the casino. Or we could go the other way and I'll shove your miserable bloody face under the Rochdale Canal?' He pointed to the bridge just past the Briton's Defender pub. 'Make your mind up.'

I had to laugh. It was comforting to know that I wasn't the only one capable of a dramatic gesture.

'That's more like it,' he said, happily leading me to the casino entrance. We went down the stairs until greeted halfway down by a burly door man.

'Afternoon, Mr Cullen, would you care to sign your guest in?'

Cullen did so. 'The wife and I joined,' he said by way of explanation. 'I find it convenient to bring a guest here occasionally. There's not too much chance of meeting many folk from Bootle Street Nick in here. Some of the younger sparks in the CID infest those wine bars and French restaurants around Albert Square and Deansgate.'

'I suppose it's all right as long as you don't blow a month's salary at the blackjack table,' I said with a smile.

'Chance would be a fine thing, the Old Queen never lets me out with more than ten quid in my pocket. I have an account with the restaurant here and they do a bloody good steak.'

I noticed that everyone seemed to know him very well. The maitre d' led us to a nice table overlooking the gambling area. Even at this time in the afternoon there were a few elderly Chinese and young Asians at the tables. Anglo-Saxons seemed to be in short supply unless you counted the croupiers.

His promise about the steaks turned out to be true enough. Cullen ate his so rare that he had to wipe traces of blood off his mouth before he spoke.

'We've been doing a bit of work on your two holy friends, Polk and Tyler.'

'Have you raided Meldrum Street?' I asked hopefully.

'In your dreams, Dave. No, we've been in touch with the FBI, trying to trace them through their passport details. It turns out that neither of them officially exist.' He licked his finger and made an invisible number one in the air.

'Great,' I muttered.

'However,' Cullen said sharply, annoyed at having his flow interrupted. 'They were able to come up with a match for one of the photos in the passports, that of Rufus J. Polk, esquire. He turns out to be one James Forrest Mattingly, and a very interesting gentleman he is too.'

'Criminal record, links with the Miami Mafia,' I said quickly.

'Why do you say that?' Cullen asked, looking at me through narrowed eyes.

'Oh, just a guess,' I said nonchalantly.

'Well, you're wrong, though he does have links with Miami. It's listed as his last American address. No, your old mate

Rufus was dishonourably discharged from the US Army special forces – the Green Berets of John Wayne fame – for being a little too enthusiastic in disposing of the enemy in Vietnam. It appears he routinely rubbed out little Orientals in black pyjamas who wouldn't tell him what he wanted to know. No one minded about that much, a bullet in the brain was apparently standard operating procedure in backcountry operations, but it seems that Rufus got carried away with enthusiasm and was also too inventive. He started torturing people on his own account. There was a congressional enquiry in the offing and his CO thought that Rufus, or *Lootenant* James Forrest Mattingly, had to go. They gave him his cards after a quick court-martial in San Francisco in 1968 . . . By the way, did you know that the Forrest in his name is from the founder of the Ku Klux Klan, Nathan Bedford Forrest, a slave dealer and Confederate general?'

'Yeah, I saw the film too,' I drawled. 'So Gump this guy ain't. Did you know that Nathan Bedford Forrest was also responsible for the Fort Pillow massacre in 1864 in which almost three hundred black soldiers who'd surrendered were shot or buried alive? Giving your kid his moniker for a handle is like some German calling his child after Hitler.'

'OK, Mr Smarty Pants,' Cullen said with a grin. 'I bet you didn't know that President Polk . . .'

'. . . was a Southern slave-owner who launched an unjust war which led to the USA annexing half of Mexico,' I interrupted.

'And he was the President who succeeded Tyler, who himself annexed Texas including a huge chunk of land that had never even been previously counted as part of Texas. Isn't education wonderful, Girolamo?'

'Right . . . Enough!' I pleaded, lifting my hand to call a halt to the *Mastermind* competition. He'd probably got his information off the same Internet pages as I had. 'So Rufus isn't exactly in *Burke's Peerage*, but what does that tell us?'

'Only that he seems anxious to live up to both his given name and his chosen alias,' Cullen replied.

'So what are you doing about proving it?' I asked.

'I went up to Meldrum Terrace this morning for a word with

the Great White Chief Arkwright – who, by the way, is an Englishman with impeccable antecedents; his father was a bishop – and asked to see them. Arkwright apologized profusely. It seems that Polk and Tyler aren't living there at the moment. They're on a recruiting trip in Europe and can't be easily recalled or reached.'

'Try Interpol,' I suggested.

'No use, there's no record of them actually leaving this country.'

'So, what now?' I asked.

'Nothing really. We can't actually arrest Arkwright for lying to us. There's nothing much we can do if we catch them apart from deporting them for entering the country under false passports. I doubt if we'd even get the chance to question them without a lawyer objecting. They've already answered all our questions about finding Fred Travis and if we tried to re-open that, their briefs would want to know why we were still looking for Clint Lane.'

'So you're up a gum tree without a paddle, as it were?' I suggested.

'You could put it that way. Mr Sinclair's uneasy. He feels that you ought to be very careful.'

'What about Peterson?'

'What about him? There's nothing we can do without evidence and as the gruesome twosome didn't in fact turn up at your parents' home to repossess Miss Melanie Muffett, he's in the clear for now.'

'Do you really think he's the only officer who might have been attracted by the Repeal 98 clap-trap?' I commented cynically.

Cullen summoned a waiter and bought himself a fat cigar and began puffing fumes in my direction. I didn't know he smoked and put it down to imitation . . . One of Sinclair's favourite tricks was blowing smoke from his pipe into a suspect's face.

'So what's the old man up to, then?' I asked, flapping away at the blue clouds.

'Nothing really, he's still hoping something will turn up from all these tests they're doing on Monica Withers and

Irvine Varley but that seems to have turned into a doctors' squabble. Jeremy Matthews says one thing and three others say another.'

'What if they weren't the only unexplained deaths connected with the C of L?' I asked. I slipped him the piece of paper on which I'd written the names of the possible victims Janine remembered.

'Nice one, Dave,' he said as he pocketed the piece of paper, 'I love the way you have of broadening an investigation until it includes half the CID in England.'

'Two of those names lived in Scotland,' I said with a smile. I didn't tell him that Everald Mallick was the ultimate source of the list. I didn't want to be laughed out of the casino. Cullen was in a very mellow mood when we parted company. He'd washed his bloody steak down with two pints followed by a large brandy and I was pleased to see that the GMP hadn't gone completely overboard for faddist anti-alcohol hysteria but it meant that I had to catch the metro to get home. I didn't mind. I was in a fairly mellow state myself.

When I got home I spent what remained of that Friday afternoon slumped on the sofa in my living-room. I woke about five with a throbbing headache and went to take a shower in the hope of diminishing the hangover. It didn't work and I was in the kitchen making myself a ham sandwich when the phone rang.

'Melanie's done a runner again,' Paddy announced flatly. 'I've told Jock but he doesn't want to know . . .'

'The best-laid plans . . .' I muttered sarcastically. Cullen's words now made sense. He was preparing me for the news that Sinclair could do no more.

'All right, but the fact remains that you delivered her up here and it's your responsibility to find her,' he said menacingly.

'I don't see how you work that one out,' I replied. 'It was your buddy Sinclair who had the bright idea of using her to trap Peterson. He should do something about it.'

'It was my idea, actually, Dave, and I still think it might have worked if we'd given it more time but Jock's got to account for every second that he uses someone on surveillance. I don't how the Chief expects them to catch anyone these days . . .'

'Of course you know,' I said sharply. 'You find some mug of a private detective, send him in and then call him an informer.'

'Even if that was true we're still responsible for that young woman.'

'We're not. She wished herself on to Janine White who was hoping to get more dirt on the Children of Light out of her. By the way, has she said anything about her experiences to you?'

'Funny you should mention that. Your mother was only just saying how tight-lipped Melanie is.'

'There you are then. Just relax and be glad that she's cleared off.'

At this point a low rumbling sound like a distant volcanic eruption emanated from the phone.

'I swear by King Dick's hat-band you're too irresponsible to be near children and families,' my parent complained.

'Dad, those days are gone! We're no longer responsible for every female who happens to stray into our orbit. You're being patriarchal. Melanie owns herself. She won't thank you for sending a posse after her. And what's King Dick's hat-band when it's at home?'

There was silence for a moment while this torrent of rebuttals was pondered.

'I suppose you may be right,' Paddy finally admitted. 'But I'd feel happier if I knew she'd come to no harm. I'd go myself but the problem is your mother and me are stuck here with the children. Their grandmother's due here tomorrow, which should be some relief, but I don't feel able to leave your mother on her own. You'll have to do it. You'll have to find her and see that she's come to no harm and if possible get her to make an informal statement before a witness to that effect.'

'Covering your butt, eh, Dad?'

'Yours, you mean.'

'She could be anywhere.'

'No, it's not so bad. I got the number of a hotel she called. You could start there.'

I grudgingly agreed. Obviously the old man wasn't going to

give up and I had landed him with Janine's children. The hotel was in Bradshawgate, Bolton. I wrote the details down.

'What am I supposed to do if I find her?'

'I told you, get her to sign something.'

'I mean, should I try to persuade her to come back to stay with you?'

'No Dave, that would be adding insult to injury. Let her stay where she is or look after her yourself but don't bring her up here. I swear your mother will nut her if she has to pick up one more thing for her . . . Never once offered to wash a pot the whole time she was here.'

'OK, message received,' I said preparing to hang up, but there was more.

'Shame about Melville Monckton, wasn't it?' he said.

'What was a shame?' I asked.

'Don't you ever listen to the radio or watch a TV news bulletin? The man's dead, killed in a boating accident near Miami. There're massed choruses of celebs wringing their hankies out on telly at this moment. Very nasty it was, apparently Melville fell out of the boat he'd gone marlin fishing in and another powerboat passed over him. The poor bugger didn't have a chance, he was chewed up by the propeller. Reading between the lines, I'd say they were having difficulty finding enough bits of him for a funeral.'

I don't know what I felt at this bit of news. Melville had certainly been very frightened when I met him but I couldn't honestly say that I was in the mood for any of that 'for whom the bell tolls' stuff about his death. He'd been willing to try to turn a penny by involving himself with the Mob and then had put himself back into their orbit by going to Miami. I wondered about that. Had he been summoned back to the Sunshine State . . . ? Perhaps there was an offer he couldn't refuse? Whatever had happened – and I seemed to remember seeing pictures of fishermen on those cruisers wearing massive safety harnesses to prevent themselves being dragged overboard – there was nothing I could do about it.

I got dressed and went down to the car. On the way over to Bolton I tuned into the local radio station and learned more about Melville's appointment with the fishes. A spokesman for the Metropolitan-Dade police announced that they were investigating the possibility that Mr Monckton might have been under the influence of alcohol at the time of his accident. That would account for him not being strapped in. My local station, GMR, was playing a selection of his hits and had even dug out a government minister to say what a sad loss Melville was to the region and the nation. The government had been considering appointing him to a committee to find worthwhile activities for unemployed youth.

That turned my mind back to my own current employment. Searching the north-west of England for someone who didn't want to be found was a pretty hopeless task. Fortunately I had a few friends in the form of the twenty-pound notes Bob Lane had given me. I turned off St Peter's Way and found myself in the centre of the industrial town. Bolton may be smaller than Manchester but I found it no easier to park my car. Eventually I found a car park off Bradshawgate and walked to the hotel in Nelson Square.

'I'm a private detective representing the mother of Miss Melanie Varley. I wonder if you could check if she's registered here?' I asked discreetly, proffering my very nicely produced private detective's identification card. For some reason there was a twenty-pound note tucked inside it. 'Melanie has recently inherited a considerable fortune and her mother is worried that she may be attracting undesirables. She sent me to check that she's OK.'

My request produced a great deal of head-scratching and consulting of higher powers before eventually I was told that Melanie had indeed registered and paid in advance with a platinum credit card. She'd brought a large basket with her and then gone out and returned with a pile of clothes. She'd told the receptionist that she wouldn't be coming back but they were still holding the room. Would I care to look?

I would.

I was led to Melanie's room by the hotel security man, an ex-copper. He opened the door and then turned to me. 'No wonder her mother's worried, look at that all over the floor.'

He got down on his hands and knees and began picking up pieces of dried mushroom.

'Is she on dope?' he asked. 'I'd say this bit is magic mushroom – *amanita muscaria* – but what the others are I wouldn't like to say.'

'She had a pile of them with her?' I asked.

'A blooming great basketful is what I was told.'

'Where are they?'

I checked the waste bin. There were more pieces of unidentifiable mushroom and also lots of labels, hangers and wrappers from expensive clothes. I took out the bank roll provided by Bob Lane and fumbled with it for a moment, and then pulled out a handkerchief and wrapped up some pieces of the mushroom.

'Seems to have been having quite a spending spree,' the ex-copper said with an obliging smile. 'She can't have been under the influence when she did that.'

'Is there any chance that I could speak to the receptionist who dealt with her?'

'Sorry, she's off duty, but the cabby who picked her up is still on the rank. You could probably find out where she went. She was on the phone for a long time too, but we wouldn't have a record of where she called because she used one of the public booths downstairs.'

'Thanks,' I murmured, slipping him a twenty which he trousered with practised deftness.

'Has the young lady been in trouble over drugs? Is that why her mother's concerned?'

'You could say that was part of it. Did she meet anyone while she was here? Any undesirables or anyone at all?'

'I could ask the staff if you like, while I'm bringing in that cabby. He's just on the rank outside.' He touched his hand to his pocket. I took the hint and slipped him another twenty.

His well-rewarded enquiries produced the information that Melanie had been an unlikely hotel guest when she arrived, lugging a large basket of mushrooms, and so she'd been required to pay in advance. She'd departed in designer clothes carrying two expensive suitcases, hadn't spoken to anyone and had been dropped at Manchester Airport by the cabby. When I showed the hotel security man yet another picture of Michael Faraday he managed to discover that there had been one phone call from the bedroom. It was to the Children of Light headquarters in Blackley.

On the way to the airport I tried to pull things together. Melanie had spent four days in the moorland wilderness, managing to thoroughly annoy my far-from-intolerant parents. Usually it was only my trifling faults that got up their noses. Then she'd taken herself off to Bolton, got kitted out in the most expensive shops and departed, presumably lugging her mushrooms with her. She'd made one call that she knew could be traced but the others were made from the public phones. Very curious. There might be a simple explanation for it, but what?

When I pulled into Terminal Two, international departures, where Melanie had been dropped, I was certain that I'd find her waiting for a connection for a flight to Australia. She wasn't. I had her paged. I checked all airline booking offices and drew a blank. Then I wondered if she'd have had her passport with her, so I went to Terminal One, internal flights, and went through the same process with the same result.

It was too late to phone poppa bear back in his hillside lair when I got home. It would be interesting to learn what 'King Dick's hat-band' was; and how the man who swore by it took the news of what a helpless little darling Melanie was. I turned the television on instead. I found the late night BBC news channel and Melville Monckton's departure from this life was still the main item. I listened to the recital of his achievements: gold discs, charitable deeds, love of sport, local boy made good, etc., etc., until it wearied me and then I went to bed. No one had mentioned his desire to turn Manchester into Sin City.

'There is no doubt that soccer has replaced religion as the great mobilizing force of popular emotions in our society. If there was ever any truth in Marx's sneer that religion was the opium of the masses it applies with much more truth to soccer. Perhaps the bishops could try to form a Christian soccer team. (*Laughter and applause.*)'

Debate in the Church of England General Synod

20

Saturday, 31 October (Halloween)

Saturday morning was bright and cold and when I remembered that it was exactly two weeks since the death of Fred Travis it felt colder still. I got up, fed my face on the fat of the land, showered and took another look out of the window at the ice on the car windscreens and decided that my usual Saturday routine of a bike ride or run on the Meadows would have to be deleted from today's programme.

A call to Sergeant Martin over in Stockport produced Dr Matthews' home address. Having accompanied Matthews to Northampton, Martin had become a partisan of the good doctor's opinions about the deaths . . . now apparently officially discounted. 'Didn't I say to you that I thought you were like your father?' Martin said smugly. 'Never relented once he got his teeth into something, that's what they said about him. Mark my words, murder will out.' He hung up on that cheery note.

I put on a grey business suit, went down to the car, scraped the ice off and set off on a round trip that would take me first to Stockport and then up to Blackley to see the guru Arkwright. All this busy activity stopped me from thinking once about Janine White; except that it didn't. Fleeting thoughts kept coming and going. I ought to visit the hospital. I should go to Bolton and see if the old man needed any help with installing her mother. Perhaps I could take the children in to see Janine. Every time my thoughts tended in that direction I snapped them back and worked out some other much more important task that needed my attention.

Dr Matthews opened the handkerchief full of mushroom fragments rather gingerly as if he expected them to explode in his face. 'I don't see the connection with the deaths of Dr Withers and Mr Varley,' he said cautiously, after poking them with his finger for a few minutes.

'There probably isn't except for the cult connection,' I said dismissively. 'If it wasn't for that I wouldn't be interested in identifying them.'

Matthews looked at me wonderingly.

'Monica Withers's sister, who according to Sergeant Martin still hasn't been traced, is a full initiate in the Children of Light. Irvine Varley's daughter was about to be made an initiate. Both their deceased relatives had objected to giving financial support to the cult. Both died from what your forensic colleagues insist were natural causes. I think there are grounds for being interested in what Melanie's doing with these fungi. According to my father, she spent last week doing little else but scouring the woods and fields for them.'

'I still don't see it,' Matthews said. I could have shaken him for being so obtuse. 'My theory was that the cause of death in both cases was due to some physical intervention . . . something like *burking*. You know when Burke and Hare, the body-snatchers, used to recruit anatomical specimens. They'd go out and round up a convenient drunk, lure the poor soul back into their lodging-house and then sit on his or her chest and asphyxiate the victim by covering the mouth up.'

'Lovely,' I commented. 'So if someone had shown you the blanket that Burke and Hare used for the job you wouldn't have been interested. Only the cadaver would have been of any use to you.'

Matthews looked at me closely, trying to work out if I was being deliberately offensive. I smiled at him. He was on my side, after all. It must have taken some guts to dispute the prevailing opinion. He looked like a bit of a swinger himself, dressed in designer jeans and a navy Cashmere sweater. The room we were in had a smokeless-fuel fire blazing and walls, surfaces and desk were crammed with Victorian ornaments. There was a slight time-warp effect, as if I'd stepped back seventy years.

'Pretty direct, aren't you? My Home Office colleagues refuse to be convinced that the bruises on the backs of the wrists are conclusive evidence that some degree of violence accompanied the two deaths. I think both of them were held down, but as for these mushrooms . . . well, poison's been ruled out.'

'I'm not saying there's a causal link. I just think that it would be interesting to find out what the cult's up to with these things. Do you know that Arkwright, the director of the cult, drinks a special cordial containing a tincture of digitalis?'

'Digitalis is toxic but you'd have to consume several grams to get a lethal effect,' he said and then lapsed into silence for a minute and drummed his fingers on the desk top. 'Still,' he continued, 'it is worrying if these people are playing around with poisons. I'll send these mushrooms to the forensic labs. They'll have a botanist there who can identify them. I could ask him to do it as a personal favour. If there's any startling result, I'll let you know. Otherwise, Mr Cunane, I'm afraid I have a paper to write and I must get on.'

He transferred the mushrooms into plastic sandwich wrappers and sealed them.

'When will you hear?' I asked, perhaps a shade too eagerly, as he showed me out.

'Not a high priority, I'm afraid. It might be several days, perhaps a week, but if there's nothing of interest you won't hear at all.'

I wouldn't like to say that Blackley was looking its best – it probably hadn't done that since the eighteenth century – but the winter sunlight did improve the valley of the Irk. Nothing ventured, nothing gained, so I drove directly to Meldrum Terrace and parked at the end of the line of 4WD vehicles outside the cult HQ, got out and boldly knocked on the door.

There were no blonde elf-maidens with rustling bell-like

voices this time. A burly male youth of about nineteen opened the door.

'I want to see Mr Arkwright,' I announced. 'Tell him Dave Cunane's here.'

The young man took this in, nodded and then shut the door in my face. I remained on the doorstep. A few minutes later the door opened to reveal the beaming countenance of Aldous Arkwright himself.

'Delighted to see you, Dave,' he said and in an odd way I believed him. His face was wreathed in the usual seraphic smile. It required mental gymnastics to tie this man in with the events of the last two weeks. He was dressed in his leisure kit of long Russian-style shirt and velvet trousers. 'Have you come to join us?' he asked. Again he seemed to be speaking with perfect sincerity. My finely tuned antennae could pick up no jarring note of falsehood. Perhaps they were too finely tuned. These days I often found myself disbelieving routine news items.

I shook my head.

'Sorry, Aldous, not this time. I just came to see if you'd heard from Melanie Varley. She's gone walkabout again and various people are worried about her.'

'Dave, you won't be offended, will you?' he said. 'I'd invite you in but I'm sensitive to something about you. You're not at ease, are you? There's something disturbing your spirit, I can tell.'

'Look Aldous, no offence likewise, I'm sure, but have you seen Melanie?'

'There's such a lot I want to talk to you about,' he said evasively, 'but I can't admit you to the premises when you're in this state.'

I was starting to get rather nettled. To hear him speak, you'd think I'd been rolling in manure or was filthy drunk. However, I knew that grabbing his shirt and bouncing him off the wall a few times would not produce the result I desired.

'Aldous, my old fruit, I know that Melanie phoned here yesterday. Just tell me where she was going and I'll trouble you no further . . .'

Much to my embarrassment, not to say alarm, Arkwright leaned forward and linked arms with me. 'Just because you're too disturbed for me to admit you doesn't mean I can't speak with you,' he said in a rather lower voice than before. 'Let's get in your car and talk there.'

Some of the same emotions that had troubled my boyhood breast when a schoolmaster once cornered me for a little chat about homework now flashed through my mind. I'd no one to blame but myself, as usual. Arkwright opened the car door and installed himself on the passenger side. I went round to my side and got in. Glancing at the shaded windows of the C of L HQ, I saw no sign that we were being observed.

'They're all at their morning devotions,' Arkwright explained when he saw the direction of my glance. 'Impure worldly affairs are polluting your thoughts, Dave, I can tell.'

'Just a minute,' I snapped, 'I didn't come here for analysis. The last time I visited you the woman I was with died shortly afterwards and I'm not entirely convinced that you weren't involved.'

'In what, my son? Death comes to us all. It isn't the end . . .'

'God! You do go on.'

'Precisely, that's my message,' he said clapping his hands with glee. 'We're all god, the whole cosmos is evolving towards consciousness of its own divinity and if your friend was aware that she possessed a tiny spark of the god-stuff in her she will live on. Everything we see around us is in the process of becoming god.'

'What, even that lamppost over there?' I said scornfully.

'Of course,' Arkwright said with an expression of joy on his homely, knobbly countryman's face. 'Matter is the stuff of the universe, we partake of matter and every atom of us has been inside stars. Organic matter is merely the most advanced stage that the unconscious universal pressure to develop a godhead has so far evolved into. Don't you see? That's what I'm trying to do with my followers, make them conscious that they must raise themselves to the next plateau in our journey onwards.'

'Do you often get carried away by your own verbosity like this?' I asked. 'I only want to know if you've heard from

Melanie. Save the spiel for the schmucks.'

'I look for the signs, Dave, the signs of the times. It was no accident that brought you to me when Fred died.'

'It was a card that a murderer stuck in his fingers,' I said angrily.

'No, no, that wouldn't have done it. I sense that you're a troubled soul, Dave. I feel that the essential *you* – call it soul, spirit, mind – whatever you will, that thing which will become the *only you* when this husk has worn away,' – and here he gave my shoulder a hard pinch – 'is here for a higher purpose than the well-being of Sister Melanie. You bear some message that I must read if the Children are to survive on this plane.'

I shook my head in dismay. I was getting the recruiting pitch full blast and it was working. Arkwright had a peculiar scent to him, some blend of musk and spices that was quite distinctive and not at all repellent. It certainly wasn't something you'd want the passing breeze to quickly disperse.

Arkwright was right, I was troubled about Janine. Even so, I decided that I wanted to get his peculiarly cloying aroma out of my nostrils. Some instinct told me that it wasn't the odour of sanctity. I wound the window down on my side and took a deep breath of clean Blackley air. At least Arkwright had mentioned Melanie, so I was making progress, but at this rate, with him up on his 'higher plane', it would be hours before I got any useful information.

'You know that your two buddies, Polk and Tyler, are a pair of cold blooded killers, don't you?' I said matter-of-factly.

The intense 'spiritual' expression on Aldous Arkwright's face remained frozen there for a full minute and then gradually dissolved into a look of foxy calculation. Which was Aldous's essential '*you*', I wondered?

'Is this the message you're destined to deliver?' he asked eventually.

I wanted to tell him that the police knew all about Polk's shady past, but caution intervened. There was no sense in tipping him off that the police were investigating Polk and Tyler if he didn't already know. Judging by their failure to show up at the Corless Farm, he did already know.

'Tell me what Melanie's up to with all these mushrooms,' I demanded.

'What? Is she still carrying on her duties? The dear, dear child, I knew the divine spark was strong in her.'

'What do you need the mushrooms for? Do you all get high as kites?'

'Nothing like that. In certain combinations, certain doors of the perception are opened, certain barriers lowered. That's all. The mushrooms are merely an aid to meditation.'

'So why does Melanie need to mess about with them if she's not at your headquarters with the rest of your loonies at this moment?'

'She isn't with us,' he said sadly. It was hard to read his eyes but I thought he was telling the truth. 'I haven't seen her since you so roughly removed her.'

'At her own request. Not everyone likes being caned.'

'Dave, I sense there's a seeking and a searching about you. Join us. If you fear that your worldly lusts won't be catered for, you needn't. There are many of our young women who would gratify you. One road to deeper perception is through wholesome sexual desire.'

'That's the funniest proposition I've ever heard,' I said with a laugh. 'Anyway, I thought you were all for celibacy?'

'Only for the full initiates in the final stage of development. The animal urges can be a helpful means of development or a road-block on the way to enlightenment. We encourage our followers to develop through and beyond them.'

Looking at him, I realized that he was fully in earnest. 'Aldous, Clive, St Paul or whatever you're really called, you talk the biggest load of crap. Are you going to tell me why Polk and Tyler and Shannon Withers feel that they're entitled to go around knocking people off? . . . No, I can see that you aren't. So perhaps you'd like to get out of my car.'

'Dave, you must come to our meeting next week at the Nynex Arena. I feel that you may find the answers you're seeking there and I may find them as well.' He opened the car door but before he got out he fished an invitation out of a side pocket and handed it to me. Nothing I'd said had rattled him or made him deviate by one iota from his sales pitch. It was an awesome performance.

I drove away as if the devil was on my tail, as my grandmother would have said . . . Old Nick himself, in the form of the grinning, imperturbable Aldous.

The blend of half-truths, sincerity, total conviction and even the frank offer of sexual favours in exchange for membership made a potent brew. How many had fallen for precisely that pitch, I asked myself? Monica had hinted that her sister was recruited by a form of sexual entrapment. The constant repetition that I was a troubled soul . . . As if everyone isn't troubled by something. If you were slightly off your gimbals, for whatever reason, that kind of talk could be immensely attractive.

It was one of those low moments. There was just no way forward.

The investigative trail led straight into Meldrum Terrace but I couldn't bring myself to drink the proffered chalice. Arkwright's brew of sex, 'natural' drugs and total certainty was too strong. How long would it be before I was compromised and became a committed seeker of the 'higher plane'? I didn't think that people like Shannon Withers had joined with the intention of becoming a skilful killer, but look at her now. The trouble was, I was the only one who could see it. Sinclair wanted Repeal 98 suppressed for public order reasons. He'd like to wound the Children of Light as well, but he feared to strike openly.

So what to do? I couldn't go back into the private detective business with a string of question marks hanging over me. The GMP had abandoned efforts to snare Polk and Tyler, no one seemed to have any knowledge if they were even in the country. Charges still stood against Clint Lane. Forensic pathologists were treating the deaths of Monica Withers and Irvine Varley as some kind of abstruse intellectual puzzle. The weird founder of a local cult wanted to recruit me as a soul in need of healing. Melanie Varley, a young woman barely out of her teens, had given me the slip although I'd scattered money over the landscape in pursuit of her. Worst of all was Janine White. I now wished that I'd never laid eyes on her. Why had she chosen me to lean on, only to let me know that she didn't even like me?

I drove through town. It was a match day, as I soon discovered when I neared Old Trafford. I suppose that showed how far gone I was. I must have been the only individual over a ten-mile radius who wasn't aware that United were at home. The usual rules of match days were in force. Young and not-so-young men were walking into the traffic as if their status as football fans conferred invulnerability from impact damage. Turning into Seymour Grove I almost ran over a group lurching out of the Tollgate, a recently tarted-up pub on the corner.

'What you doing, you sad bastard?' a pimply fan, almost dwarfed by the immense red coat that enveloped him, bellowed. He banged the flat of his hand on the bonnet of my car. An answering flare of aggression surged through me. For a second all I wanted to do was to get out and pound the youth's ugly features into jelly. My hand went to the door handle but even as I moved other fans dragged the youth away. Perhaps they'd seen the dangerous glint in my eyes. I drove on up Seymour Grove, breathing deeply and turned into the crowded car park of the Throstle's Nest pub. I needed to drink in company and cool down. I knew that if I got home in this state I wouldn't stop drinking until I ran out of whisky. I elbowed my way to the long bar and bought a pint of lager which I swallowed in one gulp.

The excited movement of fans, surging in and out like a restless sea, took my mind off my troubles. Why didn't I have a cause to follow, a team to support? Why couldn't I arouse myself to awareness of what the really important thing in life was? What was lacking in me that all these earnest souls meeting friends and discussing the club's prospects had? Sinclair's fears that Repeal 98 might become a dangerous political movement seemed laughable when you compared the pitiful ranks of Arkwright's followers, enthusiastic though some of them were, with the solid mass of United fanatics. The management could fill the fifty-eight-thousand-seater stadium twice over and still leave many disappointed. It was interesting that the Children of Light had scheduled their rally for a Saturday when United were playing away. Even Arkwright must have realized that he couldn't hope to lure fans away from a home match.

I pushed my way through the cheerful mob to a public phone and called my father. He objected to calls from my mobile because he claimed that charges went on his phone bill.

'I can't find her,' I admitted. 'She went to the airport but where she's gone from there is anyone's guess.'

'Rather clever of her, that, isn't it?' Paddy commented. 'You'd almost think someone had told her the best way to shake off anyone who might be interested in her movements. Are you sure she's not with Arkwright?'

'Short of breaking into Meldrum Terrace again, or taking the veil as one of the Children of Light myself, there's no way I can tell. Arkwright says not. Look, can you get Janine's mother to pass a message on for me? To Janine, I mean . . .'

'Go on then, your mother's taking her to the MRI tonight.'

'Tell her I won't be visiting again and that I'm sorry but I won't be able to follow up any more leads for her . . . She'll understand.'

'Will she? I'm not sure I do!' he exclaimed. 'Honestly Dave, you've lumbered us with this girl's children and her mother as well, and now you say you don't want to have anything more to do with her.'

'It's only for a few more days. I'll make it up to you,' I said evasively.

'Is not just a matter of money, although I was intending to speak to you about that . . . These plastic nappies and things come expensive . . . Your mother's become quite fond of those little ones . . .'

'That's not my fault,' I insisted angrily.

'Who else's?' he asked. 'Janine's spent the night with you . . . I know because Fiona Salway gave your mother a call.'

'Janine spent a night on my sofa – by herself. Fiona's got it completely wrong,' I said hotly.

'Listen lad, in my young day if a bloke did certain things . . . made certain undertakings . . . .Well, any man worth his salt . . .'

'You've got everything back to front,' I said petulantly. 'Janine's the one who isn't interested in me.'

'That's not the way it looks. Get a grip on yourself,' he ordered before hanging up.

I forced my way through the crowd. By now the fans were almost frantic for ale as match time drew near. I bought another couple of pints. I felt as if there was a fire raging inside me which needed to be extinguished.

'Drowning your sorrows before the game even starts?' a genial Reds' fan asked as I poured lager down my neck.

'What do you mean?' I asked sullenly.

'I can see you don't follow United,' he said indicating my grey suit. 'You must support the opposition.'

'I can't even support myself, let alone go and watch a bunch of overgrown adolescents kick a pig's bladder full of air round a field.'

This remark produced a noticeable chill in the air. I suddenly found that there was plenty of space round me. I started on the third pint.

'Leave him be, Jed, sad bugger's not worth it,' I heard someone counselling the heavy-set man who'd questioned my status. As I turned to leave, my drinking neighbours took the opportunity to demonstrate their skill with the four-letter lexicon. I couldn't even summon up enough hostility for a menacing glare in return.

I wasn't in much fear of getting done for drunken driving – the pace of the traffic through Chorlton was glacial. Hot and angry thoughts kept stirring in my brain. A dozen perfect rebuttals of Paddy came and went. I told myself that I wasn't in this world to satisfy the vanity of the old man of the moors. What *was* I here for, though? That was the interesting question. I didn't seem to be making much of a success of anything.

By the time I reached Thornleigh Court the streets had cleared. I poured myself out of the car and headed up to my flat ready to flop on to the bed. When I reached the middle landing I heard a familiar voice. 'Are you all right, Dave? You look a bit flushed,' Finbar Salway asked.

'I thought you were looking after Fiona up in Cumbria,' I said sharply.

'Bored stiff, old chap. I've left Fiona up there. She has a higher tedium threshold than I do.'

I looked at his bright eager face. In my present mood I felt like kicking him down the stairs but something obliged me to be civil and it wasn't the nobility of my character. Perhaps it was drink-induced lethargy.

I must have been staring stupidly at him.

'Are you sure you're all right?' he asked again.

I nodded my head.

'I got here just after nine. You weren't in, so I thought I'd pop down to Sale and see if anything was brewing.'

I goggled.

'Yes, well,' he continued uncertainly. 'That copper went out and then two men arrived. They drove off in their Toyota Land Cruiser, taking Mrs Peterson with them. I decided to follow them but I lost them in Wilmslow. You know, that road off the motorway near the airport. I'm sorry, Dave.'

An hour later we were still cruising round the back lanes of Wilmslow, looking for the Toyota. We were in Finbar's car with him driving. Starting at the spot where he'd lost Polk and Tyler, we checked out all the nearby side roads. I was sure from his description – 'one tall and broad, the other broad and short' – that it was them. It was a hopeless task. As Bob Lane had discovered, large numbers of residents in the Cheshire suburbs feel the need to drive around in massive cars with off-road capability. God help the environment if the price of armoured vehicles ever comes down.

When we got back to Thornleigh Court Finbar wasn't inclined to quit. 'That Mrs Peterson's got to go home eventually. If I go and keep the house under surveillance I might be able to pick up the Toyota when it comes back.'

'Listen, Finbar, you know as well as I do that you've been on that road too long. Someone's certain to spot you.'

'I'll move to a different spot,' he argued. 'Anyway, there are people coming out of the church car park all the time.'

I could see that he was determined. Whether it was the drink, general depression or just plain stupidity, I don't know. I let him go. I gave him my mobile to report developments with and returned to the flat on my own. I couldn't even summon up enough enthusiasm to go in the kitchen and polish the work surfaces.

I wasn't in the flat long, gloomily staring at four walls, before the phone rang. I expected that it was Finbar reporting that Anne Peterson had returned on foot and that he was coming home.

It was Rufus Polk. 'Hi there, good buddy,' he said. 'We've got a friend of yours here and he wants to speak to you.'

'I'm sorry, Dave,' Finbar croaked. 'I seem to be in a sort of POW situation.'

'Recognize the voice?' Polk interjected. 'Well, my cheap friend, I can tell you that I'm just about sick and tired of you snooping on us. If you don't come along down here for a chat I might just be tempted to switch the light out on this good old boy of yours.'

'Listen, you, harm him and you're dead,' I informed Polk.

'OK! Just joking!' he chuckled. 'Where's the sense of humour you Limies pride yourselves on? Why should I harm him? You're going to come down and see us, aren't you?'

'Yes,' I snapped.

'Listen, little guy, all we want is to get you off our backs. There's a dozen ways we could arrange that but you're kind of high profile. We'd like to see if we can talk some sense into that pointy little head of yours before things go too far.'

The drive to Sale was a nightmare. The football game had just finished and the world and its wife was on the road. I felt tempted to mount the pavement at times and race there but that wouldn't have done Finbar any good. A thousand scenarios had gone through my mind. I was keyed up for violence. The first thing I'd done when Polk broke the connection was to try to get Bob Lane's automatic out of the weird ornament. Yet again I'd failed and now the frustrating object sat on the seat beside me. I'd look a total fool wagging a curious sculpture in Polk's face, but having it gave me a certain comfort.

At last I reached the turning for Harboro Road. I raced along as far as the church, desperately scanning both sides of the road. Finbar's car was in the church car park. I pulled up alongside. The old soldier was in the car. He was slumped against the wheel. I leaped out and flung the door of his car open. He appeared to be asleep. I stretched my hand out to turn his face towards me, expecting the worst.

'I'm sorry, Dave,' he said weakly. 'I seem to have let you down.'

'Oh, you're alive!' I shouted with relief. I could have kissed his withered old features, then I wanted to smack his face for taking such a chance. 'You mad old bugger!' I yelled. 'They must be able to see you plain as day parked here.' The car was in a small car park between the church and the parish hall. It was the only car in the car park. The cul-de-sac where the Petersons lived was directly opposite.

'I wasn't parked here,' Finbar said shamefacedly. 'I was right down the road. I thought I was well out of sight. I was watching the house in my driving mirror when suddenly the door was flung open and that oversized Yankee . . .'

'I don't think he'd like to hear you call him a Yankee. I think he's some kind of heavy-duty Southerner,' I interjected.

'Well, whatever, he made me phone you and drive here. Then he took the phone and the car keys and he said if you go over the road you can have them back.'

'Right, I'll sort this out. You take my car and I'll collect your keys.'

'Be careful, Dave. If they've lured you here it must be for a purpose.'

'I don't think direct assault is Mr Polk's style. He prefers to sneak up on people.'

I helped him out of the car and pressed my keys into his hand. I could tell that he was badly shaken. His face was green.

'Dave, if you're not out after a few minutes I'll call the police.'

'And tell them what? That we were watching a copper's house and someone strolled down the road and asked me in for a chat? No, Polk's clever . . . He's avoided anything that might give Mr Sinclair an excuse to go charging in. I'll have to go and see what he wants.'

'At least take this,' Finbar said. He picked up the ornament, passed his hand over it and the automatic popped out. I took it and put it in an inside pocket. It didn't make a very large bulge.

The Petersons had a very neat front garden. It was too neat. Everything was regimental with neat straight lines and carefully clipped hedges. The flower beds were lined with bricks laid on their side and painted white. I took this as a sinister feature. Their front door was nicely painted too. I could almost see my face in the shiny white gloss. As soon as I rung the bell hounds began baying and then large bodies charged the door. I nervously touched the gun wondering if I'd be able to get it out in time if Anne Peterson set the German shepherds on me.

'Down, Trixie! Back, Prince!' a shrill voice within commanded, and the barking died away to a mere dull growling. The door was opened by a plump red-faced woman of about thirty. Her dyed blonde hair was permed into a wavy nest of snakes and with my classical background I immediately began thinking that she might petrify me with a glance. It was soon clear that I had nothing to fear from Mrs Peterson. 'You're the one who's been causing all this trouble,' she said fretfully. 'You'd better come in.' She didn't meet my stare but turned to busy herself with chivvying the dogs back into the kitchen. 'Go through, they're waiting for you.'

I strode into the large front room. Rufus Polk and John Tyler were seated in two large armchairs with the failing afternoon light streaming in behind them. They were an incongruous pair to meet in an English suburban drawing-room. Clad in similar dark business suits, at a pinch you could have taken them for a pair of undertakers come to advise a family in its hour of grief. Certainly their expressions were lugubrious enough. Polk's face still showed signs of the battering I'd given it at our last face-to-face meeting. They eyeballed me, making it plain that this wasn't a reunion of old friends. I looked back at them and then shrugged. I made no effort to seat myself. It was up to them to open the conversation. I was tensed for whatever their first move might be.

Neither of them stirred or spoke as I glanced round the

room. It was utterly conventional, almost like a museum display – floral pink wallpaper, with a similar pattern on the carpet, the upholstery and the curtains. The Petersons seemed to have the complete set of Royal Doulton balloon sellers. They were everywhere, jostling for space with sporting trophies. If the room was typical, the pair facing me were anything but.

'Hi,' Polk said at last. Tyler made no attempt to say anything.

'Doesn't he speak?' I asked Polk.

Polk gave a hearty laugh. 'John prefers me to speak for him, but when he does talk you'd better listen, little fella. He's a man of few words but each one is carefully chosen . . .'

'Get on with it,' Tyler muttered. His voice was so low and gravelly that I couldn't make out his accent.

'There now, you see Mr Cunane, you've got us arguing already. What are we going to do with you?'

'Yes, sit down!' Tyler said. He seemed to have far less good humour than his partner. He looked at me closely and noticed the bulge in my pocket. 'Hey, Jim boy,' he said to Polk. 'This guy's tooled up.'

'Oh Mr Cunane, you've not come here to do us violence, have you?' Polk asked in mock surprise. 'We were hoping for a reconciliation.'

'Really?' I said.

'Hey, John, listen to him! "*Re-al-ly*"', he drawled. '. . . That's authentic Limey-speak for "go fuck yourself".'

'If you're so keen on reconciliation, why don't you tell me your real names?' I pressed.

'Oh gee, golly gosh! You mean you don't believe we share the names of two of our greatest presidents?' Polk mocked. 'For a cheap gigolo, you're *re-al-ly* sharp, Mr Cunane. When we came through your Customs we thought those good old boys would spot us in an instant but we're just two more tourists to them.'

'What is your name?'

'Jim Mattingly,' he said with a smile. 'John here is called Tyler . . . Tyler Mathers.'

'Just what sort of a scam are you two pulling?' I asked.

'Oh David! Now that we've been properly introduced don't you think you could try to interface with us properly? We were rather hoping that you could be our friend. You can stick with Polk and Tyler if it makes things easier for you.'

'Thanks.'

'You've got entirely the wrong idea about us. We just help the Children of Light with fundraising. There's nothing in it for us.'

'You help them with fire-raising and you like smacking women around. The pathologists haven't been able to discover how you killed Irvine Varley and Monica Withers and half a dozen others, but they will.'

'There's not a scrap of evidence for any of that,' Polk said. This time his jocular tone was a little more forced. 'If there was we'd have been arrested by now. All we do is raise funds for Aldous Arkwright by legal methods.'

I wondered for a moment why they were bothering with all the explanation. Was it *folie de grandeur*, perhaps? It's a cliché but it must get very frustrating being a criminal mastermind and having no one to brag to.

'The police are looking for you,' I informed them. They looked bored. 'It's an offence to enter the country on a false passport.'

'And how would they know they were false unless you'd told them?' Tyler chipped in. He seemed far more hostile than his partner. 'I told you, Jim boy. We should have taken care of this cheap punk as soon as he stuck his nose into our business.'

'Was it you who took care of Melville Monckton?' I enquired. 'Or was it your friends in Miami?'

'There,' said Tyler angrily. 'I told you he wasn't the sort to back off just because we smashed his car up. You've got to come down hard on trailer-trash like him.'

'No, no,' Polk said, with a wave of his arm. 'Simmer down, Ty! You always were too hasty. David and me will sort everything out.'

He turned to me with an intensely frank and open expression on his face. His pudgy features were straining to convey honesty and sincerity. I wondered if they taught classes in dissimulation in American high schools. 'Listen, Cunane, we were as shocked as anyone when Monckton cashed in his chips. We've no reason to believe that it wasn't an accident. All we were trying to do was facilitate a deal which would have put the Children of Light on a secure financial basis. With the money we'd have made from the deal with Monckton and your awkward friend Lane, we could have supported dozens of candidates for the higher life.'

'Are you totally bananas?' I asked contemptuously. 'Do you expect me to believe that all this has been because you want to support Aldous Arkwright's crazy little cult?'

'That's exactly what we're trying to do,' Polk said and this time I didn't think the sincere expression was feigned.

I shook my head in wonder.

'I can see you're a scoffer. You probably don't believe in anything except filling your belly and finding yourself a nice lay.'

'Your pal, Aldous the pimp, offered me all the sex I could cope with this morning,' I said.

'Watch your mouth!' Polk shouted. His sudden anger was startling. 'Don't you bad-mouth the Director. He's worth a hundred cheap Limies. He saved my life.'

'Oh yes,' I sneered. 'What did he do? Offer to hold your hand on a free ride to Fairyland?'

Polk's chest rose and fell several times before he could bring himself to speak. His face turned a flat white shade that contrasted with the colourful decor. I knew it would only take a word and Tyler would be at my throat. They looked like a couple of Dobermans getting ready to savage a rabbit. I kept my hand on the gun.

'Nice one, Cunane!' Polk said eventually. 'You think if you provoke me it'll give you the chance to put a bullet in me.'

'Much as I might like to let a little air into that confused little brain of yours, Polk, *old boy*, I'm here because you threatened a harmless old man.'

'We'd never have hurt him.'

'I know that he's not about to leave you any legacies,' I said.

'Let me shut this bastard up!' Tyler exclaimed. He put a

hand in his inside jacket pocket and I pulled out the Heckler and Koch automatic and pointed it at his stomach.

'Cool it, Ty!' Polk warned with a growl. 'He's trying to provoke you.'

'No,' I said, 'but I would like a bit of information. If you claim to be a pair of harmless fundraisers, just what is friend Arkwright's attraction? I mean, why do you need him? The guy's well round the loop.'

'I was in the Stockade in San Francisco when I met him. I was waiting to be busted out of the service and was expecting to get time in a federal prison.'

'That was because you got a little too enthusiastic about killing people . . .' I said smugly. It was a mistake. Polk and Tyler exchanged glances.

'Now just where would a ladies' man like you learn that, Cunane?' Polk asked grimly.

'Never mind where,' I blustered. 'I just know that you didn't exactly cover yourself in glory in Vietnam, not that anyone else did.'

'Hey, buddy! Do you think the British Empire was built by men following the rules of cricket?' Polk snapped. 'You guys exterminated whole races.'

'Yes, but not me personally,' I said.

This led to more chest heaving and snorting from brother Polk. His eyes were like two little black buttons. If looks could kill, I'd have been mutton long since.

'OK, smart ass, have your little joke for now,' he muttered. 'You asked me why I needed Aldous Arkwright and I'll tell you. It's probably more than a cheap mercenary little gigolo like you can ever understand. I was feeling more than slightly pissed off about the good old American dream back in 1969. I was on trial to save some general's stars. They told me I ought to get a chaplain to speak up for me . . . I did. I was so pissed off with the US Army that I said I belonged to the Church of Satan. Clive Roper, as the Director then was, turned up. He spoke for me all right. That guy spoke so well, showed up their hypocrisy so convincingly, that they reduced my sentence to time served and a dishonourable discharge. I think they wanted to see the back of me.'

'So your leader is a saint and you're his apostle,' I said with a laugh. 'Some religion!'

'Sneer away, cheapie, I've heard it all before. But listen up good. This is the deal. Leave us alone and we'll leave you alone. You're wrong about those deaths. We've killed no one . . .'

'What about Janine White? You said you had undetectable methods of killing and that you'd kill her children.'

'Shit! The bitch asked me if I'd killed people and I just played back her fears to her.'

'You tried to kidnap her children!'

'No, we just wanted to make sure that she didn't get too carried away with what she wrote in that paper of hers.'

'Yes, after you almost beat her to death.'

'We all make mistakes,' he said with a sigh. 'If it makes you feel any better, why don't you shoot me in the leg or the arm? You've already smashed my face.'

'I can't stop the police being interested in you,' I said.

'I don't think we need to worry too much about the constabulary, do we? Our good friend Anne Peterson lets us know where they're up to.'

I looked at him for a long time. Polk had dark eyes as if there was some Mediterranean blood running through his Southern veins. He and Tyler watched me trying to make up my mind. Their faces were as expressionless as those of a pair of alligators in one of their native bayous. There was something so cold and calculating that all I wanted was to get out of that room with a whole skin. I didn't doubt that if the opportunity arose they'd crush me like a bug.

'Can I have the car keys and the mobile?' I asked.

'Does that mean you're butting out of our affairs?' Polk asked in a voice of quiet satisfaction.

I nodded.

He handed over the keys and phone. As I walked to the door and into the hallway I saw Mrs Peterson standing in the kitchen doorway. She looked terrified.

I knew that nothing was over.

Renegade Cult Preaching Violence

Despite denials by Children of Light officials, police sources in Manchester are convinced that breakaway elements in the cult's associated Repeal 98 movement – a group categorized as 'so right wing that they don't know the Stone Age is over' by one officer – are behind the recent increase in assaults on would be criminals.

Headline and article in the *Observer*

21

Saturday, 31 October – Sunday, 1 November (All Saints Day)

Finbar seemed to have recovered when I got back to the car. I gave him his keys and we drove in convoy to Thornleigh Court at a very sedate pace.

'So it's over?' Finbar asked when I handed him a glass of whisky.

'It is for you,' I said. 'You can get yourself back up to Cumbria.'

'You need someone to watch your back,' he said earnestly.

I suppressed a laugh. He meant well.

'Why can't the police sort all this out? I thought you were close to Assistant Chief Constable Sinclair.'

'He's not close to anyone, even his clothes hang loose on him. He just wanted to use me to discredit the Children of Light. That's what all this is about. The Children are behind the Repeal 98 people. The police are terrified that some kind of genuine vigilante group is going to get off the ground. There's a hell of a lot more support for the Repealers and their romantic 'back to the past' movement than anyone likes to admit. Law and order's got political sex-appeal these days. Did you know that since their volunteers have been patrolling the cash points in Withington and Didsbury muggings of students have gone down by ninety per cent?'

'Isn't that a good thing?'

'When you were in the Army, would you have liked to have been asked to move over by a bunch of unpaid volunteers?'

'No, I suppose not, but I still don't see why we can't phone the police now and tell them where Polk and Tyler are.'

'Assuming that they're still where we left them, how long do you think it would take someone to tip them off? Listen, Finbar, why do you think that little meeting took place in a policeman's home? They were telling us that whatever move the police make, they'll know about it.'

'You're too suspicious, Dave. There's no evidence that Detective Sergeant Peterson is giving them information.'

'Of course he is. Mrs Peterson's scared out of her wits. They've definitely got something on her.'

'I still think we should do something,' Finbar persisted.

'Listen, mate, I'm tired of playing the concerned citizen. What has it ever got me except a chance to inspect the cells at half a dozen police stations? If we interfere, the odds are that we'll be arrested and our transatlantic friends will come up smelling of roses. We're not exactly squeaky clean ourselves, are we?'

'What do you mean?' the retired officer asked in his most correct military tones. One of the fascinating things about Finbar was the way he could revert to the clipped Sandhurst accent quite unconsciously when he thought he was representing authority.

'*You* were spying on them. *I* did go into the house with an illegal firearm in my pocket,' I explained wearily.

'Damn it!' Finbar snorted. 'There must be something we can do.'

'I promised them that I'd keep out of their affairs,' I told him.

An expression of disgust momentarily clouded Finbar's face.

'It's not like you to haul the flag down,' he muttered.

'Tell me one thing that I can feasibly do to nail them and I'll do it,' I challenged. 'Anyway, it's only a truce. I'm sure that when the coast is clear they'll try to sort me out. That

Tyler had trouble keeping his hands off my throat . . . It crossed my mind that it would have been a lot simpler if I'd just shot the pair of them when I had the chance and enlisted you to help me bury them in some remote spot, but then I'd have had to shoot Mrs Peterson as well.'

'Yes. You'd never do that, though, would you?' he asked trustingly.

'Needs must, when the devil drives,' I said.

'Don't become all hard-boiled and cynical. It doesn't suit you, Dave.'

'I can't keep going round and getting embroiled in everybody's business but my own. I can't pay my creditors with good intentions.'

'That's true, I suppose, but I thought you were helping Janine White with her story. Surely there'll be money enough if you can show that the Repealers and the C of L are involved in a conspiracy?'

'Finbar,' I said curtly. 'I've tried; the police have tried; Ms White has tried. So far we've achieved nothing. Sometimes you have to admit that it's time to give things a rest.'

Finbar considered this for a while.

'Right!' he said. 'That gun, by the way, you'd better put it somewhere safe.'

Whether I really would have stayed out of the affairs of Polk and Tyler and Arkwright was something I never really put to the test because not long after a very disgruntled Finbar had departed and I'd made myself an evening meal of sausage and onions the phone rang.

'Is that *Dive K'nine*?' the voice asked.

'Yes, Mrs White,' I said softly, 'it's me.'

'I just called to let you know that Janine's a lot better. They'll be letting her out tomorrow. We're going to stay with your parents for a day or two and then we'll go back to London when Janine's well enough to travel.'

'That's great news,' I said in a non-committal voice.

'You don't sound all that pleased,' Mrs White said sharply.

'I am,' I said hastily.

'Janine's very upset about you dropping everything like a

ton of bricks. She was depending on you . . .'

'For what?' I asked patiently.

'Well, you know . . . her story . . . everything!'

'The story they had about me in the *Guardian* wasn't very flattering.'

'Janine thought it was that. She says she told you it wasn't her fault . . . the diary editor got out of the wrong side of bed that morning.'

'Mrs White, that's all water under the bridge now. Was there anything else?'

'Just that I didn't think you looked like the sort of man who would encourage someone and then just drop them.'

'It's not me, it's your daughter. She told me that she doesn't even like me.'

There was a sharp intake of breath at this.

'Janine's like that. She wouldn't like you to feel you were doing her a favour or anything. She had a bad time with that creep Henry Talbot.'

'OK, I'm sorry, but I don't quite see what I'm supposed to do.'

'You can at least talk to her, can't you? Visiting is from seven thirty tonight!'

It was twenty to eight when I got to the MRI and almost eight before I reached Janine's bedside. They'd moved her back into the main ward and she was sitting up looking rather forlorn in her white cap when I arrived.

'I suppose this is mum's doing?' she asked sharply. 'I got your earlier message.' Her expression was hardly welcoming.

'Yes, according to your mother and my father, I'm Mr Nasty in this little story.'

She looked at me with those determined blue eyes. Her face looked a lot better. The colours were almost normal. I noted that she made no effort to contradict my remark.

'Janine, I've spent an unpleasant half-hour in the company of Polk and Tyler . . .'

'Looking for a better offer, were you?'

'That's it!' I exploded angrily. Visitors at other bedsides

turned, ears were tuned to our conversation right along the ward. 'I'm sick and tired of everyone telling me that I'm only in this for the money. Practically the only person who takes me at face value is Aldous Arkwright and he wants me to join his cult and become a . . . oh, I don't know what.'

'What does he want you to become?' Janine asked unsparingly. 'Don't be bashful on my account. I know all about the little ways of the Children of Light.'

'He said that all my sexual desires would be catered for.'

'Well, what's stopping you? Go!' she snapped. 'That's what you're supposed to be good at, isn't it?'

'I don't want that, and I don't want them! The cult's just a front for a lot of drug dealing and money grabbing, however sincere Arkwright may be.'

'What do you want?'

'I'd like for once to meet someone who judges me by what she sees and not by what someone's told her.'

'And did you think I might fill the bill? Is that why you've turned all petulant?'

I kept my mouth shut.

'That's a turnaround, isn't it?' Janine asked with a laugh. 'You couldn't wait to get shot of me on the first two occasions we met.'

'I'd hardly had time to get to know you then.'

'And now he's seen me lying helpless in bed, big, tough Dave Cunane would like to slip in alongside me?' she said scornfully. 'Well think again, sunshine. It'll take more than an expression of sympathy before you get your leg over with me!'

I turned on my heel to get out of there as fast as my legs would take me.

'Wait!' she snapped. 'I've not finished with you yet. You say you were with Polk and Tyler. Did you ask them why they beat me up?'

'I'm sorry, Miss White,' I said sarcastically. 'It wasn't that sort of discussion. Having a chat with those two isn't like an editorial conference at the *Guardian*. The type of argument that pair appreciate is much more final, much less qualified by ifs and buts. They like to see their opponents in the cemetery. Fortunately, I let them know that I was quite prepared to put a bullet in their brains. It's the kind of reasoning they appreciate.'

'There you go!' she said with withering scorn. 'Typical macho exaggeration. I'll bet you'd run a mile if you even saw a gun.'

I looked over my shoulder to check that I wasn't overlooked and then took the Heckler and Koch out of my pocket.

'Do you think I'd have hesitated a second about killing the men who put you in here?' I asked quietly. 'The only trouble I have with it is that a quick death is better than they deserve.'

Her eyes went very round and then filled with tears. Her face lost the hard look.

'Dave, you wouldn't, would you? It's illegal.'

This comment was so off the wall that I had to laugh. 'Listen to her. The woman who's perfectly prepared to let two hardened murderers escape justice because they threatened her and her kids telling me what's illegal. You're a joke, Janine. What sort of game did you think we were playing? Didn't you see me smash Polk's face with a car jack? Those kind of people don't let you off with a flea in your ear and a pat on the back.'

The gun was back in my pocket when the sister bustled over to see what all the fuss was.

'Now, now, what's going on? We can't have family quarrels in here,' she clucked.

'It's nothing, sister, we're just sorting something out,' Janine said.

'Don't you go upsetting your partner,' she told me, giving me a sharp poke in the arm to emphasize the point. 'We don't want to see her back in here, ever!'

'Sorry,' I muttered.

When she'd gone Janine turned to me. 'Everything I said came out the wrong way. I didn't mean that you were a stupid posturing male. Don't go getting yourself into trouble on my account.'

'You know there's one way you could sort all this out,' I

said hopefully. 'If you'd tell Sergeant Culpepper the names of your attackers she'd leave no stone unturned for them to crawl back under. That woman's mustard on jailing violent males.'

'I can't take the chance. You've already told me that those two mean business,' she said sadly. 'But Dave, please don't pretend that if you killed them you'd be going on a vengeance mission for me. When you hit Polk with that jack you did it for yourself, not for Melanie, and if you killed them that would be for you too. I don't want any blood spilled on my account even if they did kill . . .'

'All right,' I said quickly. 'I get the message. I'm not some kind of crazy cowboy, whatever it says in the *Guardian*. The gun's for protection.'

'You like it though, don't you?' she asked accusingly. 'I saw your face when Polk went down. You were really happy.'

'Yes, it's a rough old world, isn't it?' I said coldly. 'I was happy that it was him and not me on the floor. Am I supposed to apologize for that?'

Her eyes flashed angrily again. She lost the woebegone look of a moment earlier.

'You'd be better thinking of some way we can get out of this mess,' I said quickly before she could lacerate me with her tongue again. 'It's mainly your fault that we're in it.'

'What do you suggest we do? Emigrate? I could always go to Beverley Hills and look for darling Henry Talbot, I suppose.'

'I shouldn't advise that. The C of L have a coven on the West Coast.'

'Don't be so literal minded, Dave,' she said with the first smile that I'd seen from her on this visit. 'You're a fool at times. Will you come and help me to get out of here tomorrow? Eleven a.m.? I'm supposed to be going to stay at your parents' farmhouse but I'm dreading it.'

'It's a glorified weaver's cottage, not a farmhouse,' I said.

'Whatever . . . I hate receiving hospitality when I know I'll never be able to return it.'

'Now who's striking attitudes?' I asked. 'My parents have

loved looking after your children and they're naturally curious about what you're like. I think my poor mother has me wedded off to you in her mind. It's about the hundredth time she's tried to see me hitched to a decent woman but you're the first that's come with a ready-made family. It's added to your attractiveness.'

'"Decent woman", am I? I suppose that counts as a compliment coming from you but your mother's going to be disappointed, isn't she?' Janine said with the merest trace of a grin on her face. 'I didn't mean to slight your parents. I'm sure the cottage is nothing like Cold Comfort Farm . . .'

'Oh, but that's exactly what the Corless Farm is like,' I interrupted. 'You're not going to be disappointed at all.'

At that moment the bell rang to signal the end of visiting.

'Eleven tomorrow,' she said. 'Be here, macho-man.'

I took myself off to a pub in Didsbury for the rest of the evening. There were one or two people I was at school with in the pub. They liked to gather there on a Saturday night mainly to discuss the day's football match. United had won so the mood was jovial. I stayed until chucking-out time and then went for a curry. It was well after midnight when I returned to the flat.

As I turned into the car park a figure sitting on the low surrounding wall gave me a wave. It was the elusive Melanie. It was quite a cold night and she wasn't wearing a coat. I could almost hear her teeth chattering as I approached her.

'I need your help,' she said. She was clutching a tissue in one hand and sniffing as she spoke. Despite the expensive clothes she was wearing, she looked a mess. Yet I hesitated.

'Is there anyone with you?' I asked sharply.

'What?' she said, sounding vulnerable and confused.

'Why are you here? Who sent you?'

She started sniffing and dabbing her eyes with the tissue . . . 'I thought I could get away from the Children of Light but they tracked me down to your parents' house. There was a phone call when your parents were out on Friday morning. They must have found where I was. I knew I just had to run

... I don't want to go back. It's horrible. You've no idea of the things they put you through. Conditioning they call it. It's more like torture.'

'Melanie, love, you've got the resources to go anywhere you want. Why did you run away from that hotel in Bolton?' I asked in a slightly less harsh tone.

'I phoned the Director to ask him to stop Rufus and John pestering me. He said he had no power over them. I thought I'd leave the country but when I got to the airport I remembered I'd no passport. It's at Meldrum Terrace.'

As she spoke her breath formed a cloud of fog in the cold night air. I was getting cold myself. I looked up and down the street. There was no one visible, no large figures lurking behind cars.

'You'd better come up before you freeze to death,' I invited gruffly. I wasn't pleased. Melanie's presence added yet another complication to my life. I didn't look at her but walked to the entrance and turned the key. She followed meekly with head bowed, in what no doubt was the approved posture for young females among the Children of Light.

Once in the flat I carefully fastened both the high-security locks on my door and put the keys in my pocket. Short of prolonged attention with a sledge-hammer, no one was going to get in easily.

'Do you usually lock the place up like that?' Melanie asked in between sniffs. She had a couple of carrier bags with her.

'Only when I'm receiving uninvited callers.'

She started wailing at this.

'It's all right. I didn't mean you. I only meant it as a joke,' I assured her. She dried her eyes.

'Where did you go after the airport?' I asked. I walked into the kitchen to make coffee and she followed.

'What do you mean?'

'I lost you at the airport. It's a very good place to avoid someone following you. Did you know that? All those people coming and going, no one would be able to trace you.'

'I went to a hotel in Wilmslow. You can phone and check if you like,' she said.

'It's not really where you went but who you met that worries me, Melanie. Did you meet up with Polk and Tyler?'

'Of course not! What a dreadful thing to say,' she protested. 'It's them I'm running away from. The Director had said I should have a child by John Tyler . . .' She started crying. I made no move to comfort her. I ripped a piece of kitchen tissue off the roll and handed it to her without a word. 'I couldn't stand the idea, Tyler's repulsive,' she explained after wiping her eyes.

'I can't make you lot out. It's only this morning that Arkwright told me that the higher initiates swear off sex.'

'You saw him?' she said feverishly. 'I love the Director and if he'd asked . . .'

'What? You'd have his child. So he absolves himself from his own rules?'

'He has done before, but only very rarely . . .'

'Typical!' I said contemptuously.

'Not really. There are lots of us who would be willing but he rarely allows himself to be joined in the body with one of his disciples. He says it's bad for discipline . . .'

'Why didn't you tell me all this before?' I said grimly. 'We could have had the police and social services and God knows what all over Meldrum Terrace like a rash.'

'I told you why when you helped me to escape. They have their lawyers on call day and night. There's nothing illegal about a woman having a child by a man she isn't married to.'

'There is if she's being put under duress.'

'You don't understand what it's like. After you've been with them for a while it becomes hard to think about going back outside. They tell you that the world's such a dreadful place and you start to feel so superior. Those who've been initiated, well . . . they're so confident. I've seen some of the older ones die. They're so sure that they're going on to the higher plane of existence that they die smiling and so happy to go.'

'You don't say . . .' I murmured sceptically. The coffee was ready and I poured her a large mug and added a generous shot of whisky for both of us.

She looked at it dubiously.

'Drink it,' I ordered. 'It'll bring you back to earth.'

We went back into my living-room. Not for the first time I was aware that the carpets were threadbare. Melanie had stopped sniffing and something of the fragile faun-like character that I'd noted on our first meeting had returned. She poised herself delicately on the edge of the sofa. Suddenly it and the rest of my furniture looked tatty and out of date – something I hadn't felt the other week when Lisa Lovegrove was squirming about trying to give me the best view of her cleavage.

I mentally pinched myself. What was happening? Melanie wasn't wearing her green fairy robe yet she was casting a powerful spell over me. I reminded myself that I was just about old enough to be her father. She was dressed in a kind of Indian costume, or at least that's what the embroidery on the material reminded me of. Her jacket was one of those high-collared efforts that the Indian leaders wear, only in Melanie's case simplicity wasn't the objective. It was made of a beautiful hand-embroidered pale blue linen. She was also wearing matching linen trousers. Delightful wear for a salon in Knightsbridge, but hardly the kit for wandering round Manchester on a cold winter's night. However, she'd stopped shivering now and only her bright red nose served as a reminder of the state she'd been in a few moments earlier.

She watched me observing her and gave me a shy smile, eyelashes fluttering. I took a deep draught of my coffee.

'Have you really left the Children of Light?' I asked roughly.

'Oh, I have! I have! I don't know why you keep going on about it. Didn't you help me to escape yourself?' Her eyes were brimming and I prepared for another outbreak of wailing but I was determined to find out exactly what had brought her to my door.

'Drink the coffee!' I ordered again. She swallowed a mouthful with an expression of extreme repugnance on her face.

'Drink it all. You'll catch your death of cold. What have you got in those bags? You should have put something warm on.'

She tipped out the carrier bags, revealing bras, knickers,

another trouser suit and a dress, a make-up kit, a couple of bottles of scent, and a toothbrush.

'Well, at least you're not carrying any deadly weapons,' I told her.

'That's horrible!' she exclaimed. 'How could you say that? You know I'm trying to get away from the Children of Light. Since I inherited Daddy's fortune all they've wanted is for me to sign over my money to them.'

'So you say,' I muttered.

'I shouldn't have come. I'll go. I'll get a taxi and book into a hotel.'

'Just answer a few more questions and I'll stop being awkward,' I said. 'What was the name of your hotel in Wilmslow?'

'The Swiss Village,' she said without hesitation.

'Why did you leave there when you were safe?'

'I'm a fool. I phoned the Director this morning to beg him to call off Rufus and John. He said he would but he must have traced the number to the hotel and I saw them at the reception desk this afternoon. I panicked. I just ran out of the hotel down the road and got on the first bus that came past. All I could think about was you. You would be able to get me away from those two again. I came to Chorlton but you weren't in so I went to the cinema at Salford Quays. I've been there all day. At eleven o'clock I walked here from Salford Quays and waited until you came home. I've not been in touch with anyone else.'

She opened her pocket and took out several cinema tickets which she threw on the small coffee table in front of me.

'There, check for yourself!' she said.

I did. The timings on the tickets showed that she'd spent eight hours in front of various screens at the multiplex.

'What is it you expect me to do?' I asked wearily.

'I don't know,' she said almost hysterically. 'You're working to bring down the Children of Light ... Help me. Get them off my back. I can't go on being followed everywhere I go.'

'Do you want to join your mother? She's gone to Australia.'

A look of extreme disgust crossed Melanie's face. 'She's mad. I can't live with all that wildlife. She's probably got kangaroos and wallabies crawling all over her by now. I'd rather go back to the Children and have John Tyler's baby.'

I laughed at this. 'Maybe you don't have to go that far, but I'm tired and I need sleep. I'm going to bed and you can sleep in here.'

She looked slightly more cheerful at this. She fished another tissue out of her sleeve and wiped a last drip from the end of her nose.

'I'll sleep with you if you like,' she offered.

'Yes, Melanie, I would like it,' I said jovially, 'but it would be wrong. You've been through enough tonight. Get a good night's rest and we'll work out what to do with you in the morning. Everything will look better then.'

It didn't take me long to get ready for bed but all the time I was acutely aware of the beautiful young woman in the next room. Before turning out the light I put the automatic under my pillow. Sleep didn't come easily. I kept going over everything that had happened. I heard the light click out in the living-room. Presumably Melanie was sleeping on the sofa. It was certainly large and comfortable enough for that. I'd left her a couple of blankets. I slipped into a light doze.

At about four in the morning I was awakened by a light clicking on in the living-room and the sound of a door to the entrance hall being opened. Then there was the distant sound of the toilet being flushed. I relaxed and tried to get back to sleep. Ten minutes later the door leading from my room to the living-room was gently opened. I lay perfectly still on the bed. From where I lay I was able to see the doorway through half-closed eyes. Melanie tiptoed in. She was as naked as the day she was born. I hardly dared to breathe. Should I jump up and order her back to her room?

Duty was about to conquer lust when I suddenly saw what she was after. Moving very slowly, she picked up my trousers from the chair when I'd left them and felt in the pockets, first in the left and then in the right. It wasn't my beautiful body she was after, but my keys! She turned away to look at the small dressing-table. The keys were on the right-hand side. I heard a chink of metal on glass as she moved a bottle and then she had the keys.

I switched the light on. Instantly she swivelled to face me, the hand with the keys going behind her back.

'Dave, I was lonely,' she said breathlessly. 'I want to be close to you.'

'You lying bitch!' I said with my customary chivalry. I jumped out of bed and tried to grab her, but she was too quick for me. Her right hand flashed towards me and it was only when it came close that I saw she held a razor between her fingers. I jumped back but the blade raked across my ribs. Then she was out of the door like lightning.

I charged after her. In her haste to reach the front door first she tried to block my path by overturning furniture and slamming doors. She already had one of the two door keys in its lock and was feverishly turning it when I caught up with her. She turned with the razor at the ready, hissing like a cat. There was a rap on the door from the outside. I look at her in horror. Only the Yale lock and the hand-operated lever for the steel cross bar stood between her and whoever was waiting outside . . . as if I needed to ask who it was.

I could have dashed back to the bedroom and plucked up the automatic but I was in a blind rage. I reached out to grapple with Melanie who was all hard muscles and bared teeth now. The hand containing the razor came down with a vicious slash across my right shoulder, then I grabbed her wrist. She jabbed at my eye with her other hand, the key extended like a dagger. I twisted away. She squirmed and struggled, trying to bite and scratch. Her foot came up and she hammered at me with her heel. There was no way I could hold her. The blood from my wounds made her too slippery to hold. She was strong. In another moment the door would be open. In a rage I swung my fist. She ducked like someone who'd been sparring all her life. I tried again and caught her on the forehead with the point of my elbow. She went down with a groan.

I ran to the bedroom and scooped up the gun. If Polk and Tyler were outside that door they were going to be dead meat and to hell with the consequences. When I got back to the hallway Melanie was on her feet and the door was opening. I fired and the bullet slammed into the metal door frame and spanged off into the ceiling with a thud. I wrapped my fingers in her hair and tried to pull her back.

'Kill her if you can't get him, you god-dam fool,' the unmistakable voice of Rufus Polk echoed round the corridor outside.

The door was kicked open and John Tyler briefly bobbed into the entrance. His arm was up behind his head and then came down in a snapping motion. Something flashed from his hand. I fired, ducked and pulled Melanie down all in one motion. She shrieked. All sympathy gone by this time, I pulled her back with all my strength and leaped over her into the doorway just in time to see Tyler dive towards the stairs clutching a bloody arm. The thick white flesh of the back of his neck presented a perfect target but my finger paused on the trigger and in these situations he who hesitates is lost. With a series of heavy thuds on the stairs Polk and Tyler made their getaway. I ran back to my living-room and jerked the curtains open in time to see them roar away in their Toyota Land Cruiser.

When Finbar arrived Melanie was on the floor on my hallway sobbing and weeping and clutching the deep slash that Tyler's knife had made in her arm.

'Dave! What have you been doing?' he asked in an anguished voice.

'Not me,' I gasped. 'Ask her, she tried to let your two buddies from this afternoon into the flat so they could cut my throat.'

'No, no, it wasn't like that,' Melanie moaned. She was a gruesome sight. The blood she'd extracted from me and her own blood from the gaping wound in her arm covered her arms and legs.

'I saw them dash past me,' Finbar said. 'She must have pressed the button to open the outside door.'

I looked at him blankly. The deep razor slashes in my chest and shoulder were starting to hurt like hell and the last thing I needed was a post-mortem on what had happened. To his credit, Finbar's officer training took over. He checked the corridor and then shut the door.

'Get some towels on those cuts, Dave,' he said as he bent to pick up Melanie.

> **'Mind-set dangerous.'**
>
> **The splintered and hostile outlook of many members of modern cults such as the Children of Light is dangerous, and could lead to violence against others or even turn against their own members, Dr Sebastian Eckstein warned a meeting of the British Psychology Forum on Saturday.**
>
> Extract published in the Sunday Times

22

Sunday, 1 November

I don't know whether it's a tribute to the times we live in, or whether the National Health Service was supplying the whole block with extra-strong sleeping pills, but, apart from Finbar, none of the neighbours ventured out of their front doors to investigate the shooting.

Probably the reasons were less dramatic than I imagined. The noise was muffled by my steel front door and the next-but-one flat, belonging to the petrol hoarder, was empty. Still, as my body struggled to cope with the after-effects of shock, I couldn't help wondering what had happened to everyone. There were no wailing police sirens, no flashing lights and heavy-booted coppers demanding explanations. Polk and Tyler had vanished into the night from which they'd emerged, traceless as owls venturing out to hoot at the moon.

As I slowly came back to normal my eyes met the beguiling sight of Finbar gently bathing the stricken and still stark naked Melanie. She was standing in the bath, like Venus rising from the waves, as he slowly wiped blood off her. I shuddered.

'Are you all right, Finbar?' I asked.

'Yes,' he said thoughtfully. 'I'm just wondering if we need to get this young lady to hospital after we get some clothes back on her.' There was a mildly disapproving catch to his words which I picked up on immediately.

'Don't waste your sympathy on her, she's a murderess,' I said harshly.

Melanie whimpered in fright and Finbar gently covered her with my largest and newest towel. He looked at me reprovingly.

'Tell Finbar how you killed Fred Travis, Melanie ... You and your dear friends Polk and Tyler. It was just like tonight, wasn't it ... ? How did you get into his flat? Did the Children send you round as a special treat and did you let in his murderers?'

'Not now, Dave,' Finbar said quietly.

As I looked at Melanie she seemed to shrink and become more childlike. Taut muscles relaxed. Her expression melted back into that wounded faun look that I'd once found so beguiling. This time it was Finbar who got the benefit. He studied her innocent, pleading features and then turned to me. 'My God, Dave,' he said, shaking his head. 'A man doesn't half see life in the raw hanging about with you. What was she up to?'

Melanie responded with her familiar pitiful wail, which gradually died away to a whimper when she realized that there were no customers.

'That's better,' I said. 'Face it, Melanie, as far as Brother Polk and Brother Tyler are concerned, you're expendable. That knife of Tyler's was aimed at your heart, not mine. If I hadn't pulled you down we'd be wondering what to do with your pretty corpse now.'

She shuddered but suppressed the wails.

'Do you need to be so brutal, Dave?' Finbar muttered.

'She hasn't just tried to perform open-heart surgery on you,' I growled.

'I take it that we're not going to involve the police?' Finbar asked as politely as if he'd been inquiring about the weather, 'Because in that case I must ask you to make some arrangements for medical treatment for the young lady. The knife's cut quite deeply into her arm.'

'Yes, and what about me?' I asked plaintively. 'If you think I'm going to the casualty department at either the MRI or Wythenshawe with yet another bleeding young woman in tow, you've another think coming. That Sergeant Culpepper will lock me up and throw away the key.'

'So it seems we must see what our friends can do for us,' Finbar said with a smile.

Finbar got on the phone to Dr Jim McNeil while I watched Melanie closely while she dressed. My interest wasn't prurient. She'd taken the razor out of my bathroom and I was nervous about what she might have found in the kitchen. Wisely, Melanie kept her mouth firmly shut. When she'd finished dressing we sat watching the blood seep through each other's bandages while Finbar relayed the details to Jim.

Jim is the son of a Jamaican who served as air crew in the RAF during the war. He was born in Kingston in 1941 and has lived in Britain since he was eight. He was brought up in Glasgow and has a Ph.D. as well as his MD. This hasn't protected him from being told he's a foreigner by people half his age. I know him and his wife Margaret, a ward sister at Wythenshawe Hospital, because when my own wife Elenki was dying they'd been my main support. They live in Chorlton, about a mile from Thornleigh Court. Jim works as a medical research scientist at the University Department of Life Sciences.

'Good God, man!' he growled as he walked into my living-room. 'Have you taken up part-time butchery? The place is like an abattoir.'

I started to explain but was interrupted by a rumble of laughter that came right from the big man's stomach. Jim's built rather on the lines of Pavarotti, complete with beard. 'It's OK, Dave, Finbar's relayed the details. I know what to do – stitch you up and keep my big mouth shut.'

He waved at the door and his wife Margaret, a slim and bright-eyed white woman entered. Despite the early hour, Margaret was ready for action. She looked round the room at the blood and the gory towels, tut-tutted once, and then got to work on Melanie's arm. Melanie winced when Finbar's roughly applied bandages were whipped off. I didn't feel like smiling either, when Jim did the same to me.

'Have you had tetanus shots recently?' Margaret asked Melanie.

'I had them at school,' Melanie said. The presence of Margaret seemed to provoke a response. She began crying, not like a tragedy queen looking for an effect, but like a normal person. Her shoulders heaved as large salty tears rolled down her pretty cheeks.

'Hold still and stop blubbering, girl,' Margaret said unsympathetically. 'How am I supposed to get stitches in here unless you hold still?'

Her husband came and examined the wound.

'It's a clean cut,' he pronounced. 'You should only have a thin white line to show for your adventure when it heals. That's more than I can say for you, Dave. Those slashes on your chest and arm are jagged and they'll take a while to heal. You look as if you've been trapped in a mincer. I presume the young lady supplied you with your cuts?'

I nodded. Melanie hung her head down and cried so sincerely that I almost started to feel sorry for her. In the end the McNeils spent a lot longer patching me up than they did Melanie. They stitched where the cuts were deep and applied butterfly sutures when they were less so. I ached like hell when they'd finished, which didn't improve my temper.

'Dave, you need to get yourself fixed up with a wife,' Margaret informed me as she trundled past with a mop and bucket. 'You wouldn't have these unfortunate young women latching on to you if you had someone steady at your side to deter them.'

'This wasn't a lover's tiff, Margaret,' I said angrily, glaring at her. Matrimony is Margaret's cure for most ills, physical and mental. She gave me a warm smile. 'This so-called unfortunate young woman came here for the sole reason of letting her friends in. If she'd succeeded, there wouldn't have been enough of me left to need stitches.'

Everyone looked at Melanie. Although she avoided looking at me she seemed self-possessed, almost bored. She was wearing a sleeveless dress, her wounded arm was in a sling and she still had the bloody towel draped over her shoulders. I suppose she thought it made her look more like an accident victim. I stood up and went over to Finbar who was sitting by the phone. 'Do me a favour, Finbar,' I whispered. 'Get the tape recorder out of the spare bedroom and record everything that's said without letting Melanie know.'

He gave me a crafty nod and a wink. 'I think everyone needs a strong cup of tea after all this bloodletting,' he announced. He went to the kitchen and a moment later I heard him rummaging in the spare bedroom. There were plenty of blank cassettes with the tape recorder.

A few minutes later he returned with a tray which he put down on the coffee table. 'Shall I be mother, Margaret?' he asked before pouring the tea. I noticed that he put something down on the side cupboard and covered it with a pot-towel before turning to me with a smile.

'You do realize what Polk and Tyler were up to, don't you?' I said to Melanie.

She gave me her best frightened-schoolgirl look and shook her head. 'They said they wanted to beat you up for interfering with Melville Monckton and Bob Lane.'

'So that's why Polk told Tyler to kill you if he couldn't get me?' I asked scornfully. 'Get real, Melanie! They intended to kill both of us. Then they'd have carefully arranged things to look like some sort of lover's quarrel.'

Melanie brought her uninjured arm up and covered her eyes ... 'No, John would never have done that to me,' she said uncertainly and started rocking herself back and forward in her chair.

'This should wait for the police, Dave,' Jim McNeil said.

'What police?' I asked. 'You haven't heard the best part of this story yet ... Melanie was almost certainly at Detective Sergeant Peterson's in Sale when all this was planned. Isn't that right, Melanie?'

She gave a little whimper and a nod that could have been taken as assent.

'Still, Dave, there must be senior officers who are untainted ...' Margaret McNeil said.

'Don't be fooled by her act, Margaret,' I pleaded. 'Her own mother describes her as a tragedy queen.'

'Come on, Margaret, I think we'd better go,' Jim McNeil said. He drained his cup of tea and started packing away all the equipment he'd brought. 'We were never here, right,

Dave?' he said. He went over and took Margaret by the arm. She was still unconvinced that Melanie should be left in my care. Her husband guided her to the door.

'David Cunane, if I hear that any harm has come to that young woman I shall hold you responsible,' she warned.

'The last thing I intend her is harm. We'll have a little chat and then she can go wherever she pleases. As far away as possible from me, I hope.'

'Well, just see that you behave yourself,' she said sternly.

'I'm hardly likely to go rolling around on the floor again, am I? I've more stitches in me than a Fair Isle sweater thanks to Little Miss Melanie. Sweet as a nut she is.'

I tried to get up to thank them for their help. The effort was painful. Without them to staunch the flow I'd have certainly ended up in Casualty and eventually in front of Sergeant Culpepper.

'Stay in your seat and give those stitches a chance, man,' Jim warned before leaving.

'How did they kill Fred Travis?' I asked eagerly when they'd gone.

Melanie dropped the injured pose and asked me a question in turn. 'Are you sure they would have killed me?'

'You saw the knife, you heard Rufus,' I said. 'Those kind of guys always kill to a plan . . . *Fred Travis . . . up to something nasty with a mentally handicapped young man who cuts his throat . . . Dave Cunane, the well-known sex-maniac . . . killed in some sort of struggle with a beautiful young girl who rejected his advances . . . Sadly the girl also died.* That's how it would have been and you know it.'

She nodded her head as if accepting this. My chest felt painfully tight and it wasn't just because of the slashes I'd received. I hardly dared to breathe while she made up her mind to talk. Anger flared in my brain as I watched that look of pitiful innocence slip back on to her face.

'All you told me last night about wanting to escape was a pack of lies, wasn't it, you deceitful little bitch?' I shouted. 'You've been in with Polk and Tyler all along.'

'Dave, that's bang out of order,' Finbar said. 'Either you

calm down or I'll phone for the police and let them sort all this out.'

Melanie gave him a wan smile.

'No, he's right to be angry, Mr Salway,' she said mildly. 'I did think I was escaping and leaving everything behind me, but I found that it was all too much a part of me to give up. What I said about Rufus and John finding me at the Swiss Village Hotel was true, but I lied when I said I ran away. We went up to my room and they reminded me what I owe to the Children and the Director. They took me to that house in Sale with that horrible Peterson woman with her smelly dogs and her ghastly children. I never meant to hurt you, Dave, honestly. They just said that they wanted to punish you and frighten you off. I thought they'd beat you like they did Janine White. Then they'd let me back into the Children with no more fuss.'

'Lovely,' I said. 'You do know that Janine White only just made it, don't you?'

She shook her head timidly.

'You're an expert at not facing up to things, aren't you?' I asked in a more gentle tone. 'What did they do to Fred Travis?'

There was a long and agonizing pause while she made her mind up. The tape recorder was one of the most expensive on the market, guaranteed to be silent, but I imagined I could hear it whirring away to itself. I could feel anger bubbling up again. Despite Finbar's attempts to restrain me, I swear I'd have lashed out if she hadn't eventually spoken.

'Fred had been making a right nuisance of himself,' she said at last. 'He kept wanting more money from the Children . . . Rufus and John handled all the money matters, the Director left everything to them. You've got to understand Rufus and John are separate from the Children. We used to call them the Director's Swiss Guards. They didn't live like us. There's a rumour that Polk has a yacht in the Mediterranean. He always has a healthy-looking tan. We Children of Light hold all money in common. The whole idea is that we're going beyond material attachments.'

'How lovely for you, but what about Fred? He wasn't above a material or a sexual attachment or three, or so I've heard.'

'We have certain common goals. The Director feels society is looking for strong spiritual leadership. Fred feels . . . felt . . . that our civilization needs a return to a more directed sort of life . . . you know, like in the East . . . like Singapore.'

'Oh my God! I can see it now, public caning for dropping a piece of chewing gum.'

'Well, that's only fair, isn't it?' Melanie said defiantly. 'You muck us the streets, someone mucks you up.'

'I didn't notice you cheering when you were on the receiving end of a spot of caning.'

Melanie pouted at this and shut up.

'OK,' I said with a shake of the head, 'Fred and Aldous had a lot in common. They were both into corporal punishment. What else was there?'

Melanie studied the carpet carefully as if regretting ever opening her mouth. Then she gave me a look of loathing that was entirely unfeigned.

'You're so typical,' she said, almost spitting the words out. 'How could you understand what a man like the Director feels? The insights he's gained . . . they would be quite beyond you.'

'I don't know. Your precious Director has asked me to join the Children several times. He must feel that I'm not entirely beyond the pale.'

This seemed to make some impression, because after a pause and a long sigh she resumed her story. 'The original idea behind Repeal 98 was that Travis would recruit more members for us. His appeal was to a broader spectrum than a purely spiritual organization could hope to reach in these materialistic times.'

'Wonderful,' I muttered.

'The Director feels that we need to extend our influence among the broad masses. That's what our joint rally with Repeal 98 is all about . . . But the tail began to wag the dog. Travis got dreams of grandeur. When his volunteer movement began to take off . . . people joining to fight crime and so on . . . he started telling the Director what to do . . . He somehow got wind of the project Rufus and John were putting together with Melville Monckton. I think he tried to blackmail them into providing him with more money for his volunteers and then they found that he was diverting the money they'd already given him into his own pocket.'

'So the Children of Light employ the death penalty for anyone who tries to rip them off?'

'No, of course not,' she said indignantly, as if the very idea was ridiculous. 'We don't attach the same value to life on this plane as you do,' she explained patiently, as if to a backward child, 'but what Travis was doing was worse than stealing money. He was trying to get rid of the Director.'

'Polk and Tyler told you that?'

'We talked.'

'OK, why did you ask me to help you to escape on that Saturday if you were so well in with Brother Polk and Brother Tyler? Was that some sort of ploy to make sure I shared the blame for the Travis killing with Clint Lane?'

'No, you don't understand,' Melanie said in a low voice. I could only hope that the recorder was picking everything up. 'The Director wasn't involved with anything wrong. He's a wonderful man, perhaps the most wonderful man who's ever lived. He never knew anything about Travis's dirty game but I think he suspected that Rufus and John knew more about the killing than they were willing to admit. He summoned you to Blackley so that you could help him to find out more.'

'How sweet of him, but that still doesn't explain why you suddenly decided to run away that same night.'

Melanie blushed and looked genuinely embarrassed. I studied her carefully. This was not a pretence.

'It's true what you said before . . . I am a bit of a tragedy queen. It all got too much for me up at Meldrum Terrace. What I told you about not wanting John Tyler's baby and about them wanting all my money was true. I was supposed to keep an eye on the Director and tell Rufus and John if he was getting too upset about things . . .' Her voice faltered. 'The Director really believes everything he teaches us.'

She put her hand on her lap and looked down at it as if she might have admitted too much. The transgressions of Rufus and John were obviously a great sorrow to her.

'Melanie, that's a very interesting story but I think you've missed a few details out,' I said aggressively. She coloured a little but stuck her chin out as if to invite a blow. I could have shaken her, if Finbar hadn't been there to see fair play.

I tried another tack. 'So Rufus and John asked you to spy on your own Director and it got too much and you wanted out. I can understand that,' I said with as much sympathy as I could simulate. 'Anyone would. So Rufus and John – the Swiss Guards – what do you call them, the ugly Americans?'

'No!' she snapped.

'But they're just in it for the money. You said it. They don't live like the rest of you. They must be there for the money. I mean, why else would they hang out around the Director? They're hardly the sorts to end up on a higher spiritual plane, are they?'

'You're twisting everything. I lived with these people. They support the Director because he's a loveable, wonderful man. They'd have nothing without him. None of us would. I think in the early days back in America they really tried the path to spiritual development. It's not for everyone. There's no shame in trying and failing. Why should they cut themselves off from the Director? They found a role as fundraisers. Those on the path to the higher plane need financial support. That's what Rufus and John do . . . Find the money for the rest of us. We all owe a debt to them.'

I looked at Finbar. He rolled his eyes at this.

'After you left that afternoon,' she continued demurely. 'You know, when they threw you out . . . They tried to question me about what the Director had asked you to do. They said the Children of Light might be dissolved if you found out too much.'

'So you *were* supposed to be a sort of secret agent,' Finbar asked, 'spying on your boss.'

'Why?' I demanded bluntly. 'Why did you do it?'

'It was all Daddy's fault. He threatened to cut me off without a penny unless I left the Children. Rufus and John told me there was a way round that if I was willing to make a big sacrifice for the Children. I said I was. They train us to give up our personal life . . .'

Finbar was now looking at her with the sort of fascinated

horror that you might use when observing a boa constrictor swallowing a live rabbit.

'Don't look at me like that!' she protested. 'We all have to give up something if we hope to move on to a higher plane of reality. Parents and things like that tie you down...'

'Excuse me, my dear. You must forgive my old-fashioned ways,' Finbar apologized in his most courtly voice.

'Well, it was about two months before all the fuss with Travis started. We went to Oundle early on the Thursday after Daddy turned so nasty with the Director. We waited for the taxi to come and take Mum to Peterborough. I knew she went every Thursday. She likes to go pestering doctors with her imaginary ailments. When she'd gone I went to the door and asked Daddy to let Rufus and John in just to explain their point of view. He didn't want to but eventually I persuaded him. Then almost as soon as he'd sat down in his chair John knelt in front of him. I thought he was tying his shoe laces but suddenly he grabbed Daddy's wrists. John's terribly strong. Rufus went behind Daddy and slipped this shiny bag over his head. Daddy hardly had a chance to cry out. I couldn't believe how quickly he died. It was just like turning off a light. Later they told me that if anyone found out what had happened they'd tell the police that I was just as guilty as they were. I had to co-operate with them. I think it was after that that they put it in the Director's mind that it would be a good thing if I had John's baby. So you see, when you came along you gave me a chance to escape. I jumped at the chance.'

'Yes, you little fool, and if you'd gone to the police as Janine and I wanted, and told them all this, then Monica Withers wouldn't have died,' I said bitterly.

'I know nothing about her,' Melanie said firmly.

'I think you do. Your American pals must have told you everything.'

'I've met Shannon Withers,' she admitted.

'Another cold-blooded bitch who kills for the Children of Light!' I interjected.

'No, she isn't!' Melanie said bitterly. 'We're not like that. You don't understand... You've no commitments, no beliefs.'

'You stand by while they kill your father. With her, it's her sister. Same difference!'

'Can't you see that the Children of Light must survive? The whole course of evolution is nearing its climax, the millennium, everything. We can't let petty personal issues stand in the way of mankind taking the next step forward.'

'How noble and high-minded of you,' I sneered. 'Monica was killed for her money, wasn't she? Just like your father.'

'No, no, it wasn't like that. Monica was one of the dark forces pulling us down. The Director's warned us about them . . . "Crowbars" he calls them; evil souls who try to use their money as a crowbar to lever someone away from the Children. She deserved to die but I wasn't with the Children that week so you can't say I had anything to do with it.'

'Exactly how was Monica acting like a crowbar?' I asked.

Melanie waved her free hand vaguely. 'Oh, the usual I expect,' she said. 'I heard them talking about her months ago, but she wasn't an urgent case then.'

'Urgent case? What does that mean?' I felt as if I was on the verge of learning something important but Melanie seemed to have lapsed into vague generalities.

'We have a red list of members who're under pressure. Initiates give them maximum support. I wasn't on the red list until my father threatened to change his will. I suppose Shannon wasn't put on the red list until Monica said something to her but don't expect me to know what it was. I was only doing what I was told. I wasn't an initiate.'

'You must know something more,' I insisted. 'They must have told you more.' I was staring at her with an intensity that made my eyes ache.

'Why should they have? I wasn't even in Manchester. You and Janine drove me to Oundle, remember? I was staying with a schoolfriend in Oundle until I read that piece in the *Guardian* about you being a cowboy kidnapper and working for my mother.'

'She might be right, Dave,' Finbar said. 'The first thing a lot of these secret organizations do is to compartmentalize everything. They wouldn't have wanted an outsider to know everything they were up to.'

'So now you're an expert on crime as well as first aid,' I said resentfully. 'Melanie wasn't an outsider.' My chest was hurting but even worse was the pain of not knowing why Monica had died.

'Do I know something about security?' Finbar asked evenly. 'Yes, I do,' he asserted. He was dressed in a neat khaki-coloured dressing-gown and he looked at me owlishly. 'Dave, you're in no state for this. You're becoming overwrought. You should be in bed.'

As it happened, I was in no mood for common sense from the neatly clad ex-military man.

'I must know why Monica died,' I said angrily. I'd have shaken Melanie until her teeth rattled if the bandages round my chest hadn't prevented it. She seemed to sense my desperation.

'I did hear some things before I left,' she admitted. 'Shannon Withers doesn't live at Meldrum Terrace, she's in the Peterborough branch, but I did hear that her sister was pressuring her for the return of money that she'd borrowed from the family trust and that she'd told her that she was thinking of getting married. That would have meant that if she died her money wouldn't have come to the Children through Shannon.'

'When was this?'

'It was in the week or so before Fred Travis was killed. I can't be sure. I didn't keep a diary. They never let anyone write anything down.'

I put my head in my hands and groaned. There was a chance that Monica's death was nothing directly to do with me and Bob Lane. Monica might have hinted to her sister that she was thinking of getting married. Then, on that fateful afternoon when she'd helped me to break into Meldrum Street ... Had she phoned her sister to let her know that she'd found Mr Right? Me, to be precise. I tried to work it out. I could have ended up marrying Monica. I'm human enough to be attracted to a woman who has several million in the bank. No, that wasn't true. I'd never have married her even if she'd wanted to. I couldn't have tolerated being someone's kept man. She must have known that. Did Monica die because of some casual word? Did something make Polk and Tyler believe a fortune was slipping through their fingers? Was that why Polk had called me a 'cheap gigolo'?

No, it wasn't that, I suddenly realized. It all came back to me. 'Cunane, I've heard of you,' were the words I'd heard Shannon Withers say that night at the hospital in Stockport. Once my name was linked with a red-list member's 'crowbar', that must have been sufficient for the death sentence. In my mind's eye I could see the bag going over Monica's head.

I sighed heavily. I looked at Melanie and her outline seemed to be blurred. I realized there were tears in my eyes.

'Dave, this isn't right,' Finbar protested quietly. 'You're making yourself ill. You've lost a lot of blood.'

'I'd have lost a lot more if Melanie had had her way.'

'At least take a drink,' he begged. He poured out a tumblerful of whisky and put it next to the tea which I hadn't drunk. I took a healthy swallow of it.

'Can I have some?' Melanie asked. She spoke in that same sweet voice redolent of wind chimes that I'd first heard up at Blackley. If only she'd been croaking like a bull-frog then I might have told her to catch a bus that night when she wanted to escape.

Finbar complied with Melanie's request and poured her a generous dram.

'What about this thing Polk put over your father's head? The shiny bag, tell me about that,' I instructed her as she sipped her drink.

Finbar frowned at me and shook his head so that Melanie couldn't see him. He didn't know her. It wasn't his bedroom that she'd invaded with a razor in her hand. She was as tough as old boot leather and unless we got the story out of her now she'd come up with a completely different version which left poor Little Miss Melanie looking as pure as the driven snow.

As it happened, she wasn't put off by my question even though it concerned her own father's death. Her years with the Children of Light had apparently given her a different perspective on the deaths of non-members even if they were supposedly her nearest and dearest like the late Irvine Varley.

'It was very odd,' she said speaking in a clinical and

detached way. 'Rufus took this square of material out of his pocket. I thought it was silk, at first, but it was finer than silk. It was like a bag, rounded at one end. He slipped it over Daddy's head . . .'

'And you just sat there?'

'You don't understand. It was so quick. The bag moulded to every feature of Daddy's face. Rufus pulled it away very quickly and I thought they were just trying to frighten him but he didn't move. I couldn't believe he was dead, but Rufus just laughed and said "They go quick when I bag them" or something like that.'

'Why didn't you report your father's murder?' Finbar asked solemnly.

'Why should I have? He's gone and if I wrecked the Children I'd have lost my own chance to move on to a higher plane.'

'A practical way of looking at things, I suppose,' Finbar commented, 'if a trifle unsentimental for us ordinary mortals.'

'So what happened to Fred Travis?'

'I did nothing,' she said sullenly. 'You seem to know what happened, tell me.'

'Did Travis have his eye on you?'

'That dirty old man! He pawed me every time he visited Meldrum Terrace,' she spluttered before lapsing into an angry silence.

'Go on,' I prompted.

'It was like you said! You got it in one. Aren't you clever?'

'Tell us.'

'Rufus said Travis wanted me to spend the night with him. I had to do it for the good of the Children, so I went and slept with that noxious old lecher. I wanted to scream when he touched me, the flabby old monster . . . his great belly hanging . . .'

'All right, we get the picture,' I said. 'You don't need to use Technicolor.' I could see Finbar turning puce.

'The only thing that made me stand it was that I knew they were coming for him in the morning and I was the last woman who'd ever have to put up with him. I was to get up at five thirty and turn off the alarms and open the door. I didn't see what happened to Travis. I'd told him I had to be back at

Meldrum Terrace early so he wasn't expecting to see me in the morning.'

'Are you sure you didn't know what was going to happen?' I asked.

'Of course I didn't,' she said indignantly.

'Don't you care that Clint Lane is still being hunted for this murder?'

'He's mentally handicapped. It means nothing to him. He'll never reach the higher plane. He's like an animal, he just lives in the present with no foreknowledge of his own death or anything.'

'So that makes it all right to fit him up for murder?'

Melanie shrugged. 'Rufus says we have to be prepared to accept a certain amount of collateral damage,' she said coldly.

'Speaking of Rufus, where is he likely to be now?'

'They were at the Petersons'. He can't afford to be seen anywhere near the Director now that suspicions have been aroused.' This information was accompanied by a vindictive glance in my direction. I raised my eyebrows and stared right back at her. 'Well, it's true,' she said bitingly, 'the future of the human race is more important than whether a few rich crowbars died prematurely.'

'The Petersons . . .'

'Yes, she's a frightful frump, that Anne Peterson woman. I don't know why the Director ever let her join the Children. All she ever thinks about is her dogs and her guns and her stupid brats . . .'

'You've really got your claws into her, haven't you?' I said, intending to irritate her. 'She looked like a perfectly ordinary sort of woman to me. Perhaps you can tell us what you've got against her?'

Melanie screwed up a corner of the towel draped over her shoulder and twisted it into a knot. 'She's a silly cow,' she muttered.

'Surely, she's a pleasant and intelligent member of your group. An attractive person,' Finbar said slyly. 'I know that some of her neighbours think highly of her.'

'One of her children . . .' Melanie said in a faltering voice and then trailed off into silence.

'Well?' Finbar and I both prompted at once.

'Oh, damn you! They say the Director's the father. He's had her up at Blackley making moony eyes at him more than once.'

'You do surprise me!' I said with a laugh. 'What does her husband think about this?'

'I should think he's been more than compensated by the money that she's had off us. Do you think a detective sergeant can let his wife go hunting and shooting twice a week and run two cars? She borrows money off the Children and it's Rufus who pays out the cash.'

'I see. So you're saying that whoever pays the piper calls the tune?'

'She's terrified of Rufus. If he asked her to warm the toilet seat for him she would.'

'Lovely jubbly,' I commented. 'If Rufus and Aldous Arkwright both walked in here now, and each separately offered you refuge, which one would you go with?' I asked out of genuine curiosity.

'Oh, the Director!' she said with shining eyes. 'How could you even ask? There's no comparison. Rufus is on a much lower level of existence than the Director. He wouldn't need to threaten me like Rufus did. I'd do anything for him.'

'If he asked you to jump off a tall building, would you?' I asked caustically.

'Oh, yes, especially that! That's what we're all longing for ... To be bound up with the cosmic forces without any of these fleshy entanglements to hinder us.' She gestured at her wounded arm as she spoke.

'You need help, young lady,' Finbar told her sternly. Melanie smiled, or rather she bared the points of her teeth at us.

'Will you let me go now?' she asked with a more winsome smile. 'You said I could go wherever I pleased if I had a little chat with you.'

'You need help. You need to see a counsellor,' Finbar insisted. He looked across at me and mouthed the word 'police' silently.

'There's nothing we can do about Melanie's mental state,' I told him. 'If she wants to go, she can go. I won't be pressing charges for the murderous assault she made on me.'

'Dave, we ought to keep her here until the police have had a chance to talk to her,' Finbar argued.

'I won't be repeating any of this to the police, if that's what you're expecting,' Melanie said.

'Speaking as your Director, I must warn all members that, if I read the signs aright, the times are fast approaching when we must be ready to give the evolution of the Universe a helping hand by making the move to the next plane in a body, or should I say . . . out of the body. Yes, it's come to that! No one should be afraid! We all know what our destination is.'

> Note of an address by Aldous Arkwright to a secret gathering of C of L initiates

23

Sunday, 1 November – Tuesday, 3 November

Call me fussy if you like, but I couldn't abide to have Melanie in the flat with me a moment longer. A call to the Swiss Village Hotel in Wilmslow established that she was still registered there and Finbar agreed to drive her over.

'Are you sure this is the right thing?' he asked for the tenth time. He was as reluctant to let Melanie face the potential wrath of Messrs Polk and Tyler as he was to deprive the police of her company. What he didn't realize was that the tape wouldn't be accepted as 'probative' material by the courts. I just longed to see Melanie's neat little behind disappearing through my armoured door for the last time.

'All right, all right,' he said putting his hands up in surrender. 'Don't pull that long-suffering, Christian-martyr face at me. I get that too often from Fiona. Come along, miss. Have you got everything you came with?'

Once his mind was mind up Finbar fairly bustled Melanie out of the flat. She went without a backward glance or expression of regret. I sensed she probably felt that, having told her tale, she'd paid her dues in full. Unfortunately, I knew that she'd short-changed me in any number of ways. According to her, Aldous Arkwright was completely unaware of the activities of his closest associates and had no idea of where the money came from for all those expensive cars and building alterations. She'd hadn't told the truth about her own complex relationship with Polk and Tyler. There'd been no mention of those gentlemen's connection with the Sicilian brotherhood in Miami. It would have taken days to get an approximation of the full story out of her.

I hadn't got days. When trying to drag the story of Monica Withers's death out of her I'd decided that Polk and Tyler were going to pay in full for their tricks. I couldn't live with myself if the only thing that happened to them was a rap over the knuckles, possibly only a fine, for entering the country illegally. I considered phoning Sinclair. Assuming that he'd even receive a call from me at 7 a.m. on a Sunday morning, what could I tell him? There was nothing much that he could act on . . . Never in a thousand years would Melanie stand up before a judge and jury and say anything that might harm her precious Director.

There was harm coming to him, though, I promised myself. But that could wait. Maybe someone else would have to take care of him. Polk and Tyler were much more urgent. If they'd any sense they'd be thinking about leaving the country, and where better for two rats to start from than their bolt-hole in Sale? Peterson and his sources could tell them whether I'd blown the whistle on them. I hadn't and I reasoned that they must still be in Sale.

Using the twin track on my stereo deck, I made several copies of the tape of Melanie's confession, such as it was, and put them in envelopes. There was one each for Sinclair, Cullen, Paddy, Dr Matthews and Janine White. I labelled them all and left a note for Finbar asking him to deliver them as a last favour. Then I dressed. A dark navy crew-neck sweater went on over the white T-shirt I was already wearing. I put on black jeans and a loose black leather jacket. I went into the spare bedroom and rooted through the debris that had followed me from my office in the Atwood Building. At last I found what I wanted, a box of nine-millimetre pistol ammunition. Much to my regret I'd had to give up my legally owned Beretta automatic when the law changed, but with the squirrel-like capacity of hoarding for a rainy day that has served me well, I'd retained one box of ammo. I carefully reloaded the Heckler and Koch automatic and checked the action. Unfortunately, I only had the one magazine, so I'd have to make every shot count. I put the gun in the inside pocket of my jacket.

I hadn't got any plan in my mind as I backed the Mondeo out of the garage. I almost screamed with the pain in my chest when I had to turn to look out of the back window, but I gritted my teeth. I knew that when I banged on the door of the Petersons' home the two Americans would be waiting for me. They wouldn't be inviting me in for a chat this time. Something would happen and the pair of them, and quite likely myself, would end up dead. As I drove down Washway Road I thought about Monica lying so peacefully on her sofa with that faint bluish tinge to her face. I thought about Janine being beaten almost to the point of death.

There'd been a little rain in the night and the orange gleam from the sodium lights was reflected off the glistening pavements and road surfaces. Where the road dipped there was a fog of dense white vapour which was just thick enough to reach the tops of the street lamps. The lamps looked like giant lanterns where the light was contained by the fog. Mist curled and wreathed like a waving shroud.

Stupid, grim, mock heroics, overgrown macho-man, John Wayne gone mad – call it what you like, but I did turn into Harboro Road with the intention of ensuring that the two Children of Light enforcers troubled the world no longer. You read about these happenings all the time . . . *Tragic shooting in the suburbs . . . multiple deaths* . . . It would dominate the local news for twenty-four hours. Perhaps there'd be a brief mention on the national TV news . . . *Another dreadful Manchester killing* . . . One of the heavy-duty colour supplements might follow it up. This wasn't the nineteenth century when the public chewed over minor local slayings for years on end. Everyone would think the deaths were drug-related or resulted from some gangland feud. After a few days the story would drop from the headlines.

I hadn't gone more than fifty yards down Harboro Road before I saw that my visit was in vain. The whole end of the street near the Petersons' cul-de-sac was one solid mass of police cars and ambulances. Even as I slowed down a policeman with a Dayglo tabard over his comically short blouson was walking towards me and flagging me down.

'Do you live near here?' he asked with no lip-service to courtesy.

'No, I'm just passing.'

'Are you press?'

'No.'

'Why are you here?' he demanded.

I looked at him blankly. I could hardly say that I'd rolled up to riddle a couple of enemies with bullets.

'Clear off, you fucking ghoul,' he said menacingly. 'I'll run you in if you don't turn this fucking car round. We can do without sightseers.'

'Charming,' I said. 'I've come for the early morning service in the church.' I don't know what made me say that so glibly. The sight of the distant church steeple must have put it in my mind.

'Oh, I beg your pardon, vicar,' the officer said humbly. He was thrown completely off-balance and thoughts of an official reprimand must have loomed. 'I didn't realize. We've had a tragedy here. We're all upset, you'll have to pardon my French. There's been a serious incident here involving a police officer and we've had the usual ghouls turning up to gawp.'

'How terrible,' I said, genuinely shocked. 'It wasn't Mr Peterson, was it?' I knew the answer before he spoke.

'It was. Did you know him?'

'I knew he lived opposite the church,' I said, getting more and more tangled in my lies.

The officer looked even more red-faced and embarrassed than he had before. He took a handkerchief out and wiped sweat off his brow.

'Do you want to . . . I don't know what Anglicans do . . . Give them their rights?' he suggested.

'I'm afraid the family weren't part of my flock. I don't believe the Children of Light have last rites,' I answered with frightening fluency. I was praying that he'd guide me back on to the main road so I could make a dignified getaway.

'OK, vicar. Sorry about everything. You won't be able to get into your church car park, but if you leave the car here I'll walk you down to the church. We've got orders to turn everyone back.'

With a sick feeling coming over me, I backed my Mondeo into the space he indicated. I glanced into the mirror before I got out of the car. My facial colouring was deadly white but that wasn't what misled the officer. The white T-shirt peeping out from under the dark crew neck and the black leather jacket could be taken for some trendy sky-pilot's idea of clerical rig. I walked along through the glimmering early morning light behind the officer. He marched me right up to the church doors where I saw a notice board that stated that Holy Eucharist wasn't scheduled until eight thirty. I breathed a sigh of relief.

'You'll be all right now, vicar,' the constable said before departing. 'They're bringing the bodies out in a moment and most of us should be out of your way soon.'

When he returned to the main body of uniformed officers he pointed me out to a superintendent. I waved demurely, then earnestly prayed to God that somebody wouldn't get the bright idea that an impromptu service or a little on-site counselling might be in order. I breathed again when they all returned to their grisly job. Mist was rolling in from the river valley and from Carrington Moss. With any luck, I wouldn't be recognized.

I stood at my post until the opportunity to slip back to the car should arise. So far, I'd given no thought to what might have happened here. Chill slowly spread up my spine as I watched. Mrs Seaforth, the voluble neighbour who'd been so helpful to Finbar, was holding forth to a number of officers at her gate. Uneasily, I remembered that she was a pillar of the church in whose porch I now sheltered. Even as the thought formed in my mind, she was ushered back into her house. Then a grim succession of trolleys were wheeled out of the Peterson home and into waiting ambulances. Freighted on each was a sad burden wrapped in a green plastic body bag. To my horror I noted that the first two were child-sized. Then three adult corpses were trundled to the ambulances.

Three? I felt as if my throat was being squeezed by an icy hand. It should have been four adults, or two, or none at all.

They weren't finished. An RSPCA van pulled up close to the front door and two uniformed RSPCA men went in to the house and then staggered out again, each with a dead German shepherd dog in his arms. They loaded them into the back of their van. I could taste vomit in the back of my throat. There'd been a clean sweep at the Peterson household, but by whom?

I waited five minutes more. No other corpses were removed and all the ambulances departed. Then I slipped back along the street trying to be as inconspicuous as possible. I needn't have worried. Anyway, I don't think they can do you for impersonating a clergyman these days. Lots of people get away with it. No one gave a second glance and I was soon on fog-shrouded Washway Road again, heading for Thornleigh Court.

I was definitely on auto-pilot until I reached the flat. Finbar must have got back before me, because the tapes had all gone. I sat down to take stock. Thoughts formed in my mind with the slowness of continents drifting against each other. Gradually a feeling of imminent danger began to envelop me. I took the gun out of my pocket and checked it for the second time. I wasn't functioning properly. I glanced at my watch and realized that I'd promised to pick Janine up from the MRI at eleven. I seemed to be in a dream. Slowly though, the sharp pain from the wounds on my chest and arm began to force a return to more urgent ways of thinking.

I took a couple of strong painkillers and then made myself some coffee. I tried to flog my brain into activity. Three dead adults ... Did it mean that Arkwright had killed the Petersons and one of the American enforcers? Was the third adult Tyler, the one I'd wounded? Or was it that shithead Polk? It might even be Aldous Arkwright. Maybe he'd turned up to renew his acquaintance with Anne Peterson and his child? Possibly the two Americans had decided that he was surplus to requirements and had chosen to clear off and make a fresh start in the 'pick-n-mix' cult business somewhere else.

I rapped my forehead with my knuckles. It had to be Polk.

He was the only one with the right degree of ruthlessness. The third adult must be Tyler.

Had Rufus Polk decided to cover his tracks by removing all witnesses? But what kind of man would kill the children and the dogs? Gradually I became convinced that it was Polk. With his wonderful military record, not to speak of his numerous 'crowbar' victims, he was just the sort to go in for such a drastic clearance.

What would he do next? Would he come for me? Or might he even now be heading up to Blackley for a clear-out at headquarters?

I phoned Arkwright. There was no reply. 'He'll just have to take his chances along with the rest of us,' I thought. Then it gradually seeped through to my numbed consciousness that Janine White might be in danger. If Polk was a man who'd shoot a wounded accomplice and butcher a whole family, why shouldn't he go for the grand slam? Aldous Arkwright and Melanie Varley might keep their mouths shut – they were implicated, after all – but why shouldn't he silence Janine and myself? That had to be his number-one priority now.

I dashed downstairs, cringing every time my foot landed on a step and jolted my stitches. Once in the car and heading to the MRI, I tuned to local radio . . .

'Reports are coming in of a shooting incident at the home of the prominent black activist and anti-cult campaigner Everald Mallick . . .'

Mallick! I'd forgotten about him.

'Mr Mallick, who was unhurt, stated that a white racist gunman burst into his home in the early hours of the morning and opened fire with a shotgun. He is demanding increased police protection for prominent activists. None of his family was hurt in the incident which a police spokesman said was regarded as serious.'

Why Mallick?

Then it all clicked. I was supposed to be dead. Possibly Melanie was as well. Mallick was the only one left who could link the pair with Janine. He had to go. Perhaps they'd called on him before their visit to Thornleigh Court. But Mallick was artful, always on the alert. Anyone who offended as many people as Everald did on an average day had to be ready for a fast exit. I'd give good odds that he was out of that bedroom window before Polk got his foot on the stairs.

There was nothing about the deaths in Sale. I tried a national station and there was nothing on that either. It was still early. Maybe the news would be released later. Still, if it had been Polk who'd tried to silence Mallick, then my theory that Janine was in danger became ever more credible. I raced down Lloyd Street and into Moss Lane East. I could feel sweat breaking out on my forehead. Why had it taken me so long to work everything out?

I pulled up at the ambulance bay in front of the MRI and ran into the building.

'Get dressed!' I ordered Janine when I reached her bed. 'We're going now.'

'Dave, whatever's the matter? You look dreadful,' she said in alarm.

Out of the corner of my eye I could see the ward sister coming towards us. I yanked Janine out of bed. 'You've got to come now,' I said desperately. 'Polk's on his way to kill you and if he isn't here already, he soon will be.'

'I can't come now. I've got to be signed out by a doctor,' she said inconsequentially. She smoothed the front of her long nightie. The gesture irritated me.

'Move, woman!' I snapped, 'or the only thing that doctor signs will be your death certificate!'

'How dare you call me woman!' she said angrily, tears forming in her eyes. The ward sister popped up at Janine's side and began reinserting her into the bed.

'Go, or I shall call Security,' she threatened.

I was completely deflated. I'd imagined that I'd get Janine and be out of the hospital in minutes. I looked down at the bed, stupidly. I felt like slumping on to it myself.

'Listen, sister,' I said in my most persuasive tones. 'This isn't the way it looks. Janine's a journalist and she's uncovered information about some very nasty people. That's why she landed in here in the first place. Now the wheel's come off the cart for these villains and I've every reason to think that they're desperate and that one of them is on his way here now to make sure that Janine never tells anyone what she knows.

You've got to help me to get her out of here.'

To my surprise, while Janine shook her head in disbelief or maybe shock at my sudden advent, the sister appeared to give my remarks some credence.

'Very well, but she can't leave under any circumstances until she's been seen by the consultant. He's due at ten. Otherwise the hospital would be responsible for any unpleasant consequences. You and Janine can sit in a side ward until then.'

I didn't know if the sister was humouring me until a strong-arm squad arrived with a strait-jacket for me but she rapidly installed Janine in a wheelchair and pushed her into the same ward she'd previously occupied. She dashed out and returned in a moment with all Janine's clothes, medical folder and bedside paraphernalia. 'You won't mind getting dressed, will you, Janine?' she said. 'It means that you and your partner will be able to get away all the quicker when you've been seen.'

When the sister had left us alone Janine looked at me and then at the pile of clothing.

'This isn't just a trick so that I can see you in your underwear,' I said. 'Rufus Polk is after you. I think he's already tried and failed to kill Everald Mallick.'

Janine gave me a very thin-lipped smile. I could see that she still wasn't sure. It was very hot in the little room and I felt like swooning. I took off my jacket and then the crew-neck sweater.

Janine looked at me in horror. 'Oh God!' she shrieked, 'you're covered in blood.'

It was true. Blood had seeped from my bandages on to the T-shirt.

'It's nothing,' I said and put the sweater back on.

'What's been going on?'

I took the small tape recorder containing the original recording of Melanie's confession out of my jacket pocket, and put it on the bedside table and switched it on. The sound of that woman's voice telling her one-sided story jarred, but Janine listened in fascination.

'Look, I'll go out while you get dressed. I've got to move my car anyway. I thought we were going to make a quick getaway so I left it at the entrance. I'll have to move it or they'll tow it away.'

Janine gave me an abstracted glance. She was concentrating totally on Melanie's words.

When I slipped my jacket on I put the automatic in her hands. 'Listen, if Polk shows his face in here, wave this in his general direction. Believe me, he won't hang around.'

She took the gun but I wasn't convinced that she knew what it was for. She held it awkwardly.

I slipped down to the Mondeo which fortunately hadn't been towed away and drove round into the official car park. Polk's Toyota was there, parked right near the entrance for a quick getaway. I ran back to the ward and threw open the door of Janine's room. She was just fastening her bra when I went in. There was no sign of the gun.'

'Polk's here,' I said. 'Where's the gun?'

'Oh, I put it away,' she said with a smile. 'Don't you think it's rather an inappropriate instrument for a hospital?' She deftly fastened the buttons on her blouse.

'Not if Rufus Polk's already here with the intention of killing you. His car's outside.'

'Fiddlesticks! How do you know it's his car?' She went to the mirror by the sink and checked that the silly little cap was at the correct angle on her head.

'It's a Toyota Land Cruiser,' I raged.

'There must be thousands of those,' she said complacently and then took a pad out of her bag and began scribbling notes.

'Give me the gun, please.'

'Don't be silly. Polk wouldn't try anything in a hospital even if he was here. I've hidden the gun where you'll never find it.'

I made a quick search while she watched with a smile on her face.

'You'll never find it in a thousand years,' she said happily and switched the tape on again.

I could feel my heart pounding as if it was about to jump right out of my chest. In the end the only thing I could think to do was to sit outside her door with my hand in my pocket. Polk knew that I'd been armed when he made his previous attempt on my life and he wasn't to know that I'd been disarmed by a crazy woman.

There were a lot of people coming and going, considering it was a Sunday morning. I looked suspiciously at each person approaching my position. Once or twice, when some burly porter came near, I experienced a stab of fear. We've all seen those films where the killer gets into a hospital and puts on an ingenious disguise. I found myself inspecting the nursing staff closely. Fortunately their figure-hugging uniforms made it all too plain that none of them were male killers in drag.

The ward sister brought me a cup of tea. 'Your partner's not easily scared, is she?' she asked. 'I've noticed that she seems to have discounted her injuries very well. Take it from me, I've seen plenty of assault victims whose attackers have come in here for a second go at them. You're right to be careful.'

'I wish you'd convince Janine of that,' I said.

'It may be that denying the possibility of danger now helps her cope with what happened to her. She came very close to death, you know.'

When we left shortly after ten I was still gunless but the Toyota had disappeared from the car park.

'There,' Janine said happily. 'It was probably some doctor's. You didn't need to worry after all.'

I held my tongue. She was excited by the prospect of being reunited with her children.

We were heading east on the M62 and in the lane for the turn-off to Bolton when the news came through on the radio . . . *'Greater Manchester Police have just released a statement saying that a tragedy involving firearms has occurred at the home of one of their officers. Bodies were removed from the Sale, Greater Manchester, home of Detective Sergeant Alan Michael Peterson at first light this morning. Police are refusing to state whether foul play is suspected . . . A senior spokesperson said "At this stage enquiries are still continuing and speculation about what happened is premature. Our deepest sympathies go to the relatives and friends of the Peterson family." When pressed further, the spokesperson said that he could not deny the possibility that third parties were involved in the tragedy.'*

I scratched my head and looked at Janine. That suggested the police were considering that the case was a possible suicide in which Peterson had shot his whole family. In that case, who was the third cadaver? Was it some elderly Peterson relative?

In the circumstances I didn't feel like discussing all the gory possibilities with Janine. She was still smiling and humming to herself as she looked at the notes she'd made earlier.

For once, my reception at the cottage was completely friendly. When we drove down the hillside past the ramshackle Corless Farm we could see an excited little group forming outside the Cunane homestead.

I helped Janine out of the car and then her mother and children whisked her inside.

'Bad news about Peterson, isn't it?' Paddy said in a whisper before we went in to join them. 'I shouldn't mention anything about it to your lady friend but I hope the bastard's in the deepest pit in hell, killing his wife and kids and himself like that because he's not man enough to take what's coming to him.'

'Janine's already heard it on the radio as we were coming, but she doesn't seem to be fully relating everything that's happened to her own circumstances,' I said. 'The doctors think she's in some sort of denial or whatever they call it. She needs time to recover.'

'Well, how long were they thinking of staying?' Paddy asked in a non-combative way. 'Your mother and I don't mind putting them all up a bit longer. It gets lonely out here with only those maniacs up at the farm for company. I know they whisk them out of hospital far too quickly these days.'

'You'll have to ask Janine that,' I replied, 'but I wish you and mum wouldn't keep referring to her as my friend. She's practically a total stranger and if you're expecting things to happen, I think you're going to be disappointed.'

'Dave, are you blind?' he asked genially. 'You could go a hell of a lot further and fare worse than with her.'

I shrugged and looked at him. 'I don't know where you've got the rose-tinted spectacles from. You're not on Prozac, are you?' I asked with a laugh. I felt better than I'd done all day. At that moment, though, Paddy chose to give my right upper arm a reassuring squeeze. The yell I let out crossed the valley, came back and bounced round again. Startled crows and magpies shot into the air. My mother and Mrs White appeared in the cottage doorway, open-mouthed.

'What the hell!' Paddy snorted. He had my jacket off and my chest bared quicker than I would have thought possible. I was too weak to resist.

He looked at the bandages and stitches. His face was a study in anger, confusion, concern and something else. Eileen was simply appalled. Then Paddy tossed his head back and laughed until he cried.

'Whatever's the matter with you, *Peddy K'nine*?' Mrs White asked in a scandalized tone. 'I can't see anything funny. It looks as if *Dive's* had a really bad accident.'

'Yes, it looks as if he's had an argument with a hay bailer,' Paddy said, tears of mirth still streaming down his face. 'If you knew him, you'd see the funny side of things, wouldn't she, Eileen? There's only our David can deliver one invalid for a few days' convalescence and turn up looking like this himself. Dear Christ! If our David took up undertaking he'd want to bury himself instead of the corpses.'

I didn't see the joke myself. I could feel my legs going by this time. The pain in my arm was excruciating. I was led inside and collapsed on the sofa in the small office. It was adjacent to the large double-sized living-room that Paddy had created by knocking the two original cottages on the site into one. I just about had the energy to hand him the tape recorder before swallowing a couple of painkillers that Jim McNeil had given me and passing out in a kind of light-headed daze.

During the next day or so events gathered a momentum of their own but I was spared involvement. In one lucid moment I thought I heard Jim McNeil apologetically explaining to my parents that I was suffering an unusual reaction to the antibiotics, possibly associated with stress. Listening to my medical condition being discussed as if I wasn't there produced a weird out-of-body experience. My consciousness seemed to float eight feet above my mortal remains as my condition was discussed. Then I promptly passed back into a deep sleep.

On another occasion I heard DI Cullen arguing with my father. This time I was in bed upstairs in the cottage and the noise was carrying clearly up the circular staircase to my room.

'I tell you he's got to identify the woman. We've had a positive ID from Sergeant Martin, but Dave's the only other non-member of that infernal cult who can definitely identify her.'

'And I'm telling you that he's not well enough to be moved,' my father roared.

'Well, if you'd let us take him to a proper hospital instead of trying to treat his unreported injuries yourself then maybe he'd have recovered by now,' Cullen snarled.

I managed to haul myself out of bed. Anxiety and curiosity drove me in about equal amounts. My legs felt as if they weren't attached to my body but I pulled myself over to the top of the staircase and shouted down, 'What woman?' I shouted, or rather tried to shout. My voice sounded more like a feeble squeak to me. I ran my hand over my chin. There was a couple of days' worth of stubble there.

'Steady, Dave!' Cullen shouted. His face appeared alongside Paddy's at the bottom of the staircase.

'Hold on, Dave,' Paddy gasped anxiously. 'This is your fault,' he said turning to Cullen. 'I practically had to use a crane to get him up there and now if he falls and breaks his neck you're responsible.'

'I'm not dead yet,' I muttered. Propping myself against the metal rail, I half-slid, half-walked down the stairs. 'What woman do you want me to identify?' I asked Cullen when I reached the ground. 'Where's Janine?'

'It's not her, don't worry,.' Cullen said reassuringly.

'Where is she?'

'She's just at the bottom of the garden with her mother and the children,' Paddy confirmed.

'Yeah, the thing is, Dave,' Cullen said, 'we need someone to ID one of the bodies we found at Peterson's place.'

'Oh,' I murmured. I suddenly felt very weak at the knees again.

'I'd take you there. To the mortuary, I mean. You know the routine, you'd just have to sit behind a glass screen while they lift a sheet off the corpse's face and say if you recognize her.'

'Who do you think it is?' I asked.

'It's better if I don't say,' he replied. 'Shall I help you to get your kecks on?'

'I can dress myself,' I muttered. I struggled back up the circular stairway and found that my mother had washed and ironed the clothes I'd arrived in. There were still faint stains on the T-shirt but no one would see them under the sweater. While I was dressing Paddy arrived with a cup of coffee.

'Tell them nowt, Dave,' he advised. 'Just identify this body and then come back here. You still look as if a puff of wind would blow you over.'

'That's a bit of a change in direction for you,' I said mildly as I struggled to put my shoes on. 'You're usually so keen on full disclosure.'

'You're saying that because you don't know what happens in the Force when a copper is killed,' he said in a half-whisper. We could hear Cullen moving about below us. 'There'll be those looking for someone to blame for Peterson's death and they won't be too fussy about who they point the finger at. I know Jock's heard the tape you gave me but he's playing his cards close to his chest on this one. Closed up as tight as a spinster's drawers when I asked him what had happened to the Petersons, he did. So if you've any sense you'll keep your mouth shut until you see which way the land lies.'

'Your dad's a bit of a character, isn't he?' were Cullen's first words as we reached the road out of Bolton. 'I thought he was going to deck me when I suggested waking you up.'

'He's all right,' I agreed. I noted with interest that Cullen had chosen to go to Manchester on the old A6 via Kearsley, Pendleton and Salford rather than the much quicker motorway route.

'I reckon you've had the best of it . . . Being out of it for a couple of days.'

'What day is it?' I asked.

Cullen laughed so much at this that he made the car swerve.

'You know, I'm really happy that everyone finds it so amusing when I get clobbered, but you might try to give me a straight answer,' I said indignantly.

'No, it's not that, Dave. I didn't mean it unkindly. You hear people say it as a joke. You know, he was that dateless he didn't know what day it was.'

'Tell me,' I snapped.

'What day would you like it to be?' he chuckled.

'Tell me or I'm getting out,' I threatened.

'Actually it's Tuesday, ten a.m. You slept all day yesterday and most of Sunday. They got quite worried, but that doctor friend of yours said it was a natural sleep and you'd come out of it all the better for the rest.'

We drove in silence for a while. I was itching to know what he made of the tape which he must have received by now, but remembering Paddy's warning I was determined to let him raise the issue.

'You know, I never liked Peterson,' he said after a while. 'Pushy little git, he was. He'd probably have gone straight to the top if he'd lived. He was very politically correct, you know. We got this ruling from the top floor . . . all pin-ups have to be removed from lockers because they'll be construed as sexist. What a joke! Some obeyed, more in sorrow than in anger, but Peterson made me feel he enjoyed enforcing it. I know you shouldn't speak ill of the dead, but he was a creep.'

'A spy, you mean,' I said, unable to keep silent any longer.

'Yes, and we know what happens to them in wartime, don't we, Dave?'

I bit my tongue, annoyed that Cullen had skilfully extracted a leading comment from me.

'The thing is, Dave, Peterson didn't kill himself. He was the first to be shot, probably in his sleep. Then the kids and the dogs came next, then Mrs Peterson and then this woman we want you to identify. She was holding the gun, so she was the last to die.'

I didn't know what to think or say. I felt hot and bothered. It had been bad enough watching all those corpses being lugged out of the house without being involved like this. What did they think I knew? I was quite nervous about where our little drive was taking me. I looked out of the window for a while. Everything had changed along the old road. Once you could read the history of the industrial revolution in the buildings you passed . . . miners' cottages and pit heads . . . beach and dye works . . . textile mills, but now they'd all been swept away. All that remained was a confusing and shabby jumble of the old and the new . . . modern housing rubbing shoulders with old, new precincts jostling with mills converted into factory shops. Lowry would have seen little he recognized.

'Have you found Polk and Tyler?' I asked eventually.

'They've skipped. We searched Meldrum Terrace when we brought Arkwright and the girl in. We've checked the airports. We took up your tip about names and programmed the computers with the names of all American Presidents . . .'

'Yes, but the names Polk and Tyler chose were rather special names of special presidents . . . Southerners who annexed territory. I think you can rule out Lincoln and Grant and so on.'

'Honestly, Girolamo, I'm in awe of your historical knowledge,' Cullen mocked. My heart lifted at the way he spoke. I knew that he wouldn't be talking to me like this if I was under suspicion. Cullen, like all good coppers, was capable of being devious but not this devious. 'Anyway, we haven't got them yet. There's a big search for them in the States now. Apparently the computers there have turned up several unexplained deaths which Mattingly, as I prefer to call Polk, was involved in.'

'Oh,' I said.

'Yes, it seems that the bugger worked his way through a load of old people in Arizona. They've got this retirement city there and various oldies started turning up dead. Nothing abnormal about that, you might say. They all died of sudden heart failure and as most of them were regarded as cardiac risks anyway there wasn't much done about it until the numbers began to get way above statistical averages. It turns out that most of the deceased had used the services of an insect exterminator called Jackson. Money was missing from quite a few. They only connected this Jackson with the deaths at the weekend. His fingerprints have now been found to match Polk–Mattingly's.'

'Do you think he was involved in the killing of the Peterson family?' I asked. I was unwilling to relinquish my previous theory that Polk was to blame.

'That partly depends on whether you can identify this woman.'

Eventually the concrete towers of Salford University appeared and we reached the Crescent. Cullen had to concentrate on his driving then as he followed a complicated route to the central mortuary near the River Meldock behind Piccadilly.

Cullen had his hip flask of brandy ready for me when the little conveyor belt trundled its burden of blanched and desecrated flesh into the viewing area. He took a nip and passed it to me. I declined.

The green-robed assistant removed the shroud from the body.

A shot-gun blast under the chin removes quite a lot of the head. In this case the aim had been slightly skewed so it had removed the left jaw, left side of the face and skull. Most of the right side of the face was intact, with features twisted into a ghastly grin.

'It's Shannon Withers,' I said. I took a swig of Cullen's brandy to wash the bile from the back of my throat.

'Any doubts?'

'No, I'd recognize her anywhere. Not only does she look like poor Monica, but that hard face was imprinted into my brain when I saw her in Oundle. It's her all right.'

'I wouldn't tell anybody else what I'm going to tell you, Dave, and you've got to keep your mouth shut about it as well. It's been kept very hush-hush in the Force.'

I must have received this warning with a startled look.

'Seriously, Dave,' he said, 'this is to go no further, not even to Paddy. You'll find out why in a few minutes' time.'

'Go on,' I urged.

'The theory is that Shannon Withers was staying at the house. She received a call on her mobile and got up and dressed some time after four thirty. Then she woke up Anne Peterson. She was wearing a dressing gown when we found her. Anne wore the key for the steel gun cabinet round her neck. She must have opened it for Withers. There's no sign that any force was used. Then one of them, probably Anne, shot Peterson. He was in bed with his pyjamas on. The end of the gun was wrapped in a pillow to muffle the sound. The children and dogs came next. Again probably shot by Anne. Paraffin tests show that she had far more powder on her than Withers had. For some reason, Withers shot Anne in the kitchen. We think that Anne was holding the muzzle of the gun to her head when the trigger was pulled . . . In other words, it was a suicide pact. Anne's prints were on the trigger as well as Withers's.'

I must have been looking green by this time.

'Steady on, Dave,' Cullen urged. 'We want you to see Aldous Arkwright next. He's asked to speak to you.'

'No, I said quickly. 'I don't want to see him.'

'We can't make you, but Mr Sinclair would take it as a favour if you would. We've got Arkwright and the Varley girl in custody but we've nothing to charge them with. Arkwright denies any knowledge of what Polk and Tyler were up to and the girl backs him up. Anyway there's very little actual evidence apart from circumstantial stuff which a good brief would rip to pieces if we got them to court.

'We'd like you to ask Arkwright how he ordered Anne Peterson and Shannon Withers to commit suicide. We'll have to let him and the girl go this afternoon, but you never know, something might turn up. He's been asking for you anyway. Seems to think you're somehow linked to him.'

'What about Clint Lane?' I said after a while.

'All charges against him have been dropped, only we don't know where he and that brother of his are so we can tell them.'

'I should imagine his mother could enlighten you if you can convince her that it's not a trick.'

'I'll get on to it as soon as you have your chat with Arkwright.'

'All right,' I said with a grin. It was nice to see that some things were still normal.

'It might be helpful if you'd make a statement about the injuries Varley inflicted on you. We can't get that old military geezer you hang out with, or your personal physician, to say a word about it.'

'I can't help you with that,' I told him. I didn't want to go into a saga about illegal firearms, unreported assaults, etc.

'I thought you'd say that, my old cocker. We'll have to let her go. She's only an accessory to the Travis murder and we're going to have to bail her to Arkwright.'

'Fine,' I said, 'Do what you like with her just as long as I don't have to see her.'

The interview with Arkwright didn't take place in the grimy, white-tiled interview room on the ground floor at Bootle Street where Peterson had grilled me. That was unfortunate. I felt there would have been a certain symmetry if I'd been at the other side of the table and the Director had been perched on the hot seat. As it was, we met in a comfortable room on the top floor normally used by visiting CPS barristers.

Arkwright put on a brave front when he came in. He was trying to pretend that his serenity was still intact but I could see he was finding it difficult. He sat opposite me on a leather armchair and fixed me with that piercing look of his. I felt like smacking his stupid head. If complacency equalled spiritual power, then this customer could have lit up half of England.

'You wanted to see me?' I said sharply. 'Any particular reason, or are you still trying to hypnotize me?'

'Yes my son, you've every right to feel bitter,' he said calmly. He shifted his gaze to the carpet. He was dressed in a tweed suit as if he was ready for a day's shooting on some handy local grouse moor.

'I'm not your son.'

'A manner of speaking only,' he said quickly. 'I apologize if it offends you. I just feel that our destinies have been drawn close together . . .'

'Spare me the mumbo-jumbo . . .'

'No,' he said, lifting the palms of his hand towards me in an almost supplicatory gesture. 'We are bound together. When my misguided followers placed that business card of yours in

Fred Travis's hand it was simply a casual attempt to incriminate a stranger but on a deeper level they were hitching the destiny of the Children of Light to your—'

'If this is all you've got to say,' I told him impatiently, 'you might as well save it for your followers. If you go on like this I'll be tempted to send you to your higher plane before you're ready.'

'That's what I'm saying. I fear it may be your destiny to do just that. There have been certain signs.'

I stood up to go.

'I never intended harm to anyone,' Arkwright said.

'You must have realized where all the money came from. Had you no idea what Polk and Tyler were up to?'

He shrugged and remained silent.

'What about Melanie? Do you know she tried to kill me?'

'If you'd joined me when I asked, I might have been able to shape events in a different direction. That was why I wanted you to join us. I thought you might have been able to inform me what was happening. Brother Polk and Brother Tyler would have accepted correction if I'd been able to point to specific faults. As it was, they thought they were acting in a noble cause.'

'The noble cause of lining their own pockets.'

'I think you'll find that they weren't interested in personal wealth. They did what they did to advance the cause of humanity.'

'Did that include killing the Peterson family?'

'I wasn't aware that the police think they did that.'

'No,' I admitted, 'they didn't do it directly, but someone ordered Anne Peterson and Shannon Withers to kill themselves.'

'My followers have a different attitude to death. If they're ill they don't cling to life until every resource of medical science is exhausted. The whole meaning of my teaching is that we embrace death gratefully. Life on this plane is just a passing phase. With the increased awareness which comes from sharpened sensibility, Anne and Shannon knew that it was their time to depart.'

'What about the children and Sergeant Peterson? Did they

have an increased awareness?'

Arkwright bowed his head.

'They will be guided by Anne and Shannon into the next stage of development.'

'What rubbish!' I said angrily. 'Are you still going ahead with this meeting at the Nynex Arena? You're a danger to the public.'

'I have a mission and I will complete it. In the same way you will complete your mission.'

'Which is what?'

He shook his head. 'That will be revealed to you when the time is ripe. If you had joined us I might have been able to open your eyes but now you'll have to operate in the dark. What I wanted to tell you is that whatever happens, you're doing the right thing.'

I left.

When I went out of that room my face felt like a hard knot of wood. Attempting communication with the Director was like one of those games where they blindfold you and then put unfamiliar objects in your hand to be identified. Each statement from him led on to some further elaboration of his mysteries. No wonder the police were releasing him. Attempting to get a direct statement from him was like trying to bottle moonbeams.

> Citizens should be on the alert. A group in our midst are planning to hold a rally such as has not been seen in Europe since the days of Nuremberg. Those organizing this display of 'moral muscle' should be warned ... Any attempt to trample on the rights of other citizens will be met with stiff resistance.
>
> Editorial in the *Manchester Evening News*

24

Thursday, 5 November (Guy Fawkes Day)

Bob Lane surfaced on Thursday afternoon.

Cullen had taken me back to my parents' cottage and I stayed with them until Thursday morning, Janine, the children and her mother needed a lift to Piccadilly Station so I drove them into Manchester. There'd been little chance to get closer to Janine. She'd written a full account of the cult's fund-raising methods and sent it to the *Guardian* only to be told that as the matter was *sub judice* they wouldn't be able to use her material for the moment.

'That means they won't be paying me anything,' she said.

'There are other jobs,' I told her.

'Not that I want,' she asserted with that fierce determination.

'Try other papers,' I advised.

'Maybe,' she said with a smile. We were on the platform at Piccadilly and I loaded the pitifully small amount of luggage the family had with them into the train. Before I left, Janine gave me a warm kiss and promised to keep in touch, which was something, but not what I'd wanted. When the train pulled out I felt drained and desolate. It was my own fault. I had no right to think that life was like a romantic novel where the hero gets the girl in the end.

To cheer myself up I went to Chinatown and had a four-course lunch at the Smiling Emperor. The only effect was to leave me feeling bloated as well as miserable. I decided to return to Chorlton and spend the next couple of days sulking in my flat. With Janine, it seemed that every step forward was accompanied by a step back. She was younger than me, almost a completely different generation. She must see me as a pathetic clown. Why couldn't I stop thinking about her? On the drive through town I couldn't help noticing the fly posters for the Children of Light rally. Seeing them didn't improve my mood.

I was in my kitchen trying to summon the energy to clean the cooker hob when the doorbell rang. 'It's me, Dave,' the familiar voice of Bob Lane announced when I pressed the communication button.

'Jesus wept! Your face looks like a smacked bottom,' he scoffed when I met him at the door of the flat.

'Thanks,' I said.

'What is it? Not getting your oats or something?' he asked with a laugh.

'Something like that,' I murmured.

He slapped me on the back.

I winced with pain and bit my lip to stifle the scream. My scars were still tender.

'Sorry, mate,' he grunted. 'I came to see if you wanted to celebrate but obviously you don't. What's her name?'

'Bob, delighted though I am to see you, I've never quite seen you in the role of an agony aunt. It's just something that I'll have to get over.'

'Less of your lip, Dave,' he said with a grin. 'I'm not so insensitive as you think. I could tell you were only squiring poor Monica because of that sense of obligation you lug round with you like Quasimodo's hump . . . Hey! That's a hell of a name for a club you know . . . "Quasimodo's Hump". I can just see it in neon.'

'It's good to see you so frisky,' I said. The trip to Holland had done Bob good. He seemed to have shed about five years. The worry lines round his eyes had faded, though not the wary look. That was imprinted into his face. 'How's Clint?' I enquired.

'He's up in Langley with mum. He loved working on the farm. I might take your advice, Dave, and try to cut the cord if

I could find a farm somewhere and some hayseed who'd be prepared to put up with loading his hay bales twice. Anyway, it's you I came to see. How would you feel about going into partnership with me? I feel like whipping the clubs back into shape. They just need a fresh outlook.'

'Thanks, Bob, but I can't see myself as a club owner. I don't think your bankers would be terribly impressed by a failed private detective as a partner.'

'Failed? What do you mean? You sorted out my little problem and no mistake. That Peterson won't be harassing Clint again.'

'I'm not particularly proud about that.'

'What happened wasn't your fault,' he said. He gripped my arm. Luckily, it was my unwounded left arm. 'I wasn't thinking of you coming in with me in the clubs. You haven't got the ear for the music, Dave. No, I was thinking of investing in your detective agency. I'll put up some money and you'll run things. You could get a nice office in King Street West, hire a few assistants. What do you say? You were wasted at that college.'

'That needs some thinking about,' I muttered. As soon as he spoke I knew that I couldn't accept him or his money. The whole point about Pimpernel Investigations was that I was independent.

'Dave, I owe you. I don't know what you did to get Melville Monckton off my back . . .'

'Hold on, I had nothing to do with his accident . . . if it was an accident.'

'No, I'm sure it was an accident . . . Couldn't have happened to a nicer bloke.' Bob's expression was curious. He smiled when he spoke about Monckton, then a sort of shy look came over his face.

'What is it?' I asked.

'It's business, Dave,' he said slyly. 'You wouldn't understand.'

'Try me.'

'You know that deal I had with Monckton, or rather didn't have?'

I nodded.

'It all hinged on him making a substantial first payment for the partnership.'

'Yes.'

'Honest, Dave, the first thing I did when I got back to Manchester after checking out mum was to call you . . . but you weren't in.'

'The payment?'

'Right, well I called at the bank expecting them to tell me that they were petitioning to put me into bankruptcy, but they couldn't have been nicer. The manager invited me into his office and asked if I'd be interested in a new business account and if there was anything he could do to improve cash flow.'

'Tell me,' I muttered through gritted teeth.

'Melville made the payment – you know, on that day he offered you money? He must have been really confident that I was going to sign. He thought he had me over a barrel, you see . . . Clint was with him when Fred Travis was killed and his testimony would have cleared Clint.'

'I'd worked that out, but that still left Melville and Rufus with Travis's corpse. They'd have had to pin the murder on someone.'

Bob gave a grim little chuckle.

'Oh, I see . . . Nice one! It would have been down to me if Clint had been cleared.'

'Maybe not. You'd have persuaded the police the killing was some kind of obscure plot.'

'Thanks. I'd never have persuaded Peterson in a million years. Even if he wasn't in on the deal, he hated my guts.'

'Don't underrate yourself, Dave.'

'The money . . . You'll have to pay it back.'

'The first thing I did when I saw my statement in the black was to phone Monckton's accountant. These guys talk their own language but according to him there's no record of any payment from any account of Melville's. That deal's off. He thought I was trying to pressure him into reopening the deal.'

'So where's the money from?'

'Where do you think? Melville's friends in Miami.'

'But Bob, they aren't the sort of people who just write off bad debts.'

'I don't owe them anything.'

'But the deal . . .'

'As far as they're concerned, their money just disappeared into Melville's pocket. Apparently he was a heavy gambler. You're the only one who knows that the late Melville Monckton was crazy enough to put his money up before he got my signature. You can just picture it, can't you? Him on that fishing boat trying to tell them that he'd bought fifty-one per cent of my business and them asking him for the documents. I bet he sang a lovely tune trying to persuade them he wasn't conning them. Poor bugger!'

I must have turned green.

'Save your sympathy, Dave! He was asking for it. He must have known Travis was for the chop so he got his Yankee pals to fit Clint up for it as a side deal.'

I thought about it for a moment. If I could summon the interest it would take me days to work out just how many of these moves Bob had known in advance. 'It's nice to see that someone's landed on his feet,' I said grudgingly.

'You really are a pain in the bum, aren't you? You spend too much time sitting up here feeling sorry for yourself. What's her name?'

'Janine White,' I muttered wearily. I regretted it as soon as the name left my lips.

'Give her a call. Tell her how you feel. What have you got to lose?'

I looked at him. Despite my determination to feel sorry for myself I could feel my mood lifting. He was right, what did I have to lose? I'd never made how I felt plain to Janine.

'There you are,' Bob laughed. 'I can see the old predatory gleam in your eye again. Here's something that'll put another twinkle in your eye . . . I'm thinking of getting some lads together and paying the Children of Light a visit.'

'What for?' I asked. 'If you put a foot out of line you'll be locked up and Arkwright will get all the free publicity he needs. That man loves nothing more than posing as a victim.'

'It won't be a pose when I've finished with him.'

'There's a better way,' I said. 'He's holding a public meeting on Saturday. Maybe you could do something about that.' It crossed my mind to tell him what Melanie had said about Clint being little more than a dumb animal, but I didn't. Bob was vengeful enough without my goading.

'How do you mean?'

'The C of L are holding a joint meeting with the Repealers this Saturday, or haven't you seen the posters?'

'Oh, those,' he snorted contemptuously. 'Holy bloody rollers!'

'They're going to launch their programme for remoralizing Britain under the leadership of Arkwright's highly trained spiritual élite.'

'That's all crap. Repealing all the laws since 1953! There'd be no night-clubs; no gambling, pubs shut at ten thirty, weak beer. Who the hell would vote for that?'

'I don't think voting's what they have in mind. Arkwright wants to get his people into positions of influence where they can push these ideas forward.'

'Right!' Bob announced. 'I'm going and I'm taking a few friends.'

'It's not that easy,' I said. 'All the tickets have been allocated and most were by invitation only.'

Bob's face fell. He clenched his fist and sucked his knuckles.

'There is a way,' I declared. A spirit of vengeance seemed to be gripping me. If it hadn't been for Polk and Tyler deciding to stick that card in Travis's hand I'd still be a salaried employee of UNWIST and a man with prospects. The outfit that had sponsored those two deserved its share of grief. 'I've got the complete invitation list. All a wealthy guy like you would have to do is visit a few of them and make them offers they can't refuse.'

When Saturday evening came round I still hadn't phoned Janine, nor had she phoned me.

I drove into the car park at Exchange Station. All around me, bright-eyed and eager people were locking their cars and swapping meaningful smiles. For them, it was the dawn of a new era; for me, it was going to be the full stop that punctuated one phase of my life. I'd decided to sell up in Manchester and try somewhere else. Looking round at them I decided to leave the car in another place. It might be better not to be stuck in the middle of Arkwright's enthusiasts if things got ugly. I reversed out of the car park, drove over the Irwell and found a side-street in Salford.

That same flood of excitement I'd picked up in the car park was in full spate when I arrived at the arena. Arkwright couldn't have chosen a better place to launch his new religion. If gothic cathedrals were the highest expression of the medieval way of life, this ugly, banal lump of architecture was the complete statement in concrete of the twentieth century's ambitions. I wandered round the lofty concrete atrium which completely encircled the arena, looking for my aisle number. The odour of hot dogs and onions pervaded the air, incense of our age. Finally I found the right slot and entered the steeply tiered stadium. Four gigantic screens were suspended above the amphitheatre. A picture of a glowing, almost transcendental Aldous Arkwright was displayed on each. I took my seat. Looking down from the precipitous height I could see that a circular stage had been erected in the centre of the floor used for basketball, ice hockey and similar American sports which require frequent intervals, cheerleaders and orchestrated sound effects to work up the spectators. In a moment of vertigo, I took in the giant images, the great height and the eager multitude around me.

Arkwright's green-clad initiates were ranked on the stage. A buzz of excited conversation echoed round the interior space. I studied the faces of my fellow worshippers, spectators, or whatever they were, intently; trying to pick out Bob's infiltrators. It was hopeless. There were people of all ages and classes and races. Although this was supposed to be a gathering of those who shared Arkwright's views there were stewards from Repeal 98 in every segment of the audience, ready to suppress dissent. They all looked on the tame and weedy side to me . . . plenty of enthusiasm but not much muscle.

The PA system burst into life with a fanfare of trumpets. I was expecting to see Arkwright mount the massive podium that had been raised for him when someone did appear it wasn't him. A form of service had been designed for this religionless spiritual movement that appeared to have been derived from the advertising industry. Speakers mounted the podium and delivered messages about the corruption of the times; illustrating their remarks with either a film on the giant screens above, or a little drama on the boards beneath. It was all quite gripping if you accepted the concept that the late twentieth century was in a unique crisis of poverty, depravity, crime and corruption. A professor mounted the platform to lament the decline of educational standards in an upper-class whine. Twenty thousand throats greeted his pedestrian comments with a roar of approval but I could sense that my neighbours were growing restless. They hadn't come to see these nonentities preening themselves.

After the speakers had all taken their places on the stage there was an interval for reflection. Inspirational music was played but it only heightened the feeling of expectation. Eventually Arkwright swept out, green robes flapping, and climbed on to the podium. Hand-held cameras tracked his movement and projected his face on to the screens above. There was a solid roar of approval.

Arkwright was ecstatic. He held his arms out as if to embrace us all. His charisma lapped round the arena. He began to speak. I can't remember now what he said, the usual guff about a higher plane and the need for a disciplined group to lift mankind out of its rut. I was too tense to listen. I was beginning to think that Bob had decided against action when the first missile struck the podium.

Arkwright gaped in astonishment as a paint-bomb struck his podium with a wet splat. Blood-red paint ran down. Arkwright's look of dismay was picked up by the camera and projected into every corner. He held his hands out as if to quell the storm but suddenly a deluge of missiles and fireworks began to rain on to the central stage and his podium. At the same time the lighting went out. Everywhere around me people were standing up to express their horror. Dim emergency lights came on after a moment and revealed a struggling mass of people on the central stage.

Before the light failed, there was a last long shot of Arkwright on the quadruple screens. His expression wasn't of despair or even shock. Instead, a look of fierce expectation and hope was written over his homely features. What a trouper the man was! He could take anything in his stride and twist it into some kind of prophecy.

Bob's gang, led by himself and accompanied by Clint, had swarmed over the barriers and on to the arena floor. The poorly lit scene of struggle reminded me of one of those dramatic nineteenth-century paintings by John Martin illustrating the Fall of Babylon. Short stocky men were rolling about and tumbling off the stage, struggling with long-robed fingers. A knot of Repealers formed round Arkwright and led him out of the arena. It took over an hour for the police and the Repeal 98 stewards to expel Bob's uninvited contributors to the proceedings. I stayed in my seat absorbing every detail of the spectacle but thousands of the more timid left.

One thing did impress me. Clint, although surrounded by fighting, yelling people, made no effort to join in. All he did was to patiently peel his brother free from those who sought to detain him. Clint steered Bob out of the arena before the police arrived in force.

When the lights came back on, one of Arkwright's underlings, bedraggled in his torn green robe, announced that the proceedings were closed. I was pleased with the night's work.

The light on the answering machine was blinking when I got back to my flat. There was a remote possibility that it might be Janine, so I switched it on.

'Mr Cunane, it's Jeremy Matthews here. I got the results of the tests on those mushrooms you gave me and its urgent that you contact me.'

Mystified about what could be so urgent, I called the number he gave me.

'Oh, Cunane, thank God you've called,' he gasped when I got in touch with him. 'You haven't eaten those mushrooms, have you?'

'Of course not,' I said with a laugh. 'What's the problem?'

'Can you come round to my home? It's too complicated to discuss on the phone. I was on the point of phoning the police when you called.'

'All right, but what's all the urgency?'

'I'll explain when you get here. You know I told you that a friend was doing the analysis for me? Well, he only got in touch this evening.'

When I arrived at the pathologist's home in Stockport I was surprised to find Assistant Chief Constable Sinclair and DI Cullen were already installed in Matthews' cosy lounge. Neither of them looked pleased with himself. The roaring coal fire gave the scene a cheerful air of remembered normality. It put me in mind of my grandmother's living-room when I was three or four.

Matthews's message was chilly enough to cut through the heat.

'Right, Cunane, I got your tape,' the earnest young pathologist said. 'I believe the membrane used to kill Irvine Varley . . .'

'Just a moment, Doctor,' Sinclair interrupted. 'You know that the coroner's never going to accept that as the cause of death without other material evidence such as the actual membrane itself. You might as well say that they were killed by aliens from another planet.'

'You're wrong, Mr Sinclair,' Matthews insisted. 'The circumstantial evidence is strong enough. I've found references to a fish membrane, finer than silk, that's been used in Vietnam for silent killing since time immemorial. It clings closely to the face, cutting off oxygen immediately so that the heart stops with a jerk . . . But that's not why I called you here. Mr Cunane . . .'

'Fresh from another night's mischief, I hear,' Sinclair muttered laconically.

Matthews looked at him oddly and then carried on '. . . gave me samples of mushrooms which he'd retrieved from Miss Varley. They were a very odd mixture. Most of them were fragments of edible mushrooms, interestingly enough of cultivated varieties, implying that they were bought in a supermarket, not harvested in the fields. They were *agaricus campestris* and *agaricus aryensis*, the field mushroom and the horse mushroom.'

'Yes, yes,' Sinclair muttered. He looked as if he was missing his bed.

'What was interesting – or, if you like, sinister – enough for me to summon you all here at this time of night, was the fact that these edible varieties were mixed with others; *amanita muscaria*, the "magic" mushroom which causes hallucinations and is poisonous in large doses and *amanita phalloides*, the aptly named "death cap", together with the "destroying angel", *amanita virosa*. Now, normally I wouldn't be concerned. Death cap and destroying angel can both be found in woodlands from September to November, as can the magic mushroom.'

'Doctor, could you get to the point?' Sinclair asked with uncharacteristic impatience. 'I don't normally turn out at this time on a Saturday night for anything less than murder.'

'That's what I'm trying to say. Mr Cunane told me that this cult like to play with dangerous natural drugs. They could made a cordial out of digitalis, a strong poison. The hallucinogenic aspects of magic mushroom are intensified by small additions of death cap. Unfortunately this compound is also a deadly poison unless taken in the very smallest quantities. I believe a similar mixture called *lumina vera* or "true light" was used by a Belgian cult in the thirties.'

'So?' Cullen said, taking his sceptical tone from his chief.

'So what the hell more do you want!' I shouted angrily. 'The doctor's given you the membrane. Surely that's probative enough for the most constipated judge in the country. Hell's teeth! You can get someone over from Vietnam if necessary. It's not the other side of the moon.'

'Watch your mouth, Cunane!' Cullen snapped. 'We're not idiots.'

'Well, stop acting . . .'

'Davie! That's enough,' Sinclair ordered in his crispest Caledonian tone of command.

'No, it's not enough,' I contradicted. 'What are you doing about Meldrum Terrace? You've just heard Doctor Matthews tell you they've got enough of a deadly poison to take out half of Manchester . . .'

'There's no need to be alarmist. We've no idea that's what they're using the mushrooms for. You're always too ready to let your hyperactive imagination run away with you.'

'No, I'm not. You haven't heard Arkwright talking about the next stage of development. If Melanie's typical of his followers, they think death's just like walking round the corner to wait for the next bus. They're all keyed up to do something desperate.'

'Mr Sinclair, I really must agree with what's just been said,' Matthews chipped in, throwing his hands in the air expressively. 'If you've got people experimenting with a cocktail of lethal mushrooms you're going to have fatalities and from what I hear of this Miss Varley she's hardly the most stable type in the world.'

Cullen and Sinclair looked at each other. Their mutual expression was hard to classify. Baffled, frustrated; no, it was neither of those. It took me a moment to work it out . . . Resignation, I decided, that was the look. Resignation and acceptance. They didn't disbelieve what Matthews and I were telling them. Whatever was brewing up at Meldrum Terrace, these two law enforcers were prepared to let events take their course.

'What is it?' I yelled. 'Has someone told you that benign neglect is the best strategy where the Children of Light are concerned?'

'Of course not,' Sinclair said angrily but the way his face coloured told me its own story. 'We can't just go barging into people's homes on the off-chance that they might be committing suicide.'

'We're talking about mass suicide here!' I said.

'These people are adults and there's such a thing as religious freedom,' Sinclair argued. I looked at him in surprise. I couldn't understand the lack of action. 'From what I've heard on the police radio-net we're likely to get the most strenuous complaints, if not a summons to appear before the European Court of Justice, because of the assault on religious tolerance that occurred at the Nynex Arena tonight.'

'You were there, Dave,' Cullen added. 'Don't deny it. You were at that shambles tonight. I saw you.'

'If you saw me, you saw that I never moved from my seat,' I countered.

'Only someone with access to the C of L database could

have organized tonight's little shindig,' Sinclair added, peering at me through narrowed eyes. 'All the rioters had officially issued tickets.'

'Perhaps you've got another Peterson in the department who leaked the database,' I suggested.

'Spare me your sarcasm, Davie,' Sinclair rapped out. 'There's only you with this strong talent for organizing disasters and if you think I'm going to go up to Blackley to search the C of L headquarters again on the off-chance that there might be some poisons there, you're very much mistaken. These people have ample grounds to sue the GMP already.'

Sinclair folded his arms and that was that. There was no point in further argument.

Doctor Matthews felt he'd done his duty by informing us and, after giving another short lecture about the deadly poisons involved, he showed us out into the cold night air. Sinclair and Cullen drove off without a word to me.

I couldn't believe it. I watched the lights of their car disappearing down the street. Sinclair had become so correct in his dotage that he was prepared to allow an outbreak of mass suicide on his patch. It didn't make sense. Well, if he was under covert pressure to look the other way while the Children of Light removed themselves, I wasn't.

A horrible thought struck me. There might be children involved. Hyperactive imagination or no, I found it too terrible to picture what might already be happening. The parents of Arkwright's oddly dissociated families might be dosing their children with the lethal *lumina vera*.

I jumped in the car and raced towards Blackley.

By the time I'd jumped my fourth set of red lights, I picked up a police escort – siren wailing and lights flashing. I raced up Rochdale Road, tensed for a swerve away from a road block, or steel spikes, or whatever they were going to use to stop me. Hyperactive imagination! Sinclair didn't know what he was talking about. My imagination was feverish and turbocharged. Well, it was then. I watched the pointer on the speedometer flicker up to ninety. I've never made a habit of speeding. Passengers often tell me that I'm a sedate driver.

Working in a high risk occupation has always made crashing cars seem a pretty pointless exercise. What a joke it would be to pile up now! Would I reach the next stage alongside Arkwright and his initiates?

Despite the desperate urgency, part of me was cool.

I was so certain that I was right and that Sinclair and Cullen were wrong. There were all Arkwright's hints about signs of the times. There was his loopy suggestion that I was a messenger from a higher realm sent to warn him. Above all, there was that crazy apparition of Aldous the Prophet, fulfilled and joyful when the Nynex meeting dissolved in chaos. Arkwright had revelled in disaster. It all fitted too snugly. Aldous Arkwright was planning to stage a grand exit. He must have been preparing for months. He knew that there'd be trouble at that meeting and he welcomed it. He needed a crisis to carry his followers along with him.

Someone as intelligent as Arkwright must have known what Polk and Tyler were up to. They'd all got out of America one step ahead of the law. How long could it be before the plodding but thorough British system caught up with them? All I'd done was to speed things along a bit. Despite the sweat trickling down my back, I felt a cold shiver. Had Arkwright ever truly given up his Satanism? Did he want some kind of Viking's funeral for himself, his dead followers laid at his feet?

I was certain that he did.

The massive bulk of Our Lady of Mount Carmel church loomed above the road like a stranded ocean liner and I whipped round the corner into the side-streets of Blackley. I passed the old Anglican parish church on my right. Behind me on the main road, flashing police cars raced on, their siren wails dropping in pitch as they missed the turn. Threading my way through the winding streets, I knew it could only be a moment before they were in pursuit again.

When I reached Meldrum Terrace I knew I was right. There were cars and mini-vans and 4WDS parked anywhere, some with their doors open. I leaped out of the Mondeo and ran to the door. It was just as solid now as it had been before. I tried the windows. Reinforced glass had been installed all the way along. No one was going to break those without a sledge-hammer. Remembering my previous break-in, I ran to the back of the building. Heart sinking, I saw that it wasn't going to be my third time lucky. The Children had installed razor-wire where I'd climbed in before.

I was in a frenzy. I looked at the nearest 4WD. Could I crash it through the brick wall, ram-raider style? I dashed to the cab and jumped in. The keys were still in place. I started backing and filling to get it into position and then my eyes caught sight of a red lever marked 'winch'. Trust those homicidal rednecks to think they'd need a winch to navigate through the back lanes of North Manchester! A winch was perfect. Crashing into the building, I was likely to kill anyone who hadn't already downed Melanie's herbal mixture.

I ran the hook into the letter box of Arkwright's front door, got back in the cab and turned on the winch. Boing! The steel cable snapped taut almost immediately, but nothing else happened. I put the big vehicle into reverse and suddenly the door was flying out into the road towards me.

Then, apart from the wailing of police sirens drawing closer, there was nothing. No protesting residents spilling out into the street. Sinclair didn't need to fear complaints to the European Court. I stepped over the broken door into the building. I could hear faint music and suddenly I dared to hope. I rushed through the office suite to the assembly room.

It was like a half-forgotten scene from nursery school. The soothing music from a CD player heightened the effect. People were seated on the floor in three wide concentric circles. Beside each one – no children, I noted with desperate relief – there was a white plastic cup. No one was moving. Mouth agape, I stood back. It was too much to take in. I've seen dead people before, but there were so many now. Then I saw movement.

Striding awkwardly over tangled limbs, I reached the centre of the room. I was just in time to see Melanie close her eyes. Clad in a new green pixie robe, she gave a sigh and relaxed into death. She had a very large teapot beside her from which she'd dispensed the last unholy communion to the initiates of the Children of Light. She was leaning against her beloved Director. Arkwright wasn't dead. He looked up at me and gave a faint whisper. The expression on his face was that same benign smile that had always irritated me. I looked back at him. Then his face changed. He didn't seem to be about to expire. The look he gave me now was imploring. His fingers moved and he pointed at Melanie's teapot.

For a second I stupidly thought he was inviting me to join him yet again. Then I understood. He knew he wasn't going to die. Had long use built up his tolerance to Melanie's brew?

'Dave,' he quavered, pointing to the vessel. I could hear the police arriving in the street outside.

'Here, you bastard!' I told him. 'Go to hell!' I picked up the kettle, poured him a full cup and lifted it to his lips. He drank greedily, then fell back over Melanie and entered his own dark kingdom. As his features stiffened into the rictus of death, that enigmatic smile returned.

I looked round at the circle of death. The only familiar faces missing were those of Rufus Polk and John Tyler.

I must have frozen where I was because the next thing I remember is a firm hand falling on my shoulder. I whirled round. A traffic patrolman faced me. He had his arm extended towards me. In my bemused state it took me a second to realize that he was pointing a CS gas spray at me. I put my hands up. The man was white-faced and trembling but he was no more shocked than I was. He led me out of the circle of death and handcuffed me. He and his partner then kept their distance from me as if they feared that I was the source of a fatal contamination. The air crackled with radio messages.

Sinclair arrived not long after. He seemed in no hurry to have me released.

'If you'd had patrols here ten minutes earlier they could have stopped this,' I said reproachfully.

'Laddie, laddie, there's no stopping things like this,' he said grimly. 'If we'd driven them out of here they'd have only done away with themselves somewhere else.'

'You knew.'

He shook his head. Then it struck me. Maybe Sinclair *had* been expecting Arkwright to make his way to the 'higher plane' but he hadn't been expecting the prophet to take eighty-odd of his followers with him.

*

It must have been almost 4 a.m. when I got back to Thornleigh Court. Sleep was the last thing on my mind, certainly an impossibility. I sat in an armchair, nursing a large tumbler of malt whisky. The doorbell rang, not the outer door but the door of my own flat. I went to open it, expecting to find Finbar. The sensation-hungry pensioner must have noted my arrival. News of the Nynex riot, but not of the mass suicide, was already on the airwaves. Instead, as soon as I opened the door my hair was grabbed and I was pulled forward. Rufus Polk yanked me out of the doorway and clamped his muscular arm round my neck. I began seeing stars and flashes of colour as he squeezed. I struggled and twisted. I could feel the stitches in my chest ripping free. It was no use. Polk was like a rock.

'You wanted to see how we did it, didn't you, cheapie?' he grunted, thrusting me back into the flat. I couldn't manage a squeak in reply as I was forced down into an armchair.

'Do the honours, will you, John?' he panted as he struggled to hold me down in the chair. I felt as if I was going to burst from the exertion of trying to lever him off me but it was no use. The man was just too strong. In horror, I watched Tyler flip open the silvery bag. He carefully opened the end, while keeping the bag flat to stop air getting in. I managed to get my feet under the chair and heave it backwards.

Tyler grinned and repositioned himself for a second attempt. He was about to slip the bag over my head when there seemed to be movement in the doorway. Both men froze. I couldn't see what they were looking at but got an impression of green. I may have been mistaken or hallucinating. Certainly I was on my last gasp even before Tyler got the killing bag over my head.

'No, not now,' someone said. The tones were those of Aldous Arkwright but it couldn't have been him.

Polk and Tyler ran out of my living-room and down the stairs.

Gasping for breath and bent double in pain, I was in no shape for pursuit. DI Cullen filled in the details for me the next day. After leaving me, whatever it was that had spooked them must have continued to frighten them because they fled from

Thornleigh Court at reckless speed. At that hour of the morning there was little traffic and if they'd chosen another direction they might have escaped an accident. As it was, the avenging fury or whatever it was made them choose the road towards Didsbury and the M56 motorway. The junction at Princess Parkway is a dangerous crossing even under normal conditions and at four in the morning there's always traffic heading for the airport. They made it across though. They sailed right through a six-lane junction with three sets of co-ordinated lights all set against them. Their luck ran out at the next junction.

Their road ahead was narrow now, almost reduced to a single lane and the next intersection was at Palatine Road. This was completely blind, with buildings masking the road at either side. As before, Polk took the crossing unhesitatingly, crashing through red lights. A huge milk lorry smashed into the Land-Cruiser. The Toyota bounced off the front of the lorry like a toy and turned over twice before crashing into a wall. Polk was killed instantly. Tyler lingered for a while.

Cullen took my supernatural explanation of their flight with more than a dash of his usual derision. 'You're really losing it, Girolamo. First that scene with the boss last night and now you're claiming intervention by a ghost. Get real! When those two found you spraying blood and screaming blue murder, they panicked. All they've ever killed before were people who didn't fight back. They must have thought we were just round the corner.'

Afterword

John Tyler survived long enough for a custody battle to start between the English legal system and the American Federal Justice Department which wanted him for a string of frauds associated with unexplained deaths in the south-western states. Tyler resolved the issue as many of the surviving Children of Light were doing at that time. He killed himself by jumping through a fourth-floor hospital window. The fish membrane discovered in the Toyota was identified as belonging to one of a large species of sea ray found in the South China Seas. Microscopic analysis revealed traces of scale on the faces of both Irvine Varley and Monica Withers. There were other deaths too. It seemed that the cult particularly attracted those who had a grudge against members of their families. It wasn't, as the mainstream church leaders and rabbis claimed, that the cult was breaking up families, so much as that members of dysfunctional families were looking for something like the cult to take up their grievances for them.

No doubt some other 'charismatic' leader is already planning to step into the Director's shoes. There's good money to be made at that game. I often think of Arkwright. He wasn't all bad and I never thought that he was entirely behind what Polk and Tyler were doing. With him, I think it was a case of wilfully refusing to see what was happening . . . But how many of us do that when the occasion suits? Was he the 'ghost' that startled Polk and Tyler? As the event recedes I incline more and more towards Cullen's explanation. There's a green curtain in the living-room which flaps when the outside door is left open. What about the voice? That must have been in my hyperactive imagination. I'm not superstitious. Blood loss and fear can do strange things.

Still, Arkwright was always telling me that I was his destiny and as it turned out he was right. No one ever asked me if I'd played a part in helping him shuffle off this mortal coil.

Sinclair and the GMP were too occupied fending off the questions from a parliamentary commission of enquiry into the mass suicide at Blackley to bother with me. I think Sinclair was grateful for my silence.

Regarding my own destiny, things went well enough. My scars healed, as they do, but I couldn't shake off my feelings about Janine White. I didn't take up Bob's offer of a subsidy but did set up business in King Street West. I did keep in touch with Janine but it wasn't until the long-delayed funeral of Monica Withers that I actually met her again.

Monica's funeral was held in the crematorium at Southern Cemetery. It was a grim affair. The tall Byzantine chapel was hardly packed. There were few relatives apart from a couple of second cousins and staff attendance from UNWIST was poor. Alvin Richardson was there on behalf of the department, but he avoided looking at me throughout the brief service. I watched him studying the plaques on the walls during the short eulogy which Monica's vicar had cobbled together with my help. Lisa Lovegrove wasn't present. Maybe she was now focusing her attentions on Mr Gormally-Normally. God help him! The only touching thing about the committal was that a sizeable group of students found the time to attend.

I always find cremation unsatisfactory – a personal feeling – and I was quite angry when I left the chapel. I strode away quickly when I saw Richardson heading towards me, a syrupy expression on his face and no doubt a few well-chosen, but barbed, words at the ready. I was turning out of the chapel when someone tugged the sleeve of my raincoat. For once, the climate had managed to get something right. It was a miserably wet, overcast afternoon.

I turned. I think if it had been Richardson I might have been tempted to do what I'd failed to do before and deck him.

It wasn't him. It was Janine.

'Can I cadge a lift?' she asked with a smile. Some of her hair had grown back but there were scars that she was hiding under a Kangol beret.

'What are you doing here?' I asked. I felt as abrupt and stupid as if I was fifteen years old.

'I came to pay my respects,' she said.

I made no reply but walked with her to my car.

'Where do you want to go?' I asked.

'Actually, er . . . Thornleigh Court, Chorlton.'

I looked at her. My expression, if not actually falling within the definition of 'thunderstruck', must have been close enough to raise a smile from her. She looked a lot more relaxed, the tension of the days when I'd known her had faded.

'Get your libido down, boy!' she laughed. 'It's not what you think. I got the offer of a full-time job on the women's pages of the *Manchester Evening News*. It's not exactly the *Guardian*. The same group, though.'

'Congratulations,' I said sincerely.

'It came right out of the blue. Perhaps someone on the *Guardian* editorial team felt a bit guilty about what happened.'

'That's great, Janine, but why do you want to go to Thornleigh Court?' I asked.

'Good question, Dave. But I thought you might know the answer,' she whispered mysteriously.

I shook my head. She looked at me very closely and smiled.

'Maybe I'll have to hire you, Dave. The day after I got the job on the *MEN*, this arrived in the post.'

She handed me a thick envelope which I examined curiously. It was the lease to the flat next door but one to mine, which had been vacated by the petrol-hoarding car salesman.

'I know nothing about this,' I blustered. I could feel my face turning an unpleasant shade of red.

'Well, lad, 'appen you do and 'appen you don't,' she scoffed in a mock 'Northern' accent, 'but the chance of free accommodation is too good to turn down on the salary I'll be getting, and at least I'll know the neighbours.'

NINE LIVES

Christmas morning greets Dave Cunane sourly. Manchester's most intrepid private eye is in jail. Often known to take the law into his own hands, he now finds himself in the hands of the law.

Framed and arrested for a cold-blooded murder he hasn't commited, Cunane turns to the ever-tricky Delise, his part-time lover and full-time assistant, to save his neck and find the murderer. But as the plot thickens and the corpses pile up, Cunane realises that more than one party wants him out of the way, for good.

'Sharp, hip-shooting prose with a refreshingly nasty twist'
Arena

'Sparse, authentic and entertaining'
Manchester Evening News

RED FOR RACHEL

David Cunane is Manchester's most off-beat private eye. Fond of the booze, fatally attracted to the wrong women, champion of the lost cause, he walks a thin line...

Rachel Elsworth is missing. Nineteen years old, she has vanished into the city's seamy underworld. Her father employs Cunane to find her. Rachel's trail leads Cunane into the maze of Manchester's criminal fraternity; and right to the heart of police corruption.

As Cunane finds himself drawn further and further into a web of deceit and danger, he realises that someone will stop at nothing to find Rachel before he does. Even murder.

'This is the kind of stuff the English thriller has been begging for'
GQ

'Wicked as they say... the author should give up his day job'
Time Out

ALSO AVAILABLE IN PAPERBACK

❏ Red for Rachel	Frank Lean	£5.99
❏ Nine Lives	Frank Lean	£5.99
❏ The Reluctant Investigator	Frank Lean	£5.99
❏ Last Rites	John Harvey	£5.99
❏ The Silence of the Lambs	Thomas Harris	£5.99
❏ The House of Women	Alison Taylor	£5.99
❏ A Sight for Sore Eyes	Ruth Rendell	£5.99

ALL ARROW BOOKS ARE AVAILABLE THROUGH MAIL ORDER OR FROM YOUR LOCAL BOOKSHOP AND NEWSAGENT.
PLEASE SEND CHEQUE/EUROCHEQUE/POSTAL ORDER (STERLING ONLY) ACCESS, VISA, MASTERCARD, DINERS CARD, SWITCH OR AMEX.

☐☐☐☐☐☐☐☐☐☐☐☐☐☐☐☐☐☐

EXPIRY DATE .... SIGNATURE ....
PLEASE ALLOW 75 PENCE PER BOOK FOR POST AND PACKING U.K.
OVERSEAS CUSTOMERS PLEASE ALLOW £1.00 PER COPY FOR POST AND PACKING.
ALL ORDERS TO:
ARROW BOOKS, BOOKS BY POST, TBS LIMITED, THE BOOK SERVICE, COLCHESTER ROAD, FRATING GREEN, COLCHESTER, ESSEX CO7 7DW.
TELEPHONE: (01206) 256 000
FAX: (01206) 255 914

NAME: ....

ADDRESS ....

....

Please allow 28 days for delivery. Please tick box if you do not wish to receive any additional information ❏
Prices and availability subject to change without notice.

9 780099 594871

Printed by Libri Plureos GmbH in Hamburg, Germany